FATEL

Fatel by **Aviv Geva**

Harpushit Publishing

Thank you, Teacher Esther, for that conversation in fourth grade that changed my life.

Aside from children and other obvious and definitive elations, all the moments of happiness in your life do not compare to a single day, in a life where you are living the dream.

Prologue

The waiter of dreams came up to me and asked if I wanted to order anything else, or if I was ready to go, but I hesitated.

"Look, it doesn't have to be a big dream," he tried to encourage. "It doesn't even have to be a dream that someone else will appreciate or be impressed by. It just has to be your dream."

"I'm hesitating."

"Hesitate, hesitate. Perhaps you'd like to order a placebo pill?"

"A placebo pill?"

"Yes, a placebo pill. This is the proof."

"The proof of what?"

"The proof that you have way more power than you think. Or more accurately, when you think - you have much more power ."

"Really?"

"Really, really."

"But proof of what? Tell me again."

"Do you know what a placebo pill is or not?"

"Of course I do."

"So that's it. That's the ultimate proof."

"Proof of what exactly?"

"Proof of everything. That you can do anything just with thought alone. You think it's a cure, and in over fifty percent of cases, it actually heals. That means you believe in it, and it happens even when it shouldn't, according to your belief."

"My belief? How do you know what my belief is?"

"Um... never mind. The general belief."

"The general belief? There are a million zillion different general beliefs."

"Yeah, and most of them boil down to the fact that you're not God."

"Okay, and..."

"And it's a fact."

"What's a fact?"

"That with a placebo, suddenly you know how to create something from nothing, or in professional jargon, to create."

"Create? Create what?"

"Everything. Your health. Your commuine. Moran."

What? Moran? How does he even know Moran? I asked, but he didn't answer. Either because I asked it in my heart, or because he knows everything that goes through your mind anyway. So, to wake up— is that what I want? Is that what I need?

"One more dream," I finally requested. "But, if possible, can it have a bit of a happy ending?"

He started to explain, but I already knew the answer. It's clear that in dreams, there's no guarantee. You start, and you have no idea where it will take you.

"However," he added, "I can make sure the beginning is good. And that's also just because you're a regular customer, and all…"

"Okay, great," I replied. "But wait," I asked, and the smile that had begun to rise on his face froze. "A good beginning doesn't decrease the chanc…"

"No, no. Don't worry. The chance of a good ending never changes. Even the beginning… Like, between us, I can give it a push, but it could also turn on me, take a sudden twist…"

"A beauty that turns into a monster," I laughed.

"Yeah," his smile returned, this time as if he and the smile were an integral, complete part of one another.

"So not that, okay?"

"Not a beauty or not a monster?".

Sometimes I think he's a robot altogether. That there's no reason to make this kind of small talk with him. Just order, let him leave, and that's it. It's not like there are tips here or anything. And besides, God probably pays well. Or the devil. Then I really got screwed.

"There is no God," he suddenly said.

"Excuse me?"

"We're all made of the same energy—light and love. There is no God or devil. We are all God."

"And you forgot about brotherhood... eh?" I smiled, trying to encourage him to continue, but he didn't offer anything more. A robot, like I said. With pre-prepared answers. You just have to ask the right questions.

"But the Bible says there is a God," I tried my luck with the answer that would change the face of the universe.

"True," he surprised me and responded, "and right from the start, like I already said, we have a bit of a say; it says that man was created in His image. Exactly God."

"So what are you saying, that God created God?"

"That if there is a God, then you are also God."

"But a moment ago, you said there isn't..."

"There isn't like you think."

"So, what kind is there?"

"As it's written in the Bible."

"But in the Bible..."

"At the beginning of the Bible."

"Mr. Waiter, are you suggesting that you're currently talking to one of a million gods?"

"Well then... what would you like to order?"

1

It was on Bati's third-and-a-half birthday, my beloved daughter. Since she has no mother, I make it up to her with two birthdays a year.

I very gently held the chocolate pie my mom taught me to make, similar to the ones they used to have at the Burger Ranch fast food restaurant when I was little. You have to be really careful when you take the first bite because the filling inside is blazing hot. But what child can control the first bite of their favorite dessert? Worth a tongue-burn without wavering at all.. And I don't even like desserts. Not chocolate and not cakes. Just this pie from the Burger Ranch. And since there wasn't a Burger Ranch near our home when I was little, my mom had to learn how to make an exact fake replica of its subtle nuances so that the child wouldn't scream and throw a fit about wanting "a chocolate pie from the Bunger Ranch!!!" That's how it is when you're four years old, a 'hambunger' from the Bunger Ranch. That was also the first time I tasted mayonnaise, because it's not really healthy and my mom didn't allow it in the house, but that, for context, didn't taste that good to me.

She's a good girl, my Bati. Sitting in her chair, wearing a white nightgown adorned with flowers, with her little legs dangling in the air due to their distance from the floor, and her hair still wet from the bath, neatly combed and pulled into a ponytail as best as her father could manage. And as I take excited steps holding the longed-awaited pie toward the cutest creature in the world, who is now sitting prettily in her little chair by the table, I feel a kind of silence, both strange and stressful, that with each of my steps turns into a whimper. That too, a very quiet whimper, more like a hiccup with a bit of noise that interrupts her breathing in a steady rhythm. I hurried my steps and gently approached her until her face came into my view. She was seated nicely at the table, sobbing quietly. So sweet. There is so much goodness in her. She knows I'm doing something nice for her, so she cries quietly, that I won't see. That I won't notice.

"Hey, hey, hey," I placed the chocolate pie on the table and went to wipe her cheeks. "Why are you crying? Today is your birthday..."

"Th-a-t's not tr-u-e!" she said angrily, the words escaping her without meaning to. She had never been angry with me. She knows that Daddy always does everything for her, just like I always say. "You know Daddy will do anything for you, right?" I would repeat this several times a week without realizing it, and she would nod with a smile, playing with my hair shyly.

"But it is true, today you are three-and-a-half years old."

"And-a-half is no-t a Birth-day!" she said ,frowning, and I knew the words were coming from her mouth but not from her.

"Of course it is. Who told you it wasn't?"

A flood of tears hadn't started here. Just rapid, repeating pulls at her nose. Now I knew it was serious. Now, my ability to block out emotions collapsed under the weight of the tears that washed over her eyes, mouth, and nose. "Shhh... don't cry, my beautiful." I hugged her tightly and wiped her face with the palm of my hand. "Wait, take a deep breath and tell Daddy what happened, okay?" But children aren't good at postponing satisfaction.

"Th...Tha..." she tried to say, but her face was puffy, and tears streamed down her flushed, warm cheeks. "The...They sa-id at kinder... garten, th... that..." Her childish words were now accompanied by a type of hiccup of a children's cry. "That I don't have a mo... mo-ther... th... that... I... wi-ll... ne...ne-ver find h... her."

I always preferred to ignore that difficult question when she asked it. And what should I tell her? That I'm sorry things are this way? That it doesn't matter what's missing, it matters what you have? That as long as we have each other, we have the entire world? That she should believe me and when she's a bit older she'll realize that people who have what we have—and it doesn't matter if they are father and daughter, brother and sister, or a loving couple—they don't need anything more? But only when she truly grows up will she understand. She'll learn the difference between having everything and yet nothing at all, and having nothing at all while still having everything. But for now... for now, children are cruel. I believed that her innocent soul was too young to contain and understand, and so I distracted her with comments and phrases like "Oh, what stubborn buttons these are!" while I undid her dresses, "What annoying shoelaces... right? So bothersome. Why don't you want to open?" I would make a cute face, and she would laugh, forgetting for a moment what she had asked. That's how kids are, or at least that's how it seemed to me back then, that they forget quickly. And perhaps they are just able to jump swiftly from one topic to another.

"Shhh..." I hugged her tightly. Tears welled up in my eyes but God forbid I let them chant on my cheeks.

"Will you g…go too, Da...ddy? An…and... th then I wi...will... be all... a...lone?"

"What? No! ... Never!" Now I held on really hard to the tears in the corner of my eye. For once, I didn't know what to answer, I didn't know where... I couldn't... You will never be left alone my Bati! I will always be here, I lied. Just this once... I lied. But even when I'm no longer here, she'll always know I did everything I could for her. That we are all part of one big universe. And that we, each one of us, is exactly this universe that he creates for himself.

"You remember the story about the crabs in India, don't you?" I asked, and her gaze brightened for a moment, her eyes shimmering through the tears.

"In... In-d...dia?" she said, as a curious expression began to take shape on her face, peeking through the strands of hair stuck to her sticky cheeks where the tears had dried.

"That's right!" I charged at the sadness that subsided. "Mommy is in India, you know that! And one day we will go visit her. Do you want Daddy to tell you the story about Mommy and the crabs in India, my beautiful?"

"Da...ddy..."

"What, my love?"

"T... T... Tell me the… story about Mo... Mommy… in... Indaia..."

"Sure, sweetheart... and then we'll eat the chocolate pie Daddy made for your birthday?"

"Y...essssssss," she answered with a sweet smile. A smile, with nothing before him, behind him, or all around him in this universe, and for the sound of it, you would do anything. Anything, including anything."

"So, a few years ago, Mommy and I went to India..."

"In-da-ia!" she shouted with delight, savoring the chance to say the word again and again.

"That's right, my love."

We went to India for a kind of a late honeymoon. The one we never had. The one we didn't get to have because we were already pregnant... That's how it is at forty—you have to hurry. I remember we sat on that beach, in the shadow of the massive cliff. You know, the place where the sand in the water is almost black. And when you put your foot in, it comes out black and the blackness immediately washes off because it is actually sand. Anyway, so there we were, on our late honeymoon in Canacona Situated along the beach-lined western coast of India.

I can clearly remember the first time I dipped my whole body in the water. So cool but also warm, I can't explain it. Dreamlike. And, her belly already started to show, because I had to work fast. She looked so beautiful with that belly. So beautiful. With my little Bati. My adorable little Bati. Whenever we were near water, she would reignite this fear of crabs and sea creatures that lay deep inside her, which probably stemmed from the one time she stepped on a starfish in Sinai and her whole vacation went up in smoke because it happened on the first day. Or maybe it was a sea urchin... I can't remember, doesn't matter. Anyways, she's been scared ever since. And there are millions of crabs on the beach at Goa. The highs and lows of the tide are insane, so at night the beach floods almost up to the guesthouse line, and the water reaches the boats used for fishing and tourist trips, among them gather groups of gangster dogs that guard all the guesthouses, whose gang fights would not have shamed the good old days of the Mafia in Chicago and New York in the nineteen twenties and thirties.During the day, the entire beach, up to its edge, is actually wet sand that for a third of the day literally acts as the ocean. The crabs apparently spawn there in masses, and there are lots of small holes in the sand, so when you walk, you see the small crabs sprinting very fast and disappearing into the sand. It's fine because even if you go really fast you won't step on them, so no bites or anything like that. But girls are usually a little more afraid or disgusted or pretend to be, and she always said she was afraid of crabs. That they are scary and that they bite. So she brought it on herself. Summoned her fear. Just like the children in Stephen King's book 'It' who were slaughtered one by one until they overcame their fear, and then the evil clown died because he had no "fuel" to act on.

"But there are no big ones here," I told her.

"Eh, Hagai... if there are small ones, there must be big ones" she said, and she was right. Where do you think they come from, the small ones? And also, I saw in the restaurant outside where the fish are, huge crabs tied up. Poor thing, one of them tried to move but it was all tied up with iron wires..."

"Yeah, you're right. Although in the restaurants they're not from the beach, they're from the fishing nets. There aren't any huge ones on the beach, they come to spawn and go back to the ocean.

"Okay, so they come. You see?"

I laughed, and she smiled. The truth is, there were a few bigger ones too—ones where their big, pinching claws were already visible, and you could tell they were three-and-a-half centimeters of small pricks... and then we had a surprise. These eyes suddenly came out, suddenly jumping out. Scary!! And how fast it moves. "Shoot, stop!" she screamed. It also had like a devilish look, of an asshole. A friend of mine once sat in the shallow water at Dor Beach and played with a stone that was half stuck in the sand, and suddenly the stone moved quick as a flash and it was one huge crab that pinched the life out of him and tore off half of his pinky. Unbelievable. Half a pinky in one clack!

This startled Bati, and I could see she was really alarmed. Fear took hold of her. Seeing a frightened little girl is one of the worst things in the world, even if you're not her father.

"No, Bati, there's nothing to be afraid of. I'm just telling you the story of why Mommy would never order lobster in restaurants. Because it scares her. You know, like back then at the beach..." I remembered. The place was called Cola Beach, just like Coca-Cola. And there's also this cool stream with fresh water where you can bathe at the foot of the magnificent cliff of Agonda, a small town full of certified stoners straight out of Jamaica. By two in the afternoon, everyone has to be completely stoned. Or actually, from morning on. India. Not that it mattered much to me, since I don't smoke a lot, definitely not since I had my little girl and it was time to get serious because it's the best thing that ever happened to me in my entire life.

"So Bati'le, on Coca-Cola Beach, Mommy and Daddy were sitting on the sand, and suddenly a crab crawled out of its hole, and Mommy got really scared. And Daddy said it was nonsense and that she should calm down, but Mommy didn't calm down, and then Daddy threw a piece of chocolate wafer at it, and the crab's eyes widened like crazy and it darted for it super fast. And then Mommy got really-really scared. Super scared. And she got up and started running and slipped on the sand and fell on her belly and started crying because she was afraid something might have happened to you."

If she was six years old, I wouldn't have nonchalantly told her that Mommy crashed on the sand, right on her stomach, and started screaming and crying like crazy that "the baby is dead!" and that "I hate crabs!" And "I told you! I told you I hate crabs! And now he's dead!" And Daddy laughed uncontrollably. And that's what helped save Mommy because suddenly she calmed down. It was more like she didn't quite understand my reaction... but it helped. So why do I care how? It helped. And we quietly went to the room, and then to the hospital for tests. And there they reassured us and said that the baby is alive and that you are fine. And then Daddy cried. Suddenly Daddy cried when he heard that his baby was alive. And then Mommy laughed. Laughed at Daddy for being such a crybaby and said she loved him. More than anything in the whole wide world. And that she's sorry she shouted at him and blamed him at the beach. And Daddy said "nonsense" and that he loves her more than life itself. And to be honest, she didn't blame me. Screamed, yes. But didn't blame. I love her.

"But here, nothing happened to you, you see? Daddy's sweetheart." I stroked her chin. She still doesn't really understand everything at the age of three and a half, so we can talk about anything. What a strange thing this is. When they are babies, you can tell them everything. Literally talk to them about anything. You can tell them anything that happened to you, and over time you start hiding things from them, to round up corners. White lies. God forbid they would be hurt, that they would be burnt by the misfortunes of the great universe, making sure they will forever stay pure of mind and opinion like Teflon that nothing sticks to. As if this way, you will save them from the bitter and cruel world. But I always thought differently. I always thought about how to paint the world with a brush of light blues and pinks, while gentle clouds in the background hint at the rising of the morning sun. And this way, and only this way, I could tell her. Tell her how the most charming stork in the whole continent of Asia, placed her in my arms.

2

Suddenly it happened.

Suddenly she did it. And then she added and said that she should have married me. Just like this, when we were sitting at 'Fatel'. Here we are again, sitting here, reclining and kissing the age of forty.

It was Anat's birthday, and she invited everyone. The entire group that knows each other from almost kindergarten age, who somehow—in a way that outshines a miracle—managed to stay in touch. And then suddenly she did it. And both her aging parents who never said a word to me, even though I lived six houses down the street from them and was obsessed with their daughter and in love with her to the being of my core; suddenly they were also there because they still live in Fatel and popped by to say hello because Anat is one of the gang and all, and they even smiled, and her mother even started to rattle my brain with chatter while I was hunting around for my phone, which I must have forgotten somewhere, because their daughter, almost thirty years late, kissed me on the mouth.

Just like that, when we were sitting around the table, on high bar stools, as we were already after everything, laughed at everything, matured from everything. Suddenly she did it. The first girl to make my heart ache. Moran Dagan.

Yes, it's funny, and you can make all the puns you want, I know. I tried everything in my attempts to escape the jaws of her heart. Yes, even "moron" and whatever else you can think of. It didn't work. That kind of stuff only works when you don't care about the person. When you have feelings for someone, you can throw all your heroism into the bin. And back then, there wasn't even a recycling bin—not even those big, rectangular ones in every color. Just a small, round, orange one, rusting and hanging crookedly from the wooden pole of the telephone wires, where someone from the municipality would come by to change the bag once every few weeks. That was right there in front of the house—and then Moran and her parents moved into the neighborhood.

For years, I blamed myself. Then I justified it to myself. Then I just gave up. What could you expect from an eleven-year-old kid who as early as kindergarten, made every girl he wanted his girlfriend, and sometimes with complete and full consent, he had three girlfriends at the same time? He simply expected the universe to just make it happen, like, 'Okay, this new girl from the parallel class will be mine soon.' He thought it would just happen, like it always did.

But she, just like that, after six months of no looks, was suddenly declared, publicly and in front of the entire gym at the school's Hanukkah party, to be Benny's girlfriend and practically engaged to Benny, who was also a popular kid from my class.

"What??" The eleven-year-old in me didn't quite understand. And all this was after preparing for this event for months. There, he will talk to her. There, he will impress. And with the black jeans with the faded white pigments scattered like a cool splatter of paint, straight out of the late '80s, and those special shoes, tall and puffy with all those flashy colors, that his parents had brought him from abroad over two months ago. For two months now they've been lying in the closet and mom is asking why he doesn't wear what they buy him, and he keeps coming up with different excuses and smiles in his heart of how he will impress Moran and win her heart with his new clothes at the Hanukkah party, and it doesn't matter that mom is angry and doesn't understand. He kept it all and didn't wear any of it, keeping the whole thing a complete secret. And then, suddenly, some annoying girl—and definitely the daughter of a particularly slutty type of mother—got up on stage and announced into the microphone, while Pompeos, the local DJ, was spinning disco tracks, that Moran and Benny were a couple. She then laughed awkwardly, and with some majestic excitement, as if she had just announced her victory in the discovery of the atom, made me understand for the first time in my life something I hadn't understood before, and got off the stage with her infuriating stupidity. You fucking cunt, motherfucking whore! I loved her first!!

Flak! The knife goes in and out cleanly—only after a split second does the blood start flowing. And there I am, with the cool shoes, the jeans, and the special shirt from the Netherlands. And to Benny, of all people! Sure, Benny was a really cute kid; everyone loved him because he was a little blond adventurer with a skateboard and later on a surfboard, and that works really well in the pre-preteen years. Everyone loved Benny. To this day, in all my forty years, I don't think I've ever heard anyone say anything bad about him. And he was also sort of a friend of mine. Not my best friend in the world, but still—a friend. Because Benny didn't get involved in all the scheming and dramas of the other kids. He lived in his own world, where he was happy and smiled at everyone, which makes it very difficult for those who want to hate other children.

I remember in the days after Hanukkah vacation, I'd tell my mother I wasn't feeling well, maybe I'd just stay home. And she, a minute before leaving for work, would somehow sense my mood and only quickly check to make sure I didn't actually have a fever. While she did that, I'd add and persuade, that today was just gym, health education, and math, which Yaron could catch me up on—he was my nerdy friend from class, since Arik never did his homework. She'd understand, trusting that I knew what I was doing, muttering something that sounded authoritative like, "Fine, but make sure Yaron fills you in," just to fulfill her motherly duty, and then she'd head out. I would then immediately run to their bed because there was a television in my parents' room. It was rather small and not like the billion inches televisions that we have today, but they always broadcasted on the one and only channel that existed at the time, fun programs like *Ritch Ratch*, *A Moment with Dodley*, and *Phistuk's House*. Some of them were still broadcasted in black and white even though there were color televisions for some time. But even watching black and white television was definitely better and preferable for me than dealing with the black reality outside... From that day on, whenever we played at the regional tennis court, I would cheat him a little. And not that I was some kind of liar—I hate liars and thieves—but with him, it just came naturally. "Out!" I'd declare when the ball landed next to me and touched the line. "What?? It was in!!" he'd freak out. Especially since he was such a good kid who never cheated. "It was out," I'd repeat nonchalantly. Fuck him. He has Moran. But forget it, he is not interesting. Benny, our friend, was still the easy part. Years later, while I still carry the stain of betrayal and unfulfilled love in my heart, and as we grew into our twenties, somehow—and surely with the help of the devil himself—Moran and Arik became a couple.

Arik! My best friend, God damn it! They even moved in together, and somehow, it just became normal. And all these years, as if she didn't know. That she kills, cuts, tears apart... But by then, I was already completely over it. I accepted it as an axiom, as just a part of life. Maybe it would be more accurate to say that it was a kind of disability for life. But disabled people don't commit suicide; they go on living with the disability. And so, that's how I lived with Moran, my unrequited love since the age of eleven, who had crushed my heart with a thousand-kilogram hammer, and who, with Lucifer's generous help, was currently the girlfriend of my best friend. And don't get me wrong—I had plenty of other girlfriends. Limor, and Lihi, Sarit, Tal, Yifat, and even Anat. Yes, yes, the very same one whose birthday sparked the triggering event. But Moran... Moran was simply something else. Like a protected flower you're forbidden to pick, an unattainable being that somehow, to your dismay, you knew that no matter how much you wanted, you could never have.

The truth is that I may have known this from the beginning. I don't know, many years have passed... Years during which I tried to figure out why. Not why she didn't want me—that could have millions of reasons, and therefore it would be a terrible waste of time on my part to mull over it. After all, how many people in this world don't like sweet potatoes? Plenty. Now, if the sweet potato got offended and hurt, and started wondering what's wrong with it every time someone didn't like it, its situation would be really bad. Completely unbearable. Its entire existence would be reduced to these twisted thoughts. But why? Why doesn't he like me?? Why?!

This reminds me of the last conversation I had on that trip in India. The Indian guy from the guesthouse was a great guy, and also rich who hung out with the guys and fucked a l-o-t of tourists. He was just so skilled. Hair in a high ponytail and a stylish shave on the sides, a beard that wouldn't shame James Harden from the NBA—father of the new beard movement of Herzl's time, which became cool again in the mid-2010s, and additionally, he'd always make sure to buy drinks and smoke the strongest Indian cigarettes, 'Gold Flake'—the kind that make you want to cough and puke at the same time. He had this huge guesthouse made up of four buildings, with an elevator in the middle, and from what I could gather, he also had a couple of restaurants. And a car, and a scooter, and a badass heavy motorcycle. Rich. Probably very… And he's always saying he has a girlfriend, but every cute tourist chick who walks into the guesthouse's restaurant, he immediately sits next to her, and in his hands, two winning wild cards; first, he's the owner and says hello, which is the most natural and coolest thing in the world for an innocent European tourist looking for adventure, and on top of that he is also dark-skinned or 'black' as everyone says including black people so I conclude that apparently it's okay. And European women dig black dudes, note intermarriage, not to mention just sex, among Muslims and/or Africans and European women. But since skin color isn't everyone's cup of tea, his second wild card is that he's just "a stupid native". Wait, don't jump. It's under double and quadruple quotation marks. Not only are Indians a great people, nice and sweet, they're also very, very smart. Very. What you might see in villages are simply people who haven't had the chance for education. Think of someone who grew up in a shack with a mother who did laundry for tourists her entire life, and a father who was a fisherman. And that's at best, yes? He has no one to develop him, buy him educational games, kindergarten and school, and after school classes, and a variety of stimuli from the Internet and television. But educated and more cultured Indians excel a lot in fields like computers and technology. So what I mean is, that it's like calling someone "a retard". We do not mean by that to speak about people with a mental disability and degrading their dignity, but rather using it as an expression of thoughtless behavior. Just like this one time when we were kids, and someone found out that old Elhanan had an extra phone line on the roof of his house. A phone line on the roof! It was crazy at that time. And then someone came up with the idea that we could make free calls! At that time we still used coins for public phones, and only later did the era of phone cards begin, long, long before there was a... never mind. But a phone call was an expensive thing. My aunt Esther used to live abroad. She was in a relationship with someone, and she flew out to be with him. One day, she called while we were in the living room. My mom answered, then asked me to quickly call Aunt Hava, Uncle Haimke, the cousins, and everyone. We only had about ten minutes to speak because every minute of international conversation used to cost about a hundred shekels... And so each got to speak with her for about twenty seconds, and it was crazy. From England! Later, she sent postcards with pictures, which tied into the conversation, and at family gatherings everyone would say how she said this and that, and you could see in the pictures. Wild! As kids, it seemed magical to us. And now there's a free phone at Elhanan's place on the roof! And I love Elhanan, but we also used to swipe from Ephraim's grocery store. Later I realized that this doesn't really fly with God on Yom Kippur, and it's also not very nice... But everyone did it. It was a kind of sport. During the summer break or at Lag B'Omer when you stay up until the end of the campfire and at five a.m. you suddenly realize that everyone's going to swipe from Ephraim's or Yossi's grocery store. So what? You'll go home and tomorrow everyone will say that you were a pussy? 'A pussy' is also a mocking nickname like 'a retard', it's like someone who doesn't behave 'like a man'. It's like calling a straight guy 'You faggot'.

And so we went up to the roof because we found out others had already done it, and started making calls.

Suddenly, Elhanan showed up on the roof! Suddenly in the dark, I saw him with a flashlight, and he didn't look nice at all! The charming Elhanan was suddenly looking for these punks who climbed up his roof every day and made phone calls. For sure they are not from Fatel... I remember hiding in a corner by the plants, and probably because it was so dark, he was unable to spot me. Arik managed to escape before he came up, and Benny hid in another corner I couldn't see. But for a moment, when he turned with the flashlight and asked "Who's there??" In a threatening tone, I considered jumping. Jumping down to the other side of the house, which was already someone else's yard. And I remember that down there, there were these tall and spiky plants, with this kind of green with yellow on the sides, and each side is like a small blade, or a saw. But for a moment there I almost jumped! It was really a split-second decision, and right after that, a split-second decision not to. And what could have possibly happened? That Elhanan would have caught me, shocked as hell, maybe given me a talk, or at worst, called my mom? And then what would've happened? She'd tell him it was very serious, that she'd come right away to pick me up, and all the way back she'd be cracking up and giving me kisses on the forehead? But you're a kid. You don't want to get caught. And do you know where I called? Home. And my mom answered and I said, "Hey mom, what's up?" She replied, "I'm fine, where are you?" in a somewhat confused tone, and then I said, "Nothing, just at a friend's house, I'm coming home," and then she said, "okay," and we hung up. I went up to Elhanan's roof to call my mom and tell her that I was coming home and I was ready to pay for it with two broken legs and a broken arm and I don't even want to think about what would have happened with the spiky plants... that's why they say "a retard".

So what I meant to say was that it's one of his cards. As if no matter what he does, the girl will always say to herself "okay, he's Indian, it's a different culture, third world, it must be something I don't understand or he's 'a retard' and that's fine because he's the landlord here and everything, so I'll laugh at everything he says or does, and maybe I'll even let him lick my pussy at some point and penetrate me with the huge penis that he surely have, as all blacks do..." And then all is forgiven and forgotten. And he attacks. Straight forward like there's no tomorrow. And she, it suits her. An adventure. With a cultured, good-looking Indian with money. And between us, he really does look good, so why not? And so this jerk, who tells stories about having a girlfriend, is banging chicks in heaps. Super hot chicks, I'm telling you. Really evokes jealousy. But the thing is, he knows he's a motherfucking asshole and that I'm onto the fact that he's fucking like a fucking asshole that God has showered with a sea of blessings for life, and that's why he's extra nice to me. Invites me to go here and there, brings me this bun with some kind of filling that his grandmother makes, and I say that it's exceptional and that you can see that the bun is handmade and beautiful and delicious, and he asks if he should bring me some tomorrow, and I answer, 'Sure, thanks,' and we even text the next day when he'll bring it and I text him, 'Sure thing.' And I didn't even like that roll. The meat was sweet, and I hate meat with sweetness. Like I hate sweet potatoes. But I ate it.

So one day I promised him that I would teach his cooks how to make Shakshuka, even though they already have it on the menu and they know how to make it. Just because we were like friends and it was cool. So I made it for the entire guesthouse. I worked on about four pans while Bati's mother watched from the side and couldn't believe her eyes because I told her that I didn't know anything about food and that I had no idea how to cook anything except for a glass of water and an omelet. But I also knew how to make Shakshuka, my father used to make it for us all the time when we were kids. I wonder why it stopped when we grew up. What, isn't Shakshuka for grown-ups too? And so I made it for everyone. And every few minutes a different group of girls came to witness the 'Israeli miracle' that cooks a strange and mysterious dish. There was also a French couple who started making political comments, like, "Well, and what about..." and some Israeli guy tried to answer and explain. I preferred to stick my head into the depths of the Shakshuka and listen to the trembling of the vibrant oil from the tomato and pepper juices that melted into it. Later, when we sat to eat on the guesthouse roof, he told me that they were just anti-Semites and not even worth arguing with.

"Say," I told him, "do you know how many people hate the French? And the Germans?? Everybody hates the Germans." Every traveler I met, and we somehow talked about countries, immediately said something about the Germans. without my asking. Without European politeness, without even hinting. Hate the Germans! and the French too. Talk to English tourists—they hate them. I guess it has to do with the many wars that prevailed in Europe over the years, but on the other hand, everyone also hates the Americans. All Europeans hate Americans. Hate them. Just mention America, and it's immediately cursing and insults. 'Oh, I hate them!' Here it's not even "they're like this" or "they're like that"—"I Hate!" And it's for all sorts of reasons. There are white people who hate Black people. Plenty. And Russians. And Chinese. And Arabs. All of Eastern Europe hates the Russians, and all of former Yugoslavia hates the Serbs. Hates them. And the Norwegians? They're not crazy about the Swedes and Danes. Although they disguise it well, listen to me—they're not crazy about them. And the British?? Uh-oh! The Welsh, the Scots, the Irish, the Northern Irish, hate! Hate the Brits! So, what I'm saying is that there will always be someone who is underdeveloped, ignorant or uneducated, who will hate. The problem with such people is that they are always in denial, and people who are in denial usually deny that they are in denial, so they are required to project their self-hatred onto others. It's not about us. And that's why I say that we should stop singling ourselves out as an object of hate. And it doesn't end here. Sylvester was anti-Semitic! Do you hear? Therefore we will not celebrate New Year's Eve. We'll all sit at home and resent that... Sylvester... that he was... um... oh, yeah. A wretched oppressor and a Jew hater! So, we'll sit at home and not celebrate. Why find a reason to party if you can lean on some historical fact and bitch about it? God forbid we dishonor the memory of the Jews whom Sylvester, that Pope, yes yes, inspired others to hate.

To date, some Israelis still don't buy Volkswagens because "we won't fund the Germans". They are still living the war. They are the good guys and there are bad guys, and they are still there, fighting. Those Germans from way back are no longer alive or they are geriatrics and don't know where they are at all. They played their part in history, and that's it. And who knows if the State of Israel would have existed if they had not played their part. And maybe those who work at Volkswagen today are people just like you, who simply work for a living at Volkswagen because they live in Wolfsburg and almost the entire town over there works at Volkswagen.

"So, what are you saying, that there is no anti-Semitism?"

"No, I'm just saying that we should stop using this word, cancel it."

"Okay, and then what?"

"Look, you'll agree with me, that the German who calls himself a neo-Nazi even though he's actually an ignorant person living in some backwater place, is what you call... you know, these are people who have nothing better to do but hate, you see? So he drinks his beer and shouts that he hates cops And Jews, but rest assured that he doesn't like blacks either, nor Britts, and not even the Aryan German who drives in his new Mercedes down his street. So why call him a Jew-hater? Why put ourselves in that equation? He hates. Just hates. And let him hate. Doesn't bother me in the least. And it shouldn't bother you either. He's confined to his narrow world, and the global village protects you because the vast majority are just people who simply want to live."

"There's some good stuff here in Goa, eh?" He gave a full, justified answer.

"Fucking excellent shit."

I was glad that he didn't start a heated argument and tried to convince me. I definitely wouldn't have tried to convince him myself. That's how it is when you're a real Fatel, you don't try to convince as many people as possible to believe in the reality you believe in, in order to make it come true. It's meaningless. So many times you try explaining to someone close to you where they're completely wrong and don't understand, and if only they'd listen to you, their whole life would change, right? So maybe there are situations where it's the same, just the other way around? Here, take this person. You're certain they're wrong and you're right. So, could there not be an opposite situation where you're sure you're right but you're actually wrong? And then, what's the point of any argument at all? So let's just agree that everyone is entitled to their legitimate opinion. What's a legitimate opinion? Not encouraging the murder of babies, for example. Other than that, I believe the majority is legitimate. Everyone is entitled to their own taste.

I, For instance, consider myself to be knowledgeable about music. I even used to be a DJ in eighth and ninth grade. For real. Me and Pompeos. Yep, yep. I was lucky enough to team up with the chubby bearded guy who was about two years older than me and DJ'd for some time in the village, just like in the MTV video clips that juggled on the TV screens in those days. We DJ'd in the village's rhythmics room at parties for kids in grades five through eight, and it was awesome. We were the In guys, popular. Suddenly, in the activity room on a Friday afternoon at four o'clock, with endless long pink chewing gum wrapped in candy-colored wrappers like lollipops, with helium balloons that were discovered to the world and decorated the ceiling next to the glass disco ball with the hundreds of square fragments that, in combination with the weak lighting, created a wonderful cosmic atmosphere, between plenty of boys and girls who invited each other to dance in the center of a circle they created with their bodies, next to a meter-and-a-half-long wooden box attached to colorful foil-wrapped bulbs—red, blue, green, yellow, and one that always leaked white light from the side. There was I. With sunglasses and Pompeos. DJing, putting on music, playing it. DJing, playing music. For one magical and special moment, I was that cool ninth grader, the DJ — the one who's in that actual moment — God.

And we gave out cassettes to the best dancer and dancerette at the end of each party, and they loved it. We'd get cassettes from overseas that Pompeos's cousin would order because he was a serious wedding DJ, and we'd make copies using a double-cassette tape deck. You put a cassette into each slot, place one finger on 'play' in one slot, and one finger on 'play and record'—the red button, while all the others were black. Then, with one quick press, it starts recording. Insane! It's very important to press the buttons together at the same second for the synchronization between the tapes. Sorry, the cassettes. Until one day we got to the schoolyard to play flag football, and two eighth graders, apparently the strongest of the class, who weren't fond of the outgoing champion, started arguing with Pompeos about something. The next thing everyone saw was Pompeos running for good. He sprinted wild down the alley, and after that, we never saw him again. The guy disappeared. And so my worldly fame came to an end in a flash. But I still know a thing or two about music. These were the days of Tanita Tikaram, Modern Talking and Boy George, as well as George Michael, Michael Jackson, Madonna in her early days, and many other amazing artists. Despite all the criticism surrounding the music of that era, which clearly didn't live up to the standards of the seventies with The Doors, Pink Floyd, Led Zeppelin, The Beatles, The Rolling Stones, Janis Joplin, and countless other mind-blowing artists and bands that no one will ever reach the level of; looking back, there aren't many true artists today who've created real works like in the eighties. Oh, and Abba! With that sound of theirs that takes you right back to the moment and day it was recorded. You press play and you're simply there, in that world. And also U2. And Guns and Roses, whose last concert in Israel was one of the best I've seen, and I've seen a lot, including Lenny Kravitz with half a million other people on the Copacabana beach in Rio de Janeiro, Michael Jackson, and Sting. Okay, I made up Sting. But what I actually want to say is that I can't stand Kaveret. Yeah, yeah, I know most people really love them, if not everyone. I also like the band members personally and professionally. I'm even aware that they created a wonderful tapestry of unique sound, blending seasoned Israeli folklore with scenes from the aliyah period and the eras that accompanied it. It's even genius. I just can't listen to them. And this is my legitimate opinion, but mine only. And the members of Kaveret, they don't deal with the question of why I don't connect with their music or what's wrong with them. They are enjoying the idolization of hundreds of thousands of people for decades. It's like a person with a bag full of fresh tomatoes, and they're focused on one rotten tomato, wondering why it's like that. There will always be someone who won't be impressed by you. That doesn't take away from how impressive you are. And if we go back to our friend the sweet potato, well, unlike us, the sweet potato is smarter than that, so it doesn't deal with it at all. And really, there is no particular reason why I am not one of the sweet potato lovers. There simply isn't. I just find it a bit too sweet… and mushy. Practically melts in the mouth, and I'm not a fan of foods that are supposed to lean more to the savory side melting in my mouth. I never understood people who say their steak was tender and melted down like margarine in their throat. It's steak, for crying out loud, I don't want it melting in my throat—it's not ice cream! And how the hell do you eat this roasted chicken with all those sweet soft apricots and sticky date syrup around it, you repulsive people?! But all this doesn't matter, because for everyone like me, there are dozens if not hundreds and thousands, who love sweet potatoes exactly for this reason! And moreover, I can say with complete certainty that there is someone out there who doesn't like sweet potatoes for a completely different reason.Therefore, even if the sweet potato were bothered by the fact that I wasn't one of its fans and made me swear to explain why, in G-d's name, I don't like it and its flavor, it wouldn't matter in the slightest to its continued existence! Because many others will like or dislike it for reasons it will never know. And even if it had made everyone swear to tell the truth or even threatened them to explain why, in G-d's name, they don't like it, it certainly wouldn't have been enough to confirm that the answers it would get were even remotely close to the truth. Surely, those who don't like its smell— even after it's been washed and peeled—would avoid saying it...I have a friend who isn't considered a hottie. She would always whine to me that, because she's 'ugly' or 'fat,' she'll never find someone. And I always told her that each one of us has a soulmate, someone who's especially meant for us. That's why a relationship that's difficult is never interesting or worth fighting for—because 'when it's right, it's right,' as anyone who never agreed to compromise until 'it' happened to them will confirm. And if things are *this way*, and you were created *this way*, maybe your soulmate is one of those who loves someone just like you? Don't believe me? Look at how many people just like you are out there. And they're the ones who are the most happily married. Why? Because they found their soulmate, and he found his. And she looked just like *herself*.

And therefore, I decided a long time ago to love myself the way I am, for any reason and for no reason at all, and to never be bothered with why the hell this particular persona isn't among my admirers. But why for fuck's sake! Just tell me!!

The matter I have spent a lot of time on, was why I wanted her so much in the first place. Certainly not because of that childish thing that she didn't want me. This can only last for a limited period of time. So what was the element that made my first glance at her different from any other glance, from any other girl? After all, there were others as beautiful as her and even more beautiful than her, some more smiley, others less so. Since then and over the years, although I haven't lived with anyone, and people already thought I was gay or a certain kind of homo—even though I had something like five serious relationships, although not very long ones—but even in a time period of a year or even four months you can experience emotional ups and downs. So what is the difference between them and the dozens of other girls who seemed pretty great, where we had things to talk about, plus some attraction? What distinguished these four or five special ones, that we just looked at each other— whether it was near the lockers at the gym where I met Daria, or that magical moment by the bar at that party in the open garden where I met Yael. What is that one element that made us smile at each other instantly and was missing with all those different and other girls who were also "perfectly fine" and we could have matched? For years I thought about it. Wondered. Didn't know the answer. And then one day I just realized that there isn't one. That there's no element! And that's how you know if it's true love or not. And true love doesn't have to be with the one and only forever and ever, it can also only last two or three years. But as long as this non-element exists and you smile at each other for no reason, not because she's hot or cute or smart or rich or provides you with this or that, and the same goes for her, but because you simply smile at each other without any reason. As long as it exists, this non-element, it is true love. And it can last for a day, a week, a month, two months, a year, twenty years, or a lifetime.

And this is why love is a slippery thing. Elusive. Precisely because it has no clear characteristics. It can suddenly materialize with someone you think you even hate, someone who is 'really not your type'—with anyone and everyone. And it happens for no reason. Moran and I didn't exchange a single word before I fell in love with her. It was just instant. My breath was simply "taken away," as they say. I was enchanted by her charm. And she's really a little devil—don't let her fool you now, all nice and forty. It wasn't a coincidence that she had châtain hair. Since then, anyone with châtain hair appears to me as a devilish figure. I know châtain is with 'ch' in French, and Satan is with an 's' in English, but for me, it's the mark of the devil. The thing is, I love her. In love. Bound. My heart chained. No matter how much I hate her and complain about her terrible decrees, with just one look I melt and surrender. As if I were tied with a rope. And that's entirely of no logic! Logic that always says - to move on, to move forward, to conquer myself and my flawed, futile and adrift desires. And the heart, the heart says - to surrender. Surrender to urge, surrender to longing, surrender to desire. And so, either the desire will win, or the desire will tire. Because you gave up, you let it be. You are now down the stream, and not fighting the current. The same current you will never win, for it is one of the forces of nature.

And perhaps this current is actually supposed to take you to your destination, and your inner self sees the right path for you from a bird's eye view. It's like you see a dead bird on the floor and say "Oh, poor thing", and the bird sees dozens or hundreds of dead people during its life and it doesn't matter to her in the slightest, she keeps flying and even shits on your head. And it's not because she's a shitty creature, it's simply because she sees that despite all those who died, we still exist in masses and thrive. The only thing is, that what is upstream can be seen and therefore also be aspired to. And downstream? Who knows. That's why this fear, the paralyzing kind, creeps in... For who knows what worse things are waiting down there. It's like a couple that's been together for a long time. So if you're still doing things together and having fun, then cool. If you're a couple that's already functioning like roommates, each one looking for excitement elsewhere, and maybe every once in a while doing your own thing with some unspoken agreement and everything's fine, then also cool—there are people for whom that works. But if you're somewhere in between, then there's no certainty. And when there's no certainty, you start to get confused. To fear. Where is he? What is she doing right now? Is she cheating on me now while she's in Barcelona with a friend? Is he fucking someone at a bachelor party right now? And what will happen if we break up? The fear paralyzes due to the lack of knowledge. Just like the first trip to boot camp. Into the unknown. But the heart, it comes from the heart. It will never send me to a place that I did not wish for in the depths of my soul, to experience. And I always believed—and still believe—that the heart is wiser than the brain. That the brain is merely a sophisticated tool that filters options for action according to rational calculations and past events. It learns from experience, and from that, it proposes solutions. But beyond experience, it is driven by fear, concerns, ego, by tolerance or aversion to risk. And the worst part—it lacks intuition. And intuition is the real deal. If you check yourself over time, you will find that your initial intuition never fails. Never! And it's a truly remarkable realization when it happens to you. Suddenly, you realize there is a real inner being—an archangel, if you will, a private supervision, or whatever you choose to call it—that can actually guide you if you just listen to that inner voice of yours. If something is unclear, just close your eyes and ask yourself what to do, and the first answer that pops into your head will always be the right one. What feels right to you, even if it's deprived of all 'logic,' is what's right for you.

Arik always says about his businesses that "you don't look back, you keep moving forward," and this holds true for every aspect of life. And what would I really gain from marrying my high school sweetheart? Is it the right path, even if they promise you'll be happy forever after? Or is it actually better to experience, fuck, pursue, get dumped, get offended, get hurt, offend, hurt others, do things you'll regret—things you'd urge anyone else to avoid at all costs— and in the end, find love, get married, get divorced, and then find your truest-purest-absolutest-love and stay together forever? Did the one who experienced everything actually miss out on many years of mental peace, serenity, and love? Or is the love of youth the one that truly entails loss and the sacrifice of countless pleasures and experiences? This question simply cannot be asked and therefore has no answer. The only configuration in which it *can* be asked—is what is best for *you*. Someone who was still a child at the age of twenty-five would screw up everything, feel like they missed out, and live a crappy life. This is why they need to explore those experiences that will mature him and turn him from a boy into a man. And it can also happen at the age of forty or never at all. Many times, or many people, think that we toughen up. And this is also true to some extent, in many cases. And this is how we infer about our heart as well. When your heart breaks for the first time, you're certain that the world has ended and will never be the same again. And this, in some way, is also true. That innocence will never return exactly as it once was. But like…what I mean to say is that... with the next abandonments, over the years, you'll be less disappointed. It would be more accurate to say that you'll still be disappointed, but you'll say, "Okay... so that also happened". And even if you never imagined it, and if someone had told you a year earlier that she would forget you, abandon you, not fight for you, you would've told them they were deeply delusional, that there was no way, for she told you. That she loves you. That you don't even realize how much. And all the things that she is willing to do for you! And in the end... in the end, she didn't even do much less... which is disappointing. But hey, suddenly it's 'just' disappointing. Because after *she* already shattered your heart, many years after *she* crushed it, then it's *just* disappointing. Suddenly you find yourself not broken to pieces. The end of romance? Well, that's the thing. That's what I wanted to say. As for the innocence... which, surprisingly, still exists. In exactly the same configuration even. Which is a very nice thing to discover. It's like your heart is fenced off by branches tied around it, but it is still the same heart. With the same tenderness and the same sensitivity and the same optimism. The same innocence that makes it glow and change colors. To blink as light emanates from it, and fall in love just like that little boy. And because of that, the heart always wins. But when I was a little boy, I still didn't know how to tell the difference between that internal shiver at the sight of Moran, and a good feeling. I just felt a leap in my heart and knew I wanted her.

And perhaps, perhaps my inner voice was whispering to me some vague hint, about what was to come.

3

Because I was so in love with Moran Dagan, my heart pushed me to talk about her with Benny. Perhaps it was my young, childish heart's way of getting a little closer to her, to know something about her, something. I remember one time in the neighborhood, I told him how lucky he was and that he'd definitely get a kiss from her. That's how it is in sixth, seventh grade—you dream about your first kiss. And the most absurd part was that he didn't even want her! She, the little devil with her sharp Satanic-châtain bob and light green eyes, her budding chest that peeked through at barely twelve and her prominent tush sticking out since birth, surely sent the Pulitzer Prize winner on stage to make an announcement on Hanukkah, and suddenly everyone already surrounded them and they were a couple. What? He doesn't want Moran? But how… How can anyone not want Moran??? She's the epitome of perfection! From the first moment I saw her I knew that there was no one like her. no one. Even Michal, the class queen who was my girlfriend in first grade, was long forgotten and crushed beneath Moran's melting beauty, which poured dew and rain upon the garden of my heart the moment I laid eyes on her. Until she moved to our neighborhood from another city and another school, I had all the girls I wanted, and all I had to do was choose. I mean, not exactly choose, but always, during the Friday birthday party games, I was really good at "Kiss-Slap," and with that pillow game where you'd go through "Fan, Like, Lover," I always won, and it just so happened that whoever I wanted, wanted me back. Except for Moran. She never wanted me. I wouldn't exaggerate if I said she really, really didn't want me. The more I wanted her, I always felt that she didn't want me even more. She just told me that with every look... and what the hell are you doing now?? Kissing me as if a little kiss on the mouth because it turned out that we were sitting next to each other in these tall oak chairs with footrests in the middle, and it turned out that this little kiss was kind of wet, I don't know how... Moran Dagan! Will you hurt me forevermore?!

How do I know that the tall chairs at Anat's party are made of oak? Because that's what I do for a living— wooden furniture. Yes, yes. Despite my sometimes lofty speech, and even though I occasionally indulge in common slang, I'm a carpenter. But I love being a carpenter, and because I love being a carpenter, I also pay special attention to details. Because each type of wood reacts and textures differently. Woods like mahogany and walnut aren't suitable for bleaching because they're too dark, but pine, oak, and maple will react wonderfully. Maple and beech have a smooth texture, and oak is much rougher, even though all three share a neutral color that's great for coloring or staining. In contrast, American walnut, African walnut, amboyna, and mahogany have more unique, natural tones. Many times, carpenters or various furniture makers choose the type of wood for the piece of furniture ordered based on what they have in stock or what's cheap, without considering the deeper properties of each type. It's kind of like making Turkish coffee for an English breakfast, because after all, Earl Grey and Turkish are both types of water with caffeine... I'll give you an example for illustration. There's a term in construction called bending. What is bending? It's the behavior of the element that supports the load, like the springs that allow a jeep to drive off-road, or a girder. You can't build a good sofa that will withstand weight with wood that isn't resistant to bending, because it will simply break after prolonged use. The customer might not know it's your fault, but you've done a crappy job. The same principle applies to outdoor furniture; you can't build it out of wood that isn't resistant to weather conditions. And wood that's meant to undergo machining — that's carving and creating shapes, decorations, moldings, and so on — has to come from the category of hardwoods like beech or maple. Kitchen cabinet fronts should be made of wood with a high level of dryness to avoid warping that may occur as a result of changes in internal humidity, due to cooking of course, so that the flatness of the kitchen cabinet fronts is not damaged. Simply put, a kitchen made of pine wood, which may sound wonderful to you, is not really a good option, even though it's hard and durable. Also not the fancy, durable Ipe wood, which is great for decks or pergolas. Even teak, which is considered rare and very luxurious, just isn't suitable. Therefore, whoever convinces you that it will transform your kitchen into something else, is right, but in the end—they're screwing you over. Not that it matters to really rich people, they will buy a new one a few years later and never know you screwed them over. Just like all the antivirus software manufacturers who plant viruses in your computer themselves and then 'save' you from them. And there is no end to the 'viruses' that a carpenter can plant in your furniture and you will never know. It is possible, for example, to use Streif oak, which has a very dark brown shade, as a substitute for the rare and expensive Wenge wood, or isolate knot-free sections of beech wood, which is relatively affordable and durable, to create a low-cost butcher block. Take pine wood, for instance—it's cheap and easy to cut, so carpenters use it a lot and they don't take into account that it might still secrete resin even after drying. It's not as stable as oak or maple. Cherry wood, for example, is beautiful and unique and you can sell it at a good price because it is more expensive than maple which supposedly competes with it in the same category, but with time and exposure to ultraviolet rays just like rays from our sun, it darkens and loses the reddish tint for which it was purchased. So they cover it and prevent it from being exposed to light until it arrives at the customer's house, and then the customer can go fuck himself. He doesn't know he was fooled. But I only work out of love; I've always worked that way. Also with Moran. And don't think of her as an old single woman nearing forty—even today she's still the epitome of coolness. A really well-known DJ among those in the know, creating electronic dub music, dubstep, that anyone who doesn't understand, might think it's music for totally-zonked-out-on-deathbed people, because it barely moves, but once you get into the beat, the rhythm—surely with the right drugs at the right party and the right view— you get it.

And she, standing there with her Châtain hair that goes half to the side and half is shaved, raises clubs in the air, lives and breathes life. Kicks life. This may not tell you much, but she has performed with artists such as Skrillex, Excision and Flux Pavilion. Even Infected remixed a track under her stage name. Moran Dagan, in addition to her mesmerizing beauty, is also intelligent, understands sound, creates sound. Creates—not just samples or does all kinds of covers that leave nothing of the original work and ninety-nine percent of the time, turn out crap. What's even more annoying than samplings is singers who suddenly change the song in the middle of a show. Sing, motherfucker! What, is it hard for you so you suddenly speak the words? Letting the audience sing? Changing intonations on me? I came to hear *this*. I love *this*. *This*, is what you did that I liked, so why are you singing to me something different now?! When I sell someone a sofa that they see on display or my website, do I make something a little bit different for them? Cut corners because I can't be fucking bothered with sanding all the way or trimming the legs to the exact height so they can actually sit comfortably, without it being too high or too low? I paid money and came to your show. Work, motherfucker!

But Moran is a true artist, she's not like these full-of-crap DJs who do covers or samples. And it's not a simple thing at all, to be a true artist. You can work on something for five years and no one guarantees you anything at the end. Vincent van Gogh, whose paintings are now worth hundreds of millions of dollars, died at the age of thirty-seven after a deep depression that included hospitalization in a psychiatric hospital, he had no money for bread, and his last words were "The sadness will last forever". And this is true for every profession. In every profession, some are artists and others are not. A singer can be very successful, but he is not necessarily an artist. An artist *has* to do it—he doesn't do it just because he's really good at it or because it's always been his dream. And you might laugh now, but even being a carpenter is an art. It's not necessarily a bad student who was put in the carpentry program. Even the car salesman, he's an artist at it. You wouldn't sell a quarter of what he does if you tried. Same goes for your mechanic, who can fix in a second what you'd never manage in two months. The yoga instructor who can do a one-arm headstand, and the secretarial workers in a giant company without them, the whole company would collapse in a second. Even the one who spreads your pita bread with the schnitzel or the kebab can be an artist. If he knows how to arrange everything so that when you take a bite, even in the middle of the pita, you'll still have meat, salad, and sauce—not just shoving it all in, that's art. And it miraculously improves your enjoyment of the meal. But most people, if you tell them you're a carpenter, will think you're illiterate. And what does she, Moran, have to look for with a carpenter like me, a small-time guy? She just tossed out some dumb, sarcastic remark, maybe as a joke, about how a simple, small life would suit her just fine. What could I possibly offer her, that she'd come to my house and wash dishes?

But luckily for me, we are in Fatel. And here everyone's—in one way or another—in touch with everyone. Although our year group is something unique, even by local standards. It's practically a miracle and one of the Guinness Book records how we all kept in touch like this. From kindergarten! Sure, there is drama or mutual complaints here and there, but overall, everyone is in some kind of connection, distant or close, one way or another, gathering and meeting in certain carefully curated forums. Roy and Eleanor's traditional birthday party, who have already gotten married, the once-a-year Passover meetup where we set up a tent on the beach and most people come, and other various social gatherings. So sometimes this one is missing and sometimes that one doesn't show up, but all in all, the connection is definitely maintained. Since kindergarten! Wild...

And here we are at tall Anat's birthday, and she invited, and arranged nicely at one of the village's gardens, and I sat down... Okay, enough bullshitting, really! One of the gardens of the village, I say... THE. CENTRAL. GARDEN. WHERE. MY. ENTIRE. CHILDHOOD. WAS. SPENT. But here I am, repressing again. Telling you about Anat and her husband who had the nerve not to be in our kindergarten and not even in our school or high school. She met him at work at the age of thirty, and they came back to live in the village like many of us. But I stayed in Tel Aviv, far from this village and garden. Fatel. They say it's named after Fata Morgana and I can totally relate. A desert oasis which is also a green haven that fooled the heart of an eleven-year-old. Some village... is that a way to go? And Moran who sat next to me. It's been long since I've given any weight to it. This leg will never walk again, this room of the heart is closed and sealed and all the locks that surround it are rusty and no one has any idea where the key is. It will never be opened again. There's no telling what's inside and what has become of the wounded beast that's caged inside. Bleeding, dirty, and abandoned.

And all of a sudden her mother talks to me as if she and I were childhood friends and spoke numerous times, bursting into what feels like a continuation of some random conversation about this and that, and I'm looking for the cellphone and even get up and walk towards one of Anat's tables to try and locate it there. And she walks next to me, accompanying me and muttering something. Where have you been all these years, Mrs. Dagan?? And where is my fucking cell phone when I need it??????

"I should have married Hagai", and both her parents are smiling from the other side like everything's fine, like we're all childhood friends and everything's hilarious. Helloooooo... your daughter killed my heart!!!!!

I remember the one time I went to her house. It was back in high school, when Moran—of all places—ended up in my class when we were split into majors. Suddenly, I had to see that beautiful-ugly face of hers every day. Suddenly, I had to wrestle with my fantasies all over again. And these were not fantasies of lust. Now that I think about it, I don't think I ever even jerked off to her. She was so pure in my eyes that my mind couldn't let me tarnish her image with the despicable, vile act of masturbation. And suddenly everything went black again in the chambers underneath my chest bones. All of a sudden, everything became dark again. *Yoma Chada*—that means "one day" in Aramaic, as we thoroughly learned in the Talmudic-Realistic track I somehow got placed into, all because the teacher we had in

9th and 10th grade was fantastic at teaching Talmud and made the Gemara's debates so engaging and fascinating, and this had nothing to do with the fact that she was really hot, and that so it is, that a person's life is changed forever, because he jerked-off to the teacher from 10th grade… So one day, before some math exam, she sat next to me, all casual, and mumbled something about us going to her place afterward. Yes, yes. Moran Dagan invited me to her house, six years late. But what's six years in the life of a teenage heart? One minute, and he forgets everything. Ready for anything. Lusts for everything. Tempted by everything, yearning for everything. And so she eagerly copied the entire exam from me, and afterward we really went to her house. How many years did I dream of seeing her house from the inside, that window that overlooks the street from the house I passed by at least twice a day. Looking, hoping. Maybe Moran is there, maybe something will happen. And what does she have in her dresser, Moran? My whole life, I've been dying to know what's inside, be it the worst of the worst. Lo and behold… Except that when the dream came true, the event lasted no more than twenty seconds. Her mother was in the kitchen and said nothing to me except a wordless subtext that I should go home. But I also stopped blaming the senior lady of the Dagan family. Looking back today, she was probably protecting her daughter from all the boys who had been courting her since she was born. A lot of girls are pretty, but the one who showed up at the Scouts in 3rd grade, from another neighborhood, wearing red shorts and a red shirt—you'll never forget. Instantly, everyone looked at her, everyone wanted. Before we knew she was sexy, she already was. How many men did Mrs. Dagan manage to fend off? Who knows. In high school, Moran used to hang out with the older kids. In the 9th grade, when we envied them because they already had their scooter licenses, we called them *Bragobikers*, and when they got their car licenses — *Bragmobilers*. But they were with Moran, and I wasn't. I don't know exactly how many or who, but someone definitely tasted her pleasures. Half a year of dating at that age with someone two years older than you? Give me a break… The window on the second floor of the Dagan house slowly turned into an enemy. I'd pass by it and turn my head. Deflecting, not looking. I know, I know. I should've forgotten about her, stopped. But how can you? And why do these scars stay so long after...

4

Fatel isn't called Fatel. It's a small village that no one knows. I mean, people know it, but under a different name. Only those who live there call it Fatel. Fatel, named after the 'fateel' that didn't burn... what an absurd story. Yes, I know that Fatel has one E and Fateel has two Es and it's in Arabic. Yeah, well... I'll tell you about it sometime. And it's a perfectly fine village too, really close to a big town, and some great people have come out of here, making their mark both across the country and even worldwide. It's just that, if you're from Fatel—you're from Fatel. There's no other explanation for it. Why do you think it's perfectly fine for me to be sitting here now with my friends from kindergarten and a few parents, admittedly a few, but one heck of a '*still…*' and everything feels natural and good? Because we are Fatel. We are all Fatel.

And that kiss was natural too. Moran's kiss. In Fatel, kissed me on the mouth. What...? What doesn't work here? It worked out perfect for me my whole life! But that's life... Life is life. Welcome to life. And in this life, you mustn't go in spite. I mean, you can. Everyone does. Even those who try not to — zigzag, trip up. But I've already realized a long time ago from life itself, that if it's going hard it's not yours. Not in a lazy way, in a psychological way. If you're stuck on something, you're stuck. The rest doesn't matter. And then you remain stuck. Irritated, judgmental, bumming out, bitter. If I had felt even a flicker of a chance with her, I never would've given up. Never. But it was just a no-entry sign. Not a 'stop,' not a 'wait, yield,' not even the kind that says 'train crossing.' And even if it was a long freight train, like those old ones that used to stop us on the roads before they paved all the 'six-lane' highways, I'd have been fine waiting.

In the end, the barrier would lift, and the whole family would wrap up their little moment of wonder with a smile. But this barrier would never rise. It was clear. Moran made it clear to me with each hollow and dead glance that said 'You have nothing to look for here'. Don't look at her like that now, all smiley and nice. And really, she's the best Fatel in the world right now. Sitting next to me and I feel like hugging her. Moran from 5th or 6th grade, I don't remember anymore, who crushed my heart again and again and again. Until about the age of thirty. Then I gave up. My heart conned me into thinking that I managed to bury it deep enough for it not to bother me anymore, or at least that's what I thought... and since then she's Fatel. Same as everyone else here. And it's fun. And everyone's talking. And sometimes sing a little. Nothing forced. Suddenly, five people talking remember a line from a song, and one starts humming, another joins in, and before you know it, all five are singing with a smile that they have been seeing since kindergarten, and it doesn't take more than ten seconds—and that's long—until everyone present hears it with that half ear always on standby for exactly such a moment, and immediately drops everything they're doing to join in, and all of a sudden there is a choir. And then someone starts another song, and five songs can flow like this until everyone's falling apart. Well, we're not fifteen with monster hormones anymore... Wow, the stories I can tell. Not stories of heroism or stories about me. Stories about the place. About Menash who once surrounded the village eighteen times consecutively, after he bet the entire class he could do it, running until he passed out and they took him to the hospital and the entire school for an intervention with the municipality psychologist or the district psychologist, I've no idea. Crazy stuff, not a bet on who can eat three teaspoons of mustard in a row... The funniest thing is the cars in Fatel. It's like those kibbutz cars, everyone's car is everyone else's. Except for those who bought something really expensive, and there's no way I'm taking their Jaguar. I'm joking, it's an Audi at best. There's also plenty of Mazdas and Hondas. Also Opel and such. Nice cars, actually. Fords. There's also Skodas. A few Suzuki jeeps, the small ones, they're nice. Drive well off-road. Many times, I take the cars for the license test because I am one of the only self-employed people, so I can. They pay like a few bucks for the time and supposedly for the work I lose, but all in all, you can't really say no. It's like reserves, Fatel-style reserves. Because I can, I must. And that's it. Everyone looks out for everyone. If you can, then you must. And everyone must with love. And maybe that's what builds and keeps our love. For each other. For ourselves.

Imagine that you live in a world where everyone does things that others can't do, without asking any questions. And then, no one is in need of anything. And over time you also do things with love because everyday people do things for you directly or indirectly. These are housewives, so they take the children out of kindergarten and look after them as long as necessary, sometimes even into the night, and that's perfectly fine. Men do it too. And there's no complaint or resentment or 'well, this time they've gone too far'. None. Because *they* work and thanks to *them* indirectly, *they* have electricity, water and they can pay bills. So they do it with love. They have no worries. And *they* don't have either. And I don't have either. I work in a carpenter's workshop, doing what I enjoy, and I know for sure that everything will be fine no matter what I do. No matter what I do! Do you get it? So I take the cars to the license test. And I already recognize the testers, and they recognize me. And it's not that I take two vehicles a month for a license test, yes? There are other self-employed folks, or people who take half a day off work or something. But every time before the test, you picture that face—the tester's. And when you get there—he's there. And you think to yourself, *What, a whole year has passed? Surely by now he's this way or that.* But honestly, where's he going to go? He's there. And so, for thirty years you see him there. And you always wonder if he recognizes you or not, so you give a half-nod-half-not. Unsure if he knows you or if you're just coming off like an idiot. Thinking it might ruin it for you if you look too smiley as if it will be interpreted by him that you are trying to suck up to him. Everyone thinks about it when they're doing the license test. How to behave most naturally, because naturally, natural people have no defects in the cars, and even if they do, it's not nice to fail them... you fucking retard. And you, shouting at the tester, "What, you failed me over the alignment blocks?! Who changes alignment blocks after ten years??" As if the tester is thinking, "You know what? Sure, let's let you drive like that on the road. Worst case, you lose control of the car, kill a few people, and my name's on the line for it. Sounds great to me. As long as you stop yelling or you seem like a good guy to me or you made eyes at me to make me think you'll blow me. Sometime. After you leave the registration office and hit the gas in your new BMW." Well, come to think of it, that last one might actually work.

One day, I came back to the village after an absence of about two years—a huge stretch of time in Fatel terms. A bit of India, a bit of Tel Aviv, Florentin area... I worked at a place that sold high-quality coffee beans, which people would come in and we ground for them on the spot. To me, it always seemed like it was all just black coffee, and that's part of the fun. I'd buy a different type each time, even the cheapest one they sell by the kilo. Those are the best—the ones restaurants buy. The nastier, the tastier. It also varies depending on the amount of sugar and how much you stir. People barely stir. They don't even swirl. Don't put in the work. They just put it in the cup, one-two swirls, and that's it, sweetened. You have to let the sugar mix with the coffee, dissolve into it. It's like a relationship—you can't just throw two people into an apartment and say, 'Alright, figure it out.' You need the pursuit, the slow element of conquest, the hints of yes but still not quite, the longing, the yearning. Only together do they create the sweet, intoxicating aroma. Don't get me wrong, I love an espresso from the machine too, just like a good fling, but you can't compare it to the depths of black coffee.

And so we were sitting like this in Fatel, while Arik is making me "mud coffee" in the small Finjan he has in his yard, which faces the main path leading to the road. He's got a small gas burner permanently set up next to the grill. Over here, we usually cook the coffee with the sugar already in the pot. That is, first the coffee brews well, then you add the sugar and let it keep cooking, and every few minutes, you give it a deep stir with one of those big, grandmotherly, honorable metal spoons—the kind you'd use for rice—and let it cook together for a few more minutes until it starts simmering. Ahhh... dreamlike. And as I'm savoring the aroma, lighting up a quality Nobles cigarette—because if I'm already smoking, it might as well taste like something bold and rich—gross enough to be weirdly enjoyable—he suddenly throws out, all casual-like:

"So, you hear? Lately... Me and Moran are like... "

Huh?"I moved my head in his direction with the smoke still in my mouth, "Which Moran?"

He said Moran, Hagai! Mo-ran! Which Moran? The one you've been thinking about your entire life!

"Moran, bro. Moran Dagan, who else did you think?" he kept going when I didn't respond, probably due to the instant freezing of all the capillaries in my body.

"What about her? You... are you guys...?"

"We are, bro," he smiled a sweet smile.

No one can help but love Arik. He's just so... cute. And kind. A good guy. Not that he doesn't love to rebel against life. He's got a heavy bike, and recently, he even started surfing a bit. Not the cool, born-to-surf kind of guy with bleached bangs from 6th grade like Benny, but a sweet kid. Always was. With cheeks like a jelly donut. And now, his true face has been revealed. Fucking asshole. You're doing this *to me*? To me?? Son of a fucking... son – of – a – fucking – bitch!!! With that sweet smile of his, always... always so innocent and such a good kid and the cutest man in the world, so to speak. Fucking-asshole-son-of-a-bitch. I knew it was all a scam, I knew it!

I remember hating her. I was in love with her, and I hated her at the same time. I wanted her to be mine forever, and I wanted her to be dead. "I love you," she'll suddenly say one day. And suddenly, for the first time in my life, I'll hear it right. "Me too," I'll answer, consciously leaving out the word "love." I won't gush right then. I won't flinch at the sound of her flute after thirty years of suffering. Still holding on to whatever tiny dignity might be left in me in her eyes—or in mine. I will then let go a bit but she will cling to me. Make me smell her perfume which always killed me in an instant, which passes like a caressing breeze, yet is elusive and forever unattainable. And now, as if it were mine. Will I be tempted? Shall I remove my defenses and stand exposed only to be hurt yet again by Moran Dagan? And will this be the last time? The final blow? The most despicable exploitation, after which she will cast me aside as in days gone by? Will my soul then be forever scarred and Lucifer's pitchfork will strike my chest in every interaction that occurs between us from now until eternity? And perhaps I should just strangle her right now? Hug her really, really tight, and then simply choke her to death in some abandoned facility on the outskirts of Fatel, where no one will ever find her body! No one ever understood her anyway. Murder… premeditated. Planned. Meticulous. Executed with the precision only I know and can. Just as she knowingly murdered my soul all these years. And in these last moments of her life, right before she returns her soul to the Creator after I slit her throat, I will ask her and she will finally say. Why, for God's sake?!?!?! What the hell is so wrong with me????? And then, oh, then… then will I deliver my elimination speech. About how she's a disgrace to God Cupid, how Juliet would have given anything just to see her Romeo one last time, how thousands of years of civilization led the universe to this very moment where you and I meet—and you… you didn't even give it a chance??? Yeah, I know this whole thing sounds a bit psychopathic right now, but believe me, it was great, because the alternative was to hate myself or at best to be very upset with myself, and at not-that-best, think that I'm just not enough of… something.

And now, Moran Dagan is once again pulling the strings. Carries me to places and horizons, and expanding them. Stretching the fabric of my limits to the edge and beyond. But for a reason I have not yet internalized, the fabric keeps expanding. It consists of an incorrigible elasticity and flexibility that I never imagined. Maybe it's because I'm addicted to her, maybe it's because of other things. You turned my world upside down at the age of eleven, sweet Morani, and you have no intention of stopping now.

But what could possibly happen *now*? A person has to be super fucking retarded and stupid, and I apologize to all the mentally challenged people, but you have to be one hell of a moron, to think that after all this she will be yours. Honestly, more than that, you'd have to be one sorry-ass delusional person to even want to be with her. And you... a piece of nothing pretending to be a real friend all these years... Line up right next to Moran, and there I shoot! Shoot the both of you, two disgraces to the entire human race who decided with deliberate intent to destroy my life. And you, too! Oh, yes... You, Mr. Benny Benjamin, the surfer with the oxidized ponytail. I will slaughter and eliminate all of you in one go!

Oh, Arik the despicable... How could you do such a thing to me? How?! After all we've been through? And the kind of friends we are? So I disappeared for a bit, I know. Okay, for two years. India, you know... And Vaknin from Rishon Lezion suggested that we take an apartment in Tel Aviv together... Florentin, not the most expensive parts. That we'd work and get by. Like Everyone does. And even if not, we'd wait tables a bit, spend a year, two, five in Tel Aviv, and worst-case, head back home happy after experiencing it all. After kicking a bit and tasting life. hooking up with some hot chicks from northern Tel Aviv. So you already managed to forget about me? You know how much it will hurt me. You know! And even if I should have gotten over it a long time ago, you are not the one who should cause me this pain, even if it will do me good at the end of the road. Even if it will save me. Thanks a lot Mr. Arik, but with your permission, I will exit the movie I live in in my own free time. I shook my head from my thoughts and realized that for a moment I actually thought them. Okay well, not seriously. Not really.

"But...like..."

"What?" He cut off the beginning of my stutter. "Hmm?" He moved his gaze slightly as I didn't respond. ""Hey, ash it off, or it's gonna fall into your coffee!"

"Hopsss!" I quickly tapped off the long ash that had nearly reached the filter since I hadn't taken a drag for a few seconds. "Did you see that?" I laughed, buying myself some time.

I changed the subject and started calculating in my head. Like... Well basically... Like, Actually... Come to think of it, no one knew that I was preparing for that Hanukkah party with those special clothes... or maybe they did? Perhaps it was a plot orchestrated by all three of them? To despise me, and humiliate me because I always took all the girls from them. And so they will now bring a unique and special model, from a different school, and that one girl, I will never have. Here here, I'm crafting the guillotine especially for you from fine mahogany wood! Do not worry, I'll sand it really well so that you don't get a thorn stuck up your butt... With my returning to sanity, I realized that I actually didn't say a thing when Benny and Moran became a couple, and afterward, us guys would always half-laugh in embarrassment about her hanging out with the older kids, but in a Fatel way, not in a gossip or jealousy way. Apart from me, of course. I was totally gossiping for a crumb of information. But no one actually knew because I was too embarrassed to say. To tell how I ended up as an idiot with the clothes and the Hanukkah, and later on that she's hanging out with the older guys anyway and why would she give me the time of day when they have a motorcycle and surely also know how to get laid.

"So like, how... well go on, you piece of shit!!" I completely changed the intonation. "so, I'm telling you, bro!" he immediately returned to an automaton with smiling cheeks. "You weren't here... things happen." "That's wild, Man... Like... So what, you guys are like... you're like banging her, or are you like together together??" Nice, continue with a few more 'like's and 'you know's, and it will sound totally credible...

"No, we're together, bro. A couple." He flashed his sweet, innocent smile. I wanted to bail, run away. Fly from there straight to damnation. Just run with my eyes closed, never stopping until something hits me and it's all over. To leap towards the length and breadth of the land until I run out of energy or until someone just shoots me in the head. Something must have given me away. My face is probably all red and tells everything. Luckily, I'm a redhead so it's hardly noticeable. Yeah, well. With muscles in my legs. When I was little, I was really good at futsal; I was even on the regional futsal team. This redhead from Fatel with muscled legs. An average height. Although between 9th and 10th grade I suddenly grew taller by about ten centimeters accompanied by terrible back pain and scary stretch marks, but in the end I stabilized at 1.85 meters. I was that freckled redhead, with reddish freckles on the spot where your cheeks curve when you smile, and a mane of slightly high red hair. But as one solid piece, not spikes of gelled hair. And now I was hoping that no one noticed my blushing from sheer sadness and the complete collapse of my internal systems, for redheads suffer from excess redness all over their bodies twenty-four-seven. But since Arik knows me well, I started pretending to be interested, asking questions. Not out of creepiness, snooping, or obsession, but as a friend to a friend. Let him talk, let him enjoy. I can't believe this is happening to me. I can't believe this has happened… And suddenly I was no longer in anger. I convinced myself that it was a small boy's infatuation and that I should stop. That this relationship with Arik has killed me for good, but also brought me back to life. A boyfriend in the 6th grade is very painful but only until the 9th grade, then the older kids, and then in the army she disappeared from my sight for a really long time. She did her army service far away and moved in with a friend-roommate, and things started to blur for me. And it was good. And then with Arik it finally finished me off for good. But it also led me to a profound realization. Like, if up until now you still had illusions or completely concealed hopes that you don't even tell yourself, now it is finally over.

"She's… She's really cool, bro. Seriously. Super cute. A good girl. We didn't get to know her when we were kids because she only came in the 5th or 6th grade, you know… and after that, she always hung out with the older kids. What did we call them, the 'bragmobilers' or something? Haha…"

"At first the bragobikers, only afterwards the bragmobilers," I laughed too.

"Right! The bragobikers… dope…"

"True, she was always a bit distant. Didn't really get to know her."

Ahhhhhhhhhhhhhhhh!!!

"And that's the thing, bro. She's Fatel! She's a total Fatel!"

"Sweet..."

Ahhhhhhhhhhhhhhhh!!!
Ahhhhhhhhhhhhhhhh!!!
Mamaaaaaaaaaaa!!!
Enooooooooooooooooooough!!!!!!!!!!!!!!!!!!!!!!!!!!!!!!!!!!!!!!!

"Yeeh, bro. she's really cute. Fun girl."

"Cool... and also hot." I added for a reason that was still unclear to me.

"Also hot... Totally, man..." he marveled with his look.

Enough.

God.

I'm begging you.

Please.

Enough.

And that was it, at that point I was completely dead. He didn't add anything, though I didn't speak and was waiting for more. For every ounce of lava to pour out from that wheezing volcano straight onto my head. But it's important to me that you know, without a shadow of a doubt, that Arik is really a great guy. A true, wholehearted sweetheart, without a hint of cynicism. And even in that moment, I loved him and wished him to be as happy as possible. And at that moment, I also wished... and hated the damn second that this girl entered the gates of our school.

5

Sometimes I wish I was one of those *casual relationshipers*. I wish I could be. That is the right place to be. Instead of being *available* all the time, lest you'll miss "the real thing," it's better to be *taken*. Everyone wants what they can't get. An apartment that has been on the market for a long time raises questions, something about this deal smells bad, a high risk. When you're a *casual relationshiper*, you get to enjoy the perks of a couple's lifestyle that fill so many of the *holes* of singlehood—you sleep next to someone at night and even have sex, and often a lot more of it than singles do, even if it's with the same partner. Don't get it wrong— singles hook up here and there, sometimes with a high turnover, but in *casual relationships*, we're talking about a stretch of months—three, four, nine—and during that time, there's still plenty of sex. Beyond that, you have someone to hang out with, you don't have to hang out in clubs until morning, get drunk and high, and fuck with a condom. That's right, In *casual relationships*, there's no condom! By the end of the first week, at best, it's already off because *"I trust her."* And after a while, you break up, because it's clearly not *it*, but by then, you've already had time to lay eyes on someone else, and someone has had time to lay eyes on you—and you're a real hot commodity that should be grabbed quickly like a hot bun straight out of the oven. And even if not, at least you've practiced being in a relationship, you've improved, you learned what you do want and what you don't want, and beyond any tangible level - you had the right energy. You transmitted the right frequency to the universe, you sang the right song. All the damn hell of me being so... absolute. Not being able to stay more than a second where I don't feel it.

And now we're forty years of age. After you got used to fucking all your life, turning forty is tough. Suddenly you don't go out that much, there are fewer people to go out with, less strength, not necessarily physical, maybe a little. And you're mainly at war with yourself to prove that you still got it. Every now and then, you win that battle. Look at that—I've still got it. And a hottie too. And twenty-three years old! And I just came on to her in the middle of the street when I went to buy cereals at the grocery outside the village. I woke up Friday morning, and no cereals. Luckily, the kind I like is only sold at the far-off grocery store, way up at the top of some steep street. Then, from a distance, I saw her. Wow. Wearing those tiny shorts everyone's into now, even though rape is still very much against the law, and walking next to her bicycle. So I picked up my pace a little—not too much, though, so I wouldn't look weird or freak anyone out—until I got close to her. "You know, it gets really cool if you ride it..." I threw it casually, and she laughed. That's it, if the girl laughed, you've got confirmation to continue. We chatted a bit more about nothing, and at some point arrived at the doorway of the grocery store. I could have carried on as if I wasn't heading there, but honestly, that was enough small talk to justify giving me her number if she was into it, so why chew her ear off? And she was down. That we'll talk. At first I thought of waiting a few days, but then I said *Fuck it, why wait? Yes - yes, no – no* and I called.

We set a date for that same day. The truth is that we didn't really have anything to talk about because all she has done so far in her life was a driving license test and army service, and no matter how mature and smart and interesting a person she is, it would be hard, if not impossible, for us to reach any depth of conversation. She just hadn't lived enough or grown enough yet. At the end of the date I walked her home, and then suddenly *she* asked *me* if I'd "*like some ice cream or tea or something*". And where is there an ice cream shop open at two in the morning 'round here? There isn't. "*I've got some great lemon verbena on my balcony,*" I said, thinking I was the one leading the moment. "*Cool,*" was her immediate reply. Unbelievable. But it's like a glorious soccer team in its decline, winning against an epic team once every few years—just like in the good old days—and immediately going back to its downfalls. You know that you'll never go back to this war. Deep inside, you know that if you come back at full power, you will win. If you live in Tel Aviv and go out to bars every day, buy girls drinks and chase the scene, you'll be a master-fucker even at fifty-nine. But who the hell is interested in that? Suddenly it's not interesting, suddenly it was a fight. How to get that one, and play the right game with this one, go to that bar and drive to that party. This one only wants something serious, and with her, you have to invest at least two dates, including a restaurant. But you fight because there's a prize for the winners. To the choirmaster, A Psalm of David. And what a Psalm... A song of praise for the victor. And what a song it is. Me and King David, we're actually part of the ginger brotherhood. Like, the real shit. Oh, man... there you are, showing her that you're in shape and not coming too quick, and even know how to turn her over to at least three positions every time and even leaning against the wall standing up. Oh, wow, she's definitely never had it like that. You can tell... yeah... well... But it was a really great prize. And now that prize is gone. And it's not just really not fun anymore because it was really fun, it's a real blow to the ego. And... and also in general. Like, what's wrong with me all of a sudden? *Is* something wrong? But just as soon as you consider returning to active service in the reserves, to the dangerous front line, the insight hits you that 'Actually, I don't have the strength anymore". What, is it because I've gotten older? But I did have the strength for that date with that girl last week. And it was fun too. And also with the one before her, with whom I had two challenging dates, but something about her interested me and I also enjoyed imagining myself screwing her... And suddenly, that constant loss in that war makes you yearn for and appreciate peace. Which is the most important thing and what proves beyond any doubt that it is also the right thing, simply because it makes you feel good. Which in my opinion, regardless of anything, is always better than war.

And so I moved back to Fatel, where the friends are. And here it's simply amazing. It really is a miracle. From kindergarten! How many people do you know or remember at all from kindergarten? And keep in touch with? Forty people? Absurd to the point of being unbelievable... No, really, it's unbelievable. Even I, who is telling you this story, can hardly believe it. But that's how it is with us. Fatel. Forty guys, plus some add-ons and half-parents, sitting around something and spending the evening. Talking, munching, chattering. The same faces you've been seeing for thirty-something years, there's no way you'd suddenly replace them. After all, it's them! There's Sagi with the stress on the first syllable, Arik's sitting in the corner with Ronit and Tuti, whom no one calls Reut for thirty years now, not even her father. And Benny and Ariel are sitting in the corner talking about surfing again. Ohad and Batya are constantly grinding and rolling joints according to protocol as usual. Ben-Dov, Asi, and Gali are cracking open another beer, and another, and another. Like this, for thirty-something years. And there were tons of messes, don't think otherwise. Almost everyone has been with everyone except "taboos" such as best friend, sister of, and so on. And even then, there were slip-ups. But it's all good. Always, always, always. Except when we were kids or in our twenty-something-plus-ego years, everything is always good. No fights and no one's at odds. And suddenly, I felt at home. The familiar surroundings from infancy give you a sense of security. You're not alone. You're part of something. Those weeping willow trees are still there, as if longing to embrace you when you come to find comfort beneath their caressing branches. And the gravestones... Yes, there are also gravestones in the village. Maybe it's also something that unites us, maybe it's because of this that we're even united. Sagi, not the one that's here, died in Givati. They hit a roadside bomb in Lebanon while securing a route. Died for nothing, just a shitty thing. I don't even want to talk about it, to spoil the atmosphere. When a soldier dies, it's always tragic. Everyone grieves deeply. Taken just like that, in the prime of his life, before he had the chance to experience, to taste anything of this life. When a small child dies, it's the collapse of all worlds. Or a little girl. So sweet. And there are pictures of her smiling, and everyone says how magical she was, how she spread a unique splash of light throughout the house. But if someone, say, a fifty-four-year-old woman, dies next to you from a heart attack in the supermarket, it will obviously be shocking, but... if you read about it in the newspaper, it won't really affect you. That same little girl, when she reaches fifty-four and is maybe no longer as cute and sweet as she once was, suddenly it will matter less that she died. It won't affect you in the same way, if at all. So what does this actually say, about death? That it's a factor of age? Or... perhaps of sweetness? What makes us feel more sorry—or less—for someone who will never know how we feel about them? And even if you believe in reincarnation or you don't, either way, it doesn't matter to them, because either they've returned to being light and love, or they've ceased to exist forever. So what meaning, really, is there in any of the emotions you feel toward them?

But the feeling of longing still exists. And therefore, once a year, a week before the National Memorial Day, we all go to his family, so that they don't go into it alone, so they know we're all here with them, and that Sagi lives on in each of us. And they are happy. Always happy. His mother even underwent IVF and insisted on having another child, almost at fifty, and named him Sagi too. Yeah, I know it sounds a bit surreal, but who are we to say anything? Anyway, so now they have another Sagi, and I swear to you, he even looks like him! I mean, I've known him since day zero—both of them. And now he's almost twenty. It's insane. He actually laughs at the same retarded jokes as the Sagi we knew from kindergarten. And it's like we're sending him messages and getting responses back—throwbacks to moments with his brother—and he tells us, yeah, he remembers. Every so often, he even says something that freaks everyone out, like the old Sagi is really listening. And then there was that girl who died in high school, about which I really don't feel like talking about... But it's okay because, in Fatel, everyone believes in reincarnation. That's why death is only sad from the perspective of longing, not because something terrible happened to the person. As far as we're concerned, something wonderful happened to them. They completed their role in this lifetime, and in their free time, they'll return as a newborn. And that's why we intentionally don't observe Memorial Day, Holocaust Remembrance Day, or the day of the remembrance for Rabin's assassination. It's not that we are right-wing or left-wing; most of the village's residents don't even vote. The nearest polling station is about a twenty-minute drive away, and even the people who live there barely go to vote because they are also, well almost, somewhat Fatel. So what's the deal? At first, I didn't get it either. I asked, I rebelled, I complained. But the adults always just calmed me down and patted my head. 'Everything's fine,' they always said, and still say. Everything's great. To this day, no one has explained it to me, but at some point, you just understand. It's like sea turtles hatching from their eggs, dozens of meters from the shore, and knowing exactly how to run to the water. It's this kind of collective consciousness that you're really happy to join the moment it lands on your head straight from the heavens.

Oh, the heavens. Full of stars and angels and all the divinities that everyone has created and shaped. Greek and Roman gods, oddly-shaped Indian deities, Cleopatras and mermaids, pharaohs and temples, Herculeses and Brahmins, and above all — God. And to commemorate, commemorate, commemorate everything that happened. That war and this one and *that* one. The Holocaust and the heroism, so that we never forget and never forgive those who have long been dead, And Jesus, who was crucified, and why, and because of whom and what. And the giving of the Torah, the Tablets, and all those things that might have been truly relevant three or four thousand years ago, and who knows what was before and why it even matters. And the afterlife... Oh. This is where everyone falls. If up until now you've rolled with me, this is where many many good people fall. Mainly because they are skilled. In thought. Because thinking back is easy. Trial and loops. Empiricism. Rationality. Analysis. In a moment, I'll bow and salute in the face of the exalted nature of words. But hey, your great-grandfather felt bad about it, so did your grandfather, and so did your dad, and so it's your duty to feel bad as well. With the few years we have on this planet, it is incumbent upon us to be preoccupied and busy with thinking carefully and remembering well, because *this* is important, and *that* is forbidden, and *this* is permitted, and only if we truly behave — we will earn the afterlife, which, somehow, we are absolutely certain of and convinced exists. An utopian axiom of an utmost chosen idea. Yes, yes. I don't know what it's called or why it is this way, but I will suffer and mortify, believe in the ancient chronicles of the galaxy as spoken by God, and then accept as an axiom this utopia called Heaven, where it will be the most amazing for me, and this is the best idea I can come up with and choose. Why? Because that's what they told me, my grandmother, and also my great-grandfather's grandpa, and if any of them also perished in the Holocaust, then it's definitely true, because if there's such a hell on earth, there must be a heaven in return. Huge. Simply huge.

And what will there be in that world with the promised Heaven? Oh... you could ramble on about that endlessly, and there will always be someone who believes. Always. And those who believe — well, they're certainly not afraid. That's what someone once said... But I say that those who believe are the most afraid. That if they don't do this or that — God will punish them. He will send them to hell or worse, 'That soul shall be cut off from among his people,' as is said in Numbers 15:31. Have you ever checked if the word hell— *Gehenom* in Hebrew — even appears in the Bible you believe in so much? So... umm... I don't know how to break it to you, but the word *Gehenom* does not appear in the Bible at all! The only thing that somewhat resembles it is a valley south of Jerusalem called *Gey Ben Hinom*, where the Canaanites used to sacrifice children to the Moloch. From there come the legends that hell's torments involve burning in fire. The concept of an underworld, *Sheol* in Hebrew, where rebellious souls are burned, is actually a mix of child sacrifice in *Gey Ben Hinom* and the mythological fire of Phlegethon, one of the five rivers of the Greek underworld. it's all a big pile of horse crap in mashed tomato sauce, cooked up by power-hungry intellectuals from three thousand years ago... But you know what? Let's take it all the way. It is written in the Bible that if you do not do so and so – "*that soul shall be cut off from Israel.*" Okay, so maybe there is no hell, but God forbid that my soul will be "*cut off from Israel*", what, am I crazy? Oh dear, you say without thinking. But wait a minute, it's not written that it will burn in the fire of hell, that soul. That, we already know. So what will actually happen, you will be born in the next incarnation as some 'insignificant Norwegian'? You think a Norwegian who lives with no worries and no wars in beautiful Oslo, in a welfare state as rich as Korach, has no significance because he's not Jewish? It's funny I mention Korach, because, in case you didn't know, Korach — according to the Bible — tried to incite the people against Moses. And because of that, the ground opened up and swallowed him whole. Probably somewhere near *Gey Ben Hinom*... One might wonder if it miraculously has something to do with 'as rich as hell' in English and 'rich as Croesus' in Greek mythology... And if we go back to our Norwegian friend, do you really think he's looking at us Israelis and thinking to himself, 'Ah, what a bummer that I'm not holy and pure?' Or is he laughing at us and the Arabs fighting over some 'holy' mountain or cave, seeing us as two varieties of some particularly Neanderthal-like primate, while he's peeing on us in a rainbow arc, while dining with his family and kids in worry-free Oslo?

Have you ever wondered how it's even possible that such a smart and sophisticated book just '*appeared*' over three thousand years ago? '*Preserved*'? simply preserved? Just like the mummies preserved? In the days when the Bible was written, people buried their dead close to the city but outside it, so as not to defile the living. This may sound a bit idiotic to you, but if you think in terms of people who lived three thousand years ago, there could be some sense to it. The amazing result of this, however, is that archaeologists today can clearly determine the borders of a specific city based on archaeological excavations. In-depth research reveals that the great Jerusalem of King David and King Solomon's time, as described in the Bible, is most likely a futuristic, utopian vision—one that only materialized during the reign of King Josiah, ruler of Judah, whose capital was Jerusalem. Josiah capitalized on the Assyrians' retreat to their homeland, prompted by a raging civil war, to expand northward and reclaim territories that had previously belonged to the Kingdom of Israel, with Samaria as its capital, and had until then been under Assyrian occupation.

Josiah wishes to unite the two kingdoms into one Hebrews kingdom, and only then did Jerusalem become the great capital as described. But the agenda was to glorify and exalt Jerusalem, presenting it as if it had always been great and mighty from the days of old, despite the fact that the kingdom of Judah was for most of its times simple and poor compared to the prosperous kingdom of Israel. Josiah attempts to implement a reform according to which there is one God and one sanctuary place - Jerusalem. This is his agenda for the purpose of uniting the kingdom, under his rule, of course. So he tells stories. And who would dare to contradict the king's word? In the Book of Kings, we are told that during work on the Temple, a scroll of the Bible was discovered by Josiah, containing all the commandments to worship the one and only God. A holy book, written by Moses himself! A sacred text! Written! '*Who is for my Lord, come to me!*'. Strengthened by the words of Moses, he immediately embarks on a sweeping religious reform, destroying places of worship throughout the land, smashing and tearing down all the altars and high places dedicated to idols. He abolishes the human sacrifices that were customary in *Gey ben Hinom* and the burning of human bones on the altar built by Jeroboam ben Nebat in *Beit-El* as well as the high places in the Kingdom of Israel. Wait, what did you say? Human sacrifices? What kind of Neanderthal, stupid, mentally ill people do such things? Go on, say it. I'm sure you are all in complete and unanimous agreement that it's absolutely horrifying. And for what? So that the pagan god in the sky will send rain? Have mercy on us? It's completely absurd, what does one thing have to do with the other? Killing a person so that 'God' will do this or that? But these weren't things that happened only in temples discovered in the jungles of South America; this was happening all over the world. Before the belief in a single God, there were polytheistic worships. Belief in multiple gods. The Baal and the Asherah, Adad and Hadad. This is a political and social move taken by Josiah—to stop being human savages who make sacrifices to the Moloch worship. But it's hard for us to accept that there was an agenda even back then. That today's politicians did not invent the schemes. That It all depends on who is telling the story. In 1945, more than fifty scrolls were discovered in Nag Hammadi, Egypt, hidden in a clay jar and dated to a period before the New Testament. These are allegedly first-hand accounts from the acquaintances and friends of Jesus, which stands in stark contrast to the gospels that were included in the New Testament and were written many years after his death. This 'Torah' developed in parallel to the established church and was passed down for hundreds of years between groups of Christians who adopted it as an oral tradition until the discovery of these scrolls. Information and knowledge that was passed down directly from Jesus through his apostles, followers, and even his true family members, not who the church decided on. But since the texts in question completely contradicted the 'truth' written in the New Testament, they were declared to be "full of errors that will lead anyone who reads them astray from the right path!", "a true abomination and desecration of the holiness of Jesus!".

One of the fundamental principles in these scrolls, which stands in stark contrast to the New Testament, is that Jesus is depicted as a mere human being. His mother was not a virgin, he had brothers and sisters, and he also had a wife— Mary Magdalene, as stated in the 'Gospel of Mary' found in these scrolls. There is no 'glorification', no 'fear of the Lord' as they try to scare us in monotheistic religions for political and financial reasons, of course. Jesus was just an ordinary man. And perhaps, in fact, we are all cyborgs of some ancient creature that our ancestors took control of and created what we are today. As it is written right at the beginning of the Book of Genesis, "*And God created man in His image, in the image of God He created him*". Sumerian clay tablets tell a story that dates back long before the Bible, according to which intelligent beings came to the earth and created us in their image. It is even told in the book of Genesis about the sons of God who came down from the sky and created the '*Nephilim*'—the Fallen Ones. "*When the sons of God saw that the daughters of men were fair, they took wives for themselves from all whom they chose… The Nephilim were on the earth in those days, and also afterward, when the sons of God went in to the daughters of men and they bore children to them. They were the mighty men who were of old, the men of renown.*" And perhaps our brain, or our soul, is actually an analogous version that the aliens of three thousand years ago implanted into the ancient Neanderthal, just as we are currently implanting a digital version into the 'modern' human with all the sciences of nanotechnology, cybernetics, robotics, and bioinformatics. Think about it. In the not-so-distant-as-you-think future, they will begin implanting robotic brains, robotic hearts, or any other necessary organs into the deceased, literally tailor-made, so they can 'live'. So, for old people it might not be that relevant, but think about parents of children. Surely they would prefer a robot child that looks exactly like their child than a grave with a headstone. And over time it will also develop a personality. This, after all, is the uniqueness of artificial intelligence technology. And people, by their nature, will start seeing parallels over time. In already existing technology, it is easily possible to match the tone of voice of the deceased to the robot from all kinds of voice messages, and even imitate facial expressions and body and facial expressions from videos. And it will learn. It will learn all the time. It will learn about the future, about the past. It will hear from conversations about what and how it was, and the body will continue to develop as usual. After all, the rest of the systems will continue to work normally, and what was replaced, whether it was the heart, the kidney, or the brain, will function as well. Only the soul. That same soul is not present. Some would prefer to forget, to part ways rather than live with a living monument that bears witness to the absence of the person. But most would surely choose something that looks like and strongly resembles—really!— An exact match. They'd treat it as though the person had suffered a stroke and was now relearning everything, even in an upgraded way. No fear of regression. But how do you decide how long it will live, the cyborg? And wait a minute, is it okay for him to fall in love or 'simply' have children from the seed of the person he replaced? Or alternatively, to get pregnant?? After all, this cyborg will undoubtedly outlast all of us because its brain is built on a system that is capable of thinking and calculating a trillion times more than us. He's a computer. Yet his artificial intelligence is still intelligence. It learns and evolves at a speed faster than light, and it's only a matter of time before the stronger species survives. Immune to our diseases just as we are immune to the diseases of ants, for example, and maybe once we weren't. And maybe in the future, diseases will be like today's computer viruses, and someone will develop one with no cure, destroying half of 'humanity' until the right antivirus is found. Or a third world war, where those with atomic weapons will blow each other up out of ego and the stupidity of thought. The next meteorite strike that will wipe out almost everyone here, just like what happened to the dinosaurs. What do you think will remain for those who survive? For the descendants who won't have anyone to tell them about the iPhone, Google, or the internet? A few structures, perhaps some works of art carved into stone. Papers buried deep under the rubble. Something will remain. And every few years, something will be uncovered. A piece of information. Someone will deduce something from something and decide what it means. And after generations upon generations, someone will dare to say otherwise, and then they'll say he's crazy. Perhaps they will even be killed or imprisoned, just as they did to Galileo Galilei for supporting Copernicus' theory that the planets revolve around the sun, not the other way around, and that the Earth is not the center of the universe, contrary to the Church's position, for this undermines the very foundation of its essence, and perhaps even the entire concept of religion. And no one wants the ground to be pulled out from under who they are or what they believe, or what they've been told to believe. Certainly not under their livelihood and status. What heretical words are these, Tfu! tfu! tfu! Touch wood! Go on, spit! Touch wood immediately! At least to ward off the evil eye. Hamsa-hamsa-tfu-touch wood! Do you even know why you knock on wood three times? Because there's an ancient belief, Christian by the way, that there are little goblins living in the trees, and so you knock on the wood to make sure they don't hear and ruin things for you... It may sound retarded, but that's how you were taught, and even your great-aunt's sister said it, so for sure there must be something to it... Once I saw a TV show where the contestants were tasked with catching tiny piglets in their mud pen. One participant, a woman who keeps G-d's commandments, began cursing at 'this cursed creature,

"Tfu! A disgusting animal!" She spat at the innocent, trapped, and frightened creature which was likely about to be slaughtered in its prime. "Tfu!", As if these tiny, innocent piglets were the vile and evil ones who came into this world solely to harm her and make her and the entire Jewish people go astray. Let us catch Kapparot roosters by their wings, break and disassemble them while they're still alive in the name of the Lord! Praise be, oh almighty, behold and see how much I love you and am in love with your entire being, Father in Heaven, TA-ATE! We'll do anything, as long as the main thing is that we're in love with God, and He — surely loves us back.

Humans have been living on Earth for about six million years. The first species associated with stone tool use are dated to have existed around three million years ago, and 'modern' humans are dated to around two hundred thousand years ago. A look at the timeline reveals that the belief in one God has existed for only the last three thousand five hundred years. It began in the fourteenth century BCE, entirely in Egypt, and reached the Israelites about nine hundred years later, with a remarkable and precise alignment with the reign of King Josiah. But no one looks at the perspective of time, at the timeline according to which things should be examined. It's like saying there is global warming while checking the climate changes on an axis of decades or hundreds of years. A thorough examination would show that over a span of thousands of years, we're not experiencing global warming at all. The Earth has undergone much greater climate fluctuations than those we see now; it has both warmed and cooled, and if you really want to be afraid of something, then fear global cooling, where everything simply freezes. Minimal crops, famine, and diseases, as occurred in the 6th and 14th centuries, when in most of the Northern Hemisphere people were forced to eat tree roots as Nostradamus foresaw, the abandonment of children in forests, and cannibalism, which later became the basis for fairy tales like 'Hansel and Gretel' and 'Goldilocks and the Three Bears'. Speaking of bears, there was a time when people believed bears were sacred and worshipped them. Real bear worship, I swear! Do you know how many beliefs the human race has managed to invent throughout history? And this is, of course, because most people believe they should fear something: God, Satan, the Evil Eye... And more than that, the establishment needs you to be afraid of something. And for those who are more 'down to earth' — well, Earth. We at Fatel believe that you should not be afraid of anything because everything always happens for the better. But people throughout history have been afraid to face reality directly. Therefore, they wove stories, legends, and fables, diverted their gaze upwards, closed their eyes, and prayed. 'Oh, God of the rain,' they would say, 'Oh... forgive us, for we have sinned'. 'And thou shalt do that which is right and good in the sight of the LORD: that it may be well with thee,' says Moses to the Israelites as he comes down from Mount Sinai. But we have never sinned; we simply faced reality and did what seemed right in our own eyes. And what is right in our eyes, there is no way it contains even a shred of evil.

If you were to tell someone who lived a hundred years ago about an iPhone, their mind would probably fry. "You must be out of your mind... Talking to the whole world for free, like, while walking down the street? Man, you're completely insane, huh?" Now, hand someone from two hundred years ago a microwave. "Dude, this... this is a box. You stick something cold inside, press a button, and it comes out hot...". Under the growing desert conditions of that era, pigs would develop parasites that caused severe illnesses in humans, therefore necessitating such a strict prohibition — no wonder it also exists in Islam, which arose under similar conditions. Cleaning the house thoroughly once a year, and performing a *kashering* ritual purification of utensils to ensure proper sanitation among people from three thousand years ago who had no concept of sewage systems, let alone bacteria. The Bible is just like the difference between a doctor talking to a patient and a doctor talking to another doctor. To the doctor, he'll explain the analysis and the prognosis, but if he tells the same to the patient, the patient will talk his ear off because he doesn't know the first thing about medicine and has been soaking up nonsense from what he's heard and random online searches. So, the doctor will say to the patient, 'Does it hurt here? Take this pill and it won't hurt anymore,' and from the patient's perspective, these are living words of God. There, the doctor said so. It's written in the Bible.

The funniest part is that, according to every religion, you're allowed to convert. For this ridicules the whole concept without anyone even noticing. Because it essentially says there's nothing inherently 'sacred' about being Jewish, Muslim, or Christian — for anyone can become one. According to Jewish law, any gentile who sincerely wishes to join the Jewish people can. The Christians spent centuries waging Crusades to spread Christianity across vast parts of the world, when in fact, anyone can become a Christian quite easily. All it takes is accepting the basic tenets of faith outlined in the 'Creed,' their statement of belief, and undergoing baptism. And even if you interpret radical Islam's jihad as a call to convert everyone or kill them, I could convert to Islam and be saved in a minute. I'd simply declare, 'There is no god but Allah, and Muhammad is His prophet,' in front of two Muslim witnesses, 'La ilaha illa Allah wa Muhammad rasul Allah' — and I'm a Muslim. This basically means that if I'm Jewish, for instance, I could, on the same day, also become a Christian and then go and convert to Islam without anyone knowing. And so what does that mean? Which God will protect me from harm? Which God is 'just'? Which prayer will keep me safe and protect me from evil? Which commandment??

I remember this one time when Arik and I flew to Amsterdam. And while we were strolling contentedly stoned through the streets, the church bell, which, on days as broken as they come, is supposed to chime on the number of hours marking the start of the current hour, suddenly rang out the melody of a song that was very popular at the time. For a moment, everyone stopped and marveled. They smiled, then continued on their way, with something optimistic and joyful now echoing in their minds. This is what the new religion should be. The new role of the church, the synagogue, and the mosque. The role of religiosity. To connect people. To create a community—not from a place of fear and awe, but from a place of light, joy, brotherhood, and love. As it has been since forever. But don't touch, they'll tell you! Stick with the beliefs we taught you at age six. No need to develop this. Instead of sanctifying love just as Jesus said, they didn't include these writings of His that conveyed those teachings in the New Testament. The missionaries took everyone who didn't believe in Jesus according to their definition and covered them with fire ants until, very quickly, they believed. They built more and more cathedrals to glorify God. Massive structures where humans are small and insignificant in comparison to the great and dreadful God. The greatest artists in history were recruited and harnessed to design and decorate His temples. Michelangelo's Sistine Chapel, St. Peter's Basilica designed by Bramante, Bernini's elliptical colonnade, Gaudi's Sagrada Familia. All this was ironically and paradoxically a counter to 'pagan' beliefs. Fuck me and call me Jesus... and say ye Amen.

For countless years the Jews have been waiting for the Messiah, longing for his coming. He - is their only hope for redemption.

One day, Jesus arrived and said, "Here I am. I am the Messiah."

"What, that's it? Is it happening now?" everyone asked. "You're the Messiah? But, but... where's the donkey? And... and what about the resurrection?"

"There is no donkey and no one ever dies and everything is love", Jesus tried but to no avail. Because if he is the Messiah then, wait... then that means we can't hope anymore. The mind cannot fathom this! Therefore, they were compelled to kill him— in order to, and if only— not to kill the hope.

Day by day, God sends more and more messengers, messiahs, speakers of sublime and exalted truth, to leave everything behind and connect to love, but this is of course contrary to everything that all the religious have grown accustomed to, and beyond that, it would utterly destroy hope.

I once saw an interview on television with a famous singer who said that he did not marry the love of his life— about whom he even wrote a very well-known Israeli emotional love song—because he is a person who believes in the Divine Creator and she isn't. People spend their entire lives in search of true love. Their entire lives! And you, who found it, loved, and even wrote an immortal poem for her - gave it all up because she eats dairy with meat and you don't because you believe that this is what is written in a book from three thousand years ago—and that this is the truth. The most tangible thing in the world is at your feet, reach out and touch it for God's sake! But you... you're convinced that God's sake has other plans for you. That God himself or at the very least with the help of the Cherubim surrounding him, keeps vigil over you and scrutinizes your every move, and heaven's sake you should live with someone like 'that'. It's assuredly better and preferable, that you spend your time on this earth, in solemn solitude. And on this it is said - God forbid.

So Rabin is dead and they even put someone in prison. If someone wants to assassinate a president or prime minister tomorrow, no memorial day will stop them. Nor will anyone really think of committing a holocaust if no one reminds them or informs them that there used to be such a thing. Most criminals, in fact, later admit that they took their inspiration from a Hollywood film. Reality doesn't surpass imagination; it simply fulfills it. And when this beautiful collective consciousness of Fatel descends upon you, you suddenly realize that if you don't believe in anything but yourself and the idea that you'll be okay—that boundless optimism about the future, that far-fetched expectation of dazzling success, no matter what—then you smile and understand that you will never again be afraid. And gently pet the head of the curious child beside you.

6

What do you mean you're leaving Moran? What doesn't work out? Who needs anything to work out? Who cares? You have Moran. Moran! She is already yours, that's it. It's not about the beginning, where you might ruin things and miss her. Two years. That's it. She is entirely yours if you just want her…

And so, Arik broke up with Moran and shattered my heart. Yes, well. If she were to be with someone, it might as well be Arik. At least then things would be under control. At least that part would be contained, it would be closed off. At least, that's what I thought at thirty-two. After she had already killed me, slaughtered me, butchered my soul, and then brought me back from the grave—or perhaps emerged from the grave I had painstakingly prepared for her, just to put me to death in final agony.

But slowly, I got used to the situation. There she is, with Arik. And they seem to be having a good time. Suddenly, it really seems to me as if they're the most compatible pair in the world. After all, a person must recognize his limitations—what he can hold onto and what he cannot, what he's capable of keeping under control and what he's not, or even able to take control of at all. And I, apparently, am not capable of controlling Moran. Not to mention, I could never really have her to begin with. But even if by some miracle, one I can't even begin to imagine, I were to somehow win her over, how would I ever be able to keep her? Every day, I'd be tormented by the fear that she might leave me, walk away, find someone better suited for her. Because I'm clearly not enough for her, and I've never been enough. 'That which I feared has come upon me,' lamented Job, who, despite his righteousness, faced the very disasters he dreaded, losing all his wealth, family, and health—without realizing that his fear of losing everything is what 'magnetized' his calamities. But Arik, he's a man. He doesn't hesitate or shy away; he goes after what he wants, and everything with him always flows smoothly. And now, too, it was he who initiated the breakup.

"Turns out we're complete opposites," he told me during that conversation, which I couldn't quite grasp where it was leading me. Am I supposed to be sad now? Happy? What, am I getting caught up in another fantasy that maybe, after all this, she'll finally be mine? And maybe it's a good thing they broke up. Let her disappear from my life again. Why do I even need this? Unrequited love from when I was eleven. Great... Maybe I'm also supposed to sit and cry over the teddy bear my dad couldn't win for me at the amusement park with that rifle game, only to discover years later that they deliberately messed with the sights, and that my dad wasn't a lousy shot or anything like that. So let her disappear. Let her go. Bye-bye, Moran Dagan. It's been hell.

🪲

I got back home from Anat's party. I smoked a joint and laid down in the hammock outside the room they had assigned to me in the village. It's not exactly an 'heir' or whatever they call it in kibbutzim, but if you're a Fatel, you'll always have somewhere to sleep and even a place to raise forty kids if you want. But for now I'm alone, so I took a sort of one-and-a-half-room setup with a small living room and another half-room that could be a bedroom or an office, or whatever, a shower and a toilet, and a front exit to the village, where everyone has a yard and usually a hammock. As I was lounging in the hammock, I thought about her. About what happened. That's how it is when I smoke—I start replaying the last few days, focusing on the last few hours, and what I surely must have done wrong. Wait, did she really kiss me, or was she just playing with my feelings again? Did I kiss her back? 'I should have married Haggai'... Did she really say that?"

When you're stoned, you're stupid. No matter how you spin it, you're stupid. So if you're sitting with other people who are smoking or with your friends, they know you're not really stupid. But if you're sitting with someone who doesn't smoke, to them, you're just stupid. And you're never going to convince them otherwise. To them, being stoned and being drunk are the same thing, and right now you're drunk. And as for drunks, they can subconsciously recognize who becomes an idiot when they drink, which probably indicates less mental stability, perhaps due to a lower IQ that can't 'hold' the system together. Once, I came back from a friend's place with someone I was seeing, and I was really stoned. Now, don't think I'm some kind of stoner—I'm really not, and I even despise stoners a bit because they're always talking nonsense. As I said, when you're stoned, you're a complete fool. So generally, I don't smoke, but these are my friends from the Tel Aviv days. They have a rooftop apartment where you can hang out, and a bunch of people from Florentin came by. We've kept in touch, and when we meet, everyone smokes a lot, just like we used to in those wild Florentin days after returning from the after-the-army trips to South America, East Asia, Australia, New Zealand, and so on, where you get to meet loads of cool people who are on the same wavelength as you, who've conquered goals around the world, navigated life in developing countries, and experienced adventures that half the world's population will never encounter in their entire lives. And for her and I, it was our big day. After nearly a month of being together, we were finally about to have sex.

We hadn't planned for it to take a month—at least, I hadn't—but for her, it seemed that the later, the better. In retrospect, it was the right approach for us. To her credit, when we did spend the night together after about two weeks, she made sure that I went to sleep satisfied. She understood that it's extremely hard for a man to fall asleep when he's lying next to someone he's attracted to. Somehow, women are able to do it. But then she went abroad with her sister for a week, a trip that had been planned for a long time. After that, a few more days passed until we met again, with work and all, and It was clear that this weekend we would finally do it. We planned to go to that party at my friend's rooftop on Thursday night, take a cab to Tel Aviv so we could let loose without having to worry about the drive back.

Here we are in the big city. That same day, there was also a huge street party, White Night or something, and the cab dropped us off at the corner of Arlozorov and Ibn Gabirol. From there, it was blocked off, with all of Ibn Gabirol turned into a pedestrian street.

And she was dressed exactly how I liked. A bit... 'slutty,' you know. Her butt always seemed to press out and split her pants with every step she took, thanks to its natural shape. Additionally, she was a bit stubby, all muscle. She was an athlete back in Serbia or something like that. Her hair was a very light blonde, a sharp nose but not pointy, with thin, inviting lips and brown eyes. While blondes with blue or green eyes might be the dream, any blonde addict like me knows that blondes with brown eyes are the real deal. She had the perfect breast size, fitting her body and slightly pointed. That day she wore white Reebok sneakers with slightly thicker soles than usual but not platform shoes, a white skirt with pleats like cheerleaders wear, and a red top.

She looked like a cheerleader for the San Francisco 49ers. We were both quite drunk, and I was also high. I was having so much fun that I lost track of time. At nearly quarter to one, she caught me on the stairs as I was heading back to the rooftop from the apartment's bathroom and suggested that maybe we should leave. On the way back, she excitedly told me that she wanted me to meet her best friend and her husband, who she'd mentioned in conversations. It was important to her. And I, in my stoned state, replied with a delayed "Sure." What a scene. She said that if I didn't care about it, she didn't know what that meant for our relationship, and that it was very, very disappointing to hear, and that she really wanted me to meet them and looked forward to it, And all that jazz and stuff and blah blah blah blah blah... And I actually said 'Sure'. But since she had never smoked weed in her life, she equated being stoned with being drunk. And when the wine goes in, the secrets come out... Gos, where's that emoji of the blonde with her hands sideways when you need it?

"Hagush!" someone suddenly called out my name. I turned my head. Moran! Ugh, enough with this unreliable script already! Now she's probably coming up to me, declaring her eternal love, that she has always loved me, ever since that Hanukkah party in the gymnasium with my ridiculous shoes, and that everything up to now with Benny and even with Arik, alongside all the subsequent drama with bragobikers and the bragmobilers, was merely to preserve her love for me and mine for her in convoluted ways.

"Hopa!" I forgot everything that had ever passed through   my   mind. "In the Hammockish?" she said pleasantly, smiling in her airy   summer   dress.

"Hammockish, yes," I laughed. "Want some?" I asked, quickly getting out of the hammock. 'Sure, fine,' she did whatever pleased her, as she had throughout her entire life, I conclude retrospectively. "But come too," she suggested, making space.

Moran Dagan and I are huddled together on the hammock, in a state of cuddling, and our bodies touch nearly every inch, due to and because of the laws of physics. The rush of emotion that took hold of me... it's hard to explain. Just a short while ago, she gave me a kiss on the cheek, tossed out a line from hell or paradise, and now she's actually here, moving towards me, coming to me, and talking to me. This was something that could have happened so many times throughout our shared history, and simply never did... Hold perfectly still, lest anything disrupt this ideal scene. And why, in God's name, did I have to smoke?

"I've always loved you, you know." Wait, wait, calm down. This actually makes sense. In Fatel, saying 'love' is more like expressing deep affection, without any romantic implication. And 'friend' is more like a buddy, not necessarily indicating a relationship. So everything's fine.

"Of course, me too. You're the best," slipped out of me, and thankfully my eyes didn't meet hers, as a tear was forming in the corner of it, if I'm to maintain a delicate composure. Yes, I was moved, ok? A surge of emotion suddenly overwhelmed me, not due to the high, but because of the sheer joy I felt seeing Moran beside me. I love her. And contrary to all the self-deceptions I've nurtured over the years, I now know with unwavering certainty that I never ceased to love her. Saccharine, childish, foolish. Go on, say it.

"Isn't this great?" she asked, reaching out to pluck a tiny kumquat from the tree on the porch, its branches stretching just above the hammock.

"Totally…" I responded with a generic answer, one that fits almost any situation where you're not entirely sure what the other person meant.

"There's no place like this—I'm in love," she said as she picked another kumquat from the tree. Wait, did she say that with a comma or a period after 'this'? And does it relate to what she mentioned earlier about needing to marry Hagai? I mean, me??

"Careful, it's sour," I hurried to change the subject."

"I'm just picking for fun," she played with the tiny fruit in her hand. "It has such a nice, refreshing smell," she brought the little kumquat closer to her heavenly nostrils and inhaled its fragrance. "I swear, it's such a blessing that my parents moved here. At first, I didn't appreciate it. You all seemed so weird to me, too good of friends. No intrigue, no ostracism… no ostracism, can you believe that?! Do you know how many times I was shunned at my previous school before I came here? By all sorts of girls who didn't like that I refused to follow their lead like everyone else. Or because I was blonde and the boys liked me," she laughed.

"Eh… being blonde isn't a reason to be ostracized," I laughed too, but I said it firmly. What?? What are you doing?! Just say 'amen' to everything she says, got it? Say amen!! Now! Go on, do it!

"Well, yeah, you're right." See? Shut up, you stoner. I scolded my own high. "I guess I've just never been willing to be like everyone else… you know?"

"What? Of course, of course. I get it." I still didn't get it at all.

"I've always gone against the flow," she continued, and maybe for the first time in my life, I began to understand what drew me to her. "At first, I was very popular. From a very young age, actually. But when I got to first grade, there was this annoying girl who insisted on being the queen of the class, and everyone in her group did whatever she said, and it just seemed stupid to me. So, while I was quite proud of standing my ground, I ended up without many friends…"

"Oh…" I was surprised and stoned at the same time.

"Yes. And from that moment on, I didn't feel like part of the crowd. For example, when everyone watched 'The Sopranos' or 'The Simpsons' or 'Seinfeld,' I didn't."

"No kidding…"

"And you see, not only did I not watch, but I actually hated it even though I hadn't seen a single episode! Of course, after years I watched it, and it was great."

"For sure… Just so you know, I completely understand and relate to what you're saying, but Moran," I smiled at her as she looked at me, "the boys must have liked you."

"Ah-ah-ah-ah," she laughed loudly, and I joined in."Well, you know…"

"Haha, so maybe that's why they ostracized you, and not just because of your non-conformity…? Though the speech was very touching."

"Ah-ah…" she laughed again with that sweet laugh of hers. The laugh that always shook my heart. Always pained me. Always reminded me. 'Ah-ah…' it doesn't quite sound like that, but if you say it fast enough and enough times in a row, you'll understand what I mean and how endearing it is.

And now I'm here, comfortably cocooned in the hammock, Well-stoned, sinking, and thinking. Wait. Why is she suddenly playing the sweet, charming, even pitiable girl who was ostracized at her previous school? I've looked at her a thousand times, and she'd always returned my gaze with a cool, if not frozen, stare. A million times! And now she's vulnerable and sweet and delicate, sitting on the hammock as if we grew up together?! I mean, we did grow up together, but completely apart. Her house is only a few doors away from mine, yet it always felt so distant. Like another galaxy. A galaxy with an entrance barred to me, fenced off. They even changed the language, so that even if I somehow stumbled in, I'd be sure to understand nothing and quickly leave... And suddenly you're so sweet? You've torn my soul apart and broke my heart! So now, at forty, you were supposed to marry Hagai?? And with a kiss on the lips? And your mother is suddenly talking to me as if I were a regular guest at your Friday night dinners, and that Yekkish woman would prepare Moroccan dishes especially for me, even though I'm actually Ashkenazi??

The only time Moran and I were ever on equal footing, the only moment I felt we were peers, was on the big class trip in tenth grade, before we were divided into majors. On these trips, I always felt terrible—one of those who gets nauseous. Chewing gum, licking lemons, nothing helped. I remember that during one of the rest stops, I got off the bus and suddenly she was there. Right in front of me. I was surprised. Maybe she'd talk to me? Then I noticed traces of vomit on her shoe. She gets sick on trips too, I thought with relief. Moran and I have something in common. Moran, she's a person too.

In the Babylonian Talmud, the tiger is referred to as 'Arya D'bei Ilai,' meaning 'lion of the upper world.' Apparently, this is because it's the largest and strongest tiger, even more so than a lion. In size, at least. I'm not sure the king of the jungle would give up his mane so easily... I once saw a video of a tiger in a sort of zoo with a glass separating it from people standing with their backs to it. Not aware of the glass, it crept up behind, crouched down, and then— leapt! No one was hurt, just some background laughter from foolish people, but because it didn't grasp the concept, it kept jumping and leaping at the glass. Then a little girl, thinking the tiger was playing, began jumping from the other side. After a few moments, it seemed they were genuinely having fun. She jumped and clapped, and so did he! He mimicked her on the glass, playing along, completely out of 'attack mode.' Perhaps, had there been no glass, after a brief game, he might have preyed on her or accidentally harmed her, but the sight was heartwarming. For that brief moment, he was just another creature like us, wanting to play, to enjoy, to love, and most of all—to be loved. He didn't choose to be one of the strongest predators in nature; he was born that way. He has no chance of surviving as a herbivore. Even the spider, catching its prey and killing them in one of nature's most horrific ways while approaching with its long, creepy legs, taking one more step of terror before it starts biting them—if they haven't had a heart attack by then—didn't choose that either! That's just what it knows to do. Even the crocodile, lurking in the water and suddenly emerging to snatch a hapless antelope trying to cross the river with no chance to even sprint away, is not evil or malevolent. It has no other option if it wants to keep on living.

An orca is a type of black-and-white whale that looks like a giant, innocent dolphin. I once saw a video of a group of such cuties dismantling a shark as if it were a sardine. In another video, a similar group was swimming near a woman in the open sea. The footage was from above, and it was terrifying. Just a moment away from making her into a stew, I thought, with a lot of red. But then, they simply started swimming around her, playing and frolicking, just like dolphins! They were probably just full, and it allowed us to see their true nature. Just like every other creature on land, in the air, and in the sea, they want to enjoy life. Even the largest and most fearsome tiger in nature is, deep down, still that playful cub wanting to have fun. That person who seems so bad in your eyes, the most evil, and wicked—though it's hard for you, and maybe even for them, to see it now—is actually just a small child who wants to play.

Here I am, looking at this girl who had always seemed to me like a haughty bitch, someone who deliberately didn't want me, and suddenly I found myself captivated by her. How desperately I had longed to hear her speak all these years. How I had always wanted to be the one listening to her. The one that is Nodding along. That is Hugging and caressing if needed. That is Kissing. That is Supporting. That is everything. The last time she smiled at me, apart from before that math test or trigonometry or whatever the hell it was because I lost all my senses before and after it, was when she was Arik's girlfriend. But then, those were smiles hidden behind a façade of why he and not you. Or at least, that's how they appeared to me... And suddenly she's so here, so... within reach. She's not here for a second and then disappearing; she's not here until I finish my coffee to then leave and then return to Arik's arms. She's simply here. With me. On the hammock. Waiting for me to smile back.

If you think about it even more deeply, I'm almost sure this was the first time I had a real conversation with her. I mean, sure, we talked here and there. Hello, hi, can I copy from you on the test, and so on, but an actual conversation? Now that I think about it, never. Never! Do you realize? I swear to you, it's only now that it's hitting me. I've never had a conversation longer than two minutes with the love of my life! Wait, love of my life? Well, that's an exaggeration. The girl, the child, this creature I've been in love with from the first moment I saw her, with no apparent reason. Absurd. Truly surreal. Just think about it—I've fallen for someone I don't know, someone with whom I've never exchanged more than four consecutive sentences, and I've been obsessing over her for over three decades without knowing almost anything about her... But despite all the illogicality and lack of understanding, something in my gut still feels right. Feels okay. Like this is how things were meant to be. I'm not sure we'll marry or be together; right now, it's a complete absurdity to even think about it, but even if nothing happens between us, it's definitely something I needed to go through. Something I still need to go through. And who knows what fate holds for you? What awaits at the end of the road. The emotional journey I've undergone since meeting Moran Dagan has undoubtedly changed my life. From being the boy that all the girls wanted, I suddenly became someone that someone isn't interested in. Someone took the wheel and turned the ship in the opposite direction with a single swipe. Boom. You get hit by the full force of the waves inside your body. Tossed. Thrown in unfamiliar directions. At first, you're scared. Anxious. Don't know what to do in this new situation. After all, it's something entirely new. But over time, you learn to recognize new directions. Learn the currents. And maybe something good awaits in them too. This is precisely how Columbus discovered America. Besides, who is wiser than someone with experience? Who knows how to handle a cake that's been overcooked in the oven? The one who has burned twenty cakes, or the one who always gets it perfect?

"Beyo... haha, are you being serious? How can you say she's amazing?" I dared to contradict her once again in the span of ten minutes during our conversation that had shifted from The Sopranos and Seinfeld to cinema and music.

"How can you say she's not?"

"Hmm... maybe because she's... awful?" I grimaced, and she laughed dismissively. "Tell me, have you ever listened to her lyrics? I swear, if no one had told me, I'd think it was written by kids in first grade... 'Parpar Nechmad' (an old Israeli kids show) has songs with more depth."

"Ah-ah-ah-ah-ah,"

"Really, I'm not joking!" I laughed as well.

"I don't know," she said, tugging slightly at her nose after finishing her chuckles, "I don't really care about the lyrics... it's just nice for me to listen to her."

"But what do you mean the lyrics don't matter to you? She's the leading figure in the genre of 'nothing music.' Just something rhythmic, with nothing but the beat. Even in your world, which is supposedly just rhythm, it doesn't cut it. Take Infected Mushroom, for example. Classical Mushroom is a masterpiece album with melodies, highs, lows, ballads... a story! Classical music in trance. Not just boom-boom-boom. Even Gothic by Paradise Lost, which might sound like a death song from a funeral, is an incredible ballad with a killer melody and crazy lyrics— artfully crafted, almost poetic. A 'poem,' from the English term for 'song'. Even though it's death metal and the lyrics aren't supposed to matter, there's artistry there. By the same principle, you won't find a single Madonna song with dumb lyrics, or a Kylie Minogue song with dumb lyrics, Whitney Houston, Cyndi Lauper—none!"

"Fine, fine. For a moment I forgot who's the DJ from the activity room..." she threw out, and suddenly we found ourselves doubled over in laughter on the hammock, clutching our stomachs and mouths. I'd never imagined that such a situation could actually happen, come true. Long ago, and from every period since, I had ceased to envision anything that could even remotely approach this in my thoughts.

"But wait, wait..." she didn't forget to press on once she calmed down, "so what do you think about Lady Gaga?"

"Oh... I'm crazy about Lady Gaga! Rah rah uh la la!"

"Ah-ah-ah-ah-ah-ah-ah-ah-ah-ah-ah-ah-ah-ah," she smiled and laughed and smiled and laughed and smiled and laughed so much that I couldn't stay indifferent and smiled and laughed along with her.

"By the way," I asked once we had calmed down, "wasn't your band always Suede? I remember you bragging in the neighborhood all the time about their first album..."

"Yooou, right!" she quickly smiled, "I used to be so crazy about them... I really carried their disc around all the time!" She laughed again, and it made me feel better and better with each passing moment. Humor is probably the fastest way to a girl's heart, or pants.

"Hey, you know what, Moran?" I asked, enjoying the sound of her name, "Let me ask you this. What do you think is the difference between McDonald's and Coca-Cola?"

"What?" she replied with a puzzled look, but still under the cover of a smile.

"Well, what's the difference?"

"Well?" she asked back, with a hint of charm, We've opened up.

"You see, a burger with Coke is probably the ultimate junk food. But McDonald's, after they got a bad rap for selling junk, started offering salads, healthy meals, changed their logo to green, and advertised themselves as a source of protein... Suddenly they're competing with Centrum. Coca-Cola, on the other hand, has always stuck to the same message. 'We have Coke. You Want Coke? Drink Coke. You don't want Coke? Go fuck yourself.'

'Ah-ah-ah-ah-ah-ah-ah-ah-ah-ah-ah-ah-ah-ah-ah,' she curled up with her amazing laugh, which was now even more charming than usual. "Okay, and how is this actually related?" she asked after finishing her laughter, with tiny tears in her eyes and a reddish tint around them.

'It's related because, okay, fine, I get it, lots of girls are into her songs and they're totally crazy about her, but come on, you've made her out to be Aretha Franklin. Seriously, come on. It's like, seriously, come on, come on! Sometimes I'm convinced it's some kind of prank that the whole world is playing on me, and suddenly everyone will say, 'Oh... how we fooled you!' So, yeah, real funny...

"Okay, I get it that you're not crazy about her," she stifled her laughter, "but listen. This is what she brings to the world, and it's amazing. It brings so much joy and fun to so many people... You don't have to listen to her; you can listen to Paradise Lost and Iron Maiden all day long... Just appreciate her as another light in the world. Light, Love, and Brotherhood, did you forget?" She ended with that melting smile of hers.

"She's not spreading light in the world; she's spreading stupidity in the world, and I'm sick and tired of the stupidity in this world." I dared to defy her for the third time and even went so far as to interrupt her words. Supersize me, just like at McDonald's. "It's not even music; it's a jumble of words with a dumb beat and weird moves. What is this crap? Just because it has lyrics about women, does that make it women's empowerment? Is it 'Girl Power' because she says the world belongs to women? What's this stupidiocity? Retarded Music with retarded lyrics, without intending to offend those with intellectual disabilities. And now you have all sorts of idiots singing nonsense and they're playing them on the radio all day long, even elevating them to judge on all sorts of shows as if they understand something about music... It's exactly like 'The Emperor's New Clothes.' Same as that Japanese author everyone considers a genius, but he never finishes his books, and I once read an interview where he said that a book with an ending isn't interesting. Great, my brother, so from now on, commit to watching every series only until the second-to-last episode, and hang pictures with a giant hole in the middle in your living room, because what's the point of seeing the full picture? Finish the story, motherfucker!"

'Ah-ah-ah-ah-ah-ah-ah-ah-ah-ah-ah-ah-ah-ah-ah,' she was now practically rolling with laughter, which made me laugh really hard too, and we both ended up cracking up, with the whole situation almost making me lose my composure from joy that I couldn't hide or conceal anymore. 'Oh…' she said, pulling a little at her nose. 'This assertiveness of yours is kind of cool, Hagai… Where have you been all these years?'

And that's the hardest part about Moran Dagan—I never really figured her out. It's easy to love or hate something defined. You can hate Ashkenazim, Jews, African Americans (even though for some inexplicable reason they're called "black" whereas their skin tone is actually brown), Women, Men, and whatnot. But you can't hate, say, aliens. For it's something you're not exactly sure what it is. So how can you hate it? And with Moran, I never knew. Did she even know I was in love with her? I'm positive she did, but I have no proof. You might think she might have wanted me, and maybe it was just my fault for never saying anything, but I know she didn't. You weren't there when my looks screamed it, shouted it, yelled it. There's no way a girl's eye wouldn't catch that. But I have no proof… I almost got into a fight because of her once. My dad's friend's son, Heni, with the Yemeni-style "H," though he wasn't Yemeni at all, was part of the 'bragmobilers' gang. Back then, they were still 'bragobikers,' around sixteen years old, and I took advantage of an opportunity on one particularly 'Fatelic' night, on one of the benches in the central garden you all know very well by now. My friends were playing some ball game on the other side of the block, and the bragobikers, how could they not, sat on the bench in all their coolness, smoking cigarettes, and if I remember correctly, even compared penis sizes. I knew there was someone there who was close to Moran, so I fixed my gaze on him. Tried to figure him out. Every time he wasn't looking, I stole a glance. What is it about him that attracts her so much? What does he have that I don't? Suddenly, he started yelling at Heni that if he didn't get 'that kid' out of there, he was going to beat me up. Well, he didn't exactly say that, because after all, we're in Fatel—Light, Brotherhood, and Love, in case you forgot—but let's just say he loudly wondered about what I was doing there and whether I belonged. And I, a true Fatel with all my heart, soul, and veins of my blood, got up calmly and told Heni, who had begun to respond unnecessarily, that it was okay, and that I was going to the other side of the garden to play with my friends anyway. But I managed to steal another glance from within. A mission deep inside enemy territory. A true undercover agent. What did I learn? Not much. Maybe they just had something more mature, less childish, that suited Moran better. I mean, definitely. We played silly ball games with stupid names like 'Posts,' with the emphasis on the "po," which was like soccer but with posts instead of goals, and you had to hit one of the garden's lampposts to score a point. Or someone would bring down a tennis racket and we'd play a sort of baseball that we called 'Stations', 'Seven Stones,' or a thousand other games that, compared to the bench with the cigarettes, seemed, and in fact were, completely childish. I get you, Morani. Maybe. Maybe, just maybe, I'm finally starting to understand. And maybe I *am* the one to blame. Who even knew besides me and my feverish mind that I prepared like this for the Hanukkah party and saved the clothes my parents brought me from abroad especially for you? Who told me to go and fall in love and build on the hope that you'd fall back in love with me? My successful history with girls up until the age of ten?? I clearly remember a situation where I was in the village deli, buying something my mom sent me to get, and suddenly Moran and the announcer from the Hanukkah party walked in. I froze. "Hey, Hagai…" the announcer said, emphasizing my name. But I was scared, trembling at the thought that something wrong might come out of my mouth, and I just said "Bye" followed by some insult towards her, and left. And since then, I'm blaming her??

"Ugh..." I was tired of my own thoughts and let out an old-man sigh. Damn this forty-year-old age. "Moran Dagan is a true Fatel," I suddenly blurted out a line from a conversation I had with Arik years ago.

"What?" She wrinkled her face with a smile.

"Nothing, you know..."

W h y i n t h e h e l l d i d I s m o k e t h a t j o i n t, a n d w h y d o e s i t a l w a y s h a v e t h a t a b s u r d i m p a c t o n m e ? ? ?

"What 'nothing'? Speak..."

"No, really. it's just... you suddenly reminded me with the light, brotherhood, and love."

"Hagai!" She kicked me on the leg, and surprisingly, it hurt.

"Ouch..." I laughed.

"Now that you said 'really,' I know for sure it's not the truth, so speak up..." She gave a serious look but still kept a smiling demeanor.

"Just, you know... you've always been a bit of an outsider, hanging out with the older kids and all... and we never really knew how to get you. And when I came back to the village and Arik told me you were together, I was in shock. 'Moran Dagan's a true Fatel.' I'll never forget that sentence."

"Who said it, Arik?"

"Yeah, "Yeah, that you're a total Fatel and that you're actually really cool and all," I said the last word with a hint of a nostalgic hug.

"Funny..."

"Heh, why is that funny?"

"Because all our arguments were about how we didn't match. That I'm not a real Fatel and I'll never be. He never really said it, but he always made me feel that way..."

"So rest assured, it's really not true, and he really loved you." Wait, what did you just say? Maybe you should just shut up already??

"I know, I know... That's why it was hard for me to break up with him. Arik is the best. But in the end, I guess we just weren't right for each other," she finished with a wistful smile.

Wait, what just happened? I told her he loved her, and she said *she* broke up with *him*? Everything's getting mixed up for me, Morani. It's definitely the joint.

"Say, is it true that you were in love with me in elementary school?" she suddenly looked at me with a smile.

What??

Hello!!

Moran!!!

What are you doing?!

"Haha, what?" I tried to buy some time. "You know, back when I was dating Benny. *Dating…*" She let out a dismissive laugh. "Sixth grade, like who cares…"

What?? Sixth grade, like who cares?!?!?!?!??!?!?!?!?!?!?!?!?!?!?!?!?!?!?!?!

"Where did you pull *that* from right now?" I tried to buy some more time to come up with an answer. What should I tell her now? Admit it? Say 'What are you talking about'? Or maybe I should just break down and start crying, fall on my face, kiss her feet, and start wailing 'I love you! I love you!' while she laughs uncontrollably and runs away?

"Well, that was the rumor. Among the girls. We gossip, you   know…"
"I thought you didn't have any friends," I tried to evade slyly.
"There are always friends for gossip…" She returned her long-standing sly smile. "And stop dodging the question."

She gazed at me. Should I kiss her? I really want to kiss her, desperately! But maybe it's better to stick with the same low-risk approach. Fuck this motherfucking stoned state. 'Of course, Kiss her!' My heart cried out in heartache. In my mind, I had long ago grabbed her and did. 'I love you, Moran! I love you!' And she kissed me back. Suddenly, Moran and I were kissing on the hammock in my small yard in the village. In Fatel. Under the lone moon, I finally understood why it is called 'lunar'. Her lips are full and soft. I slide my hand to her waist, and she continues on her own, slipping it under her dress. Her skin is soft, pleasant. I savor every second of the kiss gently. Suddenly, I feel Moran's hand moving up mine. Suddenly, the thought jumps into my head that... maybe Moran and I will have sex?? No, that's not something that has ever crossed my mind! Wait, is she now putting her hand under my jeans and underwear? Grasping my penis? Moran Dagan is now touching my organ and it's standing like never before?! I can't believe it. I can't fucking believe it. How lucky I am to have listened to my heart and not the stoned thoughts. I don't give a fuck about getting hurt, both figuratively and literally. I've already been hurt by her as much as possible. Or at least, that's what I thoght. I move my hand to my groin and caress. 'Oh... please...', she says a bit out loud and a bit with a head shake of 'no'. Okay, so no sex. I think... or at least not right now. You can never really tell with these girls if it's 'please stop' or 'please keep going'. In my opinion, it's a kind of an 'epigenetic' expression of women. A psychological development arising from an ongoing phenomenon of generations upon generations where, unlike 'genetics', there aren't really changes in DNA. A 'no' that actually is a 'yes'. It may sound sexist but it's not. A girl can't always say she wants it; sometimes she's overthinking a billion things. Issues with her body, hormones or things I will never begin to understand, and anyway, why would a girl have sex with you when you barely know each other, is she a whore? But between herself and her own desires, she does want it. But I always played it safe and stopped. I want the girl to want me, not to have sex with her by force or because she feels uncomfortable stopping. So I moved my hand a bit higher, where I already knew it was allowed. I climbed a little more, and now my hand was holding her chest from underneath. More accurately, the bra. It was rough and stiff. It really turned me on... it…

"Hagai?" She suddenly interrupted the semi-intimate scene playing out in my feverish mind, and I looked at her with a questioning gaze. "Funny guy," she said, rising to a standing position and almost toppling both of us off the hammock. "It seems like you're done for today…" She referred to the high that had enveloped and consumed me so completely that I must have appeared utterly dreamy to her. "I'll let you continue to chill here on your own, without any unnecessary interruptions," she smiled, blew a kiss to the air, and left.

Interruptions? What interruptions?? Wait a minute… Moran! I cried out in my heart as she was walking away from me. "Goodnight, sweetie!" she shouted from a distance. I just wanted to tell you that… those were the fifteen most beautiful minutes of my life! Just so you know, Moran… just know that… I haven't stopped loving you nearly at all. I haven't started hesitating about you nearly at all. "If only someone would lead astray, the barriers of our way.

7

During World War II, there were two types of soldiers: hero soldiers and dead soldiers. Those who died were considered heroes, but they were already dead when that happened, and that always carries more weight, so we're left with those who survived. And all of them are heroes. Why? Because who knows what really happened there. From the few films I've seen on the subject, everyone suffered immensely. It wasn't like today, where you're in some plane or tank that looks like half a spaceship. Head to head! Rifles with knives on the end so that if, actually not if, but when you're within arm's reach of someone, you'd be able to stab them. Crazy. Of course, there is still this kind of fighting today, but back then, it was all there was. Even the planes had open windows and half the body in the air, and you could try to choke or at least slap the pilot across from you if you ran out of ammunition...

If you really want to understand what a fantastic world you live in, open Wikipedia and read the lyrics of national anthems from various countries. You won't believe the insane things written there. "They come to kill us... We will fight for our land... For the Emperor... Save me from those who pursue me... Your dying enemies...." Everything is about battles, blood, death, and a total blowout of nonsense. But back then, it wasn't nonsense. It was life. Surviving as a nation, defeating enemies... And it's not just World War II, which most of you might know from the History Channel or various series or films; there were countless other wars long before. People fought with spears, defended their families when enemy armies took over their territories. People were slaughtered without mercy. Children, women, everyone. There were no cameras to document every atrocity and upload it to the internet with 'Look what happened to me'. An army would conquer a region, slaughter all the men, and rape all the women. Everything that's happening to you now is a brothel. Oh, you don't know what to do with your life? You're in a mid-life crisis? Oh boy... What shall we do?

What does all that have to do with Fatel? Well, I'll tell you. After our heroes returned from the battlefield, particularly the English among them, a group was sent— where else?—to the land of Israel, where the mandate was in control. And the mandate, true to its name, had the mandate to do whatever it wished, much like the French and Russians in various parts of the world. Our band was searching for a paradise, a place where they could forget the horrors of war. And they found it. They stumbled upon a sort of oasis amid all the greenery, halfway to the northern regions of the land.

The Englishman, who was so enamored by the sight before him, began to run along the paths that cut through the nearby villages, mostly Arab ones, shouting out his awe. The legend tells that, in his frenzy, he tripped over a large stone, struck his head, and lost consciousness. Arabs from the nearby village finding him battered and bleeding, took him to a house. There, as the story goes, he awoke to the sight of an Arab girl, the most beautiful woman he had ever seen, and fell instantly in love with her. Just like that, without exchanging a word.

So deep was his love that he forgot where he was and why she was tending to his head. He began to speak to her, in English of course, and told her about the place he had seen. The place where he would take his eternal beloved, where they would live forever, free from fear and war. One of the villagers who had gathered around to witness the event knew English from working as a sort of waiter and half-piccolo in a restaurant frequented by many Englishmen. He understood every word. The legend also claims he knew Russian, but this fact remains a point of contention among the storytellers of Fatel.

'Enchabat Bmuchu,' laughed the Arab and began to describe the Englishman's pained ramblings as those of someone talking nonsense after a head injury. 'Bata marjanatan, bata marjanatan!' he shouted, and everyone burst into laughter. Suddenly, the Englishman stirred, got to his feet, and began repeating the words of the polyglot Arab. But since the English have a knack for mispronouncing words, even in their own language—see entry Wales, Scotland, and Liverpool. No really, have you ever tried talking to someone from Liverpool? It's like trying to speak Circassian with an ant barking at you. For this reason and others, they turned Mumbai into Bombay, and 'Bata marjanatan,' which the polyglot Arab had shouted in Arabic, into 'Fata,' and to add an Arabic twist, since he was sure he hadn't heard the Arabic accent correctly, it turned into 'Fatel.' And from all the blows, he completely forgot the rest. He ran towards the door, not before returning to fetch the girl. But it turns out that the girl was... how shall we put this delicately? Not just any girl. She was the daughter of the village chief, a prestigious virgin by any standard, and it was intolerable for her to be taken like this, even if it was by an English soldier and Sir, no matter how senior he was. A commotion ensued, and our hero, of course, lost consciousness again after receiving a proper beating. At dawn, his comrades found him by the roadside, battered and bruised, yet breath still graced his lips.

"I found it! I found it!" he exclaimed as he got back on his feet. His comrades were eager to find out who was responsible for his battered face, intent on repaying him 'in kind', and perhaps even 'extra kind'. But he quickly dismissed their concerns, saying, "We were looking for a place of peace, a place of quiet and camaraderie. And now, we've found it. From now on, for us, there will be no more battles." And then they all nodded in agreement. "Fatel... Fatel..." He murmured, recalling the Arab's shout in his accented Arabic, and let's not forget that this was amid the chaos of blows and the haze of the experience. He shared with them what he had witnessed. 'They call this place — Fatel.'

"India? Are you serious?"

"Yeah, man. I need to make important decisions," he nodded with an unusually dejected demeanor. He was always so positive and smiley—a true Fatel-like. So what's with the sudden grim face? This is the place to point out that Arik eventually ended up with someone quite wealthy. How wealthy? Let's just say her father could buy all of Fatel and back, up to the Izrael Valley. At first, he was thrilled. What do I mean by thrilled? He felt like it was over, the end for his struggles. Not that he was looking for someone with money, but it just came his way. Some might say he 'fell into a lap of luxury.' I say he 'fell.' Why 'fell'? Because at first, it was indeed exciting. Daddy bought them an extravagant penthouse and, over time, helped him become a director at top companies, which really boosted his business. His wife is a very busy and successful lawyer, and I estimate their wealth to be of at least several tens of millions in the bank. "But what?" they ask in Aramaic so the cherubim don't understand... No, seriously. In our Kaddish, they changed a few words to Aramaic so the angels wouldn't understand; it's huge, I'm telling you, even more effective than the Christian goblins in the tree—this Talmud and Science program was totally worth it. And so they ask, "But what...?" Well, these two wealthy individuals work from morning till night, barely seeing their three children. He's dying to get back to making music like he used to, and despite their millions, they live far less well than most of you. 'But wait a minute—go on, jump in and say it: 'They could leave it all, or even just half of it, do whatever they want, and live like royalty for the rest of their lives!'. And you'd be absolutely right. 'But what...' When *her* father, directly or indirectly, is the one who provided *your* wealth, you can't just wake up one day and say, "So... listen, I'm taking all the money you set up for me, putting a flying fuck on everyone, and living like Malik (king in Arabic) 'til I drop dead." I mean, basically you can, but it just never happens. And Arik, when he's at work or just with people, he's the most vibrant person in the world—an Energizer always lifting the room, a ball of light rolling through life. But with his wife, he's someone else entirely. A different figure. Exhausted, dispassionate, a hard worker. One day, he told me that these two personas must never meet, because if they did, it would be over for him. His wife must never know he's 'happy' and that he's content. Because only the tortured persona gets his slack cut. "He's already suffering; why should I burden him with my nonsense?". I remember being in shock. So why did you get married? To live in a lie? Inside a cage where you get two meals a day and the rest is chores and occasional breaks in the yard, but at least you're considered 'fine'? 'like everyone else,' 'as it should be.' '*And the LORD God said, 'It is not good for man to be alone.'* See, it's not just written in the Bible; God himself said it! And not just any God, but Yahweh God! Remember that when you're stuck in a house with a mortgage, a wife, and kids screaming from every direction, and maybe you're not really happy. And don't get me wrong. You could be someone with four cramped walls, a mortgage, and five screaming kids and be the happiest person alive, while another might have no apparent worries and feel the walls closing in. To each their own.

In poker, there's a saying that goes, "You play the hand you're dealt." Remember Benny? Well, if you happened to wonder how he's doing and where he is now, let me tell you: after a failed hostile takeover attempt at a company he worked for, he started moving from business to business and supplemented his income by playing high-stakes poker. "Won fifteen K, lost four, won nine." That kind. At some point, he realized he was probably exceptionally good at poker, so he turned it into his livelihood. To be honest, what really interests him is mainly doing drugs and screwing around, and it doesn't matter if it's the same girl or ten different ones a week. Plus, he never uses a condom because he claims it ruins all the fun, which is true, and above all— everyone says he's a great guy. And he really is a great guy. He doesn't care what people think or what tomorrow holds; he lives each day exactly the way he wants to. When you're driving with him, he'll dramatically pull out coke or Ritalin or some other inhalable-drug-because-coke-is-expensive-and-mixed-having-passed-through-a-myriad-of-Colombian-and-Israeli-asses-before-it-reaches-your-nose. He'll sprinkle a bit of powder directly from the bottle onto the wrist, look at you, and make sure you notice that he's not planning to snort it or look back at the road until you do, and keeps his smile during. He's been drunk behind the wheel a million times, caught for alcohol around six times, and always managed to slip away. Whether by taking two quick breaths to clear the alcohol from his chest and then inhaling clean air and blowing it rapidly into the device to fool it, eating eucalyptus leaves found by the roadside without the officer noticing, or countless other stories that are probably true because he still has his license. He enjoys telling you about how he dropped a girl off at home at seven in the morning, then picked up someone else for a ride and ended up taking her to his place. He'll also recount how someone just walked out of his place after he pummeled her face with his fists because she begged and swore that's how she likes it. Well, after all, the guy is quite skinny... Oh, and the cherry on top—he doesn't want children. Not interested. 'Maybe it's better this way,' says anyone who fears anything that isn't 'normal' or 'like them.' Well, just let there be no more like him, right? May God protect us from such as these. But Benny doesn't care what you think. He enjoys himself. He loves living. He does nothing for the show or for what you might say or think about him. He couldn't care less about your opinions or judgments. He really couldn't care less. And if the world explodes tomorrow, he will have lived better than anyone. He does exactly what he wants and enjoys life. What's better, working every day from nine to six with file folders, a computer, and fluorescent lights, coming home to a woman you sleep with every two weeks, and living to ninety with dementia and a diaper in the last ten years, or sleeping with women, snorting coke, playing poker, and dying in an accident at forty-five? Who is happier, a goldfish living in a worry-free reality, swimming in circles in an aquarium it knows as its world and existence, eating regularly and resting most of the time, or a shark experiencing the dangers of the ocean, needing to hunt for its food, kill and be killed, roaming from place to place, propelling through the water with its fins to cross seas and oceans, carving through the ocean currents and blending with the weather's whims? Would you prefer to be the second-string goalkeeper of the world champion squad, sitting comfortably on the bench, or the leading player and captain of the second division team? I, by the way, appreciate any answer as long as it's honest.

"Live life," a wise person once told me. Ok, it was my mom. But she really is one of the wisest people I know. Most people I know who aren't from Fatel don't live life. They live for the future, replicate the past, and are afraid to live in the present. They're caught in some kind of chase to get an apartment. What's so special about an apartment, about this false sense of security that we so desperately need? After all, no one would want to live in the same apartment their whole life if given a choice. That's why people travel abroad, to hotels, to guest houses, to tents in nature. Part of it is due to the need to change the scenery. The same goes for moving houses every few years. It's refreshing, it's fun, maybe even a different area. What's so wrong with that? There are countless places where you can live in a four-room apartment for less than five thousand shekels a month. Plenty. You don't have to be in central Tel Aviv. There are even places close to the center where you can live at a great price if you don't want to be in Arad or Achziv, though I'd personally prefer the desert air at night or Achziv by the sea any day. So, can't two people put together five thousand shekels for rent? After all, what does it mean to live well? To be free! Free from what? From everything. That tycoon or millionaire you envy, do you have any idea how many worries and stresses he has in his life? How many enemies lurk in the shadows, authorities, competitors, you name it. Everyone is eager to dress him up in trouble. To skewer him. The one who has nothing, who knows with absolute certainty that he'll probably never have more than what he has or doesn't have now, he is free. So he doesn't live in Manhattan or St. Tropez, not even in Tel Aviv or Herzliya. But he lives in a decent place, maybe even pastoral if it's in the southern desert or the northern greenery, and more importantly—he has no worries. I mean, for sure he's convinced he has plenty of worries and no money for anything, but if he looked at his situation from a bird's-eye view, he'd realize that, come to think of it, his life isn't that bad. But wait. Ah... you need to save up. For the future. Oh, yes. And why is that? And if the world blows up tomorrow? Now you're probably laughing. Go ahead, laugh. I'm certainly not as smart as you. The most paradoxical, parodic, and Kafkaesque thing about wisdom is that every person you know is convinced that, apart from perhaps true geniuses who've won the Nobel Prize, they are the smartest person they know. Don't believe it? Ask yourselves. It's obvious to you that you're really, really smart, understand everything, or at least among the wise. Of course. At the same time, you're sure that most people are dumber than you. But you keep this only to yourselves, as a closely guarded secret, not revealing it to all the 'idiots around you.' You wouldn't want to offend them, would you? So know this: some of you are really, really dumb. It's a statistical thing, not meant to insult. You're probably laughing now, sure that I'm not talking about you specifically, but while you're laughing to yourselves, someone who laughed just like you was just hit by a car. That's right. They left the house with all their wisdom and understanding of the world, planned their future and even their children's future, and suddenly – they were gone. Have you ever thought about how many people die in traffic accidents around the world in a single day? Completely normal people who woke up for another routine day and never returned home. Hundreds? Thousands? Hundreds of thousands? How many people woke up for another 'normal' day and got news that changed their lives forever, or had a stroke in the middle of the street? Are you in love with your friend? Tell her! Grab her and kiss her! Don't wait for her to get married. Do you want a child? Have a child, don't wait for the love of your life. Are you suffering in your marriage? Get a divorce, I promise you the world won't collapse into itself. Each of us has an unfulfilled dream, aspiration, or desire. Each of us. And each of us could have a stroke in the middle of the street right this moment...

So live! Live! And maybe your son will make millions and won't need the money you're saving for him, and you're just living frugally for nothing? So live! And if aliens land here tomorrow and enslave or annihilate us all? Are you laughing again? Don't believe in aliens? Have you ever wondered why all the 'pharaohs' are depicted with the heads of dogs or birds in wall paintings? Or how they built the pyramids with so many rooms and internal mazes without any electricity? And how did the Maya disappear from the face of the earth 'one day'? And who placed the stones of Stonehenge and all those giant carved faces looking out at the horizon, at the sea? Nothing. They say 'there is God,' 'Jesus Christ,' or 'Allah Akbar,' and that's it. There was nothing before us. Dinosaurs. Aliens? Really? Besides God, most people don't believe anything but what they see right in front of their eyes. The Native Americans who lived on the American continent also didn't believe. Until one day, from a place they thought had nothing beyond it, ships of a kind they had never imagined appeared, and from them emerged creatures they had never seen, armed with weapons they could not compete with. That is, they fought fiercely, but the most serious weapons they had were considered a joke compared to the powerful weapons with the loud boom that suddenly explodes and kills everyone. So while some say that what killed the Native Americans the most was syphilis and other germs from these 'aliens,' and that 'in return' the Native Americans gave the European aliens the gift of tobacco, which has since killed many more, the bottom line is that the Native Americans were almost completely exterminated. But most people are cowards by nature. Risk-averse. So they spend most of their time bullshitting. They rationalize to themselves why it's better and more suitable for them to remain in the current state. Why not to act. Why this and that can't be done. The wisdom of the crowd.

When I was a kid, every player on the local futsal team dreamed of making it to the big league—Maccabi Haifa. The standout player on our team, far ahead of everyone else, was Tal Abada. He was so much better that he would dribble past all the players, trick the goalkeeper, then go back and dribble past everyone again before finally unleashing a rocket into the net that shook the entire hall. Futsal, after all, there's an echo. We always said that one day, thousands of fans would chant his name at the national stadium in Ramat Gan: 'Tal Abada! Ta-ta, ta-ta-ta. Tal Abada!...' and so on, in perfect rhythm. It was clear to every kid in the village. One day, Abada went to a tryout for Maccabi Haifa. His father took a day off from work at the factory and drove him to the big city to try his luck. I remember us all waiting in the neighborhood, perched on the railings, eager to hear how Abada had dazzled everyone with his skills, how he had weaved through the players and spun circles around the coaches who would surely sign him up immediately, making him a permanent fixture on Maccabi Haifa's roster. But Abada never returned. As evening fell and the sky darkened, our mothers called us home. Arik's mother told us that Abada's aunt, who was her friend, had called to say that Abada had fainted at the tryouts. Since then, no one from our neighborhood has tried out for Maccabi Haifa. Not even Hapoel Haifa, a much more modest team. Because if Abada had fainted from the effort, then surely no one else had a chance. Today, as I look back, I wonder—what makes people faint? Probably from exertion and trying to impress, the poor guy had ran non-stop in the scorching August sun without drinking, and he collapsed. Maybe if he had tried again, he would have succeeded. Maybe if someone else had tried, they might have succeeded even if Abada didn't. But no one tried. If Abada had fainted, then no one else had a chance. It's impossible.

An emulsion is essentially a mixture of substances that don't normally mix together, but with the help of an emulsifier, they do. Like egg yolk, which enables the blending of oil and water in mayonnaise. Suddenly, it's possible to mix what seemed impossible. But most people experience the world as it is, accepting it as given. They consider what is possible and what isn't, and what they can do within the confines of this playground and what they cannot. I once watched a nature film about a hyena and a cheetah. Cheetah is that tiger with the spots and a relatively small head, known as the fastest animal on land, reaching speeds of about sixty-five miles per hour, but it isn't as strong compared to other big cats. The hyena, although not yet an adult, can overpower a cheetah in a one-on-one encounter, but of course, both would prefer to avoid a fight that could be potentially lethal.

But fate had it that these two creatures lived in the same area. The young hyena, struggling to hunt alone, is a social hunter, whereas cheetahs are solitary and excellent at climbing trees to hide their kills. Each evening, the young and ambitious hyena would approach the cheetah to see what it had caught and attempt to scavenge from it. However, cheetahs are clever and adept tree climbers, often hiding their kills up high.

One day, the noise made by the hyena alerted a herd of impalas in the area. Unlike cheetahs and lions, hyenas aren't fast runners, so the impalas only went into a state of alert rather than fleeing. This gave the cheetah the opportunity to easily catch an impala since no one was expecting it. Initially, the cheetah fought the hyena over the carcass when it came to steal, but in the following days, the hyena returned. Despite the cheetah's apparent resistance each time, eventually, the cheetah managed to catch more prey, and its success rate increased significantly. And this is a cooperation that no one ever dared to even think of, and no one calculated the benefits it could produce. In the following evenings, they ate together. The hyena created a diversion, the cheetah hunted, and then the hyena would come to eat. Madness—unbelievable and utterly impossible.

A young couple with one child justifies not having more kids because they can't afford it. They need a room for each child, money for extracurricular activities, baby yoga classes, and emotional regulation workshops for a five-year-old. A family of eight manages just fine and no one is starving, but those living in central Tel Aviv cannot, they would collapse financially... And maybe the light that a newborn brings into the house would bring you supreme happiness? 'But what can I do? happiness doesn't bring money', as they might say, like Erik who has plenty of money in the bank and wants to pursue an old hobby but can't spare half a day because it's tied to so many things that we probably wouldn't understand. So, what are you living for?? When you flip back through the album of your life, which page will you stop on?

And maybe, just maybe, the so-called wisdom of the crowd is actually the stupidity of the crowd. After all, what does the wisdom of the crowd say? That if the crowd does something, then it must be right. That among a range of opinions, a collective opinion will be more accurate than any single expert. That's what Aristotle said once, and he's considered very wise, even though that actually makes him a single expert himself. But many others followed him and agreed as well. Because who's man enough to refute Aristotle? But I say that any crowd wisdom must carry with it the risk of total crowd stupidity. For example, there are certainly more people drinking cola worldwide per minute than drinking green tea. So does that mean cola is healthier than green tea? And there are definitely more people around the world per minute lighting a cigarette right now than those drinking a spirulina smoothie. So does that mean cigarettes are better for your body than spirulina? Is a hamburger and fries healthier than a salad? Is it better to get dysentery than to wash your hands after using the restroom? Is it preferable to cross on a red light rather than wait, on average, and I checked this, ten seconds (!) and reduce the risk of being hit by a car by ninety-nine percent and end up in a wheelchair for life? The probability of guessing the winning lottery numbers is something like ten to the power of forty-two. In other words, it's one followed by forty-two zeros, or a million trillion trillion trillion. Whereas a trillion, for those who don't know, equals a million times a million. On the other hand, the chance of being killed by a meteorite impact is slightly more than one in about a million and a half, and the risk of dying in a car accident is about one in thirty thousand. Yet, despite these odds, no one, including those who occasionally play the lottery, would bet on such an event happening to them, while still believing they might win.

It's a bit ironic that Benny plays poker for a living while most people don't. He plays, exploiting every card to its fullest. Most people don't play; they keep their cards close to their chest, waiting for someone else to fold or bluff, hoping not to be raised so they can survive another round. Another tomorrow. There, perhaps, something good will happen to them. What they desire. What they long for but dare to see only in their dreams. And so they don't truly participate in the game. They don't live fully. Raise? Not a chance. Only if he gets at least an ace and a king. Only when he has enough of what he considers good will he be happy; only when he has enough money will he truly start living. To bet on something? Never. To deviate from the path laid out for him? To believe in something other than what he was taught? To try and do something he loves? That's... that's just too great of a risk. To risk what he seemingly has. But he's sure to always play the lottery.

So live! For tomorrow, aliens might land here. Still don't believe it? The Native Americans didn't either.

8

"What's with India at forty? Isn't it dirty there, and doesn't everyone get diarrhea all the time?"

Honestly, I understood him a lot faster than he thought. He needed this. For his soul. And maybe, just maybe, there I could somehow influence him, convince him that it's okay to take a step, that he doesn't owe anything to anyone, and that life is too short not to do things just because they're uncomfortable. That it's completely, and absolutely allowed, to live.

"Goa, man," his famous smile reignited, "it's the Christian side of India, totally different. It's not all dirt and diarrhea; it's a whole different scene... Besides, it's just two or three weeks, why are you making such a big deal out of it?"

This is the moment to mention that in Fatel, anyone who goes abroad gets a small celebration, and when they return, there's a party waiting for them. It's a kind of tradition that ensures you never come back to an empty house, to a desolate place, even if it's just in your heart. When you come back, it's always to a party. So we threw one. Everyone came and said how cool it was, how much fun we'd have, and that we'd definitely enjoy it endlessly. Arik had already booked us a fancy guesthouse right by the beach and was sure everything would work out, and that I was definitely joining him. But I still hadn't booked a flight and wasn't even sure I was going. And then it happened.

"You know what? Count me in."

Okay.
Wait.
What?
Who's in?
You're in?
With us??
To Goa???

"Maybe we'll even throw a beach party over there," she smiled that smile of hers that I had hated my whole life. "Ha... great," I continued to stutter.

"Wow, I'm suddenly totally in. You don't mind, do you?"

"Not at all, are you kidding? Why would we mind" I replied, not entirely sure who was speaking for me.

"What. A winning. Team!" Arik declared with unwavering certainty, while my mind spun in a whirlpool of confusion. Of course I had booked a flight ticket online that very night.

"You can wait a bit, I did too," I suggested the next day. "Prices might drop."

"Ah-ah," she laughed her annoying, charming laugh. "Maybe you can book for me too? I'll give you cash. I'm terrible at this stuff. My agent always jokes that I'd still be lost at a terminal without him..."

They say revolutions happen in a single day, unlike processes that always get stuck halfway. The attempt at social revolution in Israel in 2011 remained a protest that no one cared about, in contrast to the French Revolution where the masses stormed the Bastille, dragged the aristocracy by their hair from their homes, and had their heads cut off by the guillotine. And so, suddenly, in a sharp flash, Moran and I are talking freely as if nothing ever happened. Just like old friends who grew up together. I had always feared speaking with her. I always felt as if something was separating us, a barrier. She was always surrounded by friends, partners, unattainable. Even when we talked here and there, I felt a multitude of fences between us and couldn't truly be myself. When something separates people, they behave differently.

And perhaps she didn't plan to torment my life and hurt me intentionally at every stage. I simply always wanted her, and that's why my heart would always open up again with every glance of hers that locked onto mine. Even if it happened only once every six months or even a year. Over time, a window would open here or there where our gazes would meet, and then I'd always tell her with my eyes that I wanted her. And even if I didn't try to say it out loud, it was evident. Just like the beats of the heart, I couldn't do anything to hide it. Love is an involuntary muscle. And she, perhaps, was just not on the same track. Maybe she even liked me the way she tossed me onto the hammock on my first evening with Moran. My first magical moment with Moran. Even if, to her, it wasn't. And maybe it was. Maybe even Moran Dagan harbors that same feeling for the child in me. The child who always told her that he was hers for eternity, forever, and she was either too young or too busy with other things to notice, to understand. And now she understands perfectly. She even sat next to me, kissed my lips, and said that it was truly a shame and that we should have been in the bond of marriage now. She said it, not me!

"So, did you get a backpack?" Arik asked during the next phone call.

"Uh, well... I think I have one at my parents' place, maybe from the army..."

"I'm joking!" he cut me off, bursting into laughter. "You're so funny... We're going with a rolling suitcase, and even that will be carried by the cab driver to your room for you. What do you think, we're heading off on a trek in Nepal?" He kept laughing at my expense.

"Go screw yourself..." I laughed too.

"Just don't accidentally bring along a water bladder and thermal socks..."

"I'll bring a mosquito net and put it right on your head."

"Haha..." he laughed at my pathetic joke.

"So... is Moran really joining us? Is she serious?" I asked as if I didn't know.

"Of course! What, haven't you booked her a ticket yet? She told me you..."

"Yeah, yeah, I'm booking it. Good thing you reminded me. I wasn't sure just how serious she was..."

"Serious, man, serious. Cool, right? It'll be the three of us together again... Sounds like fun, right?"

The three of us??

Again?

Together and having fun???

When were we ever three together and having fun?!

"Yeah... So, are we, like, getting a room for you and me, and she'll sleep next to us? How's this going to work?"

"No, man! Are you kidding? No, no... Listen. We're all three going to travel together, we'll get a huge room, buy loads of Charas, and forget about life…"

"Wow... Okay... Well, sounds... sounds great."

Arik, who always stays charming in every situation, remained charming now too, and ended the call with a smile.

'Did you book it for me?' a text message arrived on my cell phone.

'Just did,' I hurriedly replied.

'Great,' came the response with a smiley and a heart.

Moran... please, don't do the hearts now... please, please, I beg you. I sent a winking smiley back, which is always a great response to almost everything. Had fun? Winking smiley. Are you coming? Winking smiley. Your mother died? Winking smiley with the funeral date. I'm joking... I'm in a very hazy mood, please understand me. Traveling into the unknown, with a sense of emptiness, carrying a sack of love's cables hanging from my aching shoulders. My best friend by my side, and my unfulfilled love for three decades on my heart. And now I really have to try and squeeze through the tiny gap between them and claim a place of honor, an extremely tough starting condition by all accounts. How real it was between them I will never know. I can only assume, imagine. Imagine that once he held her and she held him, they lay together in bed whispering little words of love to each other, shared intimacy, she loved him and he loved her, and above all—he fucked her numerous times.

9

The flight was exhausting. I mean, the flight itself was perfectly fine, but what was going on in my head was far from it. We were sitting in the middle row of three seats on the Boeing plane of the national airline. When I was little, my uncle used to work for Maof. Yeah, that's right, there was another Israeli airline that flew abroad called Maof. I even had an inflatable plane of theirs that he once brought me as a gift, even though it wasn't my birthday. One day, they fired him. When I asked my mom why, she answered that because the competing company was state-owned, they could lower prices as much as they wanted until Maof choked and collapsed. So fuck them. The truth is, flights to India had just started with foreign companies, which I didn't mind supporting instead of the national airline that could go screw itself, as mentioned, and they were even shorter because they flew over Arab countries, but at this point, they only flew to Delhi and not to Bombay or Mumbai or however the hell my founding fathers twisted the name, and Arik said it was a pointless detour. After nearly eight hours of flying, he admitted that maybe it would have been better to fly five hours to Delhi and then another three to Goa.

This is the place to point out that the flight was scheduled for eight in the morning, and we Englishmen are sticklers for punctuality, arriving at least three, sometimes even four hours early, just to wander around and have coffee in the duty-free area. Usually, I tilt the seat back on the plane slightly towards me and then lean my body half to the side, with my legs almost touching the person in the seat in front under their chair. But due to the shorter flights to Delhi, the row in front of us was completely empty, but when Arik went to lie down there diagonally, the flight attendant quickly clarified that those were paid seats and that there was absolutely no way he could just lie there 'for free' for his own pleasure, even though no one would be harmed by it. The truth is, they were a slightly different color, but I could swear they were exactly, but exactly, the same size and shape, and as far as I could tell, the space between them and the next row was identical to the space we had.

The phrase 'one benefits, and the other does not lose' from the Tractate Bava Kamma in the Talmud, as we thoroughly studied in our Talmud and Science track, apparently doesn't apply to the national airline. So, I somehow had to try and shift myself to the side in an attempt to fall asleep, but that turned out to be an almost impossible task. And so, I found myself wide awake despite a sleepless night, and while I was like that, dying to sleep, our little cutie Morani, who was sitting between us, decided to fall asleep and rest her head on me.

Diplomatic stalemate. How can I even close my eyes now? Even if I want to sleep, there's no way I can doze off with Moran Dagan herself leaning and sweetly napping on my shoulder. I've dreamed about this scene, though not exactly like this, for thirty years. There's no way I'm moving her now. I looked at her. This was the first real time I could gaze at Moran from such close range for an extended period. Everyone else was asleep, and I was looking at her up close. Not exactly examining, but noticing her features, which have always seemed and still seem regal to me. Her mouth was almost entirely closed. A tiny slit allowed air to flow in and out between her full, pink-red, enchanting lips. How I wished that the whole world would just dissolve into a cloud fragment and disappear, simply vanish into some black hole, leaving only the two of us, her leaning on my shoulder, sailing together into the kingdom of infinity. As she wakes up, she'll look at me and smile, kiss my lips, and tell me how much she loves me, and then she'll hug me. And I… I'll just hug her back, my head cradling hers at the chin, as a tear of happiness rolls down my cheek. But instead, some fucking turbulence made the plane take one hell of a jolt, and everyone woke up with a bang.

We landed in Bombay at an airport decorated with wall-to-wall carpets, including on the walls. I needed to use the restroom, but I was too embarrassed to say anything in front of Moran. It's unbelievable. In the workshop, I'd literally use the bathroom in front of customers if I really had to, but somehow Moran turns me back into that scared, insecure eleven-year-old. Soon enough, I'd have to come up with various excuses, since we'd all be together in a tiny room. Just three of us in one apartment. A nightmare…

So, I signaled something to Arik when Moran went off to buy cigarettes. He immediately came to my aid and asked Moran to join him in checking if they had the specific headphones he was looking for and to help him pick the best brand since she surely knew more about it than we did, thanks to the profession she had chosen for herself. I claimed I was too tired because I hadn't slept a wink on the flight, and stayed behind, supposedly waiting for them. The restrooms were actually very clean; after all, I had expected something less sanitary in India…

After a few minutes, we met up again and began waiting for our connecting flight to Goa. Three hours. We sat in the food court. Great. So now what? Talk? Laugh? Feel awkward? As if we were a tight-knit group, born together, just heading to a beach in Tel Aviv. The longest conversation I'd had with the girl who had tormented my life for thirty years was about a week and a half ago, and before that, nothing. And Arik… well, Arik would save the day. They were a couple. And he and I were friends. And suddenly, Moran says she's hot and is going to the restroom to change into something shorter. Couldn't I have thought of that excuse a minute ago?? Arik and I took advantage of the opportunity since we had the small trolley with us and swapped our shoes for flip-flops.

"So, what do you think?" She emerged behind us a few minutes later in a red summer dress with orange flowers and a dazzling smile.

"Whoa..." I genuinely admired, "Who's that in a summer dress?". She suddenly looked so beautiful. In a summer dress and tiny red flip-flops. I bet her underwear is red too, and for a moment I think I fantasized about her for the first time. Yes. I totally imagined a tight red lace thong hugging her from underneath.

"Let's eat?" she asked with the continuation of her smile, pulling me out of the fantasy.

"Sure," Arik replied and got up.

"You know what," Moran sat down. "why should we drag around all the suitcases now, only to lose our seats later? Just get me something with meat, doesn't matter what.."

"Okay," Arik nodded.

"Don't you want something specific?" I asked, still feeling a bit awkward.

"No, no. Here, take," she began to pull out a bill from her pocket, but both of us ignored it and turned away. I'm not sure how generous Brits are, but Arik and I are the type of guys who don't let a girl pay. I don't really have a good explanation for this, and it seems Arik doesn't either. It's just a thing where we pay, and it's fine if the girl insists on leaving a tip and offers to pay sometime during the third date, which makes us gentlemen and her a cool girl who isn't after money. Personally, I don't like meeting someone who wants me partly because I have money and it makes the picture look better for her. It's not because I'm worried about what will happen if there's no money tomorrow; that doesn't bother me at all. A good couple, their financial situation doesn't matter. What bothers me is that she doesn't want only me. And I always wanted someone who would want only me, and I would want only her. And what would be most important to us is each other, having the most fun together, doing our little things, those small things that build up affection at the start of the relationship and later become the foundation and the basis upon which it's built. Small... recurring motifs, if you will. A song you heard on the way to the first date and then the second, and now it's your song even though neither of you paid much attention to it before. And something someone mentioned before they met the other side and now it's a little joke and always funny, with some teasing about something similar from the other side. Little big things. And then we'll do really big things. Very big things. We'll have a home that's just ours, in a place that feels most real to us. We'll embrace nature's way, and as time passes, your belly will gently grow. Each night, we'll fall asleep with you resting against my back, while I lie on my side, caressing your belly and holding your hand, with our other hands entwined. And how many tears of joy are now gathered and cherished within us. And suddenly, a laugh will release a tear of a smile. And we'll hug and know that the wonder of the world is near, it's really at our doorstep. And how we'll cherish and love the little one who's born. We'll bathe him and sing songs to him. And he or she will smile at us for the first time. Then they'll crawl for the first time. And one day, he'll let go of one of our hands and start walking, taking his first steps alone in the world! So money, that's what's important to you?! Take a check and go fuck with it! Money... money is for poor people.

Suddenly, it dawned on me that among the three of us, I could definitely be considered the poorest, even though I was making decent money. Moran DJs at international events, where they surely pay tens of thousands of dollars per performance, and as mentioned, Arik married into his father-in-law's wealth. His wife... well, lucky for him, she didn't step into my shop before she met him. Women like her are just waiting for the tall, strong, and intelligent guy who can explain why this particular oak is better than maple in that specific case, or even mahogany, and thus provide an artistic perspective on the purchase for their living room. He'd tell her about the techniques required for fine and precise carving using professional equipment, and even elaborate on different types of knives and their unique qualities, the specific characteristics of various woods, and even the process of preparing wood blocks for carving. Sometimes it could even extend to the back room, where I could continue demonstrating work with lathes, chisels, rasps, finishing tools, sanding, clamping techniques, wax, coatings, and finishing touches, alongside her motherfuckin moans of "Yes, yes! Harder! Fuck me harder!" echo in the background. You'd be surprised at how many sexual proposals I received from wealthy and affluent women whose attraction to me, with my broad shoulders and bulging veins from working out in a tank top, made them completely forget all the promises they made under the wedding canopy. I'd take all their wealth and crumple it, roll up their dress from behind, lean them on the lathe, and insert my dick into their respectable vaginas without a condom, and then spurt all over their dress, so they'd go home like whores. And they would love it. Just waiting for it to happen. Not giving a fuck about anything. I see it in their eyes. A strong psychological need drives them to the filth. To the breaking of taboos. "Do you like being fucked like that because you're a whore?" I'd ask them while my dick ravages their vagina, and they'd answer without hesitation, "Yes, I'm a whore! I'm a whore!" Some of them, even though they didn't fuck me on the lathe, fucked their husbands in another way. I already knew exactly how it would go when I'd get an 'urgent' call. Arriving urgently in VIP service to the house, which of course is immaculate, with various cleaners or workers always passing by. One woman comes to cook, another cleans, a regular gardener, another arranges the cars, I'm the furniture. Every day the house runs like a factory. And she stands there dressed in tight, yet elegant clothing, embodying wealth, and and perfectly polished.

"So where's the problem?" I ask while putting on my work clothes, knowing they get her all wet down there.

"Look, here… the handle jumps a bit. Do you see?" She looks up at me from a centimeter away, "And here… look," she guides me, accompanying my muscular arm with the rolled-up sleeve folded just next to the muscle, "Here, you see? Because it's connected to the entire right side of the sofa and holds it from both the side and the bottom, it's more than just tightening." In plain Language – she wants a new one.

"Yes, yes. I see. And what did you tell me on the phone about the fireplace?"

"Come," again grabbing my arm. And so we walk, of course passing by the different working people. "Do you see? It's very problematic."

"What, doesn't heat well?" I looked at the fireplace, which didn't look new anymore but could work fine for at least another ten or twenty years.

"Not at all like it used to," she answers a most answeringly answer.

"Well, that's... that's the problem with all these stoves. Wear and tear," I said what she wanted to hear.

"So what do you suggest?" I already knew the answer. She wants a new one, expensive, and mainly - in a different color.

"Replace it?"

For places like these, you go after you've already arranged the goods they're complaining about. That's what she wants. The newest and most expensive.

"It'll be ready within an hour," I smiled at her.

"Oh, you're wonderful." Now she'll grab my back hand a bit more without squeezing or anything like that, just leaning a little and continuing forward.

"What do you drink? Black, right?"

Later on, she'll sit at the desk, watching me with a pen in hand and the notebook spread out prominently. Checks from truly wealthy people always look more polished. They're bigger and tear off more cleanly. The price doesn't matter to her at all. Whatever I tell her, she'll write down quickly and immediately. To her, whether I say two thousand shekels or eighty-seven thousand nine hundred fifty is the same. "Perfect," will be her response to any amount I mention now. It's her dream that I say eighty-seven thousand nine hundred fifty. Her dream.

"For the handle, that's a minor thing—five hundred. For the fireplace, I'll check and let you know when I bring it. You know this isn't really my field of expertise, and I'm doing it for you only because your threats sounded convincing," I added, and she laughed. For anyone else, if I quoted five hundred shekels for replacing a handle, they'd call in the Feds. But here, if I quote anything less, even for something minor, it would just seem unprofessional to her. She doesn't even grasp what such amounts mean. "You're funny," she'll blush and enjoy the moment. "You know I only trust you. No one else comes in to do work for me, just you. Get used to it." Later, she'll insist on adding extra money for coming out specifically, bringing special tools, and for everything else she can think of. And that's what gives her her thrill.

So after managing to get some meat sandwiches with Arik, despite the long line at every food counter, and enduring a dreadful flight from Bombay to Goa, where we received only half a slice of bread and a tropical water-flavored drink, we finally arrived at our promised destination. As we exited the terminal, I breathed in the exquisite Goan air for the first time in my life. Ah, Goaaaaaaaaaaaaaaaa... Ahhhhh, now we're talking! Suddenly, and contrary to all the earlier predictions, I felt something good in the air.

"All in all, looks pretty okay," I said to Moran while Arik was busy on the phone with the guy from the guesthouse who promised to send a taxi. She looked at me, then around, in a slightly strange way. What is she up to now, this girl? What now, Moran? No, stop it. Enough already, I urged myself. She's probably just tired like the rest of us.

"I'm here near the Sprite machine, you see me?" Arik shouted into the cellphone, and after a few seconds, a charming Indian man indeed arrived and took us to a spacious and clean taxi. Well, so far, we can definitely call this a smooth landing. After about twenty minutes, we stopped somewhere to buy cigarettes and something to drink. Three in the morning, a shabby hut in the middle of a rather dirty street, with a few Indians sitting, some standing, smoking cigarettes and drinking some kind of coffee.

"Chai?" the taxi driver asked us.

"Yes, of course, chai!" Arik shouted back at him, "Three!"

"Okay, my friend, three chai. Yes?"

"You have no idea how good this is... It's just what we need right now."

"How fun!" Moran said out loud, and all the Indians who had already been looking at her turned to stare even more. It seemed like her crappy post-flight state of mind was suddenly swept away by a refreshing breeze.

"They're not going to kill us here, right?" I asked.

"Kill us? No way, man... These are Indians, they're good people. They're smart, too. If something happens to us, their livelihood is gone for life."

"Right," Moran and I said together, then looked at each other in surprise, smiled, and started laughing. Honestly, I was cracking up. Yeah, I know it's not that funny. It was a different kind of laugh. A liberating laugh. A laugh that shatters years of awkwardness, years of stereotypes. Here I am, in Goa, India, maybe the most freeing place in the world, with the girl who's had a grip on my soul for so long, and my best friend. And now, maybe because I don't give a damn, or maybe out of the embarrassment of an eleven-year-old kid, I'm laughing. Go on, bring it. Bring chai.

10

After our esteemed English Sir finished recounting his finest tales about the coveted place, he took them there. At first, he couldn't find the desired spot, but after another small green hill and one more, the breathtaking scene unfolded before their eyes. A small pond with a palm tree beside it—seemingly where the inventor of "the Hula Valley swamp drying" grew up—surrounded by a vast sandy field, and beyond that, an expanse of lush greenery. They all immediately looked at each other and nodded in agreement. There was something so different and unique about the surrounding landscape, surely it was meant to convey something to them. But at the same time, they knew they had to keep it completely secret. In those times, there was no internet or smartphones, and if you found a remote and isolated place, you could pretty much do whatever you desired. Just ask Hitler, Mussolini, and Stalin. Initially, they were concerned to fence off the area and would sneak out daily to patrol, each one on their shift, to ensure that no one came within a kilometer of the only road, about a kilometer away, a sort of main path. However, they soon realized they needed—how shall we put it delicately—females.

Christopher Columbus of the Mandate sought to find and bring the village girl, whatever the cost, through peaceful means and money, of course. However, he agreed to cancel the idea after his friends warned that it might cause too much commotion, with a high potential for exposing the place. At that time, talks about a UN vote and a state for the Jews in the land of Israel were beginning, and in the minds of the young Fatels, a brilliant idea was born. To cut a long story short and spare myself unnecessary details, let's just say our grandmothers were a tad bit... how shall we put it delicately... somewhat easy with the Mandate soldiers. But they were certainly fittingly Sabra! And for those who still haven't understood - possessing the ability to produce Jewish descendants with strong roots in the land of Israel. Over the years, the idea faded for our founding friends and somewhat faltered because they had to return to their homeland by order. After all, even the British have their limits on disobedience... But the place remained. And so, the grandmothers held onto their vision of their esteemed progeny and vowed to preserve the tradition forever. Some say that it's possible some of our grandparents aren't truly original, but in the early fifties, no one argued if, after two months of acquaintance, the woman's belly started to take shape. Who else could it be but you? So, here we are, thanks to our heroic heroes from Great Britain. Fatel. Like the "Fateel" that never lit. We'll get to that too.

🪲

The three of us in bed.

Moran in the middle.

I stare at the ceiling.

How did this happen? I'll tell you how it happened. It happened when that motherfucking guesthouse owner shoved a thousand dicks up our asses. "Shanti Baba," he'll teach me over the next week to relax. To take it easy. Two words. Maybe they come without explanation and without too much meaning, but they say everything. You already understand on your own. That you should calm down already, that everything is okay, that everything is fated, that what we choose could never have been otherwise or wrong because our inner self wouldn't choose something we couldn't handle or didn't want to experience in the first place. That this thing that feels hard, that your thought is weighing against it, that gives you a headache, is the wrong path. Just like that gentle pat on the head from the adults at Fatel when you were little. Shanti Baba.

So when we arrived at the guesthouse, exhausted and drained from the seventeen-hour journey from the moment we landed at the airport until now, it was the middle of the night. The driver who had dropped us off had already left, and all that was left was the night guard waiting for us. No reception, no hotel manager, nothing. He had a key to the room that was supposedly for us, and that was it. And there, instead of the spacious area with at least two separate rooms, double toilets, a marble shower, and a sea view balcony as promised, we found a square room with walls painted in the color of India, which means quite faded, a huge mattress lying on the floor with Indian fabric covers, a sofa, and a huge bathroom with a shower that they could have easily downsized to make the bedroom larger. That's it. What do you do now? But before I learned about the history of 'Shanti Baba,' I was angry. And what do you do when you're angry? You curse, of course. Even though I'm from the peaceful Fatel, after all, I'm still red-headed.

"Jesus, what's this crap?" I blurted out due to exhaustion and even with Moran's presence.

"Well, relative to India, it's okay," Arik said, noticing our astonished looks. "But there's no way this is the room. He promised me a parquet and a proper bathroom. This must be temporary," he hesitated before adding, "or he might have pulled one over on me."

"Alright, let's just go to sleep," Moran took charge. "Tomorrow we'll ask him and sort everything out."

"Yeah, you're right... worst case, we'll move somewhere else," I added.

"Cool," Arik agreed. "Do you want the sofa?" He looked at Moran.

"You sleep on the sofa," she answered with a smile.

"No, I thought..."

"Fine, I'll sleep on the sofa," I quickly intervened, God knows why. "You two have already slept together; you're used to it," I added, and they looked at each other and started laughing. "Alright, go screw yourselves, I'm heading for the shower."

"Aham... I'm sorry," Moran quickly stopped me. "Haven't you heard of the term 'ladies first'?" She moved towards me slowly and lightly pushed me with her nail pointing at my chest, which of course left me frozen at her touch. Again, I was aroused by her. Twice a day compared to zero times in my whole life. For a moment, it reminded me of a forgotten scene from the trip I took with Arik to the Far East about a hundred years ago. "Give me attention," she said when we came back from that party in Koh Phangan where the three of us had ecstasy for the first time. I even remember that the pill was called 'Apple' and had a picture of an apple on it. And then suddenly, she came back to our room with us, and then suddenly the three of us showered and got into bed, and then suddenly Arik was standing next to me with his dick hard and started pounding her vigorously from behind. Am I supposed to be hard now? I wanted to run to the bathroom and puke, but what, am I going to disappoint now? Miss out on an orgy? Are you normal?! How could you do something like that??? And she was so beautiful... a completely standard and normal Israeli who, after a Full Moon party... well, to be exact, when the morning came, she asked if I could walk her to the room where Arik and I were for... something, I don't remember what it was. The bathroom? Maybe. And even then, on the way, she started kissing me despite the fact that she had spent the whole week fucking Arik, and even more despite the fact that I actually wanted her before him and was even had a bit of a crush on her. And now we're both high from our first-ever ecstasy, and my last. I don't know what happened to her since then. I heard she got married and had a kid pretty quickly after we came back, when there was still a sliver of contact. Strange. A whole week of her and Arik fucking, and in the end, she wanted me. The truth is, I suspected from the very beginning that she wanted me, based on the looks. But she and Arik were at some beach party when I stayed in the room one evening, and over there he gave a press from which there was no turning back. But since that notorious orgy, she was always sticking to me. She even sent me messages when I came back to Israel, and not to Arik. Not that it mattered much to him. To him, she was just another hookup. Maybe like Moran was just another girlfriend to him. And I, I remember thinking really good things about her before she and Arik started fucking. That she was really beautiful and sweet. A bit like Moran, actually, but blonder. Much blonder. With big blue eyes. Really pretty. And Arik usually likes dark-haired girls. I mean, brunettes. We really don't have the same taste. Arik is also very different from me in his demeanor. With his sweet smile and his constant inner sweetness. I'm more of a macho type, a 'real man', a bit of a rough guy. Not intentionally, that's just how I am. Girls I dated would always say he was a sissy. There was something about him that really triggered strong antagonism in them. And girls who dated him would say I was pompous. "Never!" was the opener and the shorthand for our usual phrase, after which we'd always crack up laughing, "We'd never fight over a girl!'". Come to think of it, even Moran isn't his type at all; she's my type! Wait, what's happening here? Both the one from the orgy and Moran Dagan. How did Arik suddenly get all the 'girls of mine,' and dare with all his might to reject them so casually and cast them aside?! But He's really such a sweet guy. Really, he is. If you knew him, you wouldn't think what you're thinking right now. You can see it in his smile with dimples, you can see it in his eyes. I think the issue is that he's just not an overthinker. I'm a big overthinker. Always analyzes and second-guesses. And Arik just goes for it. The girl from the orgy wanted him? Cool. Moran Dagan is interested in him? Cool. And look, they ended up being together for about two years. A real serious relationship. And where was I all this time?

In the end, the couch was too short and had some worn-out spring that seemed like it was held together by nothing but faith, so we all had to squeeze into one bed. I look to my left. Moran. She's right next to me. Sleeping, serene. Beautiful, breathing softly. I want to kiss her. Should I kiss her? Sometimes you see someone you like in an elevator. Just you and her. You have ten seconds of grace where she's not going anywhere, and in ninety percent of the cases, you end up saying nothing. As soon as the elevator doors open, she disappears into the world, and you tell yourself that if you bump into her again, you'll jump on her as if there's no tomorrow and say, 'Hey, aren't you the girl from the elevator??' Yeah, idiot, it's her. And if you weren't such an idiot, you might have even gotten her number in that elevator... Arik would definitely kiss her. He'd just go for it. What's the worst that could happen if he would? That I'll wake up and not understand what's going on? So? So what?! The guy's right. If Arik wakes up and sees us kissing, he'll smile from ear to ear and either leave the room or just throw out a funny comment and turn to sleep on the other side. Or what? That she'll reject me? That she'll freak out and run away? Let her run! Who does she think she is, barging into our trip and my life at forty?? Fuck this shit!!

That's it, I've decided. I'm going to kiss her. I have to. Any outcome is a good outcome. Either it will be amazing or everything will blow up. I'm fine with either scenario. It's the right thing to do. It's the needed thing to do. It's the only thing to do. I shut my eyes tightly and tried to fall asleep.

In the morning, we got up and looked for the owner of the place. To be honest, he was a pretty nice guy, but he looked like the kind of thug who would cut off someone's vital organs if they didn't pay up. "Dis is not your room," he said with an Indian-English accent, to quickly try and ease the tension—if you could even call his tone anything remotely close to 'easing.' And sure enough, after we had breakfast, they took us to our actual room on the upper floor, overlooking the beach through a path of coconut trees that actually looks exactly like tall palm trees. Beautiful. Truly beautiful. This was the Goa Arik had raved about. The three of us sat outside on the balcony, smoking cigarettes, while Arik promised that any moment now he would score us some top-quality charas.

So many people here at the guesthouse. Some are cleaning, some are in the kitchen, and others carry your luggage. They all seem to be part of one big family—some might even call it a commune—and they live on the guesthouse grounds, too. But they live in these little nooks. Well, not exactly nooks, but once I happened to peek in as I was going down the stairs and a door in the hallway opened. To the embarrassment of one of the Indian women,

I saw that the walls and floor weren't really finished. They didn't even bother with plaster or proper tiles. It was pretty much "as is". As they built it, that's how they left it. I found it strange since they had many workers building the other rooms, some of which, like ours, were downright luxurious. So, they couldn't add plaster? A little paint? Some flooring? It's hard for me to believe it's a cost issue, especially when the workers practically cost nothing, and there's all this construction happening around. I figured it must be that they're just used to it, and they don't need more. And honestly, from a practical standpoint, maybe there's not much difference between a perfectly polished wall and a rough one. How many things do we really *need* anyway? I mean, really. Up until they figured out or invented that polio, which paralyzes kids, spreads through tap water, no one even dreamed of drinking mineral water. And since 1988, there's been a vaccine anyway, but people are still making billions even though there's perfectly fine water coming out of the taps. It costs more to recycle all that plastic afterward, and who knows what kind of carcinogenic stuff it's leaking into the water when it's sitting out in the sun or in storage before it gets to the store. So I've been drinking tap water for as long as I can remember, and nothing's happened to me so far. The simplicity of India makes you realize that, at the end of the day, nature gives us everything we need. And the son of the Indian guy, he's just a seed that was once in a dick and then in a pussy and became a kid, just like me. There's no difference between us. I just happened to be born there, and he happened to be born here. He eats and shits just like me, and he has the same needs, desires, and wants that I have, with the obvious variations that come with being different people. So why am I not content with what he's content with? Because I've been conditioned? How many things do we do out of tradition or some kind of 'doctrine'? We're the same body as humans from two thousand years ago. We've got air to breathe, sunlight, and plenty of food all around us, and water. If I drop you in a cave in the middle of the jungle and make sure no tiger or bear has you for lunch, you'll survive. You'll find something to keep warm, pick something to eat, and drink from the same stream the animals around you drink from. For this is how it was hundreds and thousands of years ago. Just like the Indians who live in conditions that would cause a Westerner to perish within four days—not because they're superhuman, but simply because they've lived in these conditions from infancy and their bodies are fortified and resilient to many more external factors. The basics are already in place; everything else is a bonus.

So after breakfast and cigarettes on the balcony, we went down to the beach. Let's see what these Goa beaches are all about, I thought to myself. At first, we considered lying on loungers like back home, but the young guy who called us from the restaurant on the beach offered free sunbeds that you could use even if you didn't order anything. He made sure to say this right away and assure us. And honestly, there's no chance I won't order something, and that's how he gets me as a customer. Because even if I start with a beer, chances are I won't move to another place to order food. He also doesn't come every minute to ask if I want to order something because Hey—buddy—what—do—you—think—I've—got—rent—to—pay—you—thought—this—is—free? He really does give you something for free! And since he's an actual stand-up guy, I'll order from him. And as for the jerk at the café in Tel Aviv who smiles at me just for the money and sends a waitress every other minute because I've been sitting there with my laptop for an hour just ordering coffee—I'll never sit there again, and let him pay his rent with bathroom blowjobs for all I care... So, is giving someone a free sunbed on the beach worth it or not?

"I drink it with ice and lemon," someone suddenly threw out from behind us.

"Beer with ice?" Arik asked.

"And lemon. It's great, trust me."

Given how incredibly hot it is in Goa, the ice really helps you drink the beer at the right intervals, and the lemon blends perfectly with the light 'Kingfisher' beer. I haven't tried the dark one, which is a bit stronger. I'm more of a light beer kind of person. I wonder what that says about me. Am I easygoing? Weak? Light-headed? Or do I just prefer a lighter alcoholic beverage? What I do know is that they brought me a really big bottle, about three-quarters of a liter, and since it was so hot, I finished it pretty quickly. After a short while, Moran said the sun had wiped her out and she was going back to the room to rest. Completely without any scheming plan, I decided to join her. The burning sun combined with the saltwater, the beer, and the fact that there are no showers on Goa's beaches, Left me craving a refreshing shower in our marble-clad bath.

All of a sudden, the situation was as follows: Moran and I stood mere centimeters apart, she in a bikini—essentially just a top and bottom—and I in some snug shorts, stretched across my muscular legs and package. Both of us blissfully inebriated on Kingfisher beer. There we stand like this, and I'm dying to kiss her. The Morranian enchantment is weaving its spell again. Up close, her face was the same as ever. Her eyes, those eyes, and her lips remain full, rosy, yearning. Her hair flowed smoothly to one side, with the other half stylishly shaved, adorned with natural Chatain stubbles. It entices me, revealing an ear that suddenly seems irresistibly alluring. Even when she was younger, she used to wear her hair like this, years before it became fashionable. I even have a picture of her from my Bar Mitzvah in that same garden at Fatel, with that hairstyle. She was simply born cool. Her gaze remains unchanged, not sure that confirms, enigmatic. I feel like kissing her. Any moment now, I might just do it. Should I? Is now the moment, after all these years? Should I just do it?

11

Sometimes something can seem utterly impossible, only to happen in the blink of an eye. Years of planning, thoughts, doubts, and existential reflections came to an end when Moran stepped out of the bathroom and suddenly threw a towel at me. "Here, you need?"

I was sitting half-reclined on the mattress in our beautiful bedroom, with its wooden floor, the air conditioning cooling the room, and the dark cream curtains almost completely hiding the outside view. I was meticulously planning how to make my move, and at the same time, it was clear to me that I would never actually do it because I lacked the courage to face what is known as Moran Dagan. Then suddenly, a turquoise towel, damp and half-wet from the shower that had recently washed Moran Dagan's body, was thrown over my face and half my body. Gently and slowly, I moved the part that covered my face, revealing Moran's image. She wasn't striking a seductive model pose or flashing me an illicit smile like in a cheap blue movie. She was simply standing in her typical Moran Daganian manner, wearing underwear, a bra, and a white shirt that accentuated her curves, throwing the towel, which she had just used to dry the inside of her intimate parts, right in my face. You unbelievable cunt. Ain't nothing like you.

I grasped the towel and rose. I know what you might say: that I should overcome this, mature. But then... then I wouldn't be myself. And I love being myself. Because that's who I am. Every time I've tried to change, to listen to others, to seek advice, I've found it never turns out well. It might suit this guy or that guy who advised it, and even that is uncertain. For me, only what comes from within is good. What resonates and feels right to me. For me, staying true to who I am, is what truly serves me best. And now the beer that's gone to my head has given me confidence. Unlike the high from smoking, which can corner you with confusion and needless thoughts, alcohol relaxes, empowers. And she's the one who kissed me in the garden just recently. So here I am, about to kiss her. I even have an excuse. In just a moment, I will muster all my courage and shower her with kisses. And she, she will go along with it. Her look will change to a slightly embarrassed smile revealing her teeth. I surprised her, intrigued, and put her in a lesser position. Then I'll gently yet assertively hold her skin and press my lips to hers. She won't immediately kiss back, but I'll continue kissing. That moment, that tiny fraction of a second in which countless other things were happening around the globe, including the subtle forward movement of her lips—even if it's the slightest nod—would be among the defining moments of my life. Here I am, the stunned child, the battle-worn soul standing silent and pained in the gymnasium on the first night of Hanukkah, who returned home and discovered only to his pillow how deeply he cried, who went to school humiliated and with his head bowed, Who would never again be the same after that event, who lost his innocence when his face was whitened in public despite the clear prohibition in the Gemara and the Book of Leviticus—this child, here he is, kissing Moran Dagan.

And she kissed me back. With passion, with fervor. Not like a shy, growing girl, but like a woman who knows her desires. This allowed me to charge at her with intense, lustful, hungry kisses. And then with the tongue. Here we were, truly kissing. Really hard. Our tongues practically licking each other. Licking in circles. In whirlpools. I started to get hard. I've already told you I never fantasized about her. As the personification of my innocent love, so she remained in my eyes. I suppose there was a part of me that might have desired more, but my love for her was greater. This love of mine for her likely clouded my testosterone. I know it seems illogical, but this was my eleven-year-old love. An eleven-year-old boy that is in love, its not because he wants to fuck.

And suddenly we're like two teenagers getting frisky in a room with the door shut. I slip my hand under her shirt and grope her breast over the padded bra. It gives her breast a firm shape, it excites me. Enough, I'm taking off her shirt. Everything—I'm removing it all! I lifted the shirt up, and she raised her arms in approval. Then I unfastened the bra with one hand because using two hands always complicates things for me, and her breast spilled out in a breathtaking display. How beautiful you are in my eyes, Moran Dagan. How I could not have imagined anything more enticing.

I remember I actually said "Wow..." out loud. Medium size, probably a borderline B-C cup, and with beautiful, slightly pointed nipples. And this sight, in which was not tanned while everything around it was... I attacked the right breast with my mouth and groped the left assertively with my hand. She moaned. I'm about to sleep with Moran Dagan!!!! I'm about to sleep with Moran Dagan!!!! Ahhhhh!!!! And I'm hard! I'm fucking hard as a rocket! Girls don't understand that when we're not hard, it's usually due to excitement, not impotence or lack of attraction. That we don't mess everything up; That we have a big enough; That... I don't know what! It's so much easier and simpler to sleep with someone who doesn't interest you than with someone who does. And then she undressed me, and suddenly I realized she was about to see me. After thirty years, Moran Dagan is going to see my dick! Will she like it? I mean, I know it's a decent size and... I've always received compliments that it's perfect, but... will she like it? And so I first stripped her completely. I just suddenly pounced on her pants and started opening them because she had already opened mine, and it was clear we were going to fuck because we're forty, in India, drunk, and... clearly going to fuck. So, hold on. Wow. Moran in panties. Wow. Now she's chatain and tanned, except for the breasts, which really turns me on, as mentioned. And now I'm facing a pair of white panties with a bit of lace, just on the sides at the top, something trendy and cool, and it tapers down to a sharp triangle. Her pussy looks really nice in the panties. The way the panties leave a nice curve on her body. Does she have a nice one? And if not, am I committing suicide now? Here I am, rapidly undressing, not believing it. Kissing, sipping, drinking, grasping, holding, licking... just don't let me disappoint now, just don't let me go soft, don't let me mess it all up, come too soon, disappoint, don't...

"Hagai!" she suddenly stopped and put her hand on my chest. I froze. It was as if I were riding a mountain bike down a slope and suddenly someone pulled it out from under me, leaving me pedaling in mid-air.

"Wha...what?" I replied as she placed her hand on my cheek, and I suddenly realized my heart was racing.

"Hey..." She looked at me with a new expression. Calm, quiet, with a deep inner peace that I had never seen from her before. A completely new and different side of her personality. "Hey..." she repeated in order to capture my attention. "Relax."

We went on kissing, but at a slower pace. My lips trembled, almost in disbelief that this was happening, holding within the vibration yearning to burst forth and seize in utmost strength. I was still kissing, but now she was definitely in control. The fingers and nail of her left hand trailed downward, grazing my tanned skin, slightly sunburned, all the way to my underwear. And then it happened. She curled her fingers and grasped the elastic of my dark green boxer briefs. Oh... No girl could understand the defining, exalted, promising sensation when her nail first makes contact with a piece of skin, no matter how small, hidden beneath the rubber of our underwear. Before I could think, her fingers were already caressing it with her nails, and the touch of her fingers was revealed for the first time to my fully erect organ. She slid down until she reached a firm grip. Up and down, she pulled. Up and down. Yes, she is smiling.

Blessed be the Name.

Blessed is His Name.

Blessed is He who has kept us alive, sustained us, and brought us to this time.

May His great Name be exalted and sanctified.

The Name of the Holy One, Blessed Be He.

I give thanks before You, King, living and enduring, who has restored my soul with compassion; great is Your faithfulness.

Blessed be the Name of the Lord.

With the help of Heaven, of course.

Hear, O Israel: The Lord our God, the Lord is One.

Blessed be His Name.

By Whose word all things came into being.

Now it's faster, and even more, and faster and faster and- wowwwww! Moran Dagan is giving me a handjob! Moran Dagan is giving me a handjob! We're kissing really hard now. I long to slip off her panties, my hands gripping their sides. Slowly, I weave them down in a crisscross motion. I have to see. Maybe with someone else, I'd just yank them down, sending my best fingers inside, and it would feel totally natural, leading after some mutual play to a quick condom, but I had to see. I pushed her back towards the bed, making sure with my right hand that she didn't trip, until we reached the table pressed against the wall, and she sat on it, spreading her legs and lifting them up, while I held each leg in one hand. How beautiful she was down there. It was truly exquisite—fresh, stretching into an alluring triangle embraced by thighs, with a delicate line adorning its center. Breathtaking, my sweet Morani. I kissed it, pressing my lips to the line that longed to disappear between her crossed legs. Then, without warning, she opened them wide. The scent was gentle, intoxicating. So pleasant. Just as creatures in the wild choose, we were a perfect match. I brought my lips close, beginning with long, meaningful kisses I so wished to give. Then they turned into deep, French kisses. The many years that had passed, along with the anticipation, must have made my kisses a full-on assault. I wanted to cash in now, immediately, on the potential—on this stock that had seemed dead for so many years. I kissed her aggressively, almost animalistically. Thirty years I've waited for this moment, thirty years! She pushed my head lower and deeper towards her lower regions. I never go down on a girl the first time. Probably not the second either. But I simply pulled down her panties, stretching them across my face, right where everything connects down there, inhaling her scent with noisy breaths, "Mmm…" I added, as she looked at me, surprised, while I stuffed the panties into my mouth, chewing and sucking on them. I devoured her inner lips, possessed and frantic. 'Hagwoiii,' she moaned, and I kept kissing her while she scratched my back with her nails. At some point, we just collapsed onto the floor, as I had leaned on her and the table simply fell apart. I climbed back up and kissed her with an open mouth, spitting the chewed-up panties onto the floor, and she grabbed me by the neck, pulling me into a lust-filled kiss. With her other hand, she grasped and caressed my erection, that threatened to tear my underwear. 'Are you putting it in?' I asked, restless. 'In a moment,' she replied, continuing to caress and kiss, and I could already feel myself on the brink of exploding. 'Just a little longer…' She grasped it and pulled it upward with repeated motions that were never quite comfortable for us but still thrilling. I was eager. I wanted to wrap things up. I wanted it to happen—nothing would stop me now! She guided it to the area, and I began my attempts at entry, trying as gently as possible to ensure that the sides would be sufficiently wet, because in just a moment, I'd be thrusting with all my strength and I really didn't want her to get hurt. Another twist, and another with the tip just inside, and now it's already damp and wet— 'Aaaaaaaaaaaaaaaaaaaaaah!' I'm inside! I'm fucking Moran Dagan! I'm fucking Moran Dagan! I'm not losing it for a moment, not for a second! I'm finding a good rhythm. She's enjoying it. I'm not cuming, I'm not cuming. Yes. I'm grabbing her breast now and kissing it, then her, over and over. Flip her? Too soon? Is she enjoying missionary? Or am I coming off as a dork, and should I just get her to stand and fuck her like those DJs probably do abroad or whoever… And I'm actually a master at standing up sex. It's my specialty. Of course. On the lathe, it's only standing up…

'Hagai!' I suddenly got slapped. 'I said, turn me over!'. Alright, alright, a slap is good, it's excellent, we've opened up. Here I am, turning her forcefully, determined to still be the man here. 'Yes, harder. Harder! Ah! Harder, Hagai, harder!!! Ah! Ah! Aaaaaaah!'

I felt she came pretty quickly, and it made me feel good. From here on out, everything's just a bonus. I didn't cum, but I've never really cared about that. What is cuming even about? Three seconds? I want to see her enjoying what I make her feel, bringing her to orgasm. I even remember that for my very first sex, I set up a sound system I bought in 11th grade with the money I saved from working at the McDonald's near the village. It was an Akai mini stereo, with a double cassette deck, a CD-radio player, and two detachable speakers you could place in different corners of the room for the best sound, just as Pompeos had explained—and he was right. I played U2's 'Achtung Baby,' which had just come out. With 55:27 minutes of disc time, I managed not to cum because Arik had warned me not to cum too quickly. So each time I was about to climax, I'd stop, pull out, as if to change positions, playing the role of the ultimate stud, and it worked. But since then, I've enjoyed it. It pleases me to see the girl relishing the experience. I lifted her legs and continued to pump with the last of my strength, and she moaned loudly. The beauty of women is that, unlike us, they can go again right away. And now, with Moran, not only are we having sex, we're having explosive sex. Later, I went down on her again, and she blew me while we continued, soaking the sheets about sixteen more times... Eventually it ended, and she got up. There she was, rising and walking away with light steps. Moran! Look at me for just a moment!! My heart cried out, but she just continued, walking naked away from me towards the bathroom. Moran!! He continued without asking my opinion as she moved farther away with each step. I love you!!!

Back when I was a child, every Thursday evening, I'd be placed in front of the TV to watch "Maccabi." Sometimes, we'd head over to Elhanan's place, where he'd set up a TV in the yard for the occasion, and all the neighbors from the nearby houses would come too. It was a lot of fun. There were always raspberry and lemon juices, snacks, and all kinds of gummy candies in various shapes and colors that Mom would let me have only a little of, because they ruin your teeth, and "The tooth fairy doesn't work every day, my dear," she'd say with a smile. And above all, there were lots of people, which created a warm, communal atmosphere. Even though I was still young, I knew there was a game, and I hoped we'd manage to beat the "bad guys" who changed every week: Cibona Zagreb, Scavolini Pesaro, Limoges, Pau-Orthez, Aris Thessaloniki, Real Madrid, Efes Pilsen, Estudiantes, CSKA Moscow. Oh, and... oh no. Just don't remind me of Jugoplastika Split...

But every time we managed to score, I'd cheer, and when we took a basket, I'd express my childish frustration with slaps of the hand, shouting "No!" and "Ugh!" and other such reactions when things went the opposite of what I wanted. We succeeded – Yay. We lost – Ugh. But in every gesture, positive or negative, I was entirely a spectator. As a child, I didn't factor in the "adult" data. We'd try, and if we succeeded - "Yay!".

Today, when I watch a game, I'm much more involved. I still cheer and get frustrated, but why is he letting that idiot handle the ball? Doesn't he see he's dribbling for sixteen seconds and then either shooting under pressure or doing a favor by passing, leaving another player to shoot under pressure because he's got about four seconds left? This player should be a shooting guard, catch-and-shoot, not dribbling the ball. And why isn't he playing with both big men together? What's he afraid of? And why did they bench that experienced Israeli player? Can't he give a few good minutes here and there and contribute, especially to bond the team in the locker room, which might be the most important thing in a team game?

And so on, and so forth, justified grievances. The one they paid a lot for isn't playing defense, and the coach is an idiot if he doesn't see all this, and especially to blame is whoever brought him in... In short, because I'm emotionally involved now and think I know everything, I enjoy the game a lot less. Once, everything was simpler. I'd tell that girl I wanted to be her boyfriend and see if she agreed. And that was it! If we succeeded – "Yayyy!" If we missed – "Ughhh!" And if she agreed, we'd be friends. For a long, long time, as we were both curious.

And now what? We slept together, so now we're together? Is it just a casual fling? Am I supposed to tell her everything I've accumulated over thirty years about her and me? Or should I treat her nonchalantly or even as some kind of a slut? After we slept we kissed a bit, and she said she loved kissing me. Wait, did she use the word "love"? Or is she just horny and wants me to fuck her again and if not I'm a loser and a failure? Perhaps to her it *was* just a fling. After all, as far as I know, she *wasn't* into me and had a million and one stories about me since she was eleven. And perhaps not. I, for long, no longer know a thing. Since that half-drenched kiss, I've forgotten my entire beingness. My existence has been sucked into a crack in the earth that's been there since that day in sixth grade when I tried to be with the girl who moaned beneath me an hour ago and kissed me passionately. The angel pushes the devil off my shoulder, and she also has an angel who wants love and a horny devil, and everyone is torn, and everyone thinks too much and reacts too much and doesn't know what to do too much. Why can't we just ask someone to be our friend like before? And when she wants, she can stop. We'd play 'kiss-tag', and 'pass the parcel, and 'broken telephone', and call people just to mess with them and laugh. "Sir, do you have water in the faucet?" And he'd actually go check, and we'd laugh, "Well, what did you want, cola?" and hang up. And the fun of it all. There's no follow-up call or caller ID, someone calls you and you have no idea who it is. Unbelievable. How I sometimes miss those innocent days when everything was much simpler. We scored – yay. We lost – ugh.

'Yes, no, black, white'—are you familiar with that? It's a game from the '80s where whoever says 'yes,' 'no,' 'black,' or 'white' first gets disqualified, and the other wins. Well, we didn't have computers or smartphones, so what could we do...

"Hey, do you know this game?"

"No... what do you think?"

"You're out," I said, and she laughed. "Why are you laughing? You're out."

"Oh, shut up..." She nudged me, and a smile kindled in her cat-like eyes. For the first time in my life, they didn't hurt when I gazed into them.

"So, what's the opposite of black?"

"Instant coffee on milk?"

"Geez... Moran Dagan... nice one."

"You think?"

"Absolutely."

"Sure?"

"Absolutely sure."

"Okay, thanks."

"Anytime."

"Are you happy?"

"Ecstatic."

"Are you always like this?"

"Nnn..".I Almost got disqualified. "Of course the answer is negative."

"Why negative?"

"Why and how come."

"What?"

"Nothing."

"Oh, you idiot."

"You."

"I'm what?"

Stunning.

The best in the world.

I love you.

"You're such an idiot."

"Whoa…" she slapped me, and I actually liked it. "You little rascal…"

"Excuse me? Is it okay for you?"

"Of course."

"And why exactly this gender inequality?"

"Exactly because you'd get a club to the head, that's why."

"Oh… someone's bringing up parents…"

"Absolutely not…."

"Hey!" I pointed at her. "You're out."

"Oh, shut up already!" She laughed, pushing me hard this time, and I laughed back.

"You're such a dork…" She turned her face away.

"Dork?? Me?? I'm a damn carpenter. Look, look at the veins in my hands," I proudly displayed what had impressed so many women over the years but never really fazed Moran Dagan.

"You, you. You're a dork… but cute." She finished and went back to the bathroom.

I'm a dork! Suddenly, it hit me. I always thought I was pretty cool, probably because I was surrounded by cool people, but I never imagined I was the dork of the bunch. Sure, my language might seem a bit high, which could come off as pretentious—definitely not a trait you'd expect from a dork... unless it's intellectual or intelligent pretentiousness, which surely wouldn't be associated with carpenters. The truth is, boys never liked me. You could even say they hated me a bit. I always ended up with all the girls. And girls, they didn't like me either, especially since I was always breaking their hearts. And so, here I am, a single man at forty. Gay people! Gay people always liked me. They'd try to convince me with their glances to give them a chance. If I were gay, girls might like me because I wouldn't be a threat to them, and boys, because I wouldn't be competing with them. Then everyone would like me. Except maybe the gays, because intrigues would probably start there too... And maybe that's why I became a dork. No one was around to pull me in different directions. And single. But cool. Wait, is "cool" a word for cool people or dorks? And perhaps it's better this way. To be the dork or the ugly one. Why should a woman need a handsome man who she'll constantly have to worry about? In the end, the ugly ones end up with the hottest girls. Their subconscious falls for them on their behalf. Wait! So... actually... wait, does this mean that...?

"Moran!" I called, but there was no reply. Probably still showering or 'primpering' or something. "Moran!" I shouted on a second and final try.

"What, darling?" she answered, peeking through the door. There it was, 'darling'. She's definitely in love.

"Do you think I'm handsome?"

"What?"

"Do I look good to you?"

"Are you seriously messed up, or what? What's your problem?" she chuckled in her usual playful manner, her head peeking from behind the door as if I hadn't just seen her naked and moaning in various awkward positions.

"Come on, I'm asking you."

"Well, you're interrupting me getting ready…" she shut the bathroom door.

But it seems that Moran sensed it from the very first second. That's what happened, for sure. She knew from the moment she saw me that I was a geek, and thus I could never provide the thrilling experiences her soul craved. Only a clingy and mundane love. For I could have easily become the center of her world. I mean, from my end. I would have wanted nothing more than to be a part of her world. In it, it seems, I had no place, since she had already experienced that as a uniquely beautiful girl, even somewhat mature for her age. But now, now it's okay. And I'm certainly going to be a good father with quality genes. Is that it, Moran? Just a good arrangement? Or maybe my theory intrigued you in a way you haven't been intrigued for years, and your endless desire to experience new things swept you away, if only for this one time, granting me the coveted advantage. Which, let's say, comes without an excess of emotions. Or maybe it does. After all, what are emotions if not getting swept away by someone? So in ninth grade, it was motorcycles, and now it's intellect. It fits me just perfectly. She'll fall for my fevered mind, never reveal its true secret. Passionate to the point of disgrace. Utterly pathetic, really. And now, for the millionth time, I wrestle with whether to speak up. To approach and simply confess. Perhaps, in a touch of divine jest, the good Lord might stir in her heart the right feeling.

Oh, well,... I must have taken a blow to the head. I'm not suffering, I kept telling myself over and over. I'm not suffering. But I remembered that even Moran Dagan was never liked. Perhaps because of this, or maybe even only because of this, we belong to each other through a hidden, well-concealed cosmic bond, hidden away for countless years. Why wasn't she liked? It's not even a faulty genetic explanation; it's an obvious explanation. Who are the women who receive admiration? The outgoing ones? The insanely sexy ones? Those with the deepest cleavage? For that is their greatest mistake of the crown. They drown. They drown in the sea of foolishness forced upon them before they even realize. They think that this is how they will achieve... what? What is it? Not even they know, or anyone knows for that matter. He'll see that you're a stunner and then he'll love you? Quite the opposite! Men don't fall in love with sluts; they just want to fuck them. But today we live in an era where women want to show how strong and independent they are. They're powerful. Badass! Bitchessss! Posting pictures of themselves doing god knows what and sticking out their tongues! But deep down, they all crave to lie under the covers with someone who will tell them he loves them. And the man, what does he perceive with his dumb and utterly unsharpened senses? What's placed right in front of his face. And since all his life he's heard that women are attracted to assholes, he's not going to be soft now, is he? So he treats the girl with toughness. Hard. And she, as much as she plays the part, that's never what she truly wants. At the end of the day, most women who project a façade of toughness are actually fragile, simply searching for love, and getting hurt time and again. But hey, this is what you put on the shelf, this is what the man sees you offering. A kind of supreme seductress or authorized whore, because, of course, it's allowed. Girls don't understand that as long as they're just a body, it's like a shawarma wrap. Oh, how you drool over that shawarma wrap. The meat is hot, and everything's dripping from it, and you add pickles, veggies, spicy stuff, and wow... It's irresistible! But after you're done with the shawarma wrap, the last thing you want is another one. But yesterday, he loved me!! What's even more laughable, is that the aggressiveness stirred up in men is minuscule compared to the hatred that arises among their sisters. Who gets sympathy and love? Not the submissive and battered one. God forbid that this would be my argument. The hottest bombshell whom you'll never get to see a hint of her cleavage, walking on the beach in a full swimsuit that reveals neither an inch nor half an inch. '*Who is the hero?*' asks the Mishnah in Ethics of the Fathers, and answers — '*He who conquers his impulse.*' And the heroine?

But Moran Dagan never conquered. And that's why girls distanced themselves from her. She never had too many friends. Perhaps that's why she turned to older guys, letting them enjoy her charms. Where did this lead her? To being single at an older age? Me as well? It's certain that you can't draw a direct line. And perhaps, just perhaps, this very path, winding through trials and tribulations, has ultimately guided her, after a labyrinthine journey, to me.

A few minutes later she emerged from the bathroom and bent down to kiss me. I closed my eyes, surrendering to her touch. Ahhhh… I shut my eyes, surrendering to her will. Sweet Lord of Bliss, is this how you truly feel? I wish this moment would never end, please. Please—please—please—stop—the-world-i-touched-red. Yes, that was another game from those distant days when computers were rare, and we played simply with each other. "Stop—the-world" was a game where you took something and declared it yours by saying "Stop—the-world-i-touched-red," touching something red. Come on, I swear. It's mesmerizing what a child's imagination can conjure. "I touched red..." And Moran knows the rules. She knows! And she understands that she simply cannot, under any circumstances, take it from me now. Because not only did I declare "Stop—the-world," I also touched red. At the edges of the small cloth that draped over the nightstand, beneath the shelf by the bed, while we were kissing, I reached out unseen and touched it. You might deny it, dismiss it over technicality. But deep down, Moran, we both know the truth. Deep down we both know—we both know I touched red.

12

I always longed to be near her. To look at her and have her look back. To offer her friendship and hear her say "yes." That's all an eleven-year-old boy wants. He doesn't even know what's on the next page, but to him, it's enough to stop right in the middle of the book. I didn't even have the chance to tell Arik about what happened that afternoon. I thought there'd be a right moment to share, no need to get overly excited, no need to make a big deal. Yet, they were together, they were a couple. I know it was a long time ago and that he's the most supportive without needing to ask, and who had the time to ask or think about anything when what you've been yearning for your whole life is unfolding before your eyes? Her years of rejection only made her more unattainable in my eyes. To me, she was second only to God. The party you weren't invited to, it's always the best one.

And besides, who cares what Arik thinks? Fuck him; he's married anyway. During dinner we exchanged a few smiles here and there, nothing too suspicious, but at night, things felt strange. All three of us in bed, with Moran, as usual, in the middle. I'm dying to touch her but I'm afraid. Reverting back to that insecure kid. And she's not initiating any contact right now. Maybe she's already asleep, and that's why? Maybe Moran Dagan is still toying with me, doing with me as she pleases? Once it was a math test, and now it's sex, but her heart still envelops me in its mystery. I want to open this up, to talk. To wake everyone up here and now and shout until someone gives me an answer once and for all! That's it, I decided. I get up, turn on all the lights in the room, and start shouting at everyone—Benny, the gym announcer, Arik, Moran. I want them all to get their act together and start giving me answers right this minute! I'm fed up with the bullshit and my heart is torn in every direction!

But something told me to keep my mouth shut. Maybe I'd caught the common Indian bug. There's something about India, something unique that draws millions of travelers from all over the world every year, and that especially soothes us, the combat-traumatized Israelis, scarred from what we went through in the army at fucking eighteen, while the Norwegian guy was playing PlayStation. And it's not just the drugs, which are everywhere here. Drugs are all over the world. It's not even the stunning landscapes or the dirt-cheap prices. There are plenty of other places with amazing views and low costs. Just a few months ago, I visited an international trade fair in Tbilisi, and even the Georgians—who, as part of their young prime minister's revolution, recently stopped being called 'Gruzins' and started being called 'Georgians' because he began paying the police more to refuse bribes and combat corruption—they're a kind of third world, too. Maybe not quite as third world as India, but at most two and a half. And a quarter, in some rare parts. It's a beautiful country, with breathtaking landscapes, and dirt cheap as hell. But unlike the Indians who are pleased with their situation, the Georgians are far from pleased with their situation. The Indians, even if it doesn't always look like it, are organized and efficient. Their rickshaws, for instance, are like real taxi stations. There's a dispatcher, they keep them clean at all times—I see how they work. The places along the coast— everyone understands their roles. How to approach tourists, who does what. You arrive at a place, and it always seems like there are too many workers, with half seemingly doing nothing, but they're not. Each one has a role, a specific responsibility. You can even leave your bag and take a stroll along the beach for an hour, and nothing will be stolen, because they are there. The whole gang. They know very well that if theft happens, no one will come back, so no one steals because they know they'll be slaughtered. Everything is in order. In Georgia, every taxi ride is an hour argument, and in the end the driver will still give you a sour look. Here, the Indian knows the price from point A to point B, and that's it. There's even a day and night rate! Here in Goa, and from what I understand, throughout India, there's a curfew. Lights out at eleven. Everything closes except for places with special permits. And everyone shuts down at exactly eleven. Everything is in order. And from that hour, the night rate applies. For us Westerners, it might seem like it's all shitty and that somehow they manage to live through it, but for them it's not. That's the difference. The Georgian taxi driver sees you and thinks, "This rich bastard on vacation. I'm sitting here in this cab and won't earn in a year what he surely makes in a month," and he's bitter. Even if you pay him what he initially asked for before the haggling, he's still bitter. The Indian is not bitter! He understands the situation and acts accordingly. 'I'll drive this rickshaw all day, it will earn me this and that amount, and I can live with my wife in our humble shack, and make a living. If I don't work the rickshaw, I won't survive, or I'll have to beg and die of illness in the streets.' He operates on autopilot. And he's nice to you when you're in his rickshaw, smiling, and just waiting for you to toss him something funny or offer him 'An American cigarette,' and he's happy as can be. It's clear that you have more than he does, but right now - he is enjoying the ride. Enjoying the journey. And it's important to enjoy the journey.

"Thank you, thank you," I hear from all directions as I stroll through the narrow streets leading to the sea. How many "thank yous" have I been saying lately? And with such sincerity and niceness, like spreading a delightful layer of sweetness. But the thing is, the Indians are just so polite and friendly. Even when they pester you to come into their shop, or ask you a hundred times if you need a taxi, it's always with that overflowing politeness and their fluent yet heavily accented English. "Yes sir, taxi? Where are you going, sir? Please come to my shop. Yes, mister. Please, mister." Feels like America. Not that it makes me feel special, it's just that everything around you is pleasant. There are no bitter Georgian taxi drivers, or the scowling locals you get in South America with all those stories about tourists getting robbed and so on. Great, now that I've said that, I'm definitely getting robbed tomorrow... But honestly, everything here comes with such a calm vibe, a kind of quiet ease. You slow down to a much, much lower pace really fast. Everything here moves at a slower pace. The music, the people, the time it takes for your meal to arrive at a restaurant—which feels like an eternity—but most of all, the time. So everything ends up being absorbed differently, more easily. More slowly, that's the right word for it. Restaurants are a perfect example. Even when something goes wrong, you don't see yelling or scolding. It doesn't even seem like it happens behind the scenes. Everyone knows they have to be at their best, because there are seven hundred million others ready to replace them at any second. So no one tries to cut out early, come in late, skip work tomorrow, or fake being sick. And everyone's sort of connected, even if not by first, second, or third-degree relations. A sort of 'communal' concept. It's not communist, because everyone earns a salary and theoretically anyone can reach higher than his friend, but there's still this sense of looking out for the 'cooperative.' And that doesn't require any formality or even a hint of diplomacy. It's just understood by everyone: you take care of each other. There's another layer, another reason, where alongside taking care of yourself and your immediate family, you're also part of something bigger.

I talk and suddenly think of Fatel. And maybe... if I think really deep and far, perhaps my fine English ancestors,

before coming to the Land of Israel, served in that same
Mumbai they used to call Bombay. Or at least heard from
friends who served in the area... No, I cut my thoughts
short, there's no way they only heard rumors. Something
like this has to be absorbed, felt for real. I've been here a
little over a week, and I'm just beginning to grasp what it's
all about. And I'm forty, not a twenty-year-old English
soldier with nonsense still on his mind. So, one thing is
already clear to me: not only were our grandfathers settled
in their minds from a young age, but they surely served here
as part of Britain's long-standing control over India. Even
today, they drive on the left side, and the steering wheel is
on the right. They lived here, absorbed it. Consciously or
not, they built a community that's truly rooted in ideas that
seeped into them from the magnificent and ancient Indian
culture. And if today things are the way they are, then surely,
family ties and tribalism were even stronger sixty or seventy
years ago. Yes, it actually makes sense. After all, soldiers are
usually very young, and my ancestors, as we know, were
around thirty when they founded the community. About
seventy years have passed since the 1950s, so surely by now,
most of them, if not all, have long left this world. But the
grandmothers know. Our grandmothers know everything.
The stories that go around... about the one who kept in
touch and even flew to England almost every two years,
back when it was a bit more out of reach. About loves that
were cut short. Bonds that were severed. Some of them had
wives or families or children they saw once in a while...
which explains the need for a substitute. And here I am. In
faraway India. Maybe closer than ever to my roots... I gaze
at the waves, listen to their soft murmurs. The gentle sound
of the waves in Goa—not exactly something surfers would
brag about, though there are a few surfboards for rent, in
typical Indian fashion, where everything is possible.
Everything is milega, possible. 'Bhaiya!' you call out to the guy

from the guest house, which basically means 'bro.' 'Chai milega?', 'Yes, sir, chai is milega,' he answers. 'Coffee milega?', 'Coffee is milega.' 'Like this, is possible?', 'Yes, sir, it is possible.' Everything here is possible. Close your eyes, spin around, and whoever your hand touches can sort out whatever you need. Even if it means walking an hour to the cousin of a cousin's cousin, who knows someone whose cousin has exactly the thing you're looking for. What are you looking for? What is everyone looking for? What is *the thing*? Everyone wants to feel good, to be moved by something, to enjoy something, a sip of joy for the soul. And why is that so hard? And how is it that the Indians, who compared to any average Westerner have barely a fraction of what we have, seem happier than all the Westerners combined? Maybe it's the togetherness, the communal spirit, the *verein*, as the Germans so aptly call it. You're part of something.

When I was little, we lived in one of the more communal buildings in Fatel, a small apartment as part of this strange three-story complex, with a courtyard in the middle. Kind of *Melrose Place* for the poor, if you've ever seen the show. And there, in the tiny one-and-a-half-room space where my sister and I shared bunk beds, while our parents were squeezed into the utility porch, I was happy. Because we were always together, like one tight-knit unit. What more does a child need? Nothing. People think every child needs their own room, and they aim to move into bigger, more spacious homes, but they're terribly mistaken. Children don't want distance or space, they crave closeness. Just like when you pick up a baby and hold them close, and they immediately calm down. Like a child who's showered with love from all sides and grows up happier because of it— that's how it was for me. The older neighbor girls would always play with me. Life was good both inside the house and out in the courtyard, a sort of small commune within the bigger commune.

When I was about six, we moved to a house of our own, much bigger, with a yard on all sides. I had my own room, and so did my sister, and it sucked. The warmth of that togetherness vanished, and outside, there wasn't anyone who would instinctively notice me, even if it wasn't direct attention. Children want to be together, to whisper in the dark even though they're supposed to be sleeping, to fight and make up, to cuddle just like cubs in a National Geographic film. We're cubs. We're animals that just happened to evolve due to the wisdom that came upon us. We are but evolved apes, that's all. The rest of our systems—digestive, respiratory, nervous—they're strikingly similar to other mammals. So, what works for them, works for us too.

And the biological systems of mammals are far more developed and intelligent than most people realize. Take, for example, a pride of lions. Their social structure is highly detailed. The dominant alpha male, along with his less dominant brothers who usually serve as his deputies, is responsible for guarding the territory, which can span dozens of kilometers. They patrol continuously, twenty-four hours a day. They also participate in hunting large prey, such as giraffes or massive buffaloes, when the females cannot overpower them alone. The dominant lion, the most powerful in the pride, exerts tremendous strength to bring down and subdue such prey.

The females are responsible for raising the cubs and daily hunting. Although all cubs belong to the dominant male, he does not interact with them until they are much older. He is aware that eventually, one of these cubs, his own flesh and blood, will challenge and displace him. Despite this, he remains distant, allowing the cubs to rub against him slightly but showing no emotion. He knows the stakes: any sign of weakness could be exploited by rival males lurking to overthrow him.

Thus, the mature cubs are usually driven away from the pride by the dominant male once they reach a certain age and begin to show interest in mating with their sisters or cousins. Yet, the dominant male's brothers still remain, waiting for their turn. The dominant lion understands that showing any hint of affection could be perceived as a weakness, leading to his immediate removal. Therefore, he is tough 24/7. His gaze is that of a fearsome killer, with hollow, soulless orange eyes. If he takes over another pride, he immediately kills all the cubs mercilessly because they are not his own, which miraculously causes the females to go into heat again and produce cubs of his own sacred blood alone. So dangerous is he that some lionesses go into false estrus to avoid being attacked. Why am I telling you all this? Because their family structure is astonishing. Truly admirable. They may seem to us like oversized cats that only know how to hunt and lie in the sun, much like how Indians are perceived as a sort of laboring class, but that is far from the truth. Just like in India, no detail is left to doubt. Everything is meticulously planned and executed. A prime example of this is how they kill their prey. Unlike hyenas and certainly unlike African wild dogs known for tearing apart their prey while it's still alive, lions have class, and perhaps even a sort of respect for their prey. They're not 'just animals.' They seize the prey by the throat until it stops breathing, and only then do they eat. Alternatively, if it's small prey, they bring it alive to the cubs so that the cubs learn to kill. They have 'human-like' traits, they are cognitive, they think. One of the lions' greatest enemies is the hyena. They compete for the same territory and prey, leading to inevitable confrontations. But the difference is that if a pack of hyenas captures a lion or lioness alone and manages to overpower it, they will eat it down to the bones. For them, it's meat just like any other meat. When lions kill a hyena, they leave it to rot. Even though it's an animal like

any other, and there's fresh meat right before them—
something they work for every day—they don't eat it. To
them, it's a message: Stay away.

Another excellent example is the older lionesses. They
might seem completely unnecessary, even burden to the
pride. Logic would suggest they should be removed to free
up resources for the more crucial members: the males, the
hunting and nursing females, and the offsprings who will
carry on the lineage. But that's not the case. And the reason
is not due to cruelty. Lion prides often engage in behaviors
that might seem harsh to us, all in the name of efficiency.
More than the murder of cubs, the abandonment of a single
cub is particularly ruthless. If only one cub survives from a
litter, the pride will abandon it, as it's not worth 'shutting
down' a healthy female that could contribute so much, just
to protect, nurse, and raise only one offspring. So
compassion is definitely not the reason why aging lionesses
aren't abandoned by the pride. But while the males patrol
and the females hunt, the 'grandmothers' stay behind to
protect the cubs. If the pride needs to go to the river to
drink, the 'grandmothers' accompany the cubs and ensure
that no jackals, foxes, or, heaven forbid, hyenas come near.
While they may be considered old and weak within the
pride, they are still formidable predators compared to other
animals and must be avoided. However, not all prides have
grandmothers. Those that don't may leave the cubs alone
for up to twenty-four hours while they're out on extended
hunts. The cubs have to hide well in the tall grass and hope
that no jackal or leopard passes by to prey on them. The
grandmothers - not only that are far from unnecessary—
they are a crucial asset. And we, as mammals with the same
basic needs, have chosen to disconnect from our nature,
resulting in less happiness. Instead of allowing what nature
demands, we throw our grandparents into nursing homes to
'die quietly,' and we send the little ones to daycare centers

where the attention they receive is almost non-existent. In a 'communal' life, the young couple can work in a profession that suits and fulfills them, thus contributing to the community because they are not doing something they hate just to make ends meet. Similarly, just as aging lionesses are not discarded by their pride, it is inconceivable that nature would allow people to live until ninety when they are 'ineffective' for about twenty years. And therefore, in Fatel, the elderly look after the young ones. This arrangement not only sustains them but also contributes enormously to the child's cognitive growth. They engage with the child continuously, benefiting from the fact that, unlike younger parents burdened by daily pressures, the elderly sleep well at night since they don't have to raise the child 24/7, which can eventually become overwhelming and frustrating. They are also not as strict or stressed as new parents; they are more laid-back, not getting worked up over every little thing, which helps the children grow up calmer.

I have a friend who, at thirty-seven, decided she wasn't waiting for a knight in shining armor and opted to have a child through a sperm donor. A woman can have everything in life, but if she doesn't have a man, she's still seen as a failure. "So at least she'd have children," she said, and I agreed. I also thought it would be good for her to get this off her chest. Maybe if it weren't such an issue, if she didn't constantly stress over it, the universe might have more easily provided what she wanted.

When her daughter was born, she faced severe financial hardship and, consequently, a fragile mental state. After all, a single career woman suddenly had many expenses, and her close family lived far away and couldn't offer much help. It wasn't easy. After about two years, she stabilized and decided to have another child before her biological clock ran out. The second daughter was born into a more stable reality—one she was more prepared for—so she was much less stressed and in a better situation overall.

What's remarkable is that in the photos she shares, the difference in their smiles is noticeable. When there was only the first child, her eyes always carried a hint of anxiety, because she was born into stress. The second daughter, however, has a natural, radiant smile that seems to come effortlessly. It's astonishing to see how, over the years, the positive energy of the younger child has balanced out the older girl's smile, making it look almost effortlessly genuine as well. I have friends, a couple who, with the birth of their first child, nearly killed each other from constant arguments about how to raise the child. Unsurprisingly, the child developed asthma and other issues, and once even started convulsing in the middle of the night and fortunately the ambulance arrived in time. Because he was born into stress. He felt stress from his immediate surroundings. It wasn't a warm environment, and it doesn't matter that he was the most important thing in the world to each of his parents.

The lion is not the king of the jungle because of its mane, which vaguely resembles a crown, or because it's the strongest animal in the wild. It's not even certain that it would win in a fight against a grizzly bear, a polar bear, a tiger, or even a gorilla. The lion is the king because it's the smartest. That's why its species has developed one of the strongest family structures in the wild. Just like in any sport, the winner isn't necessarily the one who runs the fastest with the coach yelling from the sidelines like a lunatic. The winner is the one who's level-headed and smart, making the right decisions on the field. This doesn't negate the fact that they also run the fastest—in fact, the opposite is true. The smart player also trains effectively, invests in their fitness, and thus maintains better physical condition and mental clarity, enabling them to make better decisions and sustain their tactical approach throughout the game. They're not exhausted after the first half. Even when trailing in the final minutes, they stay composed and avoid mistakes, focusing on how to optimize the situation. Similarly, their coach isn't just shouting and acting erratically but is engaged in strategic thinking. This intelligence also applies to defense: a smart, physically trained player can effectively counter an opponent's skill because they know where to position themselves and what tactics to use, rather than just running around aimlessly and charging like a wild idiot. And defense is perhaps the pinnacle of the immense advantage provided by communal tribalism. Like many animals, a lioness will take her cubs to a safe place and only reintroduce them to the pride at a certain age, hoping that no uncle, aunt, or cousin will decide that a particular cub isn't up to their standards. However, unlike most animal mothers, the lioness is protected within the pride's territorial boundaries throughout this time. A mother cheetah, for comparison, has to move her cubs to a new hiding spot every few days on her own to avoid detection by hungry jackals, lions, other tigers, hyenas, packs of wild dogs, or any other threat. If any of these predators targets her cubs—whom she has carried, birthed, nursed, and protected—the chances are high that none of them will survive, and she will have to start all over again, as that's simply the way of nature for her. She can't just rent an apartment in South Tel Aviv and go with the flow. This is a vast difference. Also emotionally. No animal is 'just an animal.' Both a cheetah mother and a lioness play and interact with their cubs. However, a cheetah mother only allows herself about five minutes every few hours to step away from her role as a constant protector. In contrast, a lioness, much like a couple living in Fatel where everyone contributes, can take a much longer break from her protective duties. The lioness benefits from a supportive community, unlike the cheetah, who lives alone and constantly relocates. If that's not impressive enough, lionesses also give birth synchronously, so when they return to the pride, the cubs enjoy a sort of family daycare.

Once, I saw a segment on National Geographic where a lioness decides to leave her pride. The internal politics no longer suited her, and so she left. At first, it seemed like a pretty good decision. After about a week, she found herself a slice of paradise, with plenty of water and impalas to hunt without giving a damn about the "good of the pride." When she hunted, she didn't have to share the spoils, and she certainly didn't have to wait until the dominant male stuffed himself before allowing her and the other lionesses – who did most of the hunting – to eat. But one day, while she was hunting a small gazelle, because she didn't have the teamwork backing her up, she was deeply gored by its small but sharp horn, right in the muscle of her front leg. The healing power of a lion is incredible – they can recover in days from injuries that would kill a human within hours. But that can only happen when the pride is there to provide protection, food, and time to rest – not when you're on your own. Unable to hunt due to her limp, it was, of course, a death sentence for her. A single individual or a small family unit that makes one wrong move in their business and collapses, or simply fails for a thousand other reasons, is in a much tougher spot than if they were part of a larger group. So why do we do this to ourselves? Instead of throwing a twenty-something couple with nothing into a life enslaved by mortgages, jobs, and a lack of sleep, picking the kids up from after-school activities and making sandwiches for school, let's keep them as part of the extended family unit. Part of the 'communine'. Just think for a moment about the power of a group, where some parents stay behind in the commune to clean and cook—not because they're lesser, but because they're better at it and actually enjoy doing it. A computer programmer isn't necessarily more skilled than a carpenter; they're just more skilled in computers. Even

Michael Jordan, Einstein, and Maradona combined couldn't carve wood like I can. Here at the guesthouse, everyone does what they're good at, and most of the time, they seem to be smiling. They joke around about us, the Westerners, who live under pressure, never getting anything done. Always running from place to place and dying from stress, though we call it by various other disease names. In Fatel, some friends go off to work and provide for those who care for and nurture the children, much like the grand lion prides that manage to retain their natural ways, even in the shadow of human populations that conquer and trample every good patch of land, for hundreds of thousands of years. Grandparents don't need to go to nursing homes or to the clinic every day, feeling useless and dying a little more with each passing minute. They're there for the kids. Responsible elders who have seen it all, experienced it all, who don't get stressed or feel the pressure and stress of struggling to make ends meet each month.

And people have been using "communal" codes for ages. When I was a kid and we'd go to the airport to pick someone up who had just returned from abroad, before there were electronic boards showing flight information, the adults would always recognize the flight by the duty-free bags. "Oh, those are from the United States. Those are from the Netherlands." Or they would ask people on the way to the exit which flight they had come in on. Even today, if you're driving on the Arava Road and a car passing in the opposite direction flashes its lights twice, it means there's police ahead. In fact, in almost every area, people still operate communally. Only in relationships have we left people 'alone.' And now this world, which has abandoned communal living, demands that we sanctify individuality. Otherwise, what's the point? Everyone needs to create their own sanctity and grandeur. To have as many friends on social media, as many fans, as many followers. Additionally, they must forge connections through the virtual realm and apps, where they're not even present, but their images will sketch out defining lines as much or as little as possible. All of these issues are solved by the commune. Why do you think religious people go to synagogue on Friday? To pray? They might think that's the case, but in fact, it's only the secondary aspect of the weekly mental health gathering. Everyone dons their finest attire. The women, clad in white and ready to welcome the Sabbath, take their place in the "women's section" above, watching and whispering. Occasionally, a young man glances upward, and a secret smile reserved solely for his beloved, brings a shy blush to her cheeks. There's also the gathering before and after services. No one will be left alone. The community will ensure you have a match. And I'm not referring to a religious "shidduch" where you meet your bride on your wedding night, but a regular, normative pairing. Check the suicide rates in the religious sector. Not the extreme ultra-Orthodox sectors that sometimes operate like cults, but the broader religious community. Look at the levels of happiness there. It's not just because of the belief that the Almighty will take care of everything, but due to the sense of security that you are never alone. There's an entire commune behind you.

'Alive' and 'Black' are two magnificent rock ballads by Pearl Jam, a pioneering band in the Seattle grunge scene of the '90s. Today, if you want to hear a song, you open the internet and search for it. In the past, you had to buy the cassette and then the CD, and listen to the entire album. And so, when listening to these songs within the album, they become part of a perfect tapestry, part of a story the band wanted to tell. The order of the songs, the tempo with which they start and end, the climax of the work, its peak—everything takes on a completely different meaning than just playing a random song. Suddenly, you discover additional tracks, perhaps less 'popular,' but ones that penetrate your soul and become part of you, like 'Release,' 'Garden,' and 'Oceans.'

Listen to rock operas like David Bowie's *Ziggy Stardust* and The Who's *Tommy*. They are psychedelic masterpieces where every comma holds a billion meanings. A statement. A creation. Art. And that's why these works are above time. Beyond time. Even if you don't listen to them regularly in the car or occasionally in your apartment, you can always put on a Pink Floyd album in the peak of your high or at the end of the world or with your girlfriend and a flashlight inside a tent, and you'll have a blast. But if you pull out a 'random' song from the middle of the album, it might sound trivial, 'meh,' simply because it lacks context, disconnected from everything. Just like songs, so too are partners in nature when 'pulled' from their natural tapestry. Whether it's a person or another animal, initially, they are charming, a lovely pair, but gradually, they lose context. They are no longer 'part of something,' they lose themselves from that natural fabric created by nature.

I remember this one day where all the adults in Fatel cried. All the grown-ups, including old Elhanan and Ephraim from the grocery store, who had gathered there for the important Maccabi Tel Aviv game in Europe on the big screen every Thursday. And at the end, the entire crowd in the hall yelled as one, "Ooh ah, what a scene, CSKA has been wiped clean! Ooh ah, what a scene, CSKA has been wiped clean!" And suddenly, all the adults—even the truly old ones—stood up and joined in as a chorus, "Ooh ah, what a scene, CSKA has been wiped clean!" with tears in their eyes. Tears in their eyes, I tell you! Then, even I and all the kids joined in, and we all shouted. Our little country was finally on the map. It wasn't the same map as Tal Brody's unforgettable quote, but a few years later, but beating CSKA Moscow, which represented the 'evil Soviet monster,' was still a historic event. It wasn't 'Oh yeah, how we fucked them' or something silly like today 'Yellow Rising' cheering applause, It came from within. This is what they—the little lion from Israel of the eighties, battle-hardened from wars, times of austerity, and the tough waves of immigration, wearing old clothes made in Israel because imports were not yet a thing—This was their say. That the almighty, fearsome CSKA, with its giant Taktshenko, had been wiped clean. And I remember those magical moments, etched in my memory forever, as a child in our little commune. And in those enchanted moments, old Elhanan felt like my father, and Ephraim from the grocery seemed stronger than Taktshenko, who stood at seven feet and one inch. And that's all. That is all a child needs.

13

'Al-fateeliya, al-fateeliya!' shouted the Arab in broken Hebrew towards the whites who seemed Jews to him. But the Englishmen on site understood nothing. They were completely indifferent to the troublesome and unruly Arab, continuing with their fence construction.

'Yes, just one more here and we'll be all set. Only one more to go,' said the second Englishman as he drove in another post, and everyone seemed pleased.

'Al-baboor, al-baboor!' he continued to shout in Arabic, and at any moment now they'd draw their guns and shoot at this nuisance, who surely could expose their celestial plot. However, the Arab, though he didn't keep the Sabbath, needed the old fuel stove that he had left behind— a stove, that according to legend, was used to heat the food of almost the entire tribe during Ramadan, before the men returned hungry from prayer. Apparently, we're dealing with a proper whopper of a giant stove.

But the Englishmen, fearing the secrecy of their location might be compromised and because the defiant Arab refused to quiet down, drew their weapons. At the sight of the drawn guns, the Arab hastily fled, but he would surely return with his entire tribe soon. Thus, while they savored their evening drink, our loyal English soldiers and our forefathers tried to cook a particularly fine stew from the food they had bought at the nearby market, which, of course, was operated by Arabs. Yet, the stove refused to ignite. The top of the wick should be ignited with a match, and the fuel ascends through the wick due to the principle of capillarity, which is essentially the ability of a liquid to flow up a thin tube without any aid from, and sometimes even against, the force of gravity.

As our armed and determined Arab friends approached the fortified British fence, the senior one suddenly raised his hand in a gesture of halt. He whispered to the closest guy next to him, a sort of deputy, if you will, and contrary to the wick, the whispered conversation grew more heated. For despite the prevalence of these wicks in the land of Israel during that time—up until the 1950s when gas stoves began to dethrone them from their exalted perch—our British friends were unaware of the type of fuel to use, and the wick simply refused to light. The hallmark of the wick is the 'petroleum' smell it emits, even though it operates on a fuel derived from the distillation of petroleum, a sort of anti-petroleum, if you will. And our Arab friend was well acquainted with the scent.

"L'a! L'aish?! Ma'am yoozbutilhum!" It's not working for them! Not working!

"Ilna!" said the sergeant, ours! "Hasa badna nukhud b'laiwah!". Now we take it, by force!

"L'a! Mish b'laiwah! Bil'akel." With wisdom, the senior officer decreed and asked everyone to tuck their weapons into their belts, except for those who came with knives, as Muslims also perform circumcision, and a second one isn't a cool idea.

"Ser!" he shouted in English with a heavy Arabic accent, and the British soldiers hurried to their feet, some even drawing their weapons.

"No, no, no. Remember, peace and serenity. We promised," the senior British officer reminded them, and everyone fell silent, remaining in place.

"Amm... yes please?" he responded amidst the quiet uproar beyond the fence.

"Ser... dis," the senior Arab pointed at the wick, "Awer," indicating himself and his companions. "But we help. Help, yes?"

The British officer looked at the Arab, turned to his puzzled comrades, then back to the Arab.

"I'm sorry?"

"We…" the Arab pointed again at the whole group. "We help. You," he pointed back at the British officer.

"With what?" the British officer replied, overly British.

"Dis!" the Arab pointed at the wick.

"Dis what?" He continued in his misunderstanding, and the Arab moved a little closer until he could point more clearly. "Oh, that! He wants us to help with that," he quickly explained to his colleagues who were still standing in shock.

"Okay," shouted a peace-loving Brit, "let them in."

"No, wait!" another called out. "Let's take it to the fence."

And so, the English brought the giant wick closer to the fence. The senior Arab realized that he alone could enter, and suddenly he noticed the assortment of meats and spices bought just that afternoon from the market controlled by his clan of people.

"Ah! Bring, bring. I make," he nodded. The English, surprised and puzzled, stood as the Arab gently moved them aside, took the meats, and began preparing them before their astonished eyes.

Meanwhile, the linguistically skilled Arab began an animated conversation with the Allies, and thus was woven the greatest diversion scheme in the history of the place, as we know it, of course. No one crosses the Arab community, the wealthy English buy their goods from the nearby market run by his people, the Arab cooks for them, and everyone's happy! And if you think about it for a moment, without the promise that those early British settlers, my ancestors, were bound to keep, a brutal, two-sided massacre would likely have occurred, leading to blood feuds and ending in horrific bloodshed. But thanks to one promise—just one!—the

English, against their very nature, were forced to win it all. Fatel—after the 'fateeliya' that would not light.

The next morning, I searched for Moran on the other side of the bed, but she was gone. 'Well, that's odd…' I thought to myself. Throughout our intertwined and twisted stay here, Moran had always been the last to wake, and even then, there was a sort of irritation on her face, as somewhat of a cosmic irritation with the universe, for pulling her from sleep. And now she was not here. Had she left? Had something happened? Was I worried for her?

"Moran?" I called. Perhaps she was in the bathroom? And even if she was, if she had been in there for a while without a sound, it might not have been the wisest question I'd ever asked. But she didn't answer. I got up to check, and the bathroom was empty. Oops, suddenly the door swung open.

"Hey," she said, surprised.

"What's up?" I asked, laughing as she asked if I was awake.

"Where have you been?"

"Oh, just out for a walk."

"What walk?" I persisted. "Just kidding," I quickly added as she shrugged and said, "Walk."

"So, what..."

"Are you hungry?" she picked up on my question.

"Uh... yeah," I tilted my head to the side.

"Well, come on, there's food."

"There's food?" I laughed.

"Yeah, I just saw Pratiksha making salad and omelets. Come on," she said and left the room.

"Alright, I'm coming," I replied to myself.

"Salad!" she said with a wide smile to Pratiksha, as I walked towards the table. "Salad," I echoed in a low voice, raising my hands up at the ever-smiling Pratiksha. She always smiles, Pratiksha. Even though I, skilled at smiling despite pain, despite hearing words that burn and scorch the soul, see something different in her eyes. And it's not a cliché. I see it, I know. I also know, at the same time, that her situation is much better—far better—than the eight hundred million Indians of her people. But she knows. She sees us and understands that she is, in a way, caged. It's not a visible cage like one in a zoo, but this, more or less, will be her life, almost certainly. A half-percent chance otherwise, and that's only because I've been exceedingly generous. And when I smile at her, genuinely glad to see her, she remains in the role of a servant. Forgive me for saying this; it's... it's hurtful. It doesn't benefit anyone. Perhaps it's better left unsaid altogether. But it's the truth. Pratiksha has no choice but to smile at me. Not that I desire it, heaven forbid. I mean, of course, I'm glad to see her, and her smile is especially enchanting—she's truly delightful and undoubtedly a good woman. Yet the fact remains that she has no alternative, unlike me. I could wake up tomorrow, sell the business, and pursue whatever I wish, try something new, something I love, fulfill myself as everyone in this generation so declares. She doesn't have that option. And so, the charming and even beautiful Pratiksha will work in this restaurant for the rest of her life—twelve hours a day with only three hours off in between, seven days a week. There are no enlightened souls here who understand the necessity of a day of rest, transforming it into one of the most sacred principles to prevent the exploitation of others. No Shabbat here. Just work. And all this for the astronomical sum of... are you sitting down? Lying comfortably under your blankets with the air conditioner softly cooling your skin? Fifteen thousand rupees! Don't ask how I got this information, but during our stay here, it's worth about two hundred and twenty dollars. Madness. Don't spend it all at once. So yes, her living costs are far less than ours, but that very fact perpetuates and confines her situation. It made me a bit sad for her, but I knew that relatively, her condition was still quite good, even very good. Besides, it's not like she's chopping wood. She mostly prepares food and helps with serving and clearing, and there are another eighteen Indians here doing roughly the same thing, so the work isn't particularly hard. What's more, unlike them, she has the option to rent her womb for nine months and potentially make a kind of exit strategy if all goes well... Her beauty will surely count in her favor, at least with me.

And perhaps it's for the best, this situation. Most people in the Western world suffer because they've been drilled into believing they can and must fulfill themselves. When I was little, I used to sell silkworms to children in Fatel. I'd collect them from the trees, along with mulberry leaves. White worms that spun pure silk from their asses. Well, technically it's from their mouths, but never mind. They grow to their maximum size and immediately fulfill their life's purpose, spinning a cocoon of pure silk and sealing themselves inside. Programmed. None miss their destiny. Inside the cocoon, they enter a sort of coma, dormancy, or whatever our scientists, who supposedly know so much more than they do, decided to call it, until they transform from a larva into a moth. Luckily for the silkworms, they don't heed those who know far more than they do, and so, once they've transformed into moths, they immediately pursue the essence of their lives: emerging from their cocoons, they venture out to lay dozens of tiny eggs, until they surrender to their fate and perish in the prime of their lives. And what emerges after a few days? That's right. At first, they're tiny, and you can have fun placing your finger until they climb up the "cliff." I would throw mulberry leaves at them that I asked my mom to take me to get on Saturday nights from one of the two outside the neighborhood, in the community center of Bnei Akiva. There was also a tree in the main garden of Fatel, right where Anat's birthday was, but that tree was too high, and I couldn't reach the branches. After all, I was only six. I sold them for a few dimes. Five. Ten. Sometimes even a few for half a Shekel or a Shekel. But I sold. And other kids could pick them up from the trees just like me, but I sold. "The kid will be a millionaire by ten," the grown-ups said, and I took it to heart and set out to achieve the goal. Because if there's brains - let's make money out of it. What else is there in life? So I excelled in math, and later in high school, I was also quite good at chemistry, but the teacher who remained the most deeply etched in my heart was Malka, the craft teacher from the crafts room in the basement of the municipal school. To the left was the art room, to the right - crafts. My first creation is still on the dresser at my parents' house, though it looks like a kind of vibrator. A sort of candlestick glued to the base in a diamond shape, with a candle holder screwed to a wooden rod that I shaped with my own hands, as if they had longed since birth to saw, glue, and sand. I remember people looking and saying directly or indirectly, "What, with all this intelligence, will he end up being a carpenter?" And only I didn't understand what was the problem. Everything is great, so what's the problem?

Back when I was living in Tel Aviv, there was a girl from the neighborhood whom I always saw walking her dog. One day, she seemed unusually upset, so I asked her how she was. "I hate my job," she suddenly said to my surprise, as she always seemed so cheerful. "Okay… so why don't you quit?" I asked with utter simplicity. And she replied with utter simplicity that her father wouldn't be able to handle it. "How old are you?" I dared to ask, despite her being a woman, and she bravely answered forty-two. God damn, the girl's going to be fifty in eight years, but her father won't be able to handle it. Throughout his whole life, he dreamed of his daughter working in high-tech, and now, how will he face everyone at work if she's no longer in high-tech!? "Your father," I answered, "will have to deal with it. And if he can't cope or loves you any less, that's his issue. In eight years you'll be fifty, for heaven's sake. Now is the time to enjoy life."

Two weeks later, I saw her again, walking her dog, and she was smiling. It turned out she had quit her job! Almost everyone else would have asked her immediately, 'So what will you do now?' or 'How will you manage financially?' But I simply smiled and told her how wonderful it was and how happy I was for her. For the entire year that followed, she was on something of a life sabbatical—traveling, relaxing, managing with the savings from her previous torturous job. After a year, she found work in something she truly enjoyed, and that was that.

One of my uncles has a daughter who was born with amazing pastry abilities. By the age of fourteen, she was baking cakes and cookies you only see on cooking shows. But her retarded neanderthal mother said, "What's with this baking? First, you need to study law so you have a real profession," and only when the talented, unfortunate girl reaches thirty, pregnant with her second child after finishing her internship and bar exams, might she remember that once upon a time, she knew how to bake cookies. In the end, and after a fierce and bold argument from the poor girl—brave enough to stand up to her neanderthal of a mother—they settled on dress design, for it's supposedly artistic like baking cookies but also considered a "real" profession...

So perhaps in old times, an adult's advice was truly regarded as wise, genuinely really smart advice. But today, it's probably the worst advice you can get. Not because most adults are clueless or square, but simply because they didn't grow up in the digital age. They grew up in a tougher, analog world, and therefore their advice was always advice of avoidance and fear. Avoid risks, follow your head, not your heart. They still live in a bygone era, before the age of the global village where anyone with a mobile device can know what's happening anywhere in the world. And in that world, the not cool people were the ones who stood out. They were the ones you saw on the news, read about in the papers. You were scared. That was the mentality of the time. In some places, it was even a basic survival condition. Every deal started with the assumption that the other side was, or would eventually be, out to screw you over. "Promises? Write them on ice. Trust no one." People were conditioned to distrust, and negotiations were conducted under a shroud of machismo; Who drove the Mercedes, who slapped a pack of red Marlboros on the table, who shouted the loudest, threatened, withheld money until... "Sue me, you screwed me over, you're taking food from my kids' mouths, send him a lawyer's letter, demand the money now!". If you insist on listening to someone older, listen to the truly old ones.

Those who have seen it all from above and understand they're at the end, so they don't bullshit. They're not 'careful'. And even then, take it with a grain of salt. And perhaps then you can trust the one who promised, knowing he will keep his word, as the world has guided him there through the social networks. For in today's world, people don't accept bullshit anymore. There's no dictatorial leader to whom everyone bows, no 'amen' to everything written in the paper or said on TV. In the past, only those who shouted the loudest received service—they'd get their demands met or be given compensation. Today, it's the opposite: if you shout, you won't get service. There's someone on the other side who doesn't tolerate being yelled at, having grown up in a world where that's unacceptable. Slowly and gradually, people are realizing they need to behave differently, and as a result, they're adapting. Consequently, the bullshit artists are dwindling, disappearing. Those who bluff are quickly met with online shaming when their lies are exposed. Everywhere you look, there are security cameras, and every phone is a camera and recording device. Everything is documented. The age of bullshit is over, as is the era of authoritative tones that frightened people sitting at home, listening to the 'national spokesperson' or 'senior broadcaster.' 'The Prime Minister is speaking!'. I remember that once a Knesset member or minister came to Fatel, right here to the big garden, to give a speech. I was really young, about seven or eight, and I don't quite recall what happened, but at the edge of the garden, there's still this weird stage made of stones and sand, and that's where he spoke. There were lights, and a set. Maybe even some music was played. I remember there was a real buzz in the village. 'Someone's coming to speak. It's so interesting what he'd say, what he was like in reality. Honoring us with his presence, Honorable Minister! Knesset Member! Mayor! These are important people, important things. The king's decree in the central square!'. They've given us the finger up the ass all these years, and we've taken it like fish. But we're not to blame. It used to be much worse, back in the cave days. Then came the Middle Ages with all the freeloading noble families. Bourgeois corruption. Compared to then, we're faring better. But it's all over now. Done. The era of innocence is over. The era of tone. A thirteen-year-old kid is less naïve today than a sixty-year-old man. You can't bullshit him. In a second he'll open Wikipedia and check you. He'll open YouTube and watch. He's known what porn is for six years already. Six. I remember back in 8th grade someone sneaked in a video tape with something gross involving semen and pubic hair. It's not like today where everything is 'flansh!' pure, she does bleaching in the ass, not just full-body laser. Lips, pelvis, and rib removal surgery. Silicone is already passé, not interesting. She's getting her pussy done, make it look beautiful. So you think you're going to bullshit this kid with your authoritative voice and tie on television? You can go suck on his dick... The centers of power, money, and control no longer belong to the elders. The young don't need an old person to get them a job, approve a bank loan, co-sign a bond, or vouch for them. All you need to control your world is a laptop, electricity, and internet, and you can make millions from a tent in the desert. When Facebook first started, a girl who had an album from Thailand was considered permissive. You could actually sit at home on your computer and see her in underwear and a bra, which somehow we managed to call 'bikini,' and be amazed. Wow, what a slut! But like our futsal coach taught us when we were kids - if one person is blowing through the defense, he'll get a red card; if everyone is blowing through, that's a team that defends hard. Today, everyone is blowing through. Everyone's a 'slut' and therefore no one is! They put their ass, tits, and pussy right in your face. 'I have a body, and I'll do whatever I want with it.' They're not afraid of stigmas or what others will say. Hell yeah, Feminism! A sixteen-year-old girl opens an online page, objectifies herself to the max, says something she's sure is right, and a bunch of fourteen-year-olds nod along with their clicks, which makes big companies pay her tons of money. She doesn't need anyone's approval, nobody's money, she's not subject to or submissive to stigma or custom. She's raking in cash without studying a minute, while there are hundreds of thousands of ultra-educated people around the world who have no idea how to make a buck. But they, from the heights of the conformist establishment, will continue to preach and shout about this girl, 'Gevvald!' disaster! trying to scare you off, dissuade you from her, so that the pinnacle of Olympus remains in their hands. Conservatism, mother of all sins, refuses to disappear. It refuses to lose. It continues to fight a daily battle for survival. It will fight until the buzzer, through extra time and overtime. It will cling with all its might to the altar's horns to avoid slipping down into the abyss of oblivion to which it belongs. To that same Gey-Ben-Hinom that it meticulously nurtures in your minds. So you'll keep nodding and thinking that only those who speak in lofty language are wise, and only those with a university degree are successful, contrary to the fact that half of the tycoons never finished high school and that there isn't a single study proving a linear connection between education and wealth. Once, a guy in jeans and flip-flops was a loafer, and a guy in a suit was a success; today, a guy in a suit is an upgraded slave and a guy in jeans owns a startup.

But the institutional conservatism will continue to tell you to wear a suit for a job interview, and also that it's crucial to take five units of math for your high school diploma, and above all—scolding you to speak its language, for it is the very essence of its dominion over you. If you don't speak 'properly,' you'll be considered a fool.

"*Spool the water, Dad!*" my daughter says when we go to the swing and find it wet after the rain. She knows it needs to be tipped over for the water to spill out. *Spool them,* logically, make it so they've been spilled, it makes sense. "*Climbed me, Dad!*" she shouts when we're at the playground and she can't reach the climbing structure made for bigger kids. But because she's full of motivation, she starts climbing and then wants me to help her—make her succeed in climbing. *Climbed me—make it so that I've already climbed.* It works. Until the system steps in and straightens her out to its standards. 'Fixes' her. As it keeps trying to 'fix' you. Just like how they suddenly decide you should say 'realized' when you're talking about something that's happening right now—like in a store, when the clerk says, 'Well, I realized you were interested in buying...' when it's obvious you're interested right now. It makes no sense, but that's what's 'correct.' Same thing with the way we used to say 'fetch me the newspaper,' because that was proper, but now at best you'll say, 'Get me the paper,' and maybe throw in a 'please' if you're feeling polite. Just like how they suddenly tell you that you're supposed to say 'whom' instead of 'who' in formal writing, even though everyone's been saying 'who' for everything, because that's just how people speak. And it's not that people are uneducated; it's the system that's stuck, refusing to evolve, refuses to die. It clings to outdated rules, refusing to let a final period be written on its page in history. Did it bother you when I said I loved you? I didn't say I loved you, I said I love you!!! While we had this conversation, I didn't say I once used to love you, I said, meaning right now, I love you! So what da fuck?!!? Or how they try to enforce 'It is I' instead of 'It's me,' even though 'It's me' is what everyone says. The system loves nitpicking things that don't matter, like insisting we spell 'fetus' with an 'o' as 'foetus,' even though no one pronounces it that way. And yes, you can say 'me and him went to the store' instead of 'he and I' not just because nobody talks like that in real life, but because languages evolve, and conversational usage is just as valid. The rules they cling to belong to another era, much like how biblical phrases were once considered 'correct' speech, but nobody speaks like that anymore. But the guardians of language will tell you not to end a sentence with a preposition, as though saying 'This is what I'm talking about' is somehow offensive to their ears. They demand you say, 'This is the thing about which I speak,' and yet we laugh, because who in their right mind speaks that way outside of a dusty old grammar book? And then there's the insistence that double negatives are inherently incorrect—because God forbid we say, 'I don't want none of that,' when the very heart of language is in how we feel, not in correct terms. They say it's wrong, but we know it's real. Then, of course, there's the matter of 'less' versus 'fewer.' They'll insist you say 'fewer than ten items' instead of 'less than ten,' as though the universe hinges on the difference. But these rules are like relics from a bygone era, enforced by the keepers of a tradition that no longer serves the living, breathing world of modern conversation. They cling to these remnants of linguistic purity, as though they can stave off the inevitable evolution of speech itself. And let's not forget the war on passive voice. 'Mistakes were made,' they say, is unacceptable, for we must always assign blame, always tie an actor to the action. They demand clarity, and yet in the passive there is poetry—there is space for mystery, for the unsaid, the unknown. Sometimes, the ambiguity is the point. The establishment, with its red pens and rigid rules, tries to fossilize language, to freeze it in time, to trap it in dictionaries and grammar manuals as though it can be tamed. But the truth is, language is wild. It bends, it flows, it dances around their rules. It refuses to be boxed in. And so, just as they once corrected our ancestors to say 'bring hither the candle,' they now try to correct us, to straighten the beautiful, crooked paths our tongues have carved through centuries of speech. But we know better. We know that the true language lives not in their rules, but in our mouths, in the spaces between breath and sound. But the conformist establishment doesn't want to be wiped off the face of the earth it rules, the very earth that has been so good to it. And so it continues to tighten its grip on the masses. *Be analytical! Be realistic!* Oh, such powerful words! Bow immediately before the almighty! There's a reality you need to accept, a seriousness to embrace. You must work hard! *There are starving children in Africa!* What, you want to enjoy life? Do you know what we had at your age? *Nothing!* And all this, of course, means that you shouldn't smile too much. What are you, a clown? How do you expect to succeed like that? And me? No, I'm definitely not a clown. But I do like to shake things up sometimes, to change people's mood. I'll toss a casual joke at the cashier in the supermarket—"Wait, two hundred and ten? Fine, let's make it two hundred and nine ninety-nine!" And she looks at me, used to arguing all day with people-who-are-far-too-serious-because-that's-how-it's-supposed-to-be, and she doesn't even understand what I want. So I throw out a small chuckle or a smile, and she just moves on, as if to say, *Not funny. What do you want from me now?* And then I'll drop in another—"Oh, well, maybe credit me for the bag, huh?" Or when she gives me my change, I'll go, "Wow, I've hit the jackpot! Look at all that money!" And in the end, she laughs from the sheer ridiculousness of it all. She remembers, for just a moment, that there's life outside of this suffocating seriousness, that perhaps not everything has to be so heavy all the time. It won't make her mother richer forty years ago, and it won't feed that child in Africa, but it'll make her day go by a little smoother, and the next person in line? They'll get a smiling cashier.

Old Elhanan never 'just' passes you by with a nod or a quick hello. Never. Every time you run into him on his mobility scooter, he stops to toss out some lines. "Hey, let me tell you about this dream I had last night. My wife was alive! Now I'm at odds with my alarm clock, heh heh..." It's obviously not funny, but he's trying to make me laugh, so I give a small chuckle in solidarity. And honestly, between the effort and his smile, I find it about twenty percent amusing, enough to put me in a better mood. I end up wearing this dumb half-smile for a few seconds, and he scoots off, proud of the joke he's shared that "amuses the youngsters." And now, everyone either of us meets in the next few moments catches some sliver of that smile too. And so on, and so on. Exponential joy. From nothing. From old Elhanan coming up with a silly joke.

But bad habits die hard. When things aren't going as planned, we tend to tuck our tails between our legs. We revert to our origins, trying to be Mom and Dad's good kids again. We've really gone overboard... Most cling to bygone sayings, finding it easier to listen to various 'wise' individuals or the quotes they've encountered along the way. This holds true across all areas of life. Someone once told me that her mother taught her that a man is a fool and needs to be worked on, to be enticed with a woman's body to get what she wants. And there are a billion other things you've been taught, thrown at you here and there, and because you love and respect your parents, you end up acting in ways that don't truly feel right to you. 'But... Dad said, and... Auntie told me so and so.' And what am I even rambling on about now, with smiles and peace-and-love? What, am I suddenly a Greenpeace activist? World-peace? A vegan, perhaps?

What, now it's global warming and all that jazz? Engineered meat? What??

'Light, brotherhood, and love.' Three words that are symbols. Symbols for what? For light, for brotherhood, and for love. They are not the words themselves. After all, how can a person truly be itself? No one is truly themselves. It's like when we were in high school, everyone cheered for 'Grande Milan,' the football team from Milan that won every title possible at that time. A few years later, it was Manchester United that captured the hearts of fans, and in the years following, by some magic spell, everyone suddenly became fans of Real Madrid and Barcelona. So what happened to all those fans of 'the great Milan'? Did they... evaporate? Vanished perhaps? Or are they hiding in the closets of their homes? The simple answer is that these were the same 'fans' of the current successful teams. And it all boils down to the unfortunate fact that most people do not choose to be true to themselves; instead, they choose to connect with whatever successful thing comes along, which is not them. They have no 'guiding thread,' no core idea, no continuous and consistent foundation that serves as the storyline in their lives; they simply react to what happens. And that's how you remain disconnected. Disconnected from your own truth. You can fool everyone, but you can't fool yourself. And when a person is not connected to their own truth, they have no chance of creating something good. Even the greatest artist is a 'phony' and the greatest fake of themselves when they are disconnected. That's what remains of them. There's simply no way to live a lie and produce something good; it is utterly impossible. It's like how most people dress in a routine fashion for routine places, thinking, 'It's just work; who cares who sees me?' But that's a mistake. Dressing in a way that you love, that makes you feel comfortable and joyful, is a privilege. It's your identity. It's how you feel most at ease in the universe. It's also how you'll be most productive and pleasant to others, simply because you're comfortable. Because at that very moment—you are yourself! Old Elhanan is always dressed nicely. Neatly. Instead of throwing on something old because he's old anyway, he dresses well. Even if it's not an Italian designer pants, it's always pants that look new and pressed, a buttoned-up shirt tucked in, and a belt that looks fresh. He doesn't wear 'standard' colors; he wears green pants with a pink shirt and a brown belt, or red pants with a sky-blue shirt and a black belt—seemingly odd combinations, but that's who he is. An amusing old man dressed beautifully. And so, wherever he goes, he's always a 'PERSONA,' not just an 'old man' passing by; he's Elhanan! And just as it's important to wear clothes that make you feel good and turn you into your true self, it's important to listen to your own music from time to time, to maintain your uniqueness. To be who you are. But most people are busy overthinking instead of seeking their own true essence. They consult with everyone and their mother about what's best, instead of going out and doing. They ask those older and more 'experienced' than them, and live with outdated notions from forty years ago. Only after wasting their whole lives will they have enough money to do what they truly want. Maybe they'll be senile, or even in the grave, but at least they have a mission, a path, an idea. Instead of simply doing what they're really good at without overthinking. And it's never too late to make a change in life. J.K. Rowling was on the brink of poverty and moved in with her sister in Scotland with her daughter after a divorce, and five years later became a multimillionaire from selling children's books. An unimaginable thing that no advisor, as senior as he was, would have endorsed as a viable plan to get her out of the mud. But it happened. Everything is possible. Always. The sages said, "Whoever draws near, distances; and whoever distances, draws near." You can spend a lifetime trying to make people listen to you, or you can simply start walking your path and watch how everyone suddenly believes in you. Because when you're free from the depths and whirlpools of thought, the universe simply has to align with you. It has no other option. If Picasso had consulted others, they would have called him crazy. What, an ear here and an eye there? Did you bump your head? Who would buy that?!

But most people are cowards. Afraid to lose what they supposedly have. But what do they really 'have'? It's usually something they're just capable of doing. It's not their dream, but heaven forbid they let it slip away, this… thing that keeps them going. Because without it, they fear they might cease to exist. By the same logic, the most beautiful women are the ones most afraid of losing their beauty, and the skinniest are the ones most likely to become anorexic. It's what they've been accustomed to all their lives, what they believe their confidence stems from, so their greatest fear is that losing it would leave them with nothing. And why on earth does the silkworm know its purpose in life from the moment it's born, and we don't? Why do sea turtles, hatching from eggs dozens of meters from the shore, instinctively know to head straight for the water, while we don't? Why do we burden ourselves by going to people who make a living telling others to follow their path? And what path are they even talking about? The path of the people seeking advice? Or their own path, the one peddled by coaches, psychologists, and mentors? How many of them are actually good at what they do, helping people improve or fulfill their lives, and how many of them wouldn't know how to do anything else but blabber on, and if one of their clients ever got a glimpse of their own lives, they'd be horrified?

So instead of quietly and peacefully asking yourself and listening, you go and do what others say is the absolute best and most suitable for you. You feed off the fears and conservatism of others. But there isn't one truth for everyone. Each person has entirely different aspirations. There are people whose job is to clean up poop and change diapers and catheters in hospitals. And that's not a job you just stumble into, saying, "Well, I'm not finding myself, so I'll go clean up old people's mess." It requires a certain intention and will. I love being a carpenter. That's where my happiness in life comes from. So when I meet someone who is very talented and successful at something, I don't envy him, I don't feel bad that I'm not in his place, and certainly not that I'm not him. Because 'He' is always a subjective measure. And who knows if tomorrow he has an appointment with a doctor to burn off a herpes outbreak with a laser or undergo surgery for a problem down below. 'He' is 'He' with everything that entails.

They say Isaac Newton died a virgin. Isaac Newton, one of the greatest scientists of all time, whose story would likely diminish his greatness by how little it reveals of who he truly was, is reputed to have never had sex. Now, assuming this is true, the question arises—would you trade your life for that of Isaac Newton? Is it better to be remembered as one of the greatest in history, even though you're already dead and it's no longer relevant to you at all, or to be a 'simple' person who earns an average salary but lived joyfully at every moment? But you might argue, 'Wait, during his lifetime, he must have enjoyed prestige, honor, and glory...' Perhaps, but even if he did, after that honor he went home and didn't get laid, whereas you did. But of course, no one will appreciate that. The average person on the street might know, at best, that an apple fell on Newton's head and that's how he discovered gravity, and even that half-remembered thought is forgotten within a second as they gaze at the butt of a girl in jeans who just walked by. No one will truly appreciate you, and even if they do, it will be for no longer than a brief moment. Therefore, the greatest advice for you and for the entire universe is to do something that makes you feel good. I don't envy a successful singer when he stands on stage and fifty thousand people cheer for him. I mean, sure, I'd like to be cheered for like that too, but for building some wing in the Sagrada Familia, not for my singing. If I wanted to sing, I would go and try; I wouldn't be a carpenter. And to me, it feels good when people appreciate my work, when I wake up without a boss breathing down my neck, and when I'm not stuck with files and a laptop under harsh fluorescent lights. And I have a lawyer friend who works with files and a laptop under fluorescent lights and makes a lot of money, and he enjoys it. The most important thing is that you feel the best for y-o-u-r-s-e-l-f. You—be you. As in, 'You' as the final answer. Nor for what the neighbors will say—fuck the neighbors. Nor for what your family or close circle will say. Because even if they're wise, good friends, or successful in what they do - they are not you. Only you wake up with yourself every morning.

Once, I saw a contestant on a TV talent show from the Caucasus region. He talked about how his mother, before meeting his father, used to perform a lot. But then his father told her, "It's either this or the family." And the whole family is sitting there, nodding along, while the father explains how she couldn't possibly have time for both. Then this kid contestant goes on to explain that now, with his success, his mother will finally fulfill herself—through him. No, my brother with minimal brain power, living in a dark cave. Your mother, the shattered and tormented soul, trapped in a Bolshevik household raising children, whose heart was torn apart daily by losing her only true self, will now suffer torments of hell while she finds joy in your happiness. You stupid family of ignorant primitives, devoid of even a trace of Neanderthal awareness. If tomorrow I drown in this Goa sea that's functioning as a swimming pool, or get accidentally run over by a herd of angry cows upset that the Indians are once again driving on their roads, at least I lived for a moment. I went to fucking Goa at forty, grabbed Moran Dagan, and kissed her on the lips in a way I never dared imagine I would.

And maybe Pratiksha is actually much happier than I am—doing her job, knowing exactly how her day will go, and having no unnecessary worries. But if you're not happy, go ahead and make a change. Or at least try. And if you're not even going to try, then sit quietly and shut the fuck up. In any field you can either bullshit or seek the truth. Your own deep, inner truth. Not what others think or recommend. What *you* feel and how *you* believe you should act—or not act. What is it that you want to say, not what would sound better or stronger. Did you come here to fuck or just to fuck with my head?

I looked at Moran, and she looked back at me while eating her salad with her mouth closed and making a slight face at me.

"Paaaaa," I laughed and flicked a bit of omelet from my mouth.

"Ew," she said with her mouth open, with salad in it.

"Paaaaa," I continued, and she laughed. "See, you've got your mouth open too."

"Ah-ah-ah-ah," she laughed and quickly shut her cute little mouth. I tried to decipher the look behind her gaze but couldn't manage. Our Moran is a pro at being unreadable.

"Nice going, Moran," I said out of the blue.

"What?" she replied in a sweet tone with an innocent look. But I just wanted to enjoy the moment, throwing something out and getting a response. She never really talked to me. Never. In my whole life, I wanted it, and it never happened. And then, yesterday, we had sex again, intensely, and she came really hard too. She was naked on top of me, and it was amazing. I was lying in bed reading a book when suddenly she emerged from the bathroom, without any prior warning. She shed a robe I didn't know she had, revealing a particularly white set of lingerie. As I watched with open eyes and raised eyebrows, frozen in place, she simply removed her bra and approached me. She took the book I was still holding, threw it against the wall, removed the white sheet that covered me, and lay down on top of me, not before commanding me to swiftly remove my underwear—a command I obeyed immediately and perfectly. She then lay down on my hardening organ, which swelled upward, stirred by the touch of her white panties. Her legs spread and I could feel the warmth from her hidden core through the thin, white fabric. Warm and intermittently moist. We kissed. Her movements forward and backward gradually pushed my underwear aside, exposing my erect organ as it pierced through her panties toward the endless valley of pleasure. I remember it was so hot inside. So moist, hot, and pleasant. And she moaned above me. Moran Dagan moaned above me. She wanted me. She craved sex. With me! And she's cuming… she's cuming! And I'm coming too! Releasing strongly inside her as she's grabbing me, clenching with her nails… It hurt but I'm not showing. It really hurt and scratched, Moran, ahhhh...! I'm not showing. I'm cuming. I'm cuming. Ahhhh... I'm shooting out the best and finest of my arsenal. "Wow, it hits my belly," she says, and I revel in the lie or mistake. I kiss her. Hold and kiss her. And can't believe it. Can't believe it. And suddenly believe in everything. Because if this happened, then anything can happen.

I love you, I say just to myself, in my heart. Not in my head, but in my heart. I love you, Moran. You know that, right? You see it, right?

"Moran,"
"Well, what?" she asked again.
"Do you like the salad?"

14

I slammed the door in panic and fled. Horror. My eyes couldn't believe what they were seeing. Behold the sense of sight, simultaneously venerated and despised. In the middle of the day, I had gone for a swim while Moran and Arik had finished lunch and retreated to the room for a nap. Turns out, when you're forty, you need to rest from time to time. What? Oh, nothing. Really nothing. Just taking a breath. And as I nonchalantly return to the room and open the door without a thought that... that... Moran, on all fours— or rather, six limbs, since that's two hands, two knees, and two feet, or more precisely, two pairs of toes touching the sheets, her gaze directed at the suddenly opening door—and Arik... Arik is pumping her from behind!

Ahhhhhhh!!!!!!!!!!

What?!?!?!?!?!?!??!?!?!?!?!?!?!?

What is this???????????????????

What a fucking whore!!!!!!!!!

What kind of friend is this!!!!!!!!!!!!!!!

What... what the fuck????????????????????

But just recently, we had fulfilled our loves that had been concealed behind fields and mists for decades, and now you're ruining everything?????? And you... you lubricious lewd street whore!!!!!! I loved you! I fucked you senseless yesterday and you loved me back while we were at it! And now... now you suddenly return to your thirty-year-old love????? Maybe you'll go back to Benny and we'll complete the circle and everything will be perfect!!!! Wait, I'm calling him. Don't move, don't let yourself be disturbed or distracted for even a moment by what I'm doing. But it seemed that it truly didn't disturb or unsettle her calm. She merely watched me with alternating wide and narrowed eyes, thanks to our dear friend's relentless and varied thrusts. She's enjoying it! She's actually enjoying it! Just like... Wait. Why does this suddenly remind me of yesterday? Could it be that... perhaps... wait. If we momentarily step away from my fevered and clearly disturbed mind concerning recent developments, and return to the entirely enigmatic headspace of Moran Dagan, perhaps she didn't love me back yesterday but merely enjoyed sex just as she enjoys it now? And maybe Arik is banging her—sorry, fucking her—sorry, making love to her—just as he apparently understood that I did yesterday. Yesterday! Can you believe it?? It happened only yesterday! I didn't even get twenty-four hours of intoxicating bliss. It's like a soccer player scoring a magnificent goal in his first professional game, only for his team to lose five-one. Five, not three. That's how I felt. Defeated. Humiliated. Utter loss Fifteen-nil, what am I saying, five. Fifty. Five thousand. A million.

I felt like Uriah the Hittite, sent to the front lines so that Arik could take my poor 'ewe lamb', my only cherished possession, my long-lost love, everything my heart had ever felt. I am Jerusalem personified in the Book of Lamentations after the destruction: "Bitterly she weeps at night, tears are on her cheeks. Among all her lovers there is no one to comfort her; all her friends have betrayed her; they have become her enemies."

Anyone with a younger sibling knows the heartbreak that strikes at a tender age. The sting of betrayal by those nearest and dearest. In one small, crystalline moment, your life is transformed beyond recognition. You might think the child doesn't understand, that if you say you love them or buy them a grand gift with the arrival of the new sibling from the hospital, it will smooth things over. It will dazzle their eyes and numb their mind. But they understand. Instantly, unmistakably, they grasp that they've been deceived. That they were not loved for who they are but for what they are—the child of these two people. And they could have been any other son or daughter, with this or that ability, this or that limitation, this or that face, and they would have been loved just the same. Simply because they are the offspring brought into the world by these two people who wished to start a family. In one moment, they understand that they—who they truly are—is utterly and completely meaningless. And so they realize that those they hold dear, who have deceived them all their lives until now, are betraying them with another child! Just as I thought I was special, that I had finally achieved something, it was revealed to me that I was merely a something, not someone. A mere fuck. Someone to be used. And it could have been anyone, it seems. The kiss in the garden that led to the charming conversation about the hammock—'the Hammockish,' as our Morani so aptly termed it—the shared flight experience, resting her head on me during the flight, the laughter we shared in the taxi—all of it converged and crystallized in my blossoming mind into the lovemaking of yesterday... Ibki alayk bek.

But it isn't my fault. We've been lied to our whole lives. And the lying doesn't stop when we start telling kids half-truths or hiding things from them, nor when the first younger sibling is born. It keeps going with the happy endings they show us in movies and books. In the end, everything will be fine. The Good will prevail. The Good always wins. But in reality, people get screwed over every single day. Good people, whose subconscious could swear it's heard a billion times in its life that the good guys win. What the top psychoanalysts in the world missed is that this is what creates a dissonance in a person's brain, sometimes even leading to an aneurysm in the brain. In foreign films, someone is always trying to say something. Maybe it comes from the desire to make it to Hollywood, to score a goal against the best team in the world, but whatever the reason, there's always a message, or at least an attempt at one. In American movies, sometimes you're just consuming junk food. Nearly half of American films are just waving their dick around, flaunting the name of the director or that actor or actress, without saying a damn thing. Even the greatest animated series ever made, *The Transformers*, was butchered by Hollywood, turning the legendary Japanese show into a stupid Hollywood film with a pathetic love story between humans. Who gives a fuck about this clichéd, moronic love story now?? Why the hell doesn't Megatron look like Megatron?! And who the hell are all these new Transformers and Decepticons you've created that I don't recognize, you fucking assholes?? An hour and a half of stench that lingers for miles and is forgotten after your next burp. Do your fucking job! Surprise me, show me something I don't know, a thought I haven't had, a wonder I haven't wondered. Whether it's an action film or a stunt movie, a romantic comedy or pure nonsense, or even a horror film. Do your fucking job! Give me something fresh! Don't shove another action flick where the villain makes the same old mistakes like arrogance, a love interest, stupidity, or some addiction, and that's what takes them down while the hero wins. Who the fuck cares if the hero wins? The hero has been winning for years! I want to see the bad guys win! The Decepticons kicking the nerdy Autobots' asses, Skeletor slicing He-Man's throat with his own sword. Explain to me why the good guy always wins! Why does the righteous win even if they go against everything you believe is right or what someone told you is right! FUCK ME OVER!!!!!! ENLIGHTEN ME!!!!!!!!!!!!!!!!!! E-N-T-E-R-T-A-I-N M-E!!!!!!!!!!!!!!!!!!!!!!!!!!!!!!!!!!!!!

And perhaps I'm just glorifying the past. This isn't the same girl, the same beauty the child in me fell in love with at eleven. Would a Tolstoy novel succeed today? Dostoevsky's *Crime and Punishment* is an incredible story with profound meanings, morals, and many thought-provoking directions, but it's not at all about what many people think when they quote "see, he did this - so he deserved what happened to him. Crime and punishment." There are also brilliant folk tales like *The Pied Piper of Hamelin*, Goethe's *The Erl-King*, and *The Emperor's New Clothes*. Masterpieces. But take the film *Taxi Driver*, for instance. If you ask most people, even those who aren't exactly film buffs, they'll tell you—'Of course, masterpiece! Scorsese. De Niro. You talking to me?? Huge.' But the truth is, when I watched it again recently, I realized that the whole thing was just about being the first film to show a scene with lots of blood and people getting shot. The finale scene. Sorry if I ruined it for most of you who haven't seen it and never will, but apart from that, it's really a shitty movie! Not sophisticated, not thrilling, really nothing at all. But at the time, it was considered 'crazy!', 'groundbreaking!', 'ahead of its time!'. Freddie Mercury, the legendary frontman of Queen, truly was ahead of his time. But when he and his band finally earned their rightful place among the greatest bands in history, thanks to the film made in their honor, they gave the Oscar to the actor who played him, despite being terrible and lacking any charisma—perhaps a trait that defined Mercury even more than his incredible singing. But everyone applauded. Hurray! The emperor is naked, but... Hurray. And what role does Arik play in my film? Am I the good guy and he the bad guy? Is he cast as King David from the story of the poor 'ewe lamb', or perhaps as God from the Garden of Eden story? Perhaps the serpent? What is the extent of his commitment to me and mine to him? Is he just the nice guy from the class? One of the guys? Is he truly and genuinely a kindred spirit of mine? When you think about it, what is the regular scope of our relationship? A call every couple of days? Does he blow me on weekends? The more I decide that our connection is closer, broader, and more genuine, the greater the conflict in my heart. And perhaps Arik is actually the brother I never had. My almost-brother versus the love of your life. On one hand, you want to share with a brother, because that's family. On the other hand, how can you share the love of your life?

I once had a friend who started dating a girl about a month after I did. This guy with the fluorescent lights and binders, who makes a lot of money—she had some legal issues, and he's a lawyer specializing in that, so I recommended him. I knew from the start he was coveting her, but since I didn't want her anymore, I didn't care. What did bother me, was that three weeks later, I heard from a mutual friend that he was dating "some loaded chick from Rishpon". "This one?" I showed him the picture on WhatsApp. "Yeah, that's her. Weird..." The truth is, I was pretty bummed to hear him describe her like that because she was actually a good-hearted person, not just a cash cow. But immediately, I called him up and even put him on speaker for a laugh. While I was sarcastically asking questions, the guy was denying he was seeing anyone. "Man, seriously? You lying fuck!" I yelled and laughed when both the mutual friend and I looked at each other in shock. Not only do you not even ask for basic respect between men or people in general, but after you've been with her for almost a month with no risk of anything 'ruining' it because you're a coward and a loser—you still can't man up and call to tell me? And when I call you, you lie straight to my face?? But later I understood it was out of necessity. Before this girl, this con artist had actually kept someone around for three years just for sex. He'd show her signs of affection when she said she loved him, and eventually he became friends with someone else, who, coincidentally, was also a client of his. After he and the client broke up, guess who he went back to... Apparently, she wasn't battered enough from the previous affair, so she came back for more. Of course he abandoned her again in an instant for the new client I set him up with. So, the logical conclusion is that if you go back to sleeping with someone you were with four years ago because it's your only option for sex, then your need for it outweighs any other impulse. And that's why he did everything to make it happen and ensure nothing, God forbid, would ruin it. In retrospect, I even remembered that he told me not to speak to her before she came for the meeting to avoid 'jeopardizing the chances of the case' and other nonsense to keep me out of the picture. But for some reason I didn't fully understand before, I didn't get mad at him. Now I see why. He came out as the ultimate loser, but he did it out of necessity. The need for sex is just as strong as the need for food, and people will kill for food in extreme situations, just like male animals fight to the death for the right to mate.

At first, I thought of Arik as a total zero and even considered cutting him off. He must have known there was something between us, even though there wasn't any real commitment or expectation tied to it or anything like that. But still, like, fuck you. Maybe Moran doesn't owe me anything, but he sure does. I pointed at him as the one to blame. And I'm the type of guy who cuts things off quickly, no problem. Even friends of many years, I've got no issue ending it. It's not that I don't care about them anymore. I changed, he changed, he didn't change. What worked for you perfectly at fifteen doesn't necessarily fit at thirty-five, and what was right at twenty-five might not work at forty. And so that was my primal thought: that perhaps also with Arik, it's over. Of course, we're still Fatel and all, but when we get back we won't be the same as before. What was fun and cool in our teens and twenties isn't so appealing to me anymore... But after wandering the stinking streets of India, which now seemed magically comforting, I realized he did it out of necessity, not disloyalty. At the end of the day, just like in the stories of David and Bathsheba and the Garden of Eden, we all yearn for the forbidden fruit. I was angry, but not enough to cut ties. Fuck him and that Moran of his. Of mine. Of his. Of hers. Moran—is apparently no one's.

And I'm actually supposed to hate her now. That's what I trained myself to do from a young age: if some girl doesn't want me, I hate her. Any girl who's ever rejected me, refused to go out with me, broken up with me, or said 'no' in any way, shape, or form, I hated them and wished for her premature death. It was my right. And I'm not talking about sex; I'm talking about someone who didn't want to get to know me. It hurt me deeply. 'I hope she dies, amen,' I'd say and for a moment feel a bit better, 'May she choke and get run over by a truck.' There, I said it again so you understand I'm completely serious. Because grief is a bottomless pit. It's better to blame, to be angry, and to hate. It's a much better mental state than being hurt or offended. You're ambitious, powerful, fighting for your place in the universe, not whining in a corner like some pathetic wretch. And what does a kid do when the girl he loves doesn't love him back? He pushes her, pulling her pigtails. That's how he expresses his love or vents his frustration. Because emotion is an uncontrollable force. Just like male animals in the wild, who spend their lives battling for females. A fight to the death. Everyone craves it. To fuck the females.

"It's all just a dick inside a pussy," a friend once said to me. "What's with you guys wanting to fuck all the time? Does it make you more of a man?"

"So put the stuff in a plastic bag," I replied. "Why do you need a Louis Vuitton? It's just stuff to carry from here to there. And why splurge on three thousand Shekel stiletto heels? Wear Biblical sandals, live in a one-bedroom apartment in Beit Shemesh, and eat bread and water. Why the gourmet restaurants and living in Rishpon? And just so you know," I added before she shook her head, as if agreeing that there's no chance of understanding between the sexes, "even the most romantic and saccharine love story you can imagine started with someone wanting to fuck someone's brains out."

Women don't value sex like men do because every woman can get sex easily at any hour of the day. Every woman. Between eighty to one hundred percent of the men a woman approaches on the street and offers to give them oral sex or just "help her carry a bag home" would agree, even if she's not a stunner. And anyone who doesn't believe this should knock on her neighbor's door right now, show him her breasts, and see what happens. Now think about what would happen if a man knocked on his neighbor's door and showed her his dick... And this is where the hidden anger of men towards women lies. It's entirely rooted in the fact that women control the world of sex but misuse it. They deceive, are indirect, hide behind a veil of pretense and insecurity, change and don't change, they lack a clear codex or operating system like men who simply need a hint and they're either interested or not, most of the time they are. A woman can dress as provocatively and revealingly as possible while simultaneously claiming that it has no connotation, hint, or connection to seduction. And even if she's a leading TV presenter, it's acceptable for her to wear a shirt with a cut-out in the middle that shows a lot of cleavage as if by accident, even though it seduces, drives crazy, and arouses. Woe to anyone who claims this is sexual harassment. Once, they filmed an angry football coach after a game threatening a fan that he would slaughter him. It really didn't look good, was inappropriate, and completely out of line. If a hundred people were asked, ninety would say he doesn't deserve to continue being a coach. A few days later, he gave an interview where he, of course, apologized and admitted that it was out of line. While that didn't make up for it and wouldn't convince the ninety people, who might have included me, he went on to add that we should examine how we would react if every day at work, people spat in our direction, cursed us, and then shoved a camera in our face. Us men are constantly faced with tempting women — whether in advertisements with them licking something with fake desire, on giant billboards on the highways, a woman at work wearing a sheer white shirt with a bright red bra underneath, another in a miniskirt, or those strolling down the street in shorts up to their crotch. Just as glittering pairs of shoes call out to women through the shop window and the tiny, expensive chef's dishes with their myriad silly names stir an uncontrollable desire that overshadows the uncontrollable urge to be as thin as possible, a strikingly attractive woman elicits two immediate reactions from the common male: one, his arousal rises to the brink of madness in a way that no creature who has never been a man could understand, and two, unlike women, who can simply open your wallet wide, he acknowledges that ninety-nine point nine percent of the time, it won't happen. These two factors combined lead the average male to a level of frustration that is extremely,

extremely, extremely, extremely, extremely, extremely great. So, those with a fraction of a brain get frustrated, sometimes even driven mad but control themselves, while those who are a bit less sophisticated respond with aggression. Just like the kid who pulls on the braid of the girl he likes the most. "Look at that cunt..." he says to his friend beside him, "how I'd fuck her fucking asssss..." He simply becomes aggressive like a wild animal.

Ed Kemper, a towering serial killer with an IQ far above average who murdered eight young women, admitted in interviews from prison that in the absence of the ability to interact with women, he was compelled to murder them, and only after their deaths did he engage in sexual activities with them. The murders of Ted Bundy were often accompanied by the mutilation of his victims' bodies, and frequently included the brutal dismemberment of their genitalia. One victim had her head sawed off, another was strangled so violently that when her body was found, her throat was the size of about half of a standard throat. Another had her nipple torn off with his teeth and her jaw broken during a brutal rape that caused tearing in her vagina. Of his thirty-some known victims, not one was spared severe beatings that shattered their bones, whether with a hammer, a club, a board, or any blunt object that the blue-eyed monster had at his disposal. In one of the 'Die Hard' movies that were popular in the 1990s, Bruce Willis was forced to walk through Harlem with a sign reading 'I hate niggers' as demanded by the villain. There's no law against it, but without the resourcefulness of 'Smhuel' L. Jackson, they would have gutted him with a butcher's knife. If I were to walk along a certain city's beach with a sign saying that all people of a certain race can go fuck themselves and their mothers are definitely whores, even though I'm not doing anything illegal, it's highly doubtful that they'd manage to get me to the nearest hospital before I bled out. A woman has the right to dress as she pleases, but one cannot prevent the reactions of certain people, albeit those reactions might be illegal. In the fourth century CE, there lived a woman named Hypatia, who was a mathematical genius in a world where such professions were reserved for men only. But our Hypatia disregarded conventions and "dared" to pursue the profession. One day, while riding in her carriage for pleasure, a wild mob of men abducted her, stripped her naked, and dragged her to a church. There, they scraped her skin with sharp shells, and while she writhed in excruciating pain, they threw her into a live fire. Ted Bundy's murders began with an extremely coincidental timing, as women's rights were starting to gain ground in the US. Bundy's trial, broadcast on television, not only demonstrated the horrifying atrocities committed by this infamous figure but also highlighted the unbearable ease with which women's suffering was disregarded at that time. This disregard led to Bundy not suffering at all in the last years of his life, and even behaving like a media celebrity. Dressed in a blue suit, he cross-examined witnesses, including surviving assault victims. When questioned about the murder of a twelve-year-old girl, he even leaned over and proposed to a woman named Carol Boone, who believed in his innocence until just before his execution, until he consulted her by phone on whether he should reveal to the police the locations of the bodies yet to be found in hopes of receiving a commutation. In all the footage from the highly publicized trial, Bundy is seen walking around like a distinguished gentleman, a well-dressed and respectable attorney. Instead of being led shackled and silent like the scum he was, receiving a daily beating in his cell for each of the young, innocent women whose lives were brutally and horrifically cut short, Theodore the Great Hero was treated with royal respect. Even the judge who read his death sentence ended with the words, "I hold no animosity against you, partner. You're an intelligent guy who could have been a great lawyer. I'm sorry you chose this path." Sophie Germain, a brilliant mathematician and physicist who laid the groundwork for the theory of elastic physics, was recorded on her death certificate as "an unmarried woman with no profession." Her name was not even etched among the names of the seventy-two scholars whose knowledge contributed to the construction of the Eiffel Tower, despite the fact that her research significantly advanced the understanding of the elasticity of the metals used in the tower, and without which it is doubtful whether it could have ever stood tall. These ingrained gender definitions were instilled in us by monotheistic religions, which depicted God in the form of a man and presented spiritual leaders, kings, and prophets as men as well. The relationship between man and God has always been portrayed as a father-son relationship: reward and punishment, divine wrath. "He who spares the rod hates his son" (Proverbs 13:24). God gets angry, God punishes, God rewards the righteous, God rules, creates, brings forth from nothing— ain't nothing like Him! Similarly, the relationship between the sovereign and his subjects is portrayed. "My father disciplined you with whips, but I will discipline you with scorpions!" (1 Kings 12:11) Rehoboam ruled harshly over the people who sought to ease the burden of taxation. This was easy for people to understand and relate to. Even today, a man who is not macho enough, or God forbid, too in touch with his emotions, is considered a wuss. In those days, there was no place at all for a different kind of energy—one that is more nurturing, more inclusive, more compassionate. A Feminine energy. It is told of Lady Godiva, the wife of the ruler of Coventry in the eleventh century, who repeatedly pleaded with her husband to show mercy to the people and reduce the taxes. Finally, he supposedly agreed, but on the condition that she ride naked on a horse through the streets of the city. Despite her strong religious faith and to her husband's immense surprise, Lady Godiva embarked on the ride. The literal meaning of 'Godiva' in Old English is 'God's gift.' Through her brave, pioneering act, the one with the most heroic audacity in its originality, Lady Godiva seeks to teach us that if we add emotion to all our power and intellect, we will receive value. This will enable us to achieve things we never dreamed of— the ability to cry and laugh, to love and to hate. Even in the toughest among us, there are intense emotions. And perhaps if we only listen for a moment, if we tune into the feelings within us, we might gain a broader understanding of the playground we all inhabit. It might sound a bit complicated, but in essence, it's "peshita d'peshita," as it says in the Talmud. Simply letting go. Feeling what is right instead of thinking about it. That's all. Such a perspective could bring us closer to the magic and beauty of a different kind of energy. The ability to contemplate, to give birth to ideas, to create. And those who are so powerful do not seek recognition of their uniqueness as 'God' does. And even if we assume that the content has been shaped by the strongest men throughout history, certain gods, or this or that deity, it cannot exist without a framework and space—a womb in which it can develop. If God is the king of the galaxy, the galaxy itself is a goddess. She is the containing, balancing force, the embodiment of all the good in the world combined. A Mother. And perhaps if the world were governed by mothers—majestic lionesses with nurturing, compassionate, creative, and balanced feminine energy, rather than domineering males with various Napoleon complexes—it would be better for all the children that we are. But this is even more blasphemous than taking the Tetragrammaton, YHWH, in vain. It's so deeply ingrained that even today, women themselves bless "May God grant you male sons, amen," as if, despite being

women, they too agree that males are superior. And so, to
this very day, the best thing a man can do in any argument
with a woman, is simply stand his ground and not apologize;
eventually, the woman will convince herself that she's the
one at fault, that she's just fucked up or something. One of
Bundy's survivors, who got into his infamous Volkswagen
Beetle to help him start the car—since he'd disguise himself
with a cast and crutches, taking advantage of the
compassion inherent in nearly every woman, especially in
young girls who wanted to 'do the right thing,'—recounted
that an inner voice suddenly screamed at her to flee. But as
she was hurriedly escaping the car, she remembers
apologizing profusely from the bottom of her heart while
running for her life. It's part of the mechanism ingrained in
women to blame themselves, to feel that something within
them is always wrong—a deeply embedded axiom that has
led to the epigenetic development of an inferiority complex
in relation to the male sex. The funniest part is the
interpretation given by men throughout history to the
women's inferior status according to the "holy scriptures."
"Your desire will be for your husband, and he will rule over
you!" it says in the Book of Genesis, "With pain you will
give birth to children!" Because Eve ate from the forbidden
fruit and even led Adam astray, all the women of the world
were condemned to eternal submission to men. Because of
you, males were thrown into the Nile! Come on, seriously...?
And what happened to that same Eve who tasted the
"forbidden" fruit? Nothing. She didn't die. She wasn't
punished. She didn't have any body parts cut off. Oh... but,
but... she was expelled from Eden, she shall now bring
forth children in pain. For real?? And before that, how did
she give birth to children? Spit them out of her mouth and
they would inflate? Bullshit. That wasn't the intent of the
allegory at all! But all our religions are based on fear, and any
advice meant to frighten or warn is necessarily the worst

kind. On the contrary, Eve passed the greatest test of all—defying the divine command. The parental command. The law's command, The tyrant's command. Thus, Eve is the first nonconformist, the first entrepreneur, the first true revolutionary. Eve is the boldest of them all. after Lilith, of course.

Oh no, he mentioned Lilith! The demonic, malevolent sprite! It would have been better to invoke Jehovah's name "in vain"! Well then, to twist allegory within allegory—in that very same allegory—according to the true allegory, which, unsurprisingly, has been distorted by men who wrote the sacred texts to instill fear... Well then, Lilith was the first woman. For before God supposedly took a rib from Adam and created 'a helper for him', it is written, right there in Genesis chapter 1: "So God created mankind in his own image, in the image of God he created them; male and female he created them" (Genesis 1:27). This means that a woman was already created before Eve, for Eve was created only in chapter 2! And who was this woman? Lilith was. Yet, according to legend, Lilith was a feminist. Indeed, indeed. And thus refused to submit to her husband's authority, demanding absolute equality. And how could such equality align with the notion that women are inferior to men, lacking rights, can be taken by the many, and discarded at will? It doesn't add up. It doesn't fit. So, let's turn her into a demoness! And let's go further and say she devours children! Yes, indeed! Thus, every woman, by her very nature as a potential mother, will abhor her and her name, avoiding even the thought or mention of her! Genius...

And how is it that Moran Dagan "dared" not to love me back? And then, the very next day, went and slept with my best friend? A whore! A witch! Burn her! Yet somehow, in a truly devious and mystical way, some would say, Moran

Dagan escaped the punishment. The punishment of hatred and the desire for her death. Something in her gaze shattered my resolute determination. For some inexplicable reason, I didn't hate her. I was deeply angry, aggrieved, and profoundly disheartened, but the intense hatred that would normally lead me to wish for her untimely death did not surface within me.

I once had a friend—we dated for about a month, but then stayed just friends. We ended up becoming the best of friends. We talked every day for almost two years, saw each other all the time—we were like siblings. I really loved her. Every time I'd come to the center, we'd meet up, laugh, and joke around about everything and everyone. We had this shared language that felt like no one else understood, even if we were in a room with thirty other people. She was like a sister from another lifetime. And despite the huge age gap between us, we understood each other in an incredible way. And all of it—without sex. Without some external factor holding onto the body, something to hang all the emotions on, canceling them out. Pure love. Ever since we broke up and became friends, we had a billion chances to sleep together but never did, even when I stayed over a few times because it was too late to drive an hour and a half after drinking. It just wasn't relevant anymore. Then one day, she met a guy. I was over the moon for her, even told her he seemed like a great guy, but for reasons completely unclear to me, she suddenly pulled away. From calling every day or two, and endless texting, I started noticing a chill from her side, a desperate lack of initiating contact. And I'm not one to push—if it's not a fit, it's not a fit. Sometimes people need space, need time to themselves, need distance from you. Especially when they're falling in love. But at some point, I realized she was pulling away completely. For me, it was the disappointment of the decade. If someone had told me six months earlier that this is how things will turn out, I would have told them they were not just delusional but in need of psychiatric observation and hospitalization. After about two months, it was my birthday, and she called me. We chatted—what's up, how's it going, love you, not love you—I just went with the flow. A birthday is no time for any negative energy. After about an hour, her cousin also called to wish me well, since we had gotten to know each other through her. "You need to understand, he doesn't know you," she suddenly said without me asking. That's when it all became clear. The truth is, I had already drawn the obvious conclusion earlier, but sometimes you don't really get it until someone spells it out for you. At first, I was disappointed—naturally, with him too. I mean, they're telling you that for a year and a half, there was nothing between us, and I don't want anything from her except for her happiness. So what do you think? That now that she has a boyfriend and is madly in love, she and I are suddenly going to do something we never did in the trillion opportunities we had? You dumb thug?? —And You totally let me down. If I were dating someone who told me to stay away from you, I'd tell her that you're important to me, that she has nothing to worry about, and if she doesn't trust me, then we have nothing to do together. Even if I didn't say it, I'd understand that she isn't intellectually developed enough for me to want a serious relationship with her. Later, I became worried about her. You should run from guys like that like the plague. Today you can't have male friends; tomorrow, they'll be reading about you in the newspaper. Of course I still love her and want her to be happy, but my heart is no longer red for her. It has a green, cool side that will never blush again. I thought that we were true friends, true love, that nothing could ever break the invisible bond between us. And this is how you give up on me? Disappear? You don't even fight over me? Not even taking to a conversation to explain? Nothing? Just 'die'?? What, did it make you uncomfortable? What, for fucks sake?! I gave you my heart on a silver platter, loved you like a sister, and at the crucial moment, when you needed to fight for me, you didn't. It doesn't matter if tomorrow you come and say all the right things, with all the right hugs and tears, because at the moment of truth, you made your choices. In the moneytime, when it mattered, you gave up on me. And I would never have given up on you. And for this disappointment, I might eventually forget and forgive, but my heart will not. My heart doesn't know how to pretend.

But Moran, I never gave her my heart and she let it down. It was there for her, waiting for her to come and take it, but to her credit, she never did. She never approached, nor even gave a glance like the one Indian vendors use to check if you're interested in buying something. Thus, I never had legitimacy to truly be disappointed in her. It's a person's right not to be interested in me. I can be angry, disheartened, even curse "May she die, amen," for daring not to give me even a sliver of a chance... but it's her right. And if my heart still glitters for her, shines when she looks my way, then it's only up to me and how much I allow myself to be a foolish, childish dreamer, for thinking otherwise from it. As if love is something you can control or emphasize, and then it will happen, if you really really try hard. 'I wanted something serious, and he was only after sex'. What does it matter that you wanted something serious? What's with that retarded line anyway?? It's entrenched phrases like these that keep the world stuck in the gender wars. Because *you* wanted serious. And why did you want something serious in the first place? Was it because after only one and a half meetings, you somehow sensed with your keen intuition that he was the knight of your life and the love of your dreams? Or was it simply because he was enough... something-that-fits-into-some preconceived-mold-in-your-head-and-come-one-let's-get-married-and-have-children-and-if-it-doesn't-work-out-at-least-you'll-pay-me-tons-of-financial-support? And maybe he did want something serious too, just not with you? Or maybe he did want something serious with you, but then you had an unpleasant odor from your vagina? Or maybe you had a delightful scent and were the most charming girl ever, but he simply didn't develop feelings for you? Huh? But if a man and a woman have slept together, and then he's not interested, he can never come out of it well. He's always the jerk and the asshole, and she's always the one who ends up 'hurt.' Even if he didn't tell her the real reason in order to avoid hurting her feelings and he's actually acting like the most honorable guy, it doesn't really matter. If a woman isn't interested in you, it's legitimate; if you're not interested, It hurts and insults. Women say they want equality and straightforwardness, but when they encounter them, they don't know how to behave. They always prefer the bullshit. To bullshit and to be bullshitted. For when you meet someone, there's always a chance you'll sleep together, but too often you hear that she's 'really not like that,' that 'there's no chance,' or 'don't expect anything to happen.' It's always some defensive and protective statement. 'Listen, I don't know what you're thinking, but I'm not one of those girls who goes home with you from the bar to have sex.' As if, unlike her, there are girls who come up to you and say, 'Oh, I'm glad I ran into you. So, listen up! I'm one of those girls who come home with you from the bar and want to have sex!'. Additionally, they don't take into consideration that we men have already heard these lines a million times, even from those we slept with on the first date. So, they just come out foolish. Either we'll sleep together or we won't, so what's with all the bullshit? 'I smiled at him, and he smiled back at me, and wait... what... does he want me seriously? Does he just want to get me into bed? Will he cheat on me?

It's known that men are a shitty lot. So I'll play hard to get! I'll be this, and that, and this, and that, and that, and especially not myself, the person he's trying to get to know.' It's same as with the sweet potato. Those who like sweet potatoes will love them, and those who don't, won't. But for those who do, they do. So let him know that you're a sweet potato!! With gay men, for example, there are apps for 'let's have sex in a minute and then you'll fuck off,' and no one gets hurt because everyone gets what they want. What's the element missing from their interactions? Women. They don't say one thing and mean another. For, you can't just walk to a woman and ask her directly if she wants you to fuck her and then she'll fuck off—zero women will say 'yes' to that question, even if it's exactly what they want. And since men have long understood that over-directness is a blessed recipe for lack of sex, they're forced to bullshit. They ask for a date. And then the woman thinks, "Oh, he's interested in me." After two or three dates, she "gives it up," and then he disappears because he got what he wanted. Then the woman says, "What a jerk," and when it happens a few more times, she thinks, "All men are jerks." But they're not jerks. They just don't have a way to be direct with women. Someone once told me that she actually wanted to sleep with a guy she was seeing, but it didn't happen because he didn't invest enough, didn't say enough, was only aiming for that, and so on. She doesn't sleep with whomever she wants; she sleeps with whomever deserves it! Why?? Is the guy who sweet-talked you, wined and dined you, better than the one who was direct and honest with you, and if you had been direct and honest with yourself, you would have slept with and enjoyed being with the one you really wanted? Just like in a wildlife documentary I once saw, featuring a Tasmanian devil—a type of marsupial—who approaches a female living in a tree hollow during the mating season. At first, she attacks him when he tries to enter, but after about half an hour, he returns with a bird in his mouth and is allowed inside. They then feast together and then fuck. We have women fighter pilots, heads of government, central bank governors, Supreme Court justices, and CEOs, but in sexuality, like a genetic flaw that refuses to fade, most women remain just like the most basic female animals in nature. Pay up—get laid, body for something clear-cut and one-to-one. In money time, women revert to their roots. When it comes to the crunch, the 'how' matters more to them than the 'what.' And even if you only went on one date and it wasn't right for you, you should at least send a text and 'be a man' because 'a girl needs that closure.' What's unclear about both sides not making contact and maintaining their mutual dignity, as if it's not right for either of them? What? Is she waiting by the phone? Crying perhaps? Unable to move on with her life without that 'closure' because you went on one fucking date?? And what about my closure?! Did anyone ever care about me when they flaked out on me with some ridiculously lame excuse or simply didn't respond? You set up a date with someone for the next day, and an hour before, you send a final confirmation message. Suddenly, she tells you she's made other plans because "you didn't talk to me today." "But we scheduled." "Yes, but you didn't talk to me today." But we scheduled!! So what does it actually mean that we scheduled?? What's the meaning of 'we scheduled'? Nothing?? That we scheduled tentatively?? Yes? Am I getting close? So what would it mean if we actually did schedule tentatively, that we didn't schedule at all?! How far can you go back with a woman's reasoning without falling into a pit? What causes a woman's brain to stubbornly refuse to act as a brain? I once scheduled with a girl who had a super-hot ass in her online photos to come over, and half an hour before she was supposed to arrive, she texts me she was running late because she was stuck with a private student, and maybe we should reschedule for next week since her student was a bit slow. I replied with "let him f^@$ off!" with a smiling emoji, as if it were part of a joke, and in the end she canceled and didn't even reply to another message I sent, and the next day she said it was totally not okay to say her student should fuck off, that it wasn't funny, and that it was offensive. Offensive! Me going out and buying two bottles of semi-dry white wine that she said she liked, ice cream and chocolate, cleaning up the whole house and myself, waiting like a dog on the couch while she didn't even respond to my messages— that's not offensive?! You fucking bitch, slut, piece of whore! So what do I care if you wanted something serious?! I once dated a girl for a year who was supposed to be the mother of all ultimate flings, and a bunch of 'serious' and 'respectable' girls who seemed perfect on paper didn't lead to anything. So what does it matter if he said he was serious or if he didn't say anything at all? Is he here now? Is it nice? That's it! Maybe tomorrow he'll die in a car accident, but right now, at this very moment, you're both looking at each other and sharing a smile— that's all there is to it! Don't ask questions now! And if it's not working out, then goodbye, no matter how much you wanted something serious or how much he said he was serious, the most serious, and only serious. And this complaint goes for both genders, of course. And to myself when I needed it. Moran never owed me anything. And even if we slept together a thousand times, it doesn't mean she has to develop feelings for me! Yes? Are you still with me? Because I myself have lost myself...

Perhaps Moran Dagan is right, was right all along, and I'm the immature, childish fool, in love to the point of disgrace like some baby. Maybe it really is time for me to grow up, to be a 'real man's man,' strong and tough, as they say. All the more so, as befits my masculine and Sisyphean profession. And maybe Moran Dagan is actually calculated like a senior lioness, knowing exactly what she needs to do and how. She's different, always steering the course, never led, the senior lioness. And perhaps Moran Dagan is simply different. Not bad, not good, just different. From the moment she landed in our elementary school, I felt she was some sort of an alien. On the other hand, that's how people from other schools always seem at first. Dressed differently, styled differently, an alien. Only with her, it lasted and didn't change. Always enigmatic, not deciphered. A riddle. And now I need to get out of the maze, stop thinking in my usual way, and for the first time in my life, stop thinking altogether. Let things happen as they will. Let it be. Believe in the good. Believe that things will be good. After all, what good does it do a person, even if they have problems, to be troubled by them? To be pessimistic instead of optimistic? If you're doing everything you can to fix and improve things, and not just sitting at home getting drunk and sorrowing over your fate, the result will inevitably be the same outcome—only you'll have lived your life feeling good and light rather than in stress and fear. Wrong. The result will actually be even better, and I say inevitably again, because the stress that causes almost all of our illnesses and problems—as the waiter of dreams told me—will inevitably decrease your productivity. For when you're relaxed, you're light. You breathe air. You're not trapped in your cave of fears.

Just as I thought of going back to 'The treasured past,' Moran made it clear to me that there's never any point in looking back—only forward. And now I must return like a humble, contented beggar to my room and be lighthearted. Not to pretend to understand what in the devils hell is going on here.

Here I am walking on this narrow path, which also serves as a pavement, leading from the main axis of Palolem to that stone gateway-like entrance descending to the sea. Suddenly, it feels as though all the Indian street vendors are watching me from the side, feeling pity for me and sending signals of love and kindness. They are good people, the Indians. They can sense and feel you. Full of emotion and compassion. A truly special nation. Another small step and behold the waves unfold before my eyes. Those waves that have seen it all and will see so much more than we ever will. We think we're so special, so important, that our opinions matter so much, and that it's worth arguing and standing firm because we're right! But the waves... they just keep flowing and rolling, looking at you without even blinking. Tomorrow, there will be another one like you, and another, and another, and so on, endlessly. People who thought, who argued and debated, who discussed and fought. And for what? None of it will last. The Romans of today are not the Romans of the past, just as Mexicans are not Aztecs and Egyptians are not Pharaohs. But the waves, they remain. They are the same waves. Flowing. Unfazed. "Grab a board and join us," they seem to whisper. Everything else is nonsense.

Now that I come to think of it—against my will of course—it somehow makes sense. For reasons of convenience and all. And also since we're traveling, so a bit of sex is just right. And also, they've been together before, so... honestly, it's even somewhat called for. And Arik's wife is cool with the 'what happens abroad—stays abroad' in a quiet sort of way. That's how they are. Both of them. Abroad, questions aren't asked. And I'm on board with it. But because I'm in love now, I secrete the hormone of misunderstanding. Like... how can you know if someone isn't possibly screwing your wife right now while she's on a trip with a friend in New York? Just a casual shopping trip, you thought. But I get it. They've been married for several years... And I'm on the hormone... So it makes sense. What's certain is that I'm never touching her again. I know I'm supposed to be a man now, strong and cool and a carpenter. I take a log, saw it, and carve it into furniture. I work with my hands, I've got goddamn bulging veins in my arms, more pronounced than a dozen black guys' dicks in a blue movie combined. The last thing anyone could say about me is that I'm a crybaby... But with Moran, I just can't manage it. Next to her, I guess I'll always be that eleven-year-old kid, standing mute in the school gymnasium, wearing new clothes from Holland and glittering shoes in all sorts of colors.

Here I stand once more, perhaps now cast in the role of the women from eras past, before revolutions and bra burnings. The one without even the right to vote, who swallowed her dignity and dreams for the sake of her husband. Her owner, whom she obeyed from the dawn of time, as dictated 'from on high'. Her sole joy lay in sewing curtains and cooking for the children, her only hope that her master would cherish her. Uneducated and confined, her world was a narrow realm of ignorance, warmth, and love. Now was I that tear-stained woman from the shadowed annals of the past. Devoid of rights and hope, nor shall her sobs at night be told. So was I, so shall my cry, be left untold.

15

When Moran was eleven, just a week before her birthday, which fell close to the Hanukkah party they were celebrating at her new school, her mother gave her a gift. It was an old, unwashed sock, but it still carried a faint scent of delicate herbs. It was brown, with a red tip. "This belonged to your Grandmother," Mrs. Dagan said, "actually, to your Grandmother's mother. She gave it to her before... before..." And so, Mrs. Dagan told her eldest daughter the story of the sock that was never returned.

After the story with the Primus stove, the guys opened up, grew closer, enjoying each other's company. And our explorer, let's call him Fatelique, was still in love with the village head's daughter, the renowned virgin throughout the kingdom, from the sea to Aram Naharaim.

"Laaa..." the singing waiter told him. "It's not gonna happen. The village head, well... that's an honorable match. Only from a respectable family. Maybe royalty." Legend has it there was even talk of the son of the King of Jordan. One day, he will inherit his father's throne, and what more does a king need than a stunningly beautiful wife to flaunt? And our explorer, let's call him Fatelik, was still in love with the village headman's daughter, the most renowned virgin in all the kingdom, from the sea to Aram-Naharaim.

"Nooo," the singing waiter told him. "It won't work. The headman, it's... a dignified match. Only a respectable family. Maybe royalty." Legend has it there were even talks about the son of the King of Jordan. One day he'd inherit his father, and what does a king need more than a stunning wife to flaunt? That's how things were back then. Some would say nothing has changed to this very day. And what about the girl's mouth? No one even dared to ask. But she asked. She didn't want. And the village head, how could he kill her in the name of family honor? For even if he could, everyone already knew of the shame. His name would be tarnished. A devastating blow. And the British Sir, well, maybe it's not such a terrible idea after all. One thing led to another, a meeting was arranged. A highly secret and confidential meeting between the Sir and the royal. The village head dispatched an elder uncle to convey and negotiate. And surely he did—guiding the talk with elder wit and grace, setting the pace.

"Half the land," he said without Batting an eye or a wink.

"What??" the sir exclaimed. "That's not even mine to decide! How, but... what?"

"Ya nus il ard ya ma basqir aishi," the Arab ruled, marking with his right hand on his left. Half the land. Or no deal.

And so the meeting came to an end. "Fash ash ansawi," nodded the intermediary, that singing waiter, in surrender. "There's nothing I can do," he said to the sir, who was beside himself. After all, the land was not his to decide, and there was no doubt in his heart that he would not give up on that beloved one. In secret, they met several times, completely risking her life! For if this were to be revealed, the daughter of the tribe was neither a virgin nor married! Even God Himself could not change the fate that would inevitably arise from such disgrace. But she loved the sir. A love she never knew she could feel. With him, she found happiness, freedom—she discovered her heart's true treasure! And he? He would have given all of Great Britain, including Scotland, Ireland, and Australia for her. And what

would they do now? Where would they go? They would go!
Suddenly, the answer leaped into their hearts. They would
simply run away from here and never return. And so it was.
The English were in control of the land, with their weapons
and full army, and the village head, no matter how great, he
still wouldn't risk that big of a conflict. And the great
kingdom? It would manage without him, without that
wayward soldier who had deserted. One night, as arranged,
she sneaked into a nearby truck, and he was already waiting
for her inside under the many bare old army 'scabies'
blankets that lay in a jumble. Sure, he waited. He waited all
night long in the biting cold that gripped the Jezreel
Valley—the closest thing that sounded like Israel and a state
these days—that, thanks to the fairly good road connecting
the coastal plain to the Jordan Valley, was part of the
continuation of the ancient 'Way of the Sea,' a route that had
existed since the Bronze Age, linking the two great empires
of Egypt and Mesopotamia.

And she came. Escaped. The singing waiter might pay
for it with his life, but the money the sir gave him would
ensure a good future for his family and even his
grandchildren. At that time, before everyone wanted only to
fulfill themselves, that was enough for him. Only her mother
did she tell. And even that was an hour before she left
forever. There was no other option. The mother simply
kissed her and embraced her. Her eldest daughter. Her
senior partner in the silent alliance among those deprived of
rights and choices. For an hour, she simply stroked her face
and kissed her. They both wept and cried for a whole hour.
Parting forever in the name of love. Nothing was harder for
the mother, but she wanted what was best for her daughter.
Just one thing she asked. 'Take this,' she pushed it into her
bra. 'One day, send me this sock. Only then will I know for
sure that you're okay, that you're alive, ya binti!' There were

no phones back then, of course. Barely a radio—and that was only because the father was the head of the village. Regular electricity was out of the question. 'Ana bawaidak, yama!' she vowed, promised and kissed with fervor. Tears flowed freely as she tenderly traced her mother's damp cheeks, kissing and kissing and kissing. At the stroke of midnight, a soft knock echoed at the door.

‛Cigarette?’ Arik asked as I returned. 'No, bro, thanks. Just going to shower. Hey, what's up?'I gave Moran a kiss on the cheek and stepped inside, defeated and humiliated yet smiling on the outside, perhaps managing to hide my feelings like a seasoned Georgian taxi driver. Well, the truth is I ran away pretty fast, but step by step. It's not good or possible to jump from one extreme to another without falling into the abyss in between. As I showered, I noticed a condom in the trash. Not mine. Moran and I had been together without a condom. In the background, I could vaguely hear them laughing while my stomach tightened. Moran and I had been without any form of protection, and she hadn't mentioned any pills. I also hadn't seen her taking any here and there. Usually, I spot those little pills of theirs, and I was certain I had came inside because I really didn't care, how shall I say, to solidify our relationship forever. Who even thought about it? Who could think about anything when your biggest dream, something you never imagined could ever come true, comes to life right before your eyes after thirty years of earthquake debris piling on top of it?

The beach in Goa is nice. Pleasant. We arrived at a place called Palolem. November. Just before the season kicks in and tourists start flooding in. Arik said this is the best time to travel because it doesn't yet feel like a semester break in Thailand. Suddenly, right in the middle of the sunshine, rain. A downpour. Monsoon? The Indians say it's the effect of the cyclone swirling somewhere to the south. Did you just say Cyclone? One that blows away houses and everything around?? God forbid. What is there for us to complain? Back home at worst it rains heavily, and even that, once in a long while... People live with typhoons, erupting volcanoes. Volcanoes! Cyclone! What is there for us to complain?

"The cows try to find shelter, to take cover. The Indians, who normally treat them with reverence, shoo them away from shop entrances with sticks. No risks taken. Store oversight takes precedence over Sabbath observance, even that of Shiba. Bom Shankar. I couldn't quite grasp what was tradition here and what was just nonsense. Probably, I'll never understand. And perhaps it's all just one big mix-up. Like in ours, like in everyone's. The weak seek to believe in something that will save them from their unfortunate fate when the time comes, while the relatively wealthy also seek divine assistance to preserve the status quo, hoping to maintain their vast wealth, or they thank Him for the good He has bestowed upon them. One day I asked an Indian guy I met who seemed educated and from a high status why is the issue of caste is so strong there, why is it felt so acutely. After all, India has a truly feudal system. Castes. You're born into a certain social class, and you can't escape it. The high are above, the low are below. Hard to believe, but even in the twenty-first century, there's a class that's actually called the 'untouchables.' Oh, yeah. Gandhi did call them the 'children of God,' but that hasn't changed the fact that it's forbidden to touch them or get close to them, and they exist in a class that essentially has no status. Not to mention the rape and abduction of women—more accurately, girls—

who have no chance of receiving justice if the perpetrators are from a higher caste.

There's the damn cleaner again, scuttling around underfoot. Come on, move! Can't you see I'm sitting here, crossing my legs like a woman, my balls getting crushed alongside my 'fuck-me-in-the-ass-Elton-John-glasses' and my slicked-to-the-side-picture-perfect-hairdo, just like the shirt? The pants are white, and maybe the shoes too. Hell, they might even be crocodile leather. And he's the CEO of some goddamn fuck-me-in-the-ass-nonsense, some bullshit invention that some mega-swindler sold to some investment fund. Fuck you, you sweater-wearing son of a bitch! Wanking off to cans…Move, give this poor guy a break. He's been working since five in the morning, after sleeping in a room with four others, no plaster, no putty, no paint. Let him pass with the broken broom and dustpan they gave him in order to break his back a bit more. That's who you're tough on? Big boss man? Do you bark at your investors and company owners too, or do you just whimper like a little poodle, just as white as your disgusting sweater? Fucking asshole…Be a man and get up, let him pass and even say sorry, please, or thank you. Let him feel like a human being for a moment! Benny once had a bar, a small place in the Krayot area. One day, I was there just before closing, jumping in for a beer with him after a failed date while he was counting the money. One of his partners was there too, along with a girlfriend he had. Suddenly, while we were sitting there, engrossed in our own matters as the staff wrapped up, one of the cleaners, who was of African descent, asked if he could have a soda. Just a can of coke, like you can do a hundred times a day if you feel like it. But then, the partner's girlfriend chimed in from the height of her wisdom, "Why soda? Let him drink water." It just slipped out without anyone asking her or even thinking to consult about it. I remember we all looked at her in amazement. But it just came out automatically. And Benny, what the fuck does he care? Let him have a soda. But for her, it just didn't register. For he was born in Africa, so he should drink water like a dog. Maybe we should just pour him the dirty water from the mop and let him lick the floor, because why waste a glass on that half-person who came to clean and is barely making twenty Shekels? Who cares what happens to him or how many other jobs he has to juggle just to get by? Just let him be gone already, with that stench of his. Give him a moment to feel that he's not just garbage, and then toss your white sweater with the embroidered braids to the trash. White sweater isn't cool. But he certainly didn't look like the type to get rid of it; and even gave a convoluted explanation. "First," he said, "if both of us had nothing but fifty rupees, and he spent it on beer and since then is working as a waiter for fifty rupees an hour, and I bought a notebook and studied, then while he was sitting there with a beer in hand, laughing at me while I was destitute, so now let him serve me for fifty rupees. The second explanation is karmic. Indians believe that someone who is destitute has done bad deeds in this life or a previous one, and that's why karma is chasing them. The wealthy, on the other hand, are in their position because they deserve it karmically. The rich also don't want the poor's bad karma to rub off on them, so they treat the poor with distance. Oh, well...

Meanwhile, the rain had stopped. We finished breakfast and decided to head down to the beach. Moran said she needed to go up to the room for a moment, and we figured it was a girl thing, so we didn't ask questions. We spread out a lounger. I didn't mind sitting in the deck chairs with the umbrellas, but Arik said he wanted to relax a bit, like back home. We strolled along the beach until we spotted a few people lying on loungers, so we set up nearby. It quickly became clear that we were next to a couple of tourists and a group of Israelis. How did it become clear? Because the Israelis were playing some supposedly Middle-Eastern singer with supposedly deep lyrics that everyone recited and praised, even though, at least in my humble opinion, it was complete nonsense. But she was belting it out. The singer sang better than she did, to be honest, but she was shouting the words at the top of her lungs. I was thinking about what's going through the minds of these tourists. I mean, I've never encountered a couple of tourists blasting music and shouting, let's say, in Finnish for illustration. I closed my eyes and hoped she'll shut up soon enough. She doesn't. It's really tempting to get up, smack her hard, grab the speaker, and toss it into the sea, not before smashing it violently on the ground and kicking it fiercely. "Should we move somewhere else?" I ask Arik. "No, what? Does it bother you?" he replies, hidden under his hat and sunglasses. Him, he's oblivious to everything. Back home he has a billion things on his mind—business, kids, wife. Here, he's lying on the beach, smoking hash and getting laid. Just a moment ago, he smoked a joint, and Moran gave him her ass, which was wide open for him, and he eagerly took her in a wild rush. How long has it been since he's been in a scene like this? So he doesn't give a fuck about anything at all. An Indian woman passes by, asking for the millionth time if we want to "come to her shop." "Buy one ting, yes? Yes, mister?" I blink in refusal. The girl next to us continues to scatter words, but now it's old-school rock. She's still wailing at full volume, raising her arms in a victorious gesture. The fellas next to her appear to be in a light slumber. Am I the only one hearing her? The Indian woman stops to look at her. "Hey, sir," she seizes the chance since I glanced her way, "Any nice jewelry?" Honestly, this particular one is getting really annoying. You just turn your gaze in her direction—boom! She pounces on you. Even if she's already asked you a hundred times today. For her, half a percent chance is better than nothing. Where else does she have to go? But as annoying as the Indians hawkers can be, urging you to buy something, it still doesn't come close to the perfume saleswomen at drugstores. What's going on with you all, for heaven's sake?! Who at the academy for perfume sales decided that harassing customers was the way to go?? And what's the end result? That I'm not nice to them! Me, Haggai from Fatel, light, brotherhood, and love, behaving unpleasantly toward someone, and I'm not even to blame! "No, I'm fine," I reply, trying not to avoid their gaze. Sometimes I don't even take my eyes off the perfume shelf because I can sense out of the corner of my eye—or even the corner of my mind—that in just a few hundredths of a millisecond, someone's going to pounce on me with a question. So I pretend to be focused and don't even look. It's something I've automatically developed after years of psychotic harassment by perfume saleswomen. Why do you jump on me in two-point-four seconds, you Ben Johnson on speed?! Let me look around, search for my perfume, or something new, and if I can't find it, I'll come to you. I see that you're here. You're here! Do you hear me? YOU! ARE! HERE! We both know it, we both understand it. We also know how it works if I want perfume, just like all the other salespeople in every other field who don't pounce on customers know how it works. "Excuse me, do you work here?" — "Yes, can I help you?" That's it! We all know, we're all skilled at it. Rest assured - Y O U W I L L N O T G O U N N O T I C E D ! ! !

Ah... well, I got it out of the system. Is it nerves? Resentment? Typical ginger traits? Do I feel bad? Am I frustrated? The Charas in India, although it's considered relatively low-grade here in Goa compared to the stuff from

Rasol and Malana up north, messed with our heads. Suddenly, we're less cheerful, each of us caught up in our own thoughts, annoyed about something. The body, craving the substance again and again, won't give us a break. Of course it's not the effects of cocaine or heroin, and maybe that's the problem. The effects are there, but you just don't notice them, don't give them any importance. It's definitely not that; it's just a joint. No stoner will ever agree that their habit has destructive effects on their life. They're addicted—addicted to the most insidious drug of all. It has its winning qualities, but it comes at a price: pessimism, passivity, insecurity. It feels like just another cigarette, certainly not an act of a junkie like sniffing or shooting up. Just a joint. And don't get me wrong, weed can be an awesome thing. It calms you, releases you, is an excellent pain reliever; you don't press your brain and thus let the universe allow things to happen. It's no wonder millions of people around the world have consumed it for ages. But I'm talking about being enslaved to something—dependent on it, addicted to it. Then, this wonderful thing—becomes a drug. But good luck convincing a girl that her nerves are because of her period. It'll sound terrible, and ultra-feminists will surely compare it to the yellow star from the Holocaust. But I genuinely believe that if women on their periods wore some red collar or something, millions of mental anguishes could be avoided every day around the world. 'Why is she acting like a lunatic? Oh, she's on her period...'. Well, maybe a collar is excessive, but... how about a bracelet? An earring? Some other thing? An india bindi?? "Has nothing to do with it I'm telling you!!!" But it has. For sure. I see what's going on. Suddenly, Arik makes a face at something, Moran heads to the sea alone for hours and barely comes back. Only in the evening, when we all sit together on the terrace overlooking the sea and smoke, do we all calm down. The holy grail we've been waiting for has arrived. I know I have to get this out of here, to rid us of this wicked deed. Only then we'll be able to go back to being... amm... well...

And perhaps it's part of learning to surrender. And honestly, how can you not? I look to the left—just sea and rocks. To the right—coconut palm trees towering into the distance and vast patches of water rushing in from the sea. It's peaceful here on the beach of Palolem. Calm. My mind is a bit occupied, but I'm starting to settle in. 'Saloly, saloly', 'India time,' as the locals say. 'Shanti baba.' Everything will come to you. Just relax. Don't think. Don't think about anything. Not even about Moran's face moaning in pleasure as Arik handles things from behind, thrusting and withdrawing in rhythm. Not even that. Though the image flickers constantly in my mind, I try to forget. To suppress it. Something new is starting to develop in my head. A new thought. I take another sip of the black coffee they served me here, a kind of American filtered coffee with an Indian aroma. Surprisingly tasty. To my left, a girl sits alone, drinking a local beer and fiddling with her cellphone. There's Wi-Fi in every restaurant, so no problem there. She's been at it for an hour, not lifting her head even a little. Just lift it, even a bit. Maybe you'll see something. Maybe you'll notice. Maybe you'll see me too, sitting here just like you. Not alone, but still lonely. Trying to push away my nagging thoughts. And maybe she has her own nagging thoughts that she's trying to drown within the depths of the device. Shanti baba, I keep on telling myself, shanti baba.

I hit play on my playlist through my phone. It's on shuffle, so songs flow randomly without any order or choice. And suddenly she sang. Playing with that delicate strumming on the guitar, she sang "Little Girl Blue." In that moment, with the earbuds snug in my ears, I finally understood Janis Joplin and why so many people loved her.

Why her darkness and melancholy felt like light to the soul for so many—a beacon at the end of the tunnel, guiding you toward a deeper consciousness. Suddenly, I felt she truly understood me, singing just for me. Janis, who passed away over forty years ago, through parallel worlds and galaxies, I now know she still exists, beating alive and singing just for me right now. Especially for me. I swear, in that instant, I realized someone out there truly understands me and embraces me. Here I am, Hagai the carpenter from Fatel—I am Little Girl Blue.

16

After about half an hour, Moran joined us. It was supposed to feel strange, but it didn't. Maybe I'd let something go. When the world crumbles, you stop caring about anything. But before we could enjoy her company, some tourist showed up and started talking to her. *"You damn slut..."* my inner bad boy, the wounded and offended one from way back, began muttering. But I didn't say a thing. And neither did Arik. He just smoked his cigarette in silence. He's married and all... I mean, what? Is she his girlfriend now? But she and the tourist were talking about his club in Australia, how he really loves her music, and supposedly knows it, dying for her to come perform there sometime. To her credit, she made sure to say *"totally"* or *"yeah, right"* in Hebrew every so often, just so we'd know she was still with us and not with him. *Dude, don't you get that she's not interested? You're not even circumcised, and your dick is probably gross, so would you mind just getting the hell out of here already?!* the child I used to be kept on ranting. "So..." He finally broke eye contact with Moran and asked out loud, "Drinks?". "Of course!" We all answered together. We ended up walking him back to his room. All in all, a nice guy trying his luck, I concluded with the alcohol slightly numbing my frayed nerves. Then he sort of turned toward her and whispered something, and I gave her space and stepped back. If you want him—go with him. If you want me—come with me. And she came. After a bit of polite small talk, she kissed him on the cheek, though he aimed for her lips and even tried to grab her, the cheeky bastard. Well, let's be honest, we'd all been drinking, so it's somewhat understandable. But she turned him down with that charming smile, tilting her face away, threw in a couple of words, he replied with a few more, and tried again. Then she allowed a brief brush of lips, as sight would have it, which almost made me explode, but that was it. Alright, she handled it well enough. No need for drama. Goa. Shanti Baba.

We smoked a joint the tourist pulled out, since it felt rude to say "no" twice in one minute, and said our goodbyes. And now what? Should I tell her I've been in love with her since I was eleven? And if so, should it be serious and heartfelt, or should I lace it with humor? Should I Just throw it out casually as if it's nothing, risking that she might dismiss it like just another Arik or a tourist with an explicit uncut dick? What do I do with that now? Sometimes in the haze of being stoned, you do something you're sure you would have done if you weren't high. So I decided to just ask her. Damn it, how long am I supposed to wait to open up everything with her, until we're sixty? I'm going all in like in poker, double or nothing—there's nothing to lose. And she explained to me that with Arik it wasn't really planned at all, since he's married she hadn't even thought about it, and she even told him it wasn't appropriate because she knew his wife and all, but since his wife isn't a real Fatel, and Moran is always abroad anyways and unlikely to cross paths with her and he also swore that they were living an 'abroad everything is fine' kind of way, and that in a twisted sort of way, her subconscious will even be a bit pleased to know it was her and not just some random tourist with AIDS, syphilis, hepatitis—because, of course, those tourists are probably parading around like walking health hazards across the world—then it happened. And lasted a bit longer than they expected, and then they cut it off because it didn't feel right. Like, what, there was something between them, and now what? Are they remembering it? Is something surfacing? Perhaps in his mind? Is he getting paranoid about me? In short, it feels less suitable. And then this tourist with his alleged club in Australia started hitting on her at the beach, babbling about how he was an artist, and wait—she's an artist too—and "Wow, you must come see my art," or whatever the fuck. But Long story short, they didn't hook up because he's not circumcised, and that totally grosses her out. Surprisingly, that detail actually made me feel a bit better, despite the image that rose in my mind, which kind of repulsed me. So great! So basically, she's not a slut; she's... she's a person. And that suits me way better than a slut. For no one wants to be in love with a slut, That is why we play games, of course. What, am I gonna lick her ass on the first date? Am I a creep? A pervert?? Am I fucking disgusting?! She's gonna 'let you have it' on the second date? That's way too soon. What, is she gonna let you shove your dick down her throat the first time and come in her mouth or on her face, with everything dripping down the frames of her glasses while she makes hurt faces of a damaged clay doll? What, is she a whore?

"So, like...? You're cool like this?" I asked as we walked back to where Arik was left on the beach, probably already back to napping in our shared bed that I now call mother of all sins, the land of sun and moon, light and coveted evil.

"Like this? How, like this?" she wondered, giving me an unreadable look—definitely not defiant, but not amused either. Apathetic? Something like that.

"You know, like..." Oh, aiming to be apathetic. Yeah, that's it.

"I think so," she laughed. Damn you, fucking little whore! For a moment that kid inside me who'd one day become a carpenter, pushed aside the hidden child buried deep within my Hanukkah spirit. I laughed too. After all, we were stoned.

"Ah-ah... I get it," she laughed her royal laugh, which sounded particularly devilish and unusual to me right now. "I had fun, yeah. And you?"

And me??? And me???? You whore! You fucking whore! You slut! You piece of slutty whore! Yells that crazed kid again. You royal piece of filth from another land... a piece of... muck... that God himself sent to me from the fires of hell...... I've been in love with you my whole life, you... like...

"But... How is it possible? I mean... to live like this?" I asked, completely dry and lost.

"I don't know..." she blinked, and her smile faded a bit. "How can one live any other way?"

Well, we always knew there was something different about Moran Dagan. How can anyone live differently? Well, everyone lives differently! I mean, I know a few like, swingers... I have one friend who is one of those with his wife, but that sounds terrible to me. On the other hand, he and his wife have four kids, and according to him, they have sex every day. From my many years of knowing them and frequent visits to their home, they have a house full of light and love. It sounds strange, but... is it weirder than having to sleep with the same person your entire life, even if you really, really love, respect, and appreciate them? What is a relationship, at its most basic and fundamental level? A couple choosing to be together. Two entities. Not two people becoming one, not two halves completing each other. And that's what everyone forgets. With the immense gravitational force of Hollywood, we've turned relationships into a kind of communism or fascism, if you will, where the good of the system is above the good of the individual. No, the individual is always above the system. Because only if each individual is well—will the system function. Now what's the messed-up thing about all this? That in addition to a value system, we also have a system of needs. And one primary and basic need in that system is sex. The need to get laid. To fuck someone's brains out, for someone to fuck your brains out. To shove your dick down her throat, to cum in her mouth, on her face, on her tits, on her ass, on her belly, on her feet, on her pussy... Aside from maybe the knees, I've heard it all. And all of a sudden to get some new dick, or in the ass, or have someone go down on you and lick the core depths of your beautiful ass, and let everyone know how beautiful it is, to let someone whip, tie you up or just hit you, or even simulate rape... The thing is, most of the stuff listed above is a bit hard to implement after ten years of marriage and three kids. Thank goodness we have sex once or twice a week because we swore at least to keep that up. And once every month and a half, an unexpected—even—exciting—sex—miracle miraculously happens. Or maybe during a trip abroad or a vacation—whether it's without the kids. So you have to do it with a different partner! But wait a minute, hey... we swore. I swear to you that we swore. The moment this love enters the realm of fulfillment, we discover there's a price tag we didn't expect. It's unavoidable. It clashes with the concept of partnership and the idea of dad, mom, family. So we're all living a lie. Ninety percent of the world's population is sexually frustrated. Living in self-castration. With a constant suspicion hanging over us—"Where have you been?" "Where are you going?". How many times have you asked that question in the past year? In the past month? In the past week? And why is it even supposed to be asked? Did we come here to live a lie and deceive? To constantly trick the person who matters most to us aside from our kids? But... but I need it! I'm horny! I need excitement... conquest... something! Why do you think the dog keeps coming to the table and begging? Pouncing at something that falls on the floor or that he suddenly finds on a walk, while we yell at him "What are you doing?!" and "No! No!! Bad dog!!"? But he's not a bad dog; he's a good dog. He watches over us at every moment and would throw himself in front of a drawn knife for us without having a one hundredth split second of a thought. He just does it because he has to. He can't keep eating that same dog food, even if it's with rabbit fat and salmon, he can't! He eats it every day. Every day, and preferably even just once a day according to some damn veterinarians who decided that this is the healthiest for him. Fuck you that it's the healthiest—he wants to live! Enjoy the food! Enjoy life! Do *you* eat only healthy stuff all day?! You fat fuck who shoves shawarma with extra fat and fried eggplants into your mouth and smokes two packs of Marlboro red? It's also really healthy for you to have three proper meals a day and run ten kilometers twice a week. And you, who steals chocolate rolls from the drawer at work even though you've been on a "diet" for five years, it's also healthier for you without bread and sweets, snacks, munchies, and ice cream and chocolate before bed, you mister and missus ass fuckers! But the important thing is that the dog, with his poor fifteen years he has, will live a life of excellent health. Give the dog some meat, you assholes!! So when there's a glimmer of a chance for something else—he charges at it. Doesn't think twice. He eats and that's it, and now screw you. Yell as much as you want, you sons of bitches, giving me the same damn Iams for five years... The only difference between us and our dog is that the dog is exposed. He shits in front of us, pees, fucks if he can, and eats in secret. We say everything is fine while rubbing on a porn where two 6.5 feet black guys are banging a tiny blonde eighteen-and-a-second-year old while another one is choking her with his enlarged cucumber and simultaneously slaps her in order for her to show how much she's enjoying it, or two bodies-enhanced-by -surgery-girls-sex-dolls-alike eating each other's after- bleaching-shines-like-a-pearl-butt-holes... And then everything's fine. Look at us, a loving couple. We have three kids, and just yesterday we celebrated our tenth anniversary since the wedding, kissing in public. Charming, really charming. Right this minute, a stunning lady is sitting at home, maybe even someone very famous whom half the world would love to go down on for hours on end without stopping. But in reality, her husband has already done her thoroughly and from all angles and they only get intimate at most twice, in a 'good' week. Now explain to me how this isn't a market failure... but no! It's betrayal! We swore...

And how can we sustain a relationship with all this progress? With this 'not enough' feeling? You still love her and know she loves you too, but something beyond the sex—which is, of course, the tangible marker and thus the most obvious—something about this 'pen' isn't healthy for us anymore. It leads to too much anger between people. Hostility. Resentment. Hatred. And all of this in the name of love? For, after all, we both still yearn for and need love. Crave love. Crave a relationship. Crave a family. Crave sex. And sex with someone you've slept with two hundred times is as exciting as eating porridge for a holiday meal. And don't let anyone tell you those stories like, 'It gets better with time, bro, you learn what she likes, she learns what you like...' with that dumb grin. What does she even like? Having fingers shoved up her ass mid-action? Or wait, sorry, maybe that's what you like, but a strap-on is only for real gays, right? And after you've both 'discovered' what the other likes—wow—and done it two hundred thousand times— enough already! You're turned on just imagining that woman in front of you in the supermarket line suddenly reaching back and grabbing your dick, feeling your pants, then glancing back with her tongue out. Even if your wife is a hundred times hotter. Am I right?? And you, too, dying for some 18-year-old Peruvian native to give you forty centimeters of dick on your girls' trip to Thailand. Ahhhhh... how long has it been since you had a dick like that... Ahhhhh!

In all of us, there's that spark, but most of us don't let it roam free. One of the most enjoyable things nature has given us is the pleasure of each other's bodies. Some love tall women, others prefer thin, some like curvy, and some go for men. And admit it, you've never had or enjoyed sex like you do when you're fantasizing. Oh, yes... that's where you... wow. That's where you really let go. Licking the insides of her ass, cumming on her face, maybe even a couple of vaginas enter the scene, maybe a dick or two, but you cum like you never do in the 'real world.' Because in the real world, you have to be responsible and act like an adult. Someone once told me that he'd never finish on his wife's face, even though he loves it and has done it with plenty of other girls throughout his life. But heaven forbid he tarnish the pure and innocent face of his wife, because he respects her. So why did you want her in your bed every day, you stupid fuck, just to hold back?! But he's not to blame; that's how he was raised. And so became sex—or eroticism, to be exact—the leading cause of relationship breakdowns in this world. For what is more erotic than the unknown, the hidden, the revelation? This is likely why most affairs occur with people nearby, making the whole situation incredibly ugly. But it's not out of malice; it happens out of necessity. People don't fantasize about the actors in porn films; they fantasize about those they know. This is simply because they are already familiar with them, have already interacted with them, having seen how they look into each other's eyes and what those eyes have said or hinted at at some point. During one of my strolls with Arik on that trip to Amsterdam, we wandered through the red-light district, each with a joint in our mouths, as hot girls pressed their asses against the display windows as we passed by. It's clear that besides the money, they also want to get laid by a handsome guy; they're human, after all. Across the way stood some seventy-year-old German guy, with a blonde towering at six feet tall on one side, looking every bit German, and on the other side, a short, dark-skinned woman. He was giving them instructions alternately. We were outside and didn't really hear, but it was definitely something like, "You tie me up here, and then you fuck me with the dildo, and afterward, I'll lick both your pussies and ass while you piss on me and punch me in the head. Hard as hell though you hear? You hear that, you whore?!". Suddenly, I notice a girl from the other side standing an inch away, telling me, "I'll let you fuck me, suck you, fuck me, suck you, let you fuck me." She repeated it so many times, so close that somehow I find myself following her up the stairs, while Arik is in total shock, knowing I never go to hookers. But once inside, she asks for fifty euros, settles me in the light on some bed with a rubber mattress, plastic covering under the sheets, and comes to suck me off with a condom. I got up straight away and left. There's no story here, nothing interesting. It didn't do anything for me, even though she was a knockout. I couldn't even see her body. I'm dying to fuck my friend, the interior designer, who's desperate to get divorced but paralyzed by fear— a hundred times over. She's from Beit She'an, clinging to an old-fashioned mindset, even though I can see she's a total slut in bed. But coming from Morocco—or wherever the hell—she wouldn't dream of cheating on her husband. And as much as I respect that, there's no escaping it. Our connection has deepened over the two years she's sent me work; we've become more than just colleagues, we're tight friends. We talk about everything, sharing laughs and secrets, talking on the phone. And I'm dying to fuck her senseless because we have this deep familiarity, and I want to penetrate her essence. I want to show her how much she turns me on as a person with my cock burried deep inside her, and right in the middle of doggy style, she'll turn her head back to me, overwhelmed by how good it feels, our bodies pressed together, making it clear that at this very moment — I'm fucking her. So I picture myself gripping her by the neck, my hand sliding down to tease her through her pants, and then she's in nothing but her black lace panties and bra—wait, no, pink. Pink. Damn... But that's the core of the fantasy—its tantalizing potential to become reality. Even if it's on a very, very distant level, the chance must exist. That's what amplifies it and drives us to grip our genitals tight. How I ache for my intern to walk into my office one day, lock the door behind him while signaling 'shh' with his finger at my slightly stunned gaze. He'll approach me and then unzip his tailored pants, and just like in every respectable 'romantic' novel, pull out a massive cock while I'm wide-eyed and probably protesting the situation and slide it into my mouth, pushing it all the way down my throat as I choke, drool spilling from the corners of my lips. Then he'll lift me onto the desk, hoist my legs up, and after licking my high heels, he'll greedily suck my entire vagina into his mouth for half an hour straight, then leave me like that and walk away. How I wish to walk into my apprentice's room, pick her up, turn her, knock her hard from behind, and end up cumming on her ass while everything's dripping in her squirt and leg while she goes back to grading exams... Every now and then there is a story in the news about a teacher who was arrested because she had sex with her student. It's forbidden! Obviously, if that's why his grades are up then it's a little beside the point, but except for this unfortunate fact... I wish some teacher had opened up new worlds for me at sixteen! What could possibly happen? That I'd come out fucked up? Scarred forever? I got fucked up and scarred forever anyway. I once heard a quote from a football coach in Argentina. He was offered to coach the national team, and his response was: 'the national team is like a fourteen-year-old girl — you can't say no to her.' Fourteen! And no headline screamed 'pervert, rapist, or pedophile.' It's fun to have sex — so they have sex. But they are considered a third-world country. They take siestas in the middle of the day, are allowed to sleep around with everyone, and we call them primitive. Go ahead, say it. It will help ease your conscience for at least a couple of seconds. Do you know how many girls told me that at the age of fourteen she 'blew her big brother's friend'? Or slept with her father's best friend at the age of eighteen? And that's before any eleven-year-old had a phone and in one click she sees four black dudes fucking an eight-hundred-CC silicone Trans woman from four directions... But the political correctness conformism has other plans. You're in your forties and attracted to someone who is only eighteen? Pervert! That's... that's just unacceptable! For... for... for she's just a child and you're taking advantage of her! Even if she's done laser in her pussy at sixteen and masturbates seventeen times a day on the laptop in the room with the handle of the comb smeared with K-Y gel and that her father was dying to fuck no-matter-which-of-her-girlfriends-that-are-walking-around-the-house-in-shorts-and-sprouting-tities-emerging-from-fourteen-year-old-at-best... What I am saying to fuck, he would love to shower them and lick their whole bodies, including the pussy and the asshole, for two hours straight, and then dress them in Pluto nightgowns—not before licking their whole bodies again with emphasis on the pussy and the hole of their asses a thousand more times, and each of them has a fantasy that some friend of their dad's will do something to them that they're not quite sure what it is, but it really makes them scratch in the depths of their peepee when they think about it at night while they can't fall asleep, wearing only a shirt, and the whole sheet is already wet and barely dry by morning from touching themselves all night...

Once, I met someone at the local hair salon who looked familiar, and I stole glances here and there. 'Hagai?' she suddenly asked, much to my surprise, and for a moment, I was excited, thinking maybe something cool could happen between us now. 'Naama... Benny's sister?' she continued before I fully registered what was happening. 'Naamonet??' I exclaimed with a smile. 'I can't believe it... The last time I saw her, she was about ten,' I said, as if explaining to the hairdresser and the other people in the salon who didn't really care, but represented in my subconscious the conformist audience that insists everyone does what's 'acceptable' or 'allowed.' 'I've known her since she was a year old!'. But even though she was pretty hot and already about twenty, once we started talking, my desire to be intimate with her quickly faded. I'm not sure what it was exactly, but something about her felt innocent... youthful. Maybe even virginal. I felt the need to protect her rather than haunt her. And believe me, it wasn't just because she was Benny's sister; I would have been happy to screw his sister after he took Moran from me. But I simply recognized, consciously or subconsciously, innocence. She still seemed like a child to me. However, from the institutional perspective, age equates to sexual maturity. Isn't it possible for a fifteen-year-old girl to be mature and ready, just like a twenty-five-year-old can be innocent and unprepared? Beyond that, if the eighteen-year-old sleeps only with twenty-year-olds, none of them will know how to bring her to orgasm. Most will pump like a train and finish after a second, unlike an experienced man. Just like a fifty-year-old woman might seem less attractive in her perception and that of others, but an eighteen-year-old boy who is excited by everything that moves and is just discovering the world of sex would be very happy to aggressively bang her in ways her husband hasn't for years. In addition to that, when two people of roughly equal ages are sleeping together, whether they are both twenty, thirty, or forty-nine, there is immediately a mix of sex and love. 'Wait, we just had sex, does he love me now? Is she mine now? Did I give it to him too quickly? Does she think we're in a relationship now? Is he obsessing over me now???'. In age-gap sex, there are no illusions. A twenty-year-old girl understands that the forty-five-year-old man is not going to marry her because it probably doesn't suit either of them, and certainly that twenty-year-old who just finished shoving his penis in the vagina or anus of the forty-five-year-old woman—who knows that anal sex can be fun because she's no longer twenty and fixated on it being painful—doesn't want to marry her, and she as well, how should I put it, has nothing more to do with this young, refreshing treat after she's been satisfied. As a result, all the aforementioned participants can continue with their lives without frustration and unfulfilled urges. Much to the dismay of the gods of Puritanism and political correctness——nature has decided it works.

But it's forbidden! Tsk tsk tsk! Shame on you! Forbidden! Put on a suit and stand really close to your wife, who is also fantasizing about someone—or forty someones... yes, yes, hold hands, like that... that's right. Wait, maybe put your hand on her waist, or actually on her shoulder, because a waist isn't appropriate around the kids who have been masturbating since they were nine, and now... now you can all smile for the family album picture. D'fak, w'rmad, w'butscha 'aleik! Okay, that's just something I made up. But it sounds really good. Almost as good as the never-ending nonsense of our pathetically ridiculous existence... Certainly better than the democratic legislator, who is not only a genius, but his unparalleled genius is beyond nature and incomprehensible for 'ordinary' people such as myself, just like the concept of divinity and the first day of the creation of the universe. According to our legislators, being horny is a sin, just like in the Dark Ages,

and so they went even further and made prostitution illegal.
Which is about as smart as the law that gives pedestrians the
right of way when crossing the street. Is it really wise to
make the average person think they have the right to barge
into the road when there's a car coming with other vehicles
behind it, each with its own momentum? For, in the best-
case scenario they won't get run over, someone will slam on
the brakes, and the car behind will crash into them. But hey,
the legislator is surely tens if not hundreds of times smarter
than me, so it's probably just that I'm not sophisticated
enough to understand, let alone grasp, the true rationale
behind all of this. The latest cutesy pilot venture of the
genius democratic legislator stated that following
encounters between a number of rebellious children and
rebellious elderly people on the sidewalks of Tel Aviv, all
children with electric bikes should be moved to the road.
This ended with the deaths of several children. Certainly not
something the all-powerful legislator would be impressed by
while he continues to devour another bourekas.

In Germany, one of the most developed and successful
countries in the world, there is no right of way for
pedestrians, but you are allowed to cross on red if there are
no vehicles around, as they recognize that you are an adult
with a brain. However, if there are children nearby, you're
not allowed to. There, the law is a product of thought. And
lo and behold, prostitution is legal. Now go ahead, say it:
"It's an infringement on women! It's sexism!" Go on, say it.
Until less than fifteen years ago, human trafficking was
considered mere pimping, with a maximum penalty of five
years in prison, and now it's only sixteen years. Less than
murder. With a good lawyer and a third off for good
behavior, thanks to the astounding genius of the
incomprehensible legislator, the human scum who
destroyed many more lives than just one—who trapped
fourteen-year-old girls from Albania and Moldova, sent

them in the belly of a cargo ship in cages with a bucket for food and a bucket for shit and pee, to a country where they don't know the language, and locked them in a room where they are raped about twenty times a day—will be released. That's infringement on women, not the escort girls charging a thousand euros a night with flashy websites who choose to live that way, undergo medical checks, and pay taxes. In Germany, they understand that you won't make prostitution disappear from the world, just as the Prohibition era in the United States didn't stop alcohol consumption, and just as all the laws in the world won't stop drug use. The law doesn't change anything. And it certainly cannot restrain one of the greatest urges of any living being. But no! It's forbidden! Forbidden, forbidden, forbidden. We'll remain sexually frustrated but politically correct. What *is* allowed, is to continue living in a lie.

Well, maybe I'm exaggerating. You are certainly more virtuous than I am. But there is that one at work who, in a different situation, it would be appropriate for something to happen, the sexy neighbor, or the one who always compliments in messages and invites for coffee. And one time she might say, 'Wait, I'm raising three kids, I work hard, my husband sleeps with me once in a blue moon, I deserve to enjoy life too,' and she will respond to that guy from the messages, just because it's flattering. And maybe she and the guy from work will end up alone in the office one day… At some point there will be a moment when someone who really didn't intend to 'betray' anyone, especially not their life partner, will say, 'Fuck it, what the hell,' even if in slightly different words… But until that happens, human beings do what they generally do when they have no solution —They shut their mouths. Act and stay silent. Cheat and get cheated on. They'd rather bury their heads in the sand and make excuses. "When you get married, you'll understand. It doesn't work like that. When you have a wife, you'll see what it's like. You'll see you have to compromise, bend, be bent, cut corners." They send sleazy videos on their phones, their only escape for their workplace lust. "Man, did you catch that? He totally nailed her! She's a babe, huh? Awesome." Awesome? What's awesome?? You barely want your wife, you have sex once a month, maybe once a week if things are good, and I've heard from some rare exceptional souls that twice a week is an insane, perfect achievement. So, what are we living for?? To betray... What a pathetic word to describe a desire that can't be tamed. You ate something other than what Mom made?? Traitor! Playing with another friend in the sandbox, not just me?? Traitor! Yeah, but... this is intimate. Its dick inside a pussy with all that juices and that feeling that "Oh... it feels so good to be inside her..." or "when he's inside..." But wait, that feeling, that special sensation, it doesn't exist anymore! And that's exactly the problem, right there. That this "oh..." won't be reserved just for you anymore, and that's why it's betrayal, but it doesn't even exist anymore anyway! No matter how much 'bullshit' tries to fool 'crap', you won't even convince yourselves if you look deep inside, that as partners who don't cheat or swing and indulge in those trendy hip alternatives, you have good sex. You cracked up Pepo, Grandpa Geppetto, and the immortal Brazilian striker, friend of Romário, Bebeto. You don't! And that's what creates eighty percent of the frustrations in the world. A person needs food and sex just like any other animal in nature. Without one of them, it ceases to exist. But somehow, we've agreed that it's okay to go without for a long time. No, it's not! People without sex become frustrated and bitter. It shows up as excessive irritability, resentment, anger, rage, depression, and violence. Look at how many people sit in prison, literally lost their freedom, because of sexual desire. Don't believe me? Think they're all just deviants? Think about how much time you've spent in porn, finding yourselves sweating with tissues all around for a catharsis of five, maybe ten seconds. That's why people cheat. Not because they want to 'betray' the person they love most, but simply because they're animals. Just like in nature, only in homes. And they're wither without sex. Medical studies even indicate that a woman's vagina actually becomes vulnerable without sexual intercourse. And anyone who doesn't experience this and isn't fooling themselves or their surroundings is truly a special and blessed individual, and I hope for their sake they truly appreciate it. But aside from them, the rest become hungry for something else.

You know what the real moral of Dostoevsky's brilliant book, *Crime and Punishment*, is? In the end, what ultimately overwhelms Raskolnikov who escaped murder, isn't that 'the good' closed in on him, but rather his own conscience that won't let him rest. It's greater than you. The more you try to shake it off, the more it turns into a whirlpool, like quicksand—the more you struggle, the deeper you sink. Once we studied a Talmudic issue called "This One is Not Benefitting, and This One is Not Losing." If you've benefited and no one's been harmed, then all is well. According to our-sages-blessed-be -their-names — you're off the hook. Therefore, the only question that should arise, in any field by the way, is whether this thing we're pondering brings us more bad than good, or more good than bad. If you've betrayed your husband, but aside from slight guilt pangs, it truly brings joy to your home, as now you're calm and content, then all is well. But if guilt weighs heavy, and you feel worse than good, then it's not. If it keeps your wife awake at night, because though she knows not for certain, as her mind won't rest for she feels your betrayal, then it brings more bad than good.

Let me tell you a horrifying story, a truly disdainful act. A real disgust. This is, by no means, proper behavior according to any code of conduct. For years, I've had a fantasy of lying with a pregnant woman, but of course that's a bit problematic. One day, I got out of the car to save a parking spot in Tel Aviv, and suddenly I realized that the girl in the vehicle, pulling out of the space I intended to fiercely guard, was a not-so-familiar girl I once met at a rooftop party. I remember we chatted a bit; I don't recall what about, but I do remember that in a moment of drunkenness, she revealed to me, perhaps half-jokingly, that aside from kids and animals, she's done it all. What I didn't recall was her having such a huge chest, and from a bird's-eye view, I spotted ample breasts. Oh! My mind awoke in full force and vigor.

"Wow, congrats!" I said with joy.

"Thanks!" she replied, smiling and joyful too.

"When did you manage to get married?" asked the tactless part of me.

"I didn't," she answered, still under the veil of her smile.

"Oh, cool…" I nodded for a moment, then a thousand identical messages flew through my mind, flashing with the blinding light of projectors that could illuminate all the oceans of the world combined— 'It's ok to fuck her!!!!!!!! It's ok to fuck her!!!!!!!!'

"Listen, it's my fantasy," continued that part of me without a hint of tact before I could even respond.

"What??" she let out a prolonged laugh. "I'm in a relationship, silly… just without the rabbinical stuff."

"Ah, damn…" I kept my charming smile.

"Alrighty, let me get out of the parking space. The crazy carpenter…" she stifled her smile.

"Ok, we'll talk then!" I shouted as she drove away, waving goodbye.

But a few days later, after a series of texts whose intentions I hadn't yet grasped, she popped by to say hello at the workshop because she had 'happened to pass by.' At first, she seemed shy about her body, even though it was one of the sexiest I'd ever seen. Her breasts were like a pair of eight hundred erect CC's. Sorry, not erect—rigid! Her butt was big and round, perfectly taut, with full and muscular thighs.

"I'm repulsive," she said, unaware that my sexual deviation for pregnant women is in a completely different sphere. "I'm fat."

"You're not fat; you're pregnant! And you're stunning..." I added.

"My husband is disgusted by me," she suddenly shot out, to my utter surprise. "He doesn't touch me."

The entire following day, I was consumed by thoughts of "What have I done?" that it wasn't cool, and that I might have even harmed the baby, and what kind of certified, foolish pervert I was. Only later did they reassure me that it's actually very healthy for a woman to have sex during pregnancy, and that I had done her a great service. Psychologically, I even helped her, as instead of feeling ashamed of her body as she had until now, she would now present it with pride. But the horrifying and grotesque story didn't end there. After the birth, I would come to her house a minute after her husband left for work, and she would squirt milk from her breast onto my dick, then lick it all up. She made sure to refresh the supply every few minutes so that my essence would mix with the milk in her mouth. Ugh, disgusting... Go on, say it! What a disgusting cheating woman and a piece of shitty wanker who sleeps with married women. Yuck! What a couple of repulsive people... Revolting. Just after the baby was born... and her husband is at work... definitely not sleeping with anyone, and here we are, with the mixing and the cum and milk and dick in the mouth... Ugh! Sleeping with married women is also bad karma, right? Go on, say it. But what you don't know is that we also had talks—talks about life, like you always do after sex. And in those talks, she told me she wanted to break up with him. That she wasn't happy. That it was boring. That their relationship was dead. Today, they have four kids. So did the affair do her family bad or good?

What if they promised you that your partner would never know, and therefore would never be hurt, and there would be no chance of your relationship being ruined because of it—almost as if the affair was in a time capsule? If you could leap into a parallel universe or return to a point in the past before you met your current partner, sleep with someone, and then return to the present—would that still count as cheating? And if not, then what's the difference? Most of the married women I've done on the lathe then talked to over coffee later told me they absolutely love their husbands, that he's their best friend and soulmate, and that they wouldn't even consider replacing him with any other man. He simply no longer appears as a 'hunter' in their eyes anymore. They just wanted passionate sex that doesn't exist in their marriages. It doesn't! What can you do? It's like love—either there are feelings or there aren't. You can't fake a hard-on or a mood. And people who have sex are much happier than those who don't. Just look around and see who's smiling by default and who's frustrated by default. Those whose lips are constantly curling at the corners, are the ones with the sex.

And if you're such macho-men who are against infidelity and—'Who, me?' and 'My wife would never,' and 'My husband? no chance…'—then let's create a DNA database just like those 'siblings' groups that find people who are actually siblings from the same sperm donor. Let's all enter a global database and see who is the child of whom, how many children each father has around the world, and whose children belong to each mother. Agreed? If not, then from now on, shut your mouth. Liars and deceivers, cowards and dream-quitters who comfort each other with pathetic trash phrases. Phrases of fear that trap us all in this damn norm, in the fenced farm they built for us, where there and only there are we considered legitimate and okay.

But what do we do with all this in practice? Talk about it? Not talk about it? Him being your best friend is the foundation of your relationship, and what will happen if he gets hurt? Gets offended? Or just won't go along with it? And maybe just like Arik, whereas the person he is with others and the person he is with his wife are two completely different identities that should never meet—perhaps therein lies the problem. Why shouldn't the person I'm supposed to love the most, the partner I've chosen for life, the one I freaking sleep with every night and take a dump beside, why shouldn't he be happy when I'm happy? Why? What, for fucks sake, is the solution?! Well, besides polyamorous people and swingers, there's another group of people who are happy in their relationships and are always having plenty of sex—those in their second act. Arik's mom, in the spirit of neighborhood gossip, always boasts about how her sex life with Ruby, her new boyfriend who's sixty-five just like her, is not only alive every day but also truly wonderful! And they really do look like a vibrant and in-love couple. They're always going on hikes together, going to the beach, going out... How many forty years of marriage couples do you know that behave like that? What if we could build ourselves a platform where nothing is destroyed because, from the start, there's nothing to ruin? Everything is built in a flexible space with the utmost elasticity, just like the iron beams of the Eiffel Tower. In the communine, we have an infinite love for the group, yet at the same time totally maverick. No one is dependent on anyone, no one burdens the other, and everyone is free. Want to be a loving couple within the communine? Wonderful. Feeling a bit tired of it? You can step back without needing to make 'life-altering' decisions. You can embark on second acts without the kids getting hurt because their lives aren't changing even a millimeter. The same dad, the same mom, the same structure, because after all, we live in a kind of extended family, and besides, most affairs happen with people close by, so there's a good chance that second acts can emerge within the extended communine, as this person or that has always appealed to you, and you know them quite well. Of course, at first, there will be those who will grumble about the hand of fate. What, no marriage and no seven blessings from the rabbi? How can you live like that? But when they're given an elastic space that allows them to live—but really live, including love, passion, raising kids, and a communal space where you never feel the weight of the world on your shoulders, a place where you only do what you love and excel at, and financial security is no longer an issue, suddenly, both you and they will smile much more.

But our society, in all its foolish puritanism, preaches both directly and indirectly for conservatism, rooting in us fears and a sanctification of the past, subtly embedding within us horrendous and terrifying expressions. 'Destroying a family!' 'Tear the children away from their parents!' They've ingrained panic in us as if the day of divorce is, at the very least, akin to an Aktion in Auschwitz. How many happily divorced people are there in this world? And where do you think more people get hurt? In 'normal' and 'safe' relationships? Or in open relationships, polyamory, and all those other things that the horny have invented? What percentage of people are hurt by betrayal, insecurity, humiliation, violence, or abandonment anxiety, and how many people cling to this damaging and hurtful relationship as their foundation for security in life? It's a joke! The joke of human existence since the establishment of monogamy. But hey, Grandma said it's not good to get divorced... And what do you suggest happened to those kids who were 'torn' from their parents? Have they lost their humanity? Lost forever in the abyss of oblivion? When I was a kid, I had a friend named Assaf. Long before Arik. Assaf and I were such good friends that one time, after school, I went to his house, and he came to mine, and we met halfway back, laughing and delighted by our telepathic friendship. Then one day, out of the blue, his parents decided to move. And an eight-year-old child suddenly has to disconnect from his entire environment. No one thought about how perhaps both our lives were falling apart at that moment, even though for us, as eight-year-olds, they were indeed ruined. And there was no internet and no smartphones with video calls. A phone call once in a while... until that too got disconnected and ended. Fuck your motherfucking asses... So get divorced! I have two friends who both needed to get divorced. Why? Because they and their wives don't match anymore. Once they did, now they don't. People will tell themselves a thousand stories, a thousand emotional manipulations, to avoid risk. 'I'll be seen as a failure, what about the kids, who will take me, what will happen to me?' All because they fear change more than they fear their own shadows. So they stay in the shit. One friend listened to me, and today he lives in a dream. He found new love, and they even brought a stunning girl into the world because they're so happy, despite their older age. The other is still spinning tales. 'What can you do? That's just how it is with women after kids. It's like that for everyone. Everyone. That's just how it is'. The wisdom of the crowd... They all stay together for the sake of their kids and don't realize that the best thing that can happen to their children is for their parents to be happy. It sounds shocking, but maybe, just maybe, when the child is with the dad, he's 'daddy of the year', and when he's with his mom, she's 'mommy of the year', because they both miss him and don't take him for granted like in 'normal' and 'healthy' families, and also, and mainly—because when he's not there, Mommy and Daddy can walk around naked at home and have sex with whoever they want, or just pleasure themselves with ice cream and porn in front of the computer. You are hereby free to be free...

Nature, God, fate—whatever you choose to call it—has woven for us two types of apes that look almost the same but behave entirely differently when it comes to conflict resolution- chimpanzees and bonobos. When two chimpanzees fight over food, a stick, a female, or whatever, it results in a brawl, just like us 'civilized' humans. Bonobos, on the other hand, are a type of ape that is constantly having sex. That's how they resolve conflicts. Whenever tensions rise—over food, a chosen branch, you name it—everyone has sex with everyone. And not only does everyone have sex with everyone, but they are also very liberated in terms of their sexual preferences. Males and females, two males, two females, adults and young ones; sexual relations among relatives are also accepted. This sexual promiscuity allows bonobos to enjoy a high quality of life, low stress levels, and rich social relationships. Imagine a man and a woman arguing over a parking space, and the obvious option for both is for her to turn around, lift her skirt, and enable him to bang her from behind. The man-would gladly give up the parking spot and also get to have sex with a complete stranger in the middle of a workday, and the woman-would enjoy both a pleasurable sexual experience and a parking spot, and the universe would benefit from less conflict and more positivity moving forward. And this goes for every issue. Perverts? Mentally ill? Not acceptable to you? Well, bonobos would disagree. To them, you can continue to argue about anything just like chimpanzees and have sex with the same person once every two weeks. By the way, those who lead the bonobo community, are the females.

And perhaps Moran Dagan is simply a more evolved model of every girl I've known until now. And until I reached her level of insight, I must have seemed like a child to her—someone she couldn't do anything with or about. But now there is, now I understand. I understand everything completely. Suddenly, in one moment, everything falls into place. The necessary transformation for our species that lost its way, unwittingly severing itself from nature during that flawed yet wondrous industrial revolution. And now, with the united forces of knowledge, information, and understanding, we will embark on a new path. No need to force it. That's all. This magic, it has its due day, and in time it fades away. And that's perfectly fine. I used to have this cool hatchback, packed with horsepower. It was a killer car. The only thing was, that every few months something would break down, and I had to take it to the shop. But when it ran, it ran like a dream. So, was it a good car or not? We often try to change the person in front of us, to fix them— if only they'd change *this*, if only she'd act more like *that*. We hope the person we love will eventually be just a little bit more like what we want, just a tiny adjustment, a fine-tuning. But they won't. This is the car, that's how it drives. It's comfortable here, but it causes trouble there—it won't change. That cake, it's sweet here but sour there—that's how it comes. Now you have to decide if it works for you or not. Do you know how much it costs to kill someone? Twenty-five years in prison. That's the price. Now think about what it costs to live with that person. Often, people say, "Wait, I have a stew simmering that's not quite right, but with a pinch of spice here and a dash of this there... See? It's changed a little, it's cooking." But that stew is spoiled, not to their taste. The moment they toss it out, a new dish will arrive, one far more fitting. Even if that stew once tasted divine and longed for shared joy, life shifted. People change, people don't change; they make mistakes, decide, regret, hold on, don't hold on, it doesn't matter what. At this moment, it simply doesn't fit. "But he said this, but she did that, I think it should be this way." Everyone's wrapped up in their thoughts, instead of their emotions. I once dated someone, and every time we met, we genuinely had fun; there was something magnetic between us. But when we talked on the phone, she was preoccupied with overthinking—what was wrong, what didn't fit. "Wait, why did you say that? Why are you like this?" But all of that is irrelevant. What truly matters is whether this person brings you joy or pain. Are you comfortable, or do you have a headache? This is the car; this is how it runs. Like this. Does it suit you? Yes or no? Is it worth 'putting up with' this for the 'reward' of that? If so, then shut up and pay the price. If not, then goodbye. And if it doesn't suit you and you can't say goodbye then just shut your fucking mouth and pay the price for being a gutless coward afraid of your own shadow. I see people fighting for their relationships. They go to counselors, psychologists, guides—all in order to "save the relationship!" To battle for it! But a relationship isn't something that requires a "battle." There are things we get excited about, really captivated by, but after a while it can fade, feel less right, less suited for the time, and it's okay to view it that way! No one wants to do that to someone they loved so much, someone they fell for and were crazy about, especially when it felt so right at that moment! He didn't con you! She isn't a fucking whore who ruined your life; it's just something that was incredibly cool, maybe the coolest in the world, when you stood under the canopy. Believe it or not, no one planned to turn into a piece of shit and a nightmare for the person smiling at them now, as if two fingers were stuck up their ass. And maybe the sex at first was explosive. You'd dive in with all your might, really fast, and wow, how she would moan! At first slow, then a bit faster, and more. Then suddenly she realizes you're in the peak rhythm, and maybe it hurts a bit more, or she feels more, so she goes, 'Ah! Ah! Ohhh!' And you keep going, turning it up, pumping! How you're pumping! Like a machine! Ta-ta-ta-

ta-ta, and then ta-ta-ta-ta-ta-ta-ta-ta-ta! Bang! Bang! Hell yeah, how you're pounding! Oh, yes... how you're pounding your future wife. You took MDMA and you're on vacation! In a cabin, or you flew to Prague! Amsterdam if you're really crazy or cool! Bahamas if you've got loads of cash. Bora Bora! Fucking New York!!!!!!!!!! G-U-A-T-E-M-A-L-A!!!!!!! Totally wild you are... And you're drinking, and going out, taking a little more MDMA, and you're crazy about her, and she's crazy about you, and every second you tell her she means everything to you, my liiiife! And she loves you, and you love her back, you swear you love her, my life, you are, my dear! And now you're in the room, and you're pumping, you've got power! And you're drunk, and she is too, and the MDMA... and music playing from the bar outside or what you've put in the room, and you can hear maybe the sea somewhere, and you're H-A-V-I-N-G S-E-X!!!!!! Madness... you, you're utterly wild... Now, can you get up to the child?!

17

In Fatel, there's an ancient custom that if someone is in a bad mood, they are 'exiled' to reflect on their thoughts and understand what's bothering them, as a way to prevent their negativity from affecting others. Afterward, they return to share their insights so everyone can help lift their spirits. This practice is called 'going to the Isle of Demons.' Some say it's actually an English gesture from our ancestors to the Jewish people, in honor of Dreyfus, a Jewish officer in the French army who was exiled there after being falsely accused of treason and espionage. In the name of efficiency and systemic considerations, he rotted in prison and received a pardon only after years. Honestly, regardless of anything else, Goa is really boring my soul to its depths. There are no longer any vibes like before; it's all just *shanti shanti all day long*, and today it's even cloudy with no sign of the sun. Another rickshaw, another cow wandering aimlessly through the streets, and another bull rummaging through a trash can in search of a good meal or at least a decent snack, sifting through it with pleasure, undisturbed. No one will disturb His Royal Highness, the holy bull who will never become a steak or a patty. Holy, holy, holy. Another *tikka*, another *chai masala*. Relax, man, *shanti baba*. Everything's good. Everything is always good here. Even when it's crap. Even when life itself is the very juice of the garbage bag and the trash can.

So the next day, while we were sprawled out on the sunbeds at the beach in Palolem, I casually suggested moving to another beach. Like, just for the diversity of it, and I knew no one would have the energy to move. "There's still plenty of time," was Arik's expected response, while Moran, ever so sexy, nodded beneath her red straw madame hat adorned with the white ribbon she had recently bought from one of the many shops leading down to the beach, her tanned body clad in a matching red swimsuit. "Well, I think I'll head over to Patnem soon, go hang out a bit at the island of demons," I said, and both of them turned to me with confused looks. I reassured them that everything was cool, that India is a place suitable for solo travel and soul-searching, and that I'd be back in a couple of days—three or four at the most. "It's only one beach south. Six-minute ride in a slowly moving rickshaw". By evening, I was already there. I rented a house on the beach with a backyard that had two sunbeds facing a truly private beach surrounded by rocks. Classic for a couple. A dream place for a honeymoon. Too bad I am here alone.

Here in Patnem, everything is more relaxed. Maybe too relaxed. A dwarf coconut tree shades my head, along with the moon. In my country the moon always takes on a concave shape, but here it's genuinely hollow like a bowl, and even a bit reddish... Apparently, the territorial shift has affected it as well. Anyhow, I'm here. In a sort of private paradise with myself. Too bad Moran isn't here with me, and doesn't love me back. It could have been perfect for us. Well, that is, if she hadn't shattered the illusion of my existence by taking it from Arik from behind less than a day after we slept together. But at least here, I can think. Think and think and think. Except I really don't feel like thinking at all. About anything. I turned off my cell phone and didn't bother charging it. Enough. I'm in Goa, for God's sake. I just want to disconnect, to unwind, to breathe in the ocean breeze, clear as wine. I light a smoke, another joint from the stuff Arik scored. I've turned into a full-blown stoner for the time being. Drinking beers at noon, dipping in and out of the sea alternately. And the sea is fun. A tourist washes her coveted body, shimmering under the rays of the sun that rest on those drops cascading from her royal figure. And what is it to me, these advanced smoking habits? It's doubtful whether it's not this that drags down my mood, clouds my eyes, exhausts and shakes my ever-constant reflection, easily cuts through my train of thought, and strips my mind of its musings. Only lustful and morbid thoughts echo in the darkness. In total blackness. Get this stuff to hell, man, child of the divine. Take it from me and cast it away. Throw it in the nearest trash. Perhaps a certain ox will turn from being a tame one to one that is known for goring, as the *Mishnah* says. Then we could blame it all on him. Everything! Because if he did it twice, he's certainly no longer tame, and right now he's truly a threat, just as the insurance companies, well-protected by years of flawed, miserable legislation, have learned all too well. And maybe here in India, devoid of capitalism, the cart rolls downhill without eyes or a driver, millions of seekers of answers content with a long-nosed god and celestial goddess, Ohmmmm, Bom Shiva and Ganesh and Brahma, surely they will protect us from the looming abyss. Surely they know it all. Tikka masala. Henna tattoos that last two weeks and then fade like your aimless, purposeless thoughts. Blinded and trampled under herds of cattle wandering freely and unchecked. And the dogs... oh, the dogs. A constant escort wherever you go. Maybe some food will fall from your pocket. Perhaps a gentle caress. Noble creatures. All-knowing and loyal guardians. *A dog of valor, who can find? For his kennel is far above rubies.* And you're there. Almost reaching. Almost touching. Just a moment, and you're at the edge. Just a moment, and the whirling cyclone will reach you too, and you will perish along with thousands of those living in meaningless shacks and tents. Without any important thoughts. Surely tomorrow they will draw more water from the random well that serves the whole village. Who cares? *Please nourish me more of that red, red stuff!* Divine curry. And let 'em all drop dead. I, in the meantime, shall revel to the fullest. Until it sleeps. Until this, too, shall pass. Until we all pass and flow and evolve and change and die and die and die, and only then will shall live. Free as a bird, enslaved as a man. Gorillas in the zoo. Fenced in. Guarded. Just don't move. At least not too much. For then, of course, we will have to slander you in public. Maybe even slit and slaughter. For it is neither possible nor permissible to be different. Hail conservatism, hail capitalism, hail, hail, hail. Only what belongs to us and is similar. Never change. Don't ever try to change, and live. And all the rest, *shall cast into the river.* When did we lose what mattered so deeply? What once brought us the feeling of freedom and growth? When did we finally surrender to the curses of our own making, that weigh upon us from dawn till dusk? And where do all these twisted thoughts come from? It must be the drugs. For sure. After all, I'm a good Fatel boy, eco-friendly and sustainable. Or Moran. It must be that very Moran. The one who is different. The one who changes things. Pulling me in with her threads—threads of desire and longing. I'm enslaved. I know. It's certainly not for me. But right now I feel trapped. Dreaming and fantasizing, yearning for her touch. I care not for what surrounds me. I'll ignore it. I'll ignore it as I wonderfully ignore the filth and muck in the streets, savoring another 'Kingfisher' beer on the beach, accompanied by a plate of decidedly non-kosher shrimp. It tastes good to me, so I choose. Thus, I will choose it again and again and again. I want. Bestow upon me with some more. Oh, my… Perhaps we shall all pray to that same God of the coveted paradise who must be waiting for six o'clock, when millions of people will say the same words together. Then surely He will save us… Oh my…

I'm weary. Moreover, it's begun to bore me. I'm no longer a twenty-year-old kid traveling the Far East after the army, with each day feeling like a gift after spending three years in uniform, wandering through the hidden corners of some fuck-off terror town, and now discovering new worlds, new people, and learning new things about myself. Aside from a vacation at the Dead Sea or in some resort or club where you're constantly at the hotel—by the sea—at the hotel—by the sea—at the restaurant of the hotel—by the sea—at the only restaurant in the area—at the hotel by the sea, all other vacations consist of running errands. A walk here, a drive there, a trip to see this, to do that: eagle feasting, boat trips, fishing, kayaking—you name it. And it's not like there's much to work with here, anyway. Because of that cyclone some seven thousand kilometers away, about forty percent of the Europeans canceled right away. Because, you know, a cyclone... ok ok, I dropped my hand from my face and stopped shaking my head. But that was still the good part! One day, while walking alone on the beach, I already got really pissed. That day, I walked all the way to Palolem Beach and back, which is about a twenty-minute walk each way. The walk was actually quite nice. Village houses, dogs, roosters, and cows lounging around together, and I even found a path through thick vegetation leading to the beach. I thought maybe I'd run into Moran and Arik, but instead, I stumbled upon a few European girls doing a yoga class on the beach. I stopped to watch for a bit, but pretty quickly I got this feeling like they were making me out to be some kind of stalker. Like, screw you! Stay with your yoga and your pretentious selves, you fuckers... Coming all the way to India just to do yoga, like, can't you do yoga in Vienna?? And what about some men for the enhancement of the experience?! So right around sunset I arrived back at Patnem Beach, and at one of the restaurants that had dragged chairs and tables out onto the sand, just like all ninety others, I spotted some blonde girl sitting alone. I was so pissed off by then, all these European girls with their fingers stuck up their own asses, like go screw yourselves on your yoga mats, I stopped and, almost angrily, asked her if she wanted "a little company, or if you'd rather," I actually said 'rather,' "be by yourself."

'Sure, sit,' she surprised me, and it took me a few seconds—just a hundredth of a second before the other side realizes it—to sit down. Alright, cool. So, I'll sit. And we talked, and ordered beers, and suddenly I noticed she had a bunch of tattoos and was actually pretty hot—but like, an India kind of hot, with messy hair. 'I've got something to smoke too, in my room, if you want,' I threw out, even though offering someone a smoke in India is like offering the owner of Microsoft to go in on a lottery ticket with you. 'Come on dude, it's a slam dunk. You should totally.'

'Sure, yeah… Actually, I wanted to,' she literally jumped right in. So then we both hurried to finish our drinks in a surprisingly cool and mutual way, and it took the Indian waiter long enough to bring the bill so that you couldn't miss it, and we headed to my room. 'Actually, I'm horny as fuck,' I swear those were the exact words she used. 'But I'm at the end of my period.'

And I, being all hot and frustrated, even though I really dislike a period with someone I don't know because it's gross, said "Okay, I have an idea". When you're so sure that the other person is into it, I just lifted her and pulled her into the bathroom while stripping us both down, turning on the shower, and starting fucking with her standing up. There's something about it that really excites me. Maybe it's because it usually surprises and turns on the girl, or maybe I'm just used to it on the lathe, but most girls look genuinely taken aback by it. I figured that it's probably so rare that they don't fully grasp the setup and positioning I'm trying to enable them at the beginning. So after she shouted out that "You're fucking me!" and "Fuck me!", and "I'm a whore!" and "Fuck me like a whoreeee!" because like, fuck it, were both completely stoned, drunk, and wouldn't see each other ever again, so we could really let loose and say whatever we wanted, I wondered if the total liberation of women was just about shouting that they were whores. Of course she left just like she came. We both knew it was just a casual fling, and within a minute walk, she's back in her room, resting and farting alone on her bed. I rolled myself a joint stuffed way beyond the limit with some quality chars since it only costs a buck and a half here anyway, and sat in my private seaview backyard wearing only my boxers, enjoying the wonderfully salty air of Goa, puffing thick clouds of smoke towards the crescent moon, shining out its best of tune. I was making faces at myself. Suddenly, I felt good. Out of nowhere, being alone was so nice. That supposedly meaningless hookup had set me free. And now, without the weight of frustration hanging from my back, I was open to seeing and realizing that sometimes surrendering to defeat is the best thing you can do for yourself. Then, all of a sudden, you're not tormented. Not thinking. Not bothered. Not trying to solve a problem. Suddenly you're free and it feels great because you have no worries. You lost that thing, and that's that. And hey, wait a second, it's not so terrible after all, like you thought it would be. Turns out you didn't fall into any abyss, and you're still intact. Maybe I lost that battle or this set, but surprisingly, the game keeps going. The same game I've been playing since I arrived in this world, in which I'm the main player. Player of the century. Suddenly, I'm alone but not miserable, definitely not feeling lonely. Suddenly, It's like I'm alone, but with my best friend.

In Goa, the rooster crows at five in the morning, doesn't let you sleep. What do I say in Goa? All over the world. My heavy stoned mind, immersed in a dream during a kind of self-Vipassana with myself alone under the dim light of a waning moon, stirred and wondered why the rooster even bothers to crow when dawn arrives. Really, why? It's clear that it's an ingrained mechanism in him and that nothing you do will prevent him from doing it. Except, of course, turning him into a Schnitzel. So why? And it's important to point out that there are a million types of birds in the world, most of which indeed drive you crazy incessantly in the morning, but none of them go "cock-a-doodle-doo". And perhaps roosters herald the beginning of the day. And aside from transforming into chicken steak or a really juicy kebab and craft omelets, they are entrusted with the sacred task in this universe—where, for many years, alarm clocks truly did not exist—of announcing the dawn of a new day. Another day of Neanderthal people acting out of survival instinct. Carving another cave to protect themselves from rain and other weather calamities, predators, and intruders. Climbing higher on trees to get the finest, ripest fruits, and developing more advanced weapons with which they can hunt more easily and efficiently, as well as to slaughter each other of course. But at the beginning of each new morning, the king of non-flying birds heralds the dawn, with his name derived from the Sumerian language in a way that translates to 'the bird of the king,' signaling that everything begins anew. And let's see what the day will bring. Maybe they will discover gravity, maybe the atom, or perhaps Edison will finally invent the light bulb. But without our dear Mr. Rooster, none of this would happen. Do you get it? This stupid rooster, as most of us perceive him—unable even to fly—holds the title of king of kings. The true ruler of the universe. Without him, a significant portion of ancient people would not rise early, most of humanity would not be in sync, and civilization would develop at a much slower pace, perhaps even failing to survive. Because no matter how well-oiled, sophisticated, and efficient the machine is, without its smallest screw, it will eventually break down or cease to function. And that screw, ladies and gentlemen, is our friend the rooster. Up until today, you've been told stories, in the name of science, of how the melatonin in our bodies reacts to blue light and so we wake up. Yet, there are many places in the world where daylight lasts for entire months, or where it arrives very late. Furthermore, studies have shown that roosters know when to start crowing due to a cycle governed by an internal clock, not by an external signal. Therefore, the rooster is not meant to fly at all! If it did, it wouldn't be here to wake us up. And let's be honest, if it weren't so delicious and easy to catch, it would not have survived. I know it sounds like an oxymoron, but its inability to defend itself or flee, not to mention its excessive slowness compared to natural predators, would leave it with no chance at all.

"The greater good" is an interesting term—intriguing, sometimes misleading, even frightening, some might say. At the very least, problematic. It compels us to step outside our private interests, so to speak. Why "so to speak"? Because we really don't know for real. What would really happen if this or that. But what if the greater good is always good for us? Maybe if my lawyer friend hadn't been coveting that 'loaded from Rishpon', I'd just be wasting my time on her? True, they could have been together just the same without the grossness, but maybe if there hadn't been that spark between them, she and I would have kept meeting here and there for a while, dragging out some kind of chewing gum until it lost all its flavor, and perhaps I would have gone with her to Anat's birthday party because everyone here is a Fatel and it's all cool, and no one would ask questions, and maybe I would have missed that incredible moment with Moran that threw me into this delightful-abrasive mess, and I wouldn't have my Bati, who is so special to me? So what, should I be bummed out that they came out acting like total losers, or should I just say, "What a fiery surge of flames blesses my way"?

There's a story about a guy who once had a small homey restaurant at the bottom of a residential building. The neighbors upstairs couldn't stand all the noise and smells, so they sued him. If you had asked him about his situation on the day he lost the case, he would have told you that his world had come crashing down, that everything he'd built over the years had gone to waste. And so he kept selling just the hummus from the restaurant, because that's the only thing the court allowed him to continue with, and in the end, that hummus made him a millionaire. Every plague in human history has reshaped medicine in some way. Every destruction brings along rebuilding. Nothing happens to us for no reason. In every situation, even when it seems to show us a picture we'd rather not see, there's something good to find. In a sober retrospective reflection, we can see that there's nothing in human history that was ever truly better. It was never cooler to live in a cave, worry about being eaten by a bear, poop in a stream, or hunt with spears. Always, what's more advanced, even if it doesn't seem that way right now, will eventually prove to be better. Well, maybe except for pooping in a stream... So maybe everything does have a reason, and maybe everything is always for the best, and that's the right way to look at life. What do I mean by "maybe"?? I've just proven beyond a doubt, at least to myself, that even the tiny fact that schnitzel goes great with ketchup, is a cardinal factor in the survival of the human race.

I stepped inside, filled the kettle with water, and turned on the faucet in the shower. Luckily, there were no signs of blood at the scene. Freshly showered and in good spirits, with a towel wrapped around me, I headed back outside, armed with a strong black coffee I found at a local supermarket that amusingly had Hebrew on the label saying it was black coffee. Classic... After that, I put on my swimsuit and went down to stroll along the beach at Patnem. There usually aren't too many people here. A few girls doing yoga at the far left of the beach, some parents with their kids, and tourists lying on sunbeds in the sunshine. Suddenly, I saw a couple of young guys with those long chillums usually brought from northern India, branded with names like Kaio, Manu, and Alberman. There they were, on the beach, doing it without a thought, without weighing the chances of getting caught and spending who knows how long in an Indian jail. An Indian jail, damn it! After all the stories I've heard over the years, I even found a hiding place for the charas I had, deep inside my room. But that's how it is at twenty-two; you fear nothing. And maybe you don't think too much about anything either. I'll never forget how, the day before we flew back to Israel, an Israeli girl sat down next to us at the guesthouse café and started pulling out a bag full of drugs she had left, handing it around to the guys. "Maybe I'll take one hit with me to Delhi," she said, holding a piece of hashish in her hand, debating out loud. Unbelievable. The girl is willing to risk sitting in jail in India, just so that if she got to Delhi and couldn't find anyone to buy or take from—which is utterly illogical given you're an Israeli in India—she'd have something to smoke.

"Just like that, a chillum right in the middle of the beach?" I asked to their surprise.

"Want some?" one of them offered. I gave a quick look at the scene to assess the situation. Four good-looking Israelis, fit. Surely screwing plenty of tourists here. And I didn't see any cops nearby.

"Sure, why not?" I heard myself reply, uncharacteristically, without thinking too much. Suddenly, the spirit of India blew through me. I could actually feel it. It happens to you without noticing. Suddenly, you go with the flow. You do things without thinking ahead. Smoking with someone, and before you know it you're fucking in the shower, hitting a chillum with some kids on the beach. You don't plan anything, and then things just happen. That's the real India. It's not Thailand.

And maybe I just wanted to be like them. To feel twenty again, carefree, without existential thoughts. A good-looking guy with natural muscles, getting laid effortlessly—just by existing.

"Want something else?" the main stud, clearly the leader of the group, asked as I respectfully managed to handle the *safi*—a piece of cloth, like the flannel bandages we used in the army, dampened and placed at the spout of the chillum to act as a sort of filter, similar to the water in a bong.

"Something else?" I asked, raising an eyebrow at him, trying to look cool.

"Come hit a spike with us," he tossed out with enviable coolness.

"Spike?" I asked breathlessly after the smoke escaped from my lungs. One hell of a smoke cloud that chillum gives.

"Spike, will hit a party, fuck some girls..." He took the chillum from me, flashing a smile full of perfect teeth, his canines adorned with the trendy scruff of a total bastard and the world champion of screwing tourists in Goa. "LSD..." he continued with a grin and took another puff from the chillum.

"Whoa... sounds intense..." I played it cool, pretending to joke around with the guys.

And honestly, I really don't look my age. Most people here give me a max of thirty-five, and if it weren't for the slight gray in my hair, it would even be less. You heard me??

Hey, I'm not some old man! If I were twenty now, you'd see what it's all about! I wanted to scream, but it was beyond me. Go convince them that you also used to be cool like them. And I swear to you, the twenty-year-old ginger in me wouldn't just be chilling with them over a chillum; he'd take all three of them on in every competition, including fights, and he'd also be fucking their girlfriends one after the other or even all at once, so… yeah… so… that's it. The chillum… it goes straight to your head.

"LSD is the only drug that doesn't lie," one of the three cool friends of Studmaster-Major suddenly chimed in from behind.

"On coke you feel like a king even though you're not; on MDMA you love everyone even though you don't; on weed you're paranoid even though you aren't. But the LSD… it doesn't lie."

"LSD is a drug for smart people," the major studmaster eagerly interjected and ruled. "It makes you think on nineteen levels. To laugh… what am I saying laugh, to crack the fuck up and roar with laughter at the entire world…" He chuckled with clouds of smoke escaping his mouth.

"Exactly," continued the next hottie. "'Look at that dumbass who took ecstasy, bouncing around like some goat…' and you can't help but crack up. Crack I tell yaaaaaa…" He stretched out the word, leaning closer with a grin full of perfect teeth.

"Dance if you want, chill out, see some different things," threw in apparently the more sensitive one of the lion crew, bringing the conversation back to its requested seriousness.

"The thing with LSD," continued the Senior Studmaster with more seriousness, "is the quantities."

"Like with any drug," the Lieutenant affirmed.

"The number one rule with drugs, bro, is how much of a pig you are. Actually, that's the only rule. And don't let anyone tell you otherwise. Always take a little, taste it, see what it does to you. Don't be a pig. Because pigs are doomed to be...?" He turned his head back to the rest of the crew, who responded in unison, "Slaughtered!"

And then they all started laughing. Like, really cracking up and rolling around stoned on the Indian lungi decorated by that god with the trunk they had spread on the soft sand of Goa, and so was I, and suddenly I found myself having fun! Cracking up stoned as hell in Patnem with four super awesome Israeli guys, who I was just like twenty years ago.'Hell, this is India!' I told myself in my heart. 'This is what I traveled for.'The freedom. The release. The feeling that everything is open. Anything is possible. In India—everything is Milega!

And honestly, the theory of the Studmaster-Major and his comrades was completely logical. I'd even say extensively reasonable. A prickly pear is a healthy thing, right? It's a fruit, it has vitamins... right? Well, if you had any idea, you'd be talking differently. Prickly pear is a freaking superfood. It's packed with magnesium, which helps with blood pressure, communication between brain cells, intestinal mobility, and heart muscle function. It contains a mineral called selenium, which basically inhibits the oxidation of bad cholesterol, preventing it from settling in the artery walls and causing heart attacks. Additionally, studies have found that prickly pear juice helps against stomach ulcers, protects the liver from alcohol poisoning, and the extract of the prickly pear has a positive effect on blood sugar levels. Recently, there's even been documentation showing that the natives in Mexico, from where it originated, used prickly pears for diabetes treatment. Another study revealed that one of its key molecules can trigger the 'suicide' of leukemia cancer cells, which basically means that this supposedly useless cactus can kill cancer. Oh, and on top of all that, it's also anti-inflammatory and a good source of vitamin A. But if you take ten prickly pears, throw them in a blender, and drink it, you'll die in excruciating pain within a few days because your intestines will literally turn to concrete.

"The world belongs to the young" is a phrase that's a bit depressing, melancholic, and even nostalgic for anyone who's not young. With another puff I took from the chillum while the young studs cheered me on with, "Goooood, gooooooood, yeahhhhh!!!" and cracking up, I suddenly realized that the world doesn't belong only to the young; it belongs to the here and now. Here I am, just as young as them, even though I'm not, able to enjoy the situation and make the most of it, and they, the youngsters, are still not set in their minds, still don't understand the world like I do, still asking questions, pondering existential dilemmas, thinking about how to make money... Not at all sure that they feel the world belongs to them. Then a stupid paradoxical situation arises in which the world belongs to no one! The adults want to be young, and the young don't even know what they want. Therefore, it's better that each one enjoys the here and now. The young—do whatever they want without thinking about yesterday or tomorrow, and the adults—do exactly the same.

So in Goa I took LSD for the first time in my life.

18

There was no choice, no other way. After slipping away and escaping, they began their journey to the neighboring Kingdom of Jordan. Back then, the borders of the land called 'Palestina' were unclear. The British ruled from the Western Land of Israel to Eastern Transjordan. According to Churchill's White Paper, technically 'Palestina' and 'Transjordan' were still under the same mandate, but in practice, they were governed separately, especially after Britain granted autonomy to Transjordan under Emir Abdullah. On top of that, the Arab tribes were distant, with no communication—neither from here nor from there. And so, they could live together there, without fear. Yet still, the Sir eventually had to find work. His close friends had given him a few liras to get by, but even that had its boundaries— both literally and figuratively. All, of course, in the name of love. Returning to the army was not an option, but after a few months, a state was established in Israel. And the Sir, a skilled and devoted soldier, wanted to take part in the war. At that time, things weren't really organized, if at all, and after some back-and-forth with someone in the Mapai Party, a visa and residence permit were arranged for him and his young family, which now consisted of a man, a woman, and a child. A small, beautiful child. A child of mixed British and Arab heritage. Her hair was light, and her eyes were green like her mother's.

"We'll call her Rita," the Sir suggested, "it's a beautiful name. Very youthful and also fitting for the Land of Israel. It also comes from the word *return*. For one day, she'll return. Return to Fatel."

Those were more or less the Sir's last words, before he died in that war. Died for the sanctity of a homeland that wasn't his. And his wife, who was Arab to begin with, was now a proper kosher Jew, and a single mother. And what does a single mother do in Israel in the early 1950s? She finds a husband. As it happened, he was also a kibbutznik—Shlaimaleh, but from Kibbutz Hulda, the far-off and the not-at-all Fatel. Together, they plowed the land, sowing the homeland. She never got close to the village, despite her deep longing. She had a commitment. A child to raise. A good husband, a provider, and a loving man. She couldn't risk it all now. But the sock—she had to send the sock to her mother, who was waiting, bursting from waiting. Three years, and nothing. Not a trace of her beloved daughter. Maybe she died on the way, maybe she was arrested and imprisoned. In those days, who knew? But she liked to imagine that her daughter was living with the Sir in distant London, living a royal life. That's how she was—optimistic by nature. Until her last day, she waited and hoped. Until the day she died, of a brown sock with a red tip—she dreamt.

⚇

"Here, from here. From here I'm telling you!" shouted Studmaster-Major as we wandered between the winding paths from Patnem to Palolim.

"Don't you want to take a rickshaw?" I asked without pressuring the group, which started to head toward the party a few hours later. Of course I was thinking about Moran and Arik, wondering if they were still there and if I might run into them. I had been without a phone for several days now, disconnected from reality, and I felt good about it. In India, even the Wi-Fi is weak and constantly disconnecting—Indian Wi-Fi. At first, it's annoying and frustrating because it's so contrary to what you're used to, to what you've been accustomed to. But then you realize that this is exactly how it should be. Just let go of your phone already, you fucking thing.

But I did think about her. I tried to make it hurt and not hurt at the same time. At one point, imagining the mere hours when I felt authorized to be in love again with "the love of my life," and at another, finding myself once more surrounded by arrows of blame and self-flagellation, on the verge of genuine ridicule, watching the idiot standing at the door while "the peculiar pair" was getting steamy. What a bummer that you can't lie to yourself, or rather, that you can only do so up to a certain point. But it's like trying to drive backward on a train while ignoring the wall it's about to crash into with full force. At some point, it will catch up to you. So I prefer to face the pain. To feel it, to sense it, to ache through it, and only then to let it go. Let them fuck off. Let her and her Arik fuck off, or any of her other companioners. There, that's how I love myself. Yet love is an addictive drug. Not something you can just stop or quit if you want to. Not even if you're forced to. I tried to come up with a thousand logical reasons to convince my brain to make my heart stop loving her, but to no avail. You can be disheartened by someone you love, you can be angry at them, but you can't stop loving them.

"Come on, let's go left!" Studmaster-Major urged as the rest of the group hesitated. Hell, I knew he was the alpha male of the pack. Always banging the hottest chick while the rest are left to compete for the leftovers. Like any pride of lions in the wild, no one dares eat until the head lion had his fill. We turned left, and after wandering aimlessly for a while, one of the lions finally dared to ask an Indian guy how to get to Palolem Beach from here. The guy explained that it was simple—just go straight and then a little right. And suddenly, we arrived. Turns out we were so disoriented that we didn't realize we were practically a stone's throw from the beach. But somehow our internal compass, after paying honor to the king of the jungle of course, led us down the right path.

"So what's this party about?" I asked as we strolled along the beach toward where, according to Studmaster-Major, the party was supposed to take place.

"Something unplanned, man. Turns out there's some insane DJ from Israel who started this impromptu party because she's crashing at a guesthouse on the beach, connected to a speaker, and suddenly people just began..."

"What?? Which DJ from Israel?" I interrupted him without meaning to. I wasn't sure if it was me or the spike.

"I've no idea, some hot chick..." he said, and everyone laughed. I laughed too, but if someone had looked closely at my features, I'm sure they would have noticed that my blood vessels were frozen, suspended in a halt, preventing themselves from swelling and betraying the flush on my cheeks and a certain sensation in my head, or just ready to burst. Suddenly, we began to hear the bass and knew we were headed in the right direction. We could also see a crowd of people gathered at the far end of the beach, right before it ends and the jungle of coconut trees begins, where you could enter and feed the vultures at a certain time of day.

As we drew closer, my anxiety began to swell against the excitement burning among the robust pride of lions, who were already pulling out their finest joints and cigarettes, bouncing and twirling to the beat of the electronic music. This is not my playground. Moreover, it's her playground. And what, am I going to jump into a wild roll right now? To a loop where I'm once again chasing Moran Dagan and facing disappointment? On stage, she'll look like a true star, in control of everything, playing the minds of those high on drugs. Playing with my mind, once more. Then she'll come down, and what, am I supposed to approach her like the last of the fanboys? Wait for her to acknowledge me and bless me with her presence, her majesty the DJ herself? And where will Arik be in all this? With me? With her? Scouting for girls to work his charm? For Arik, it was just another lay from back in the day; for me, it was everything.

There she is on stage, and I'm captivated by her once again. By the music, by the rhythm in which she moves, by her complete command of the scene. Against my will — enchanted. And that's all it takes to know it's infatuation; you're simply entranced. You can't stop thinking about her. That's how you know it's real. That's the only way to know it's meant to be. And when it is, you no longer need to question, overthink, calculate, fret, or live in constant fear, because you know that no matter what happens, she's your soulmate, and everything else just doesn't matter. The universe will take care of the rest.

"On LSD, you think on nineteen levels; it's a drug for the wise," I suddenly recalled the words of the Studmaster-Major, or perhaps it was one of his deputies...? At every stage of life, there's someone who could be "the one," and if it doesn't align because you're not on the same track at the same time or in the same phase of life, there are plenty of other soulmates out there. Suddenly, on LSD, thoughts arise that I never imagined would come to mind... I know what you're already thinking. Great, now he's falling for her again because everything has a reason and so is for him and Moran, she remains undeciphered or maybe this time she'll tell him she loves him back, and the story will end this way or the other. But I've always thought differently than you. I've always believed that love holds a meaning beyond mere emotions—a physical significance, if you will. Mass. Like a kind of message that draws us for a certain reason. A kind of gravitational force. You can only resist it to a certain extent. But why should we? After all, if it's a message from another dimension, it must surely be a positive one, since that other dimension is necessarily higher and wiser than us, and now it's simply communicating with us in a different way, sending us to a specific place through signs and wonders, through the pillar of a cloud. Something in our bloodstream is suddenly pumping, doesn't that seem strange to you? And perhaps attraction is yet another form of extrasensory communication, through which we are drawn to a particular person to reach somewhere. Perhaps that's why people who sleep with many partners become confused. Their path branches out in a way that is composed of countless roads. And whoever is attracted to one person, their path is clear and secure, and therefore it probably also becomes somewhat dull at some point. There's a stage in life in which we seek stability, and a stage where we seek the enigma. Then comes a stage where we try to solve the enigma and return to stability. It's like from ages twenty to thirty, something stable suits you—just give you a comfortable framework and a decent salary, and everything is good. In your free time when you're not at work, you're 'free' to enjoy the money and also know how to calculate how much time you have outside of work hours each month and how much you have saved on the side. Somewhere during your thirties, most people seek independence. 'Wait, who am I investing all this energy for? And this is what I get? I'll invest it in myself and earn more'. Some, not all. Those for whom the existing situation no longer satisfies them. And in your forties, you seek that thing you're drawn to, not necessarily thinking about money, because you believe—and maybe also know a bit better—how this world operates and how to make money in more ways. You're truly drawn to a certain field, to a certain action, just as you're drawn to a specific person with whom it's good for you to share a journey. And perhaps love isn't something we invented, but a kind of coordinates for a specific map, something we still can't fully comprehend in our understanding and that is meant to lead us to the place we are destined to reach if only we listen to the signs, if only we trust in it without fully understanding. If only we follow love. *We shall do, and we shall hear.*

Suddenly, the music stopped abruptly.

'Stop everything, stop everything,' the hot DJ, who now looked absolutely stunning, switched off the switch in the minds of all the dancers. 'Come on, you,' she signaled to me with her hand. 'Me?' I signaled back with my hand. 'You, you,' she nodded and even flashed a smile. Is this stage the alternative answer to the cursed stage from the Hanukkah party? I don't know what or why she did it, but suddenly she just grabbed the microphone, along with the music turning back up, she simply said, 'Ladies and gentlemen — Hagai Binder!'

Yeah, Yeah. I know. Awesome. Been there-done that. Surely my grandfather's English friends made a feast out of it. It's like Moran and Moron... Man, we're simply meant for each other. And I'm there. Even making a gesture of gratitude to the devoted audience, and they're screaming. Cheering for me. For me!! Hagai the carpenter from Fatel! They don't even know who I am or why, but the DJ called it out and blessed it, and he, or rather she — is now the closest thing to God. I stepped onto the stage, unsure if it was under the influence of the LSD, which I was already told is the drug of truth, and she hugged me. The queen of the world. Here she is holding on tight, as if she missed me, and even giving a kiss on the lips, and I'm really resisting her wishes, as if giving in but keeping a bit of distance. They say everyone deserves fifteen minutes of fame in their lives. And I say no. Even a minute is enough. Only after it happened did I realize this. Suddenly, out of nowhere, for one brief shiny moment, everyone was cheering for me.

Somewhere at the beginning of the 2000s, the great wave of house music began to wash over the world. Sasha,

Digweed, Tiësto, Nick Warren, Anthony Pappa, Oakenfold, Dave Seaman, and many other talented DJs took over the world's stages with exquisite progressive house, providing a response to the gorgeous girls of the Goa trance parties of the nineties. On June 3, 2006, at the Heineken Music Hall, Tiësto closed the party with 'Mindcircus' by the musical group Way Out West, featuring Nick Warren and the heavenly voice of Tricia Lee Kelshall, who completely dismantled everyone and left them on the floor in the midst of the ecstasy high that was available under every lush tree back then. And this track, its uniqueness lies in the way it comes after all the high-energy tracks of the party, splitting your mind in two. One part is still at the party, in the peak of all the highs and dancing, while the other part is comfort to relax. But these two parts must never meet. They mustn't coexist. There's always a river flowing between them. Sometimes it flows gently downstream, and sometimes it crashes powerfully as the waves do in the sea, akin to the "Advata de-Yama" described in the Babylonian Talmud. But Dubstep, well, I already told you, it's not electronic music like house or trance. It's... it's something entirely different. Something magical. A kind of low-beat electro would be the closest lie to the truth if you really pushed me into a corner. And Moran ended the party in a way that left everyone's hearts on the floor, with a crazy Dubstep version of this track. It's not for nothing that they say the DJ is God. The DJ controls people's minds. And then, with a single wave, poof! It sends you flying to another place but at the same time keeps you grounded in the same spot, at the same party. With the same drugs in your brain. "Man, I'm fucking torn!!" shouted some Israeli next to me while a European with a wig that looked like a giant fur hat clutched his head on both sides, and it was clear from his eyes, covered by yellow sunglasses, that he didn't understand what had just happened to him. For a split second, he disconnected. And poof! That's it, he already experienced it. He absorbed it. There's no going back and no other option but to surrender to the new thing that the ears hear and the brain processes. Moran, she's just the kind of person who knows how to kill you in a second.

19

"I always knew there was something different about you," she suddenly blurted out as we sat on the beach, listening to the crowing of Indian roosters, while I was still coming down from the LSD high that lasted well into the early hours of the morning, in which Moran helped me get through because I had no idea where I was. The super-cool guys had long disappeared, and I found myself swaying to the beats of the electronic music, stomping my feet in the water.

The beach in Goa is deceptive. At night, the tide rolls in, 'drowning' the private beaches along the hostel strip. Sometimes, it gets to the point where, to cross a spot that would take five minutes to walk during the day, you need a boat. A boat! Indians actually suddenly show up with boats. And the funny thing is, they don't even ask for money. Just some guys who came to the party and got stuck on their way back because they didn't want to wade through chest-high water with their phones and clothes and all... So, one called another, and in India, you know how it goes, suddenly there are these young, cute Indian kids with a boat. I gave them a few wet bills I had in my pocket to make sure they were happy, while the other girls that were with me on the boat just stretched their legs and disappeared into the shadows. But she didn't. She stood there smiling, happy to see me enjoying myself or maybe just there to support. I wasn't in a state of mind to make a conscious decision about it, and definitely not to fully understand. But she was there. Reassuring me that everything was fine, that she was with me for as long as I needed, even all night if it came to that, though I wasn't worried at all.

"So, what? where... Where's Arik?" I asked, noticing he was nowhere to be seen.

"Mmm… he probably went off with his tourist. He's got a new girlfriend," she laughed, and suddenly I cracked up, because apparently that's how it is on LSD. Then Moran lost it as well, and both of us were laughing uncontrollably on Palolem Beach, late into the night, our feet in the water. And then, we kissed. Suddenly, we were kissing wildly. Just the two of us, alone on the beach, emptied of the rest of the partygoers. I've told you before, that's how it goes in Goa—lights out by eleven, unless there's a special permit for the party. And me? I had no idea where I was at all. I grabbed, clutched, anything I could. She was wearing something that looked like a galabia or a sari, and I just grabbed where her chest was until it slipped down, and I started kissing her nipple. I kissed it with my whole mouth, with all my lips, and our tongues were swirling and dancing together to the sound of the waves pounding the shore. Suddenly, this huge wave crashed over us, and we had to stop kissing because we swallowed a bunch of water. And then we just cracked up again. But in Goa, it's hot even at night, so we just kept going, soaking wet.

"Mor…" I began to say. I wanted to tell her… but then… then suddenly, I wanted to cry. Out of nowhere, I realized I was on the verge of sobbing! What is this?? I hadn't cried in thirty years. More! Who cries? Maybe at six or eight when I got into a fight with some kid and he won or something. Maybe. And at funerals, I always played the tough guy. Even when it hurts. Even when Mom called me from the hospital to say, "We've had a tragedy." That's how she put it. When her mom passed away. And I played the tough guy. Didn't cry. Even though she made a special trip out of the hospital just for my bar mitzvah, despite the fact she was already dying of cancer. She came out, just for that. For my bar mitzvah, then back to the hospital. Back to dying. As a kid, you barely appreciate it, barely understand. It's only with time that you grasp the significance of what happened. The event she, as a person, went through—not just as my grandma, that old person who's kind to me and brings me chocolates, who's the parent of my parents. But the person she was. Once a little girl who went through things, who later escaped Poland before the war, who met my grandpa, and together they built Fatel. Then my mom was born, her first and only daughter, who had two children of her own. And now her grandson is having his bar mitzvah. Her daughter's son, the one she raised as a baby, nursed, and struggled with life like everyone else. And now she makes a decision. Just before leaving this world. To leave the hospital against all medical advice, as her final act in life. She came to see me, her grandson, called up for the Torah.

I remember she was really beautiful. Made up and wearing a sheer white scarf on her head. She was beautiful. Every time she was in the hospital, my mom would ask if I wanted to come see her or if I preferred "not to see her like that." And what does a kid understand by "like that"? I thought her head had turned green or something. So I always preferred not to go. Retard, I already told you. But when I hung up the phone, I broke down crying. Just like that, on the couch in the living room. All alone with myself. But since then, I swear to you I haven't. And suddenly, suddenly my eyes got hot. I had to genuinely bend my head into my hands, and suddenly a bunch of liquid came out from between my fingers. And I didn't want her to see me start crying all of a sudden. What's with this shit now?! What, that she will want me out of pity?? Never!! Never! No! I wanted to stop and tell her to go or something, but every time I thought about opening my mouth, I realized that a sob was about to come out, and I immediately held it back until I finally just grabbed my shirt and quickly shoved my head inside before she could see. And now I was sitting on the sand with my head in my shirt and my hands gripping the collar from above, making sure it wouldn't fall. LSD is the drug of truth.

"Are you crying?" she asked as I covered my face. "Hey, Hagai, are you crying?" she asked again when I buried my head in my shirt. But I just waved my hand because I didn't want any sobbing. Let her go, let it be whatever, let it... something. Then she came over to hug me. "Don't cry, Hagai," she stroked my back, and I felt like I was about to explode, to scream with sobs and giant wails. What the hell is this now?! So I just ran into the sea. I got up like that, with my shirt over my face, and I ran like Fabrizio Ravanelli, the Italian national team striker who used to celebrate every goal like that, into the water. With the first wave I threw everything off and dove in, and then I just let loose. I started to burst into tears and wails in the water, not coming up for air, crying into the waves. No way she could have heard anything. When I came up for air, I looked at the moon and splashed water on my face, trying and struggling to calm down, but it wouldn't stop. I was sobbing and crying. Until I dove long enough for the salt to dry my tears. I stayed there like that, naked. Then suddenly, I felt her behind me. And I didn't want it. This thing I had wanted most in the whole wide world my entire life, was now right behind me, wanting me more than anything, hugging and kissing my back, caressing my arms from behind, my stomach and chest. Then I felt her nipples brushing against my back and her thigh rubbing against my butt. She was naked. She turned me around, but I wasn't in that state of mind at all. I was in a thousand hells. But she just kissed me with an open mouth, wrapping her leg around mine. My dick was already touching—getting stuck—in her triangle. While I was mumbling, she simply turned her round ass toward me, and after a bit of effort, she took me inside her. Suddenly, I was pumping her in the ocean, amidst the waves. I grabbed her breasts and kissed—biting her neck. She was moaning.

Loudly. She didn't care about anyone. And why should she care? To whom? The Indian from the guest house? The night guard who might be hearing? Some random tourist strolling along the beach in Goa who doesn't care about anything? So she fucks! She fucks in the sea of Goa, among the waves, enjoying herself, and to hell with everything else. Until that day, I lived in darkness, thinking I was having fun and that this was how things were. Simply because no one ever showed me the light. But the moment they did, I saw. Suddenly I saw it all and it was so much! We kissed passionately, and that kiss unfolded the entire world. The sadness, the joy. The pain, the anger, the disappointment. But also the love. My long-standing love for Moran Dagan. Moran Dagan, here I am saying it again, I love you. In just a moment, you'll throw me down onto the coarse sand, and I'll look at you. Only this time, it will be in the light. There I was, lying—or rather, sprawled on my back against the damp sand—and she just stood there with her perfection, moving in striptease-like movements. She had lightened her hair to a kind of platinum, and after weeks under the heavy summer sun in Goa, she was deeply tanned, looking like a mulatto model. And this time, this time I saw everything. All the curves, the nipples, the big roundness of her ass, her— nearing white gold— blonde hair falling and bouncing as she moaned above me. Suddenly, I didn't care about anything. Not about being seen, not about anything at all. We were fucking with the waves and the noise of the dogs barking at crabs or at people who seemed to pass by us at some point. What do I care about a couple of tourists or whatever... I'm completely high on LSD, in a full, complete stoneness that envelops me, wraps around me, and cradles me tight. There's no fear at all, no paranoia. I'm whole. I, and Moran, are now one. I came inside her maybe two hundred times. Or at least that's how it felt to me. So this is what an orgasm feels like, I suddenly understood in my newly awakened consciousness at nineteen levels, just as Studmaster-Major, a true Pride Leader, had explained so well. A true Leo. And what does he do right now? Screwing some tourist on the other side of the beach? Raising another chillum with the boys? And actually, what does it matter? What does anything matter now? And how did I get to this point of complete release, a true surrender, where I'm fucking and rolling with Moran on the beach, with my dick inside her for over an hour? Or maybe it's because I surrendered, because I lost to the universe and agreed to accept everything it brings my way. Afterwards, we lay in doggy style and tried all sorts of new positions. And I saw you. I saw everything. And you showed me everything. Thank you, Moran Dagan, for showing me the light. For bringing me into the light. For pulling me from darkness into light.

"What?" I asked, realizing she had said something and I hadn't really paid attention.

"Ah-ah..." she laughed that stunning laugh of hers. "Yeah, it doesn't go away with the morning coffee, the acid," she stared at me with a smile.

"But what did you say? That I'm different?"

"No, that I always thought you were different, but you're just a dumbass, forget it."

"Hahaha, stop talking like me, Moran," I laughed threateningly, and tried to understand the joke or the intent behind what she said. She paused when her eyes met mine. They revealed everything to her—my eyes. That I loved her. That I had loved her my whole life. That I had loved her for no reason from the very first moment I saw her. Now, with the lingering stoniness of the LSD, which, according to the Deputy of Studmaster-Major, serves as the truth serum, I was truly bare before her for the first time.

There's an Israeli researcher couple, who came up with a principle in nature called the principle of burdening. This principle essentially states that I burden myself, and therefore you can be sure that I'm not bluffing. Just like *the argument of Miggo* in the Talmud, which is a claim you must believe because it's a claim a person makes and it's not the strongest claim they could have made, so you must believe them because they could have lied to make themselves better off, and you would never know. So according to these two Israeli researchers, this is how it works in nature as well. A cat that a dog approaches arches its back and does not run away. Now, why doesn't it run away? It's not that it doesn't run away because it's stupid and-go-run-already-so-I-can-pass-by-with-the-dog, it doesn't run away because it's smart. It actually conveys a message to the dog. 'I see you, I can run away, but I consciously choose to burden myself, not to run away, and I arch my back really high so that you understand that I've noticed you,' just like a deer that jumps in place after noticing a tiger, effectively saying to it — 'I saw you, I'm just as fast, so let's save both of us the energy. However, what the Israeli researchers did not discover is that the principle of burdening also applies to humans. When I expose my emotions, I become more vulnerable. Here, I am composure-free, acting like a man, and pouring my whole heart out to you, and now let's save both of us some energy. Which is beautiful and could work wonderfully if humans were as connected to themselves as animals are. Because "acting like a man" in front of other men, I get. We men get it. But what does it mean to "act like a man" in front of a woman? What does that entail when dealing with a being who possesses a trillion and one complexities and sensitivities, where every little shift in a single vowel—whether intentional, accidental, or careless— can disrupt her world or, at the very least, alter her perception of you? Sometimes I think that perhaps a woman's brain is the greatest wonder in the world, greater than the pyramids and the Colossus of Rhodes. It is simply a marvel how that brain can interpret situations in an entirely different way. You go out for a meal with your girlfriend and friends, and on the way back, you discover that so many things happened that you weren't even aware of! But we don't pay attention not because we don't care; we don't notice these things simply because we're not women. Why do men have much less ability to listen to women? Because they're not women. It's like people who don't like cats. "What's with this shit? You whistle and he doesn't come, you pet him, and suddenly he goes 'weeeeeoooooow!' scratches you like hell and runs away—what a fucked-up creature." But he's not a fucked-up creature; he's just not a dog. We understand, "Okay, X happened—let's deal with it." It's not clear to us what comes from talking for an hour about X. For women, it seems to provide some value to discuss X for an hour. Maybe they learn about themselves, go through a process with X—I honestly have no idea—but men understand X and are now looking to move on. Not because we don't have the energy to listen any longer, but simply because once we understand X, we don't find value in continuing to talk about it. And perhaps acting 'like a man' in front of a creature who isn't a man is exactly the opposite of acting like a man in front of other men, and that's what trips everyone up. Because when you act like a man in front of other guys, you're brave. You say the truth to their face, not hiding anything. You speak your mind, and now it's on them to man up and deal with it. Or break. And if they break, they're labeled as 'a sissy,' or 'a pussy,' or any other term that literally means 'not a man.' And Moran... I know that... that she already has something for me. In the feelings. It started with the kiss in the garden of Fatel on Anat's birthday, and it's continuing now, after one hell of a twisted and cumbersome leap we made here in India. Every time we talk, I can feel it in my chest. If as kids it was a crush, then nerves, then fuck it, then a coma with respiration when she was with Arik, and here in India a bit of anger and tension—now I feel it. Every time we talk, I want to tell her. And now I know that she feels it too, but that's when I realized it! I need to act like a man and stay silent! Be strong and keep that bundle of emotions that's dying to explode on the world deep inside. I'm dying to grab her, look into her eyes up close, her gaze —for the first time—will be innocent towards me, naive, and questioning. She wants it, but it's still not cooked enough for her to take it off the heat. Men are like dogs, they see something and immediately bark, run, bite if necessary. A woman is like a cat. She arches her back. Just watch how a cat behaves, just like its feline relatives, when it suddenly spots a bug or a bird. Just like a tiger, it tracks it with unwavering eyes. It can follow it with its gaze for an hour. Then, it will slowly position itself in the right stance, and only when it's sure the odds are in its favor will it pounce. Like a cat, a woman has time. That's why lionesses hunt, not lions. They set ambushes, hide in the bushes, and sneak in slowly while each takes her position. They don't just run wildly at the prey; that would be a tremendous waste of energy. They have tactics, strategies. The lion only comes when it's necessary to subdue prey that's too large or in other exceptional cases. He doesn't lurk and follow the prey; he arrives after the lionesses have slowed down the victim and then pounces, unleashing one of nature's most powerful forces. A man is like a lion; he's like a dog. He runs and barks. He charges. He fucks. But a woman has time. We're so fucking retarded compared to you that it's unbelievable. Such retards. And I stumbled upon this by chance—an exception that does not prove the rule—so no woman suspects anything when she makes this move. But it happened to me. Before I started banging the Mother-to-be with the milk and the cock, she came to drink coffee with me one afternoon at the workshop, and during that time, I had just reconnected with a friend from the past who had been in a deep relationship for about five years. And suddenly I realize that both of them asked the same crafty question, if I'm there "just because you hope something will happen? Or do you also enjoy just being my friend?" And like a dumb dog jumping and barking without thinking, I immediately replied, "Of course not," half-apologetically. Only in retrospect did I come to the realization that these con artists simply wanted 'to smooth the lion's mane.' That you don't even think for a second that *they* might be in touch with *you* just for sex. Come on, fuckface. What do you think, she's looking for a friend??

"Slut…" I said, half hesitantly, half playfully.

"What?" She looked at me, tilting her head a little to the right and back, answering only after processing the data in her mind.

"I said you're a slut. That you all are."

"Me? A slut?" She smiled at me, her eyelids fluttering playfully.

"Uh-huh… screwing with me here on the beach, naked." Well, I was on acid, so I have an excuse for everything now.

"Actually, I am a slut…" she said, much to my surprise. "Very… slut." She continued and pushed me down, eventually slamming me hard to the ground.

"I'm a slut…" she said as she sat on me.

"A fucking slutty whore is what you are," I went all in. Now let's see if she's bluffing.

"Yeah... I'm a fucking whore..." she started grinding her ass while we were still dressed. "That's what I am..." She rolled her tongue but in a much sleazier tone.

'Damn, she's actually into it,' my British brain suddenly said to his Israeli side.

"A fucking bitch whore slut," the Israeli half shot back, and the British one nearly went silent, if not bolting out of the room and fleeing for all eternity.

"Yes... I'm a fucking whore slut... I'm a slut... I like to get fucked..." she chimed in.

"Little bitch..." my British half just had to chime in as well, "You love it when everyone fucks you because you're a slut, right?" I stretched all the strings tight, feeling like a few even snapped on my side as I felt her really well, struggling to get the words out.

"Yesss... I love it when they fuck me like a slut because I'm a slut..." She quickly stripped off her shirt and underwear, lying on top of me and swiftly getting rid of my pants, underwear, and shirt. Suddenly, she was rubbing against me while both of us were naked on the beach in Goa. There she was, moving back and forth as I was inside her, everything warm and wet, her breasts driving me mad as they alternately brushed against and pulled away from my chest.

"Yes... fuck me, I want you to fuck me... oh, yes... I want you to fuck me now like a whore... oh... yes..." she maintained a steady pace, alternating between slow and fast. "Fuck me... yes, fuck me... fuck me like a whore, like a slut... yes... I'm a slut," she began to grind on me hard, with a rhythm that wouldn't shame a twenty-year-old. "I'm a fucking whore... yes..." And I, with all the energy I had, just as Studmaster-Major said—you can dance for nine hours straight if you feel like it—I started pumping hard from underneath. Our rhythm was perfectly symbiotic, her going down while I pushed up in exactly the same tempo. Bam! The space around my cock met the space around her pussy with perfect force—Bam! Bam! Bam! "Yes! I'm a whore, fuck me like a whore!" she shouted, and I swear the entire beach in Goa could hear, "Yeah, like a whore! Like a slut! I'm a slut! I'm a fucking slut! I'm an Arab's whore! Yes! Yes!! Ahhhh!!!" She kept screaming, and I pumped even harder because I had run out of all the curses for whore, slut, and the fucking Arab's whore. She finally quieted down as well. Thank goodness. Like this is what I needed now, for her to start yelling curses at me in Russian, or Bolshevik, or some other language she just came up with. But she didn't. We were totally on the same level of stupidity that was turning us on. For years I've been saying this only at heart because I knew it just wouldn't come out right. Only once did I really feel it. A genuine inner voice told me the girl wanted me to spit on her face. Not a nasty, slimy snot like "hhhhhukkkk, tfu!", but a normal 'tfu' that's made from open lips and saliva—like the kind you exchange when you kiss. And I actually dropped her a hint, and it turned out my intuition was spot on. I told you, that initial instinct never lies. And it was awesome! Tfu! Tfu! And she was loving it! Later, I even slipped in a half-curse, but I quickly realized that *this* wasn't her thing. But aside from her, nothing. It always seemed to me like a fenced-off fantasy, something only "real whores" would want. But it wasn't. She just... it just turned her on exactly like it did me, precisely because she's not a whore and I'm not some master of sadomasochism with a 'Sir' title from a dungeon in Berlin. I pushed her back and moved down toward her thighs, a breathtaking sight for any heterosexual man. For a moment, they part, revealing a soft, pink slit that stretched slightly to the sides. I don't go down so often—it's hard for me. Too intimate. I'm also not a fan of all shapes, only those with a line that hides everything. And Moran's line is heavenly, divine. I send my tongue, and it parts slightly at the touch of my saliva. Inside, it's already wet, licking me back. She moans and sighs, and there's a good scent of clean skin and the salty water from the Goa sea, which occasionally splashes onto my face and washes everything away. I'm in love with the size and shape, feeling like I'm in the cockpit of a spaceship. From here, there's no need to move until you hear the final cry, announcing the arrival of spring. And while she's gasping and panting, smiling at the sight of me as I rise and lie down on top of her, I deliberately penetrate her with all my strength. With all my might. To wake her from her orgasmic slumber. After a few seconds, she's back into it. Once more, she's moaning—and how good it feels. Until she cums again, until she cums again. "Cum with me, cum with me," she's asking-demanding, even though it's clearly an utterly unreasonable command. She spins me around and takes control. On top of me, but I also make sure to pump from below. Our bodies are pressed together, dripping with salty water and sweat. We rub against each other—up and down, back and forth. We've found a good, steady rhythm. I reach my hands behind her and grab her ample ass that's thrown onto me, and she slams into my balls with every thrust. "Yes, cum with me, cum with me!" she screams, and I grip tightly, holding on as best I can, kissing her with all my tongue. "Ahhhhhhh!" we both shout as I release everything I have inside me to motherfucking hell!!! "Whoaaaaaa…...... wow!" she trembles above me, and I run my hands tenderly over her ass and back. Now she's lying on top of me. Reclined. We still don't kiss since the orgasm. Just a moment. Calming down. I want to kiss her. Here I am, grabbing her and giving her a kiss that's somewhere between short and long, with the morning star that began to rise, in the moonlit and sunlit hours of Goa, it happened. I never imagined I'd have a sex scene like this with Moran Dagan. And that we'd cum together so intensely. But now it happened. Just like that. Because I called her a slut.

20

"Il kalsat mash nafsa'hum! Il kalsat mash nafsa'hum!"
screamed the Arab woman in that same village in the Jezreel
Valley. The sock is fake.

"Ayna hiyya??" she continued in Arabic. "Wen binti??
Shu 'amiltilha?!" she asked where her daughter was and what
did he do to her.

And he's trying. Trying to explain what happened. But
she's already got the shoe in her hand, hitting him, and the
family is pulling him out of the place. And what can he say?
After all, he's just a messenger. And also, he doesn't really
know what for. A sock. A miserable sock that has long since
reeked of mold and dirt. What has it been through, he
wonders. But the guy swears. Swears that everything is fine
and that, simply put, the sock got lost. After all, fifty days in
the desert. It was supposed to be a three-day trip in an old
commercial vehicle that would make a few stops to avoid
raising suspicion in places and on roads traveled only at
certain hours. The Brits, the Arabs—who knows what
they'll do to you in this remote land of sand and swamps?
What does everyone want to be here so much for? He
swears he doesn't understand. Home. The homeland. The
land. For a moment, it seemed like everyone here had gone
mad, including Napoleon and Alexander the Great. The sun
would skip over the land of the Hebrews if it had the choice,
as Mark Twain put it so well. And where will he keep that
stinky sock now? So he threw it away. It got lost somewhere.
Is that what matters right now? Keeping the sock? He needs
to survive in the barren desert. Eat. Be careful not to get
killed by various tribes, animals, or God knows what. He
can buy another sock at the market when he gets back. He
remembers exactly what model and everything. For, she as
well did not buy it at the duty-free—a store with tax-exempt

products he heard about from the Brits that's set to open for the first time in the world at Gatwick Airport in London—She bought it at that same market from the brick vendor. There's only one like that. But she, she recognized it.

"Ai, ya binti... ya binti!!! Shu 'amiltilha?!" she cried out, weeping with a sorrow she had carried with her to the grave. She didn't know that her daughter, along with her sweet little granddaughter, were already marching back to the land of Israel.

Last night, I dreamed a wonderful dream. I was at the beach, resting my head on the shore, by the water's edge. Leaving behind a trail of ocean and foam spilling from it, almost reaching my toes resting on the sand. How delightful it is, how intoxicating the feeling. How misleading and dreamlike. How it can change in an instant. Here come the waters washing in; one bold and arrogant wave threatens to touch and sweep away my feet, along with all my thoughts. But I stand firm before it, unafraid. Here it is, nearly touching me, nearly threatening. But I have no problem letting it wash me clean from the grime that lingers here in every corner, and no one seems to care. The forces of nature, the waves, and the landscape crash against the rocks, coloring them a deep green under the sun's rays, which are now filtered by clouds. Here comes one that's truly audacious. It touches me; it's coming. I remain steadfast in my thoughts, and it almost kisses me. And then... after several hours, in which I must have fallen asleep, she woke me up. She was young and beautiful, but I didn't recognize her. By the time I awoke, it was already dark, and my head was in the water. If she hadn't woken me... but she did, as if just at the last moment.

"Do you know I've never DJ'd sober?" She changed the subject after a few seconds of locking her gaze onto mine as we walked back to the guest house. She noticed. I'm sure of it. She totally knows everything now.

"Really?" I was surprised.

"Yeah. Like... it's never planned, but there's no way I'm not offered a million things, you know,and it always turns out that I take a little something, like no biggie. But then I'm totally connected to the set, so it always works out best for me."

"Listen... you dropped a killer set last night... like, wow," I emphasized with wide-open eyes and my hands gesturing in awe.

"Thanks, Hagaichuk," she cupped my cheeks with her hands and gave me a kiss. "But don't forget you were high."

"No, it's not... like... listen, you were just amazing. You're a crazy DJ, you know."

"Thanks, Hagai!" she really emphasized, giving me a kiss on the lips, and suddenly I was gripping her neck and was hard again, and in my mind we were kissing passionately and stopping to fuck behind some stand right here in the middle of the street. "Will you show me tonight that cool market you found on the way to Patnem?"

"Sure, cool," I shook off my lewd thoughts. "Gladly".

"Yes? You'll take me?" She looked at me with a mischievous glance.

"*Of course...*" I replied in a whispery, sly tone. "Don't worry, Little Red Riding Hood... I'll take you. Come on, *I* know where Grandma lives..."

"Ah-ah-ah-ah-ah," she laughed, and it made me feel good as usual. "A dangerous guy, you are. A wolf in sheep's clothing."

"Well, sometimes dangerous guys are good."

"Ah-ah-ah-ah-ah-ah-ah... so I take it we're forgetting about the cool market?"

"No, no, I'm just kidding... But wait, let's go tomorrow," a different idea popped into my head. "Tonight, let me cook you the best meal you've ever had in your life."

"What?" was her surprised reply. And Moran isn't someone who gets surprised easily, so it caught me off guard too. "You cook?"

"I..." I nodded gradually, "I roll with it..." I ended up giving an answer that wouldn't confuse me too much.

"You what? You roll with it?" she burst into laughter.

"Oh, quit complicating things. You're being invited to a party, and you're asking what kind of mixes will be there?"

"Okay... I have no idea what you just said, but let's pretend I understood," she replied, and we both cracked up again in that acid-trip laughter. Honestly though, I'm so done with the food here in Goa. There's everything and nothing. So many flavors, but it all tastes the same. A good taste—India's taste. Slightly dirty, slightly spicy. But tasty. But frankly, almost everything tastes good to me. That's how it is when you've been single for a while. Canned tuna tastes good to you. Like, seriously! Throw in some veggies, za'atar, and a bit of cheese, and you've got yourself a great meal. And that's how it went that evening too. And she was really surprised. At first, she was surprised, then pleasantly so.

"What's this, Hagai? Are you messing with me?" She gently lifted her head toward me, unsure whether to laugh or if I was actually joking.

"Messing with you? Do you have any idea how long it took me to find this half-loaf of dark bread, like the kind they used to sell in the old grocery store in Fatel? In those brown paper bags? 'Dark or white?' Ephraim would call out to you from afar."

"You're right!" she shouted, her face lighting up with a smile, that same 11-year-old girl's smile. I loved her so much at that moment. "How I loved Ephraim from the grocery store!"

"And that green garbage can of his, full of olives..."

"And the one next to it, with the pickles!" We both shouted together.

"Wow... classic. Ephraim from the grocery store... I'll never forget that time Arik made me swipe chocolate milk with him at dawn when we stayed up late during some summer break, and Ephraim showed up and started chasing us with all his fat bouncing around in the big garden... I didn't go back to his store for years after that. Even though he knew I was a good kid. I think... But still. I couldn't look him in the face."

"You're a good boy, Hagai," she said, pulling me close and suddenly giving me a kiss. In an instant, we were really kissing, getting heated up. And in the background was the landscape of our childhood: Ephraim, the big garden. How much I wanted to grow up with you, Moran. To laugh together during recess, to jump on the crunchy autumn leaves on the path leading from the central garden to elementary school, to go to Ephraim's grocery store and buy chocolate milk together, to kiss for the first time—maybe on a bench in the garden. I was present with you in so many situations, especially during those teenage years where you talked, behaved, laughed, and cried. But I witnessed it all only as an observer... And with every one of those moments, I fell for you more, wanted you more. In every situation like that, I wanted to be there for you and for you to be there for me, because together we could be everything! How I wanted to grab you and shake you, to yell that you and I are the real deal. But I was just another insecure teenage boy... How I longed for you with every glance you turned away from me.

"Eh, eh, eh..." she grabbed my hand as it moved toward her curves. "You said the meal of all meals, you think you can fool me with dark bread and white cheese and expect it'll get you sex?

"White cheese, Moran? White cheese?? Do you know how far I traveled for this? I went all the way to Agonda to find it. Leben! Fucking! Leben!" I shouted, holding the creamy, tangy yogurt-like cheese in my hand as she looked at me in amazement. "And this..." I pulled out the green, golden bottle from under the table, "is olive oil you've never tasted in your life. It's got pieces of saffron in it!"

"Really?" she asked, her face wrinkling in curiosity.

"Well, actually, I'm not sure; maybe he was messing with me... but hold on..." I opened the leben and tore the bread into two huge pieces, black bread like they used to make, in that brown bag. "Here," I gestured to her. "Now we pour some of this," I drizzled the olive oil over the bread we each held in our hands, letting it drip all over while she stared at me. "And... dip." I handed her a big piece, overflowing with leben and Indian olive oil. She took a bite and even licked my fingers at the end after the liquid spilled out sideways.

"Mmm... wowwww, Hagwwai," she said with her mouth full.

"Hwwa?" I nodded, my mouth also full of fresh bread with leben and olive oil. "Lwike awt the Arwab's."

"Exwwactly!" she replied, and we wiped the leben and olive oil from each other's faces and, in a completely unplanned simultaneous moment, stuffed it into our mouths. And just like that we demolished the entire fresh bread with all the leben and tons of olive oil, and it was explosively delicious. Better than any restaurant I would have taken her to. And she sat there on the chair in that short beach dress, from which you could see bits of her swimsuit, her tanned thighs, and her chatain hair. I grabbed her and kissed her with lips that were still chewing, but no one cared. "Mmmmoooo, Hagwwaiii," she said, but she kept on kissing, grabbing me with her hands on my clothes while I held onto her tanned, juicy thighs. I lifted her back and held onto the remnants of her curves that protruded above the part spread on the chair. We kissed fiercely—with strength, with passion. Slowly, we devoured everything, kissing with our tongues with all our might, forgetting everything—bread, olive oil, leben that had long since smeared across the table and onto the floor. Afterwards, we lay there, sweaty, and I pulled her close to me, resting her against my chest. I gently caressed her and gave her a small kiss on the lips.

"International DJ... I brought you with leben and olive oil," I said and she burst out laughing. I hadn't even thought about it, whether to say or not. That's just me—always throwing my dirty humor into the air, and if someone can't handle it because it's uncomfortable or offensive, then we just aren't a match. Anyone who doesn't get that it's obviously a joke—because if it weren't, I wouldn't dare to bring it up on the tip of my tongue—then there's nothing for us to do together. But Moran got it. She understood in an instant. And I knew she would. I knew she was made of a different substance you don't come by often—the kind that made me fall for her at first sight. And for the first time, maybe, I think she did too.

We lay on the floor, not wanting to leave each other even for a moment. Like a couple on vacation. We were silent. I could feel it coming from her too. We both wanted it. Suddenly, and without any planning, we both wanted this—to be together. Moran Dagan, after more than twenty-five years, wanted me. And I wanted her by default. In the next moment, we charged at each other again with kisses. Wild sex. The craziest I've ever had in my life. She really was experienced, just as she had been at eleven. I always felt like I wasn't enough—something for her. And suddenly, I was. I loved her. Truly. Not that the love from when I was eleven suddenly spread its wings and returned, or burst forth from the climbing plant—the living fence behind which it had been hidden all these years. I know that's not it. I also know I simply felt a loving emotion for her. I cared for her, worried about her well-being, and wanted her to be happy. And then joyful. And then joyful with me. That's just how I felt. I wasn't angry as I had been towards her all those years. I was no longer bitter or preoccupied. There's a song by Depeche Mode called "Free Love." Is that what you want, Morani? Half love? Well, here I am agreeing.

And Perhaps I'm just rubbish. A small mire of a soul enslaved to sordid desires. But so are you. And again, that wasn't it at all.

21

We understood from Arik that we were probably unavailable for a couple of days, so they called him from home. "Something happened." At Fatel, they never tell exactly what happened. Not out of cheap gossip, but out of mutual respect. But there are levels of severity for the person being informed to understand the gravity of the situation. "Something happened" is definitely serious. It's not death, but it's serious. The news started to roll in quickly. Some virus from China. At first, they didn't take it seriously, but right now at least half the world is paralyzed, and Arik's mom is hospitalized because she has a fever, just to be safe. Are we staying here? If Arik's mom weren't in the hospital, that would probably be the answer. I never understood the people who go on a six-month trip after the army, and then they're told that their grandfather passed away, so they return home. Even if you make it to the funeral, it's just a stupid ceremony that doesn't mean anything to anyone, especially not to the deceased who's already gone and anyway you won't have the chance to say goodbye, even if you didn't get to say goodbye "properly" before you flew. "Properly..." What a hated and foolish word. Properly according to whom? *I'll* decide what's proper *for me* if you don't mind. And besides, between us, we never really get to say goodbye properly… So stay in Manali, you fucking retard!! Stay in Cusco, you moron!! What's the point of going back to the mourning tent now?! Keep your head down for the next few days, experience your sadness in one of the most magical places in the world, smoke a joint with the guys, and speak with your beloved grandma or grandpa before going to sleep or in your dreams. That's the best you can do. And keep on with your trip, because that's definitely what they would want for you.

"Will you stay here with me in Goa?" Bati's mother asked when I returned from washing my face the morning after, drying the leftover water from my face with a small white towel she had made sure to have ready.

"What?"

"We'll stay here in Goa," she shrugged.

"Okay..." I replied, turning to put the towel back. I had barely recovered from the slap that hit me yesterday, and now this? We were wrapped up in our tangled love, sweaty and dripping from our embrace. Body to body, one to one, we were one. And then he opens the door casually, as if nothing is going on. Well, to be honest, you can't really blame him. There's no way of hearing anything from outside. But once again, Arik takes her from me. Takes away that moment with her. A moment that is, after all, the accumulation and peak of all the moments that have passed since last night's kiss between the waves. And maybe it's good that he came in. Breaking the moment. Turning the page for us. It was ours, and now it's packed away and burned into our consciousness. It's there. Something in the hearts of both of us, shifted. But now what? We're gonna sleep together again, the three of us? Perhaps I'll wake up in terror in the middle of a horrifying reality whereas Arik is doing Moran while she's holding my head, suffering— enjoying it, because "How can one live any other way?" Fuck this shit! But luckily, Arik is a cool guy, and also a good friend who gets it. He sat with us for a minute and a half of small talk before volunteering to go get food for everyone.

"Come on," she quickly got up. "I'll bring it. Let's all go together. Until it's just the three of us again??". So we went down to the café beneath the guesthouse, and Pratiksha arrived with the menus. And now what, 'Let's stay here in Goa?' Like, live here?!

"'What will we work as?" I like, continued the joke. "You'll DJ for a thousand rupees, and I'll make furniture that no Indian here can afford to buy?' I asked, but she just smiled at me, not really getting the joke."

If you think about it for a moment, since everything here is really cheap, technically, even if I chose to work here as a carpenter, I'd have to sell for much less than back home, but it would also cost me way less to produce, and living here would be a lot cheaper too. Which means, in the end, this whole economy is one big load of bullshit. Trash talk that all sorts of "experts" have been feeding us for ages. Interest rates here, deficits there, fiscal year... Get the fuck outta here!! If you can produce a piece of furniture here that costs five times more to make back home, then it's all just a matter of decision. Both our wood and the Indian wood were once seeds sprouted from the ground. Charles Ponzi was an Italian who immigrated to the United States in the early twentieth century. He promised his investors an exceptionally high return on investment in a short time, when in reality, the funds presented as profits were actually the investments of the investors themselves or future investors. In essence, there were no 'real' profits, which is why this kind of scam is named after him—Ponzi scheme. But wait, what is Ponzi, really? It's creating a reality that supposedly doesn't exist. But you create it, and then it does exist! Because if no one withdraws all their money, then everyone is actually making profits all the time. Let's say that X has a million dollars, and he gets a guaranteed flat interest rate of six percent per year. So he has the million dollars, and every month he earns five thousand dollars 'out of thin air.' That's nice for someone with a million dollars. Think about it: a million dollars and you have a monthly income of five thousand dollars without having to worry about fixing your tenant's toilet. And if no one withdraws all their money but just takes out little amounts here and there, then everyone is always making profits. As long as half of them don't withdraw everything at once, then I've received real money, out of thin air, provided that we all stick to these rules. And then, why settle for six percent? You could also do ten. Even twenty. If all the economies of the world unite, or alternatively, if all the citizens of the world unite without asking any economy, we can all work only in whatever we feel like because there's no reason that many people would withdraw their money at once, because everyone is making profits *all the time*, and everyone's cash flow keeps pouring into the system, filling it up *all the time*.

Okay, stop. Think about it. Read it again. Think about it. There's absolutely no difference between a Ponzi scheme and a bank. For also in a bank, if everyone withdraws their money at the same day, it collapses. The only difference between a Ponzi scheme and a bank is that in a Ponzi scheme, the government isn't in on the deal. Still don't believe it? It doesn't add up? In the end, the money will run out? You prefer to nod along and pay half your salary for a flawed income tax that's all about robbing nearly half your earnings, with no idea where the money goes? Excise tax, sales and purchase taxes, and hold on, capital gains tax! You have to pay the government for the fact that the property you bought has appreciated over the years and its value has increased, as if the government itself took on the risk with you, participated in your mortgage payments, and shared in your deteriorating mental state due to your being enslaved to the bank, and would also share the losses if the value of the property dropped. And let us not forget about the added value, our dear VAT! Value-added tax. What does that even mean? What 'value' is exactly 'added' here? Is it like that same advertisement claiming a product is really great based on a 'public opinion poll' that no one could ever verify? Is that the added value? Who exactly does it add value to?! In addition to the value-added tax, they take a million percent in taxes on cars, and people are stuck with a Subaru from 1984 that they've had to patch up the transmission and engine at some rundown garage in some Fuckwhere town and then they wonder why there are accidents… But wait, let's not forget about social security! Which… really like… hundreds and thousands of dollars you pay every month, and the odds are you'll never see a dime from it ever again. Where does all that money go? So here's the deal: if someone goes bankrupt, doesn't pay child support, or just doesn't feel like working because they'd rather collect unemployment and there's no money to collect from, then social security pays out. That means that if someone gives a damn about everyone — everyone ends up paying! Amazing. What a fantastic democratic solution thought up by the almighty legislator, just… to sit back and flaunt from the amount of dick they're shoving up your ass without it even hurting. This is exactly the reason why Democracy turned Ponzi into a fraud. Because if Ponzi isn't a fraud, then how can we keep fucking you in the ass, in the name of the law of course? Wanna see how Ponzi can be 'a not fraud' at all? Let's take for example a country with ten million inhabitants. A thousand percent there's no economic equality among all. There are the poor, the rich, and those in between. The rich - want to keep their wealth safe from anyone touching it. The poor - want what the middle class has. And the middle class - wants what the rich have. All of this, of course, without considering the exceptions that don't prove the rule, because they are, of course, the exceptions. Now, let's try to resemble ants a bit more and ask each resident to contribute ten cents every day for the common good, which would go to a random citizen in the country each day. We might even exempt the rich if they agree, although they aren't required to. For the sake of example, let's take a thirty-five-year-old man who has about fifty years left to live. Ten cents a day equals thirty-six and a half dollars a year—less than forty dollars a year, right? But every day(!) one of the citizens will receive one million dollars, completely transforming their life. Every single day. So over fifty years, this man would have contributed just over one thousand eight hundred dollars for the common good, which is far, far less than any tax he would pay, yet over eighteen thousand people would receive one million dollars each. No taxes, no nonsense, just for the common good. Over eighteen thousand lives changed dramatically! If you could give one thousand eight hundred dollars as a one-time grant for a lifetime and turn eighteen thousand people into millionaires, wouldn't you do it? Now imagine if we could harness two billion people to behave this way. Ten cents a day. Two hundred million dollars a day. Two hundred people a day in the world receiving one million dollars. Seventy-three thousand people a year globally, each of whom could, of course, share with those close to them.

But the masses continue to believe in one of the greatest fictions in human history. Even though Stalin is long dead, along with Hitler, Mussolini, and Franco, the narrative must live on. Therefore, one of the cornerstones of democracy is to continually impose a method of sanctifying the flawed, corrupt, and abhorrent narrative— the thesis of good versus evil. In which, supposedly, the Good prevail. Who are the Good? This matter will, of course, be determined by its elected officials, as well as those responsible for its survival, such as law enforcement and the justice system. And so, if you're a border patrol officer — catch the terrible criminal smuggling drugs! Why? Because drugs are illegal. Why? Because we decided so. Why? Because this is how the Good prevail, and besides, you're doing your job and feeling good about it. Let us throw a hundred people a day into prison for ten years for smuggling, destroy families, leave two children without parents because, hey, their parents decided to smuggle cocaine from Colombia. And that Mexican guy? That wanted to score two thousand dollars and smuggled a few bags in his stomach? So what if he has a little girl and a wife and he won't see them for ten years, and the life of him and his family will be ruined? The important thing is we caught the Bad. Have you ever thought about why people use drugs in the first place? Do you think they do it to worship the devil and kill little kids? Have you ever stopped to consider that maybe they just want to let loose? To enjoy themselves? Who endorses you to decide for someone else what's good for them and what's bad for them? Democracy, the great paternalistic brother, neither darkens its rod nor sharpens its mind. If all drugs were legal, they would be regulated and wouldn't be mixed with rat poison that kills people; they would be sold in pharmacies, and the money would go to the state. At the same time, treatment could be offered to those who want to quit. Miraculously, ninety percent of organized crime worldwide would vanish overnight without putting anyone in prison or firing a single bullet. So where's the problem? Well, the only problem is, that then there would be no bad guys. And if there are no bad guys, then what do we, the Good, need to exist for?

And now fetch! Catch him! He smuggled m-a-r-i-j-u-a-n-a! Do you know what that can do to you?? Wait, why do I care? Me?! I care about you, of course. Because if I don't take care of you, who will? You? You will take care of yourself? And then... then what will I do? I need to supervise, to instruct... after all, I'm a public servant. It doesn't matter if I'm a total blockhead; I was elected. It doesn't really matter if it's for reasons of blockheadedness or nepotism; the important thing is that I was chosen. And now obey! Obey, or I'll unleash those dogs on you that can sniff out ecstasy even through cardboard and so many beautifully wrapped boxes of fish food. Ecstasy? Do you know what that can do to you?! For eight hours, you'll be the happiest person alive telling everyone you love them. Is that what you really want?? I, in the name of the law, of course, won't let that happen.

One of democracy's biggest problems is that the majority will always, always, always, by necessity and definition, be less wise than the minority. For how do we recognize someone as wise or a genius? They stand out from the rest. They are exceptional. There aren't many like them. And so, by necessity and definition, they will always be in the minority. In the Talmudic-Scientific Program, we learned many words in Aramaic. Melahekh Pinchei, or what many call Melahekh Pancha, is an Aramaic expression meaning "dish-licker," a flatterer. The legislator has been elevated to the rank of a demi-god, about whom it is repeatedly written that he does not waste his words in vain, "The wisdom of the legislature"—divine words, no less—despite the fact that he may very well be just another plate-licking-dime-a-dozen-politico-empty-suit swayed by lobbyists, who, of course, also work under the protection of the law, and this is certainly nothing like bribery, since they only "suggest." Just like pharmaceutical company representatives who merely "suggest" that doctors recommend their new drug, and then, entirely unrelated, there's an annual conference abroad at a five-star 'deluxe' hotel, complete with lavish hospitality for the doctors and their spouses. The Hippocratic Oath, too, has long since devolved into an uncontrollable "cover-your-ass" oath, and the science of medicine has been replaced by the worship of the gods of smugness and arrogance. In that same corrupt democratic structure, the doctors are the good ones entrusted with defeating the evil diseases, and only they have the superpowers to help with that. I personally took pills for excessive stomach acidity for years until one day I saw a movie where the hero takes a leaf called 'Watercress' for the same issue, so I thought, 'What the heck, let's give it a try. What do I have to lose?' Since I tried it, I haven't taken a single pill. Fifteen fucking years I took those damn pills, you bunch of fuckers in urinal color lab coats and stethoscopes up your asses... A leaf! A fucking leaf that costs a penny! Okay, so it's not scientifically or medically or cock-licking-in-the-ass proven, but it's not poison, right? It's a leaf sold in the supermarket next to the Swiss chard and hearts of lettuce in those cute plastic containers. So try, Mister Doctor-Professor-Your- Highness-The-Fucking-Asshole, offer the person to eat two watercress leaves, and maybe it'll work! If not, then start all your tests and your poison medications... Maimonides, one of the greatest jurists of all time, a prominent philosopher of the Middle Ages, who was recognized as a philosopher and physician in both Arab and European cultures, who was dubbed 'The Great Eagle,' whose genius and knowledge prompted the saying, "From Moses to Moses, there arose none like Moses." Among his many writings, he authored a work detailing the names of plants and their benefits, and lo and behold, this leaf cures something that countless industrialized and unnecessary pills have failed to resolve. But why on earth would he recommend a leaf, his highness the physician? To give a patient something completely unprocessed, that hasn't undergone a thousand trials and hasn't been written about in at least fifty prestigious journals? It hasn't been scientifically proven... What? What did we study medicine for for ten years, undergoing endless specializations and sub-specializations, just so one leaf could solve all your problems like some holy roller from a thousand years ago said? Let's perform another surgery, and another one, another opinion, another treatment, another manufactured and engineered pill full of junk and poison that you'll take for life. A leaf... Come on, like... You fucken kidding me. What do you think I am, a naturopath??

The number of people who die each year from obesity is roughly four times that of those who die from overdose, yet no one is calling for the outlawing of cholesterol and sugar. A processed hamburger served to you a minute after it goes from frozen to cooked, with mayonnaise preserved in a cancer-causing plastic bag, and ketchup loaded with sugar and preservatives in a cancer-causing plastic bag, alongside fries heated in rancid oil that's been burning for nine hours, releasing a toxic chemical called acrolein, which studies have found to have a direct link to arteriosclerosis, heart disease, and breast cancer. All of this is served on a bun made from white flour and white sugar, with canned vegetables, and for dessert — ice cream packed with sugar, full-fat lactose-laden milk, a billion sweeteners, colorings, preservatives, and whatnot, topped with whipped cream loaded with sugar, chocolate chips, and sugar-coated candies. A bomb of cocoa, crap, and shit — straight to the vain. But not only is it legal to eat this, it's also legal to get a sugar-packed drink refill and 'all-you-can-eat' buffet. But opium? Are you crazy? You smoked opium in India?! Tell me, have you totally lost your mind?? And then you lay there for a quarter of an hour, staring through the open roof at that Mama where everyone was on mattresses, and one by one, they approached with a disposable plastic straw, connecting to her pipe while she smeared something that looked like a piece of bird shit, and then you take a hit? Have you fallen on your head? Opium comes from poppies; they make heroin from it! But when I lay there, those were the twenty most peaceful minutes of my life. Yes, I know opium contains codeine and morphine, but I don't remember falling into injecting heroin since then, and it definitely didn't cause me ulcers or heartburns. I just lay there, smiled at the moon that smiled back at me, and I felt really good. And then we went back to the room and I went to sleep.

I once saw a show on TV where they didn't even catch someone with drugs; they simply searched his phone and found SMS messages about drugs, and they forced him to admit that when he was in his home country before boarding the plane, he smoked pot. From that, they concluded that this twenty-five-year-old guy might use drugs even within the borders of the U.S., exercise impaired judgment, and... are you sitting down? Cause harm to someone! After all, as law enforcement officers, their role is to enforce the law to the best of their ability. And so, they didn't allow him to enter so that no harm would come to U.S. citizens. Later in the show, they caught the guy to whom the cardboard package containing twelve kilos of ecstasy had been sent earlier, which the dogs sniffed out through the cardboard and the fish food boxes. Because, if you receive drugs by mail, in most countries, possession is presumed to belong to you. Now go prove you don't have a sister, and that you didn't fuck your grandmother... In plain terms, if you don't like someone, you can just send them drugs in an envelope and get them stuck in a mess for at least a few months, in the best-case scenario. Let me tell ya, these legislators are just geniuses. The Genius Democratic Governance. That border officer from the show later explained that they "helped save lives" today. Save lives! Honestly, poor guy. He's not to blame for being programmed to be a fucking moron with an incubator graduate diploma. The young Mexican who tried to make a quick buck and earn a few dollars to get by for the near future has a young wife and a baby girl. His ten-year sentence won't change anything. You haven't moved a single piece in the stupid chess game between the brainless democratic world and the real world. He's just another "monkey." There are millions like him who will do exactly the same thing tomorrow. The only thing you've done is ruin lives. His, his wife's, the little girl who will grow up without a father, his parents', and all his relatives. 'Okay, he's to blame for breaking the law'. Well, go on, say it. Everyone say it. That's what makes it the wisdom of the crowd, and you not off the wall. But if you actually used your brains and thought it through, you'd quickly come to the conclusion that he's not at all a threat. Because today it's simple — there's cool, there's not cool, and there are crooks. The crooks — shameless crooks. They don't swipe like they used to or pay half with counterfeits or go dark; they send you a message saying your computer is locked unless you pay a ransom. I'm a crook right in your face. And those can be identified, and there are ways to deal with them. I would suggest sawing off their hands without anesthesia, for example, live streamed to the whole world, and now let's see how many people still want to be hackers. But the establishment, of course, won't approve of that because it's... too brutal. Too horrific. It's not politically correct. Not suitable. What, are we savages? There sits the hacker at home, holding his belly from laughing at the ease and wonder of being a criminal in the democratic world. Or all kinds of gaming apps where you supposedly play against people from all over the world, except that, strangely, the 'opponent' always gets the cards or dice they need. But those apps are so... innovative, so colorful and shine at you, that you don't even consider for a second that you're actually playing against a computer that makes you lose so you'll have to buy new coins. And it's also super cheap, so it's no biggie, right? It's not like we actually need to hang the filthy kid who's now driving a Ferrari around London in the middle of the main square and set him on fire before he chokes to death... Stinking thief in a suit... But hey! Hey... it's not politically correct. Due to the fact that democracy is the governance of stupidity, nepotism, and self-righteousness, criminals are treated with kid gloves. The weak who have fallen through the cracks in your democratic folly, in the imperfect world you created, where no one was there to educate him, to lend him a hand when he needed it so he wouldn't fall, may have a heart of gold and be the first to stop and help you if you fell in the middle of the street. But he remains a fool with forms to fill, an idiot whose computer is blocked, a simpleton who is signed on official documents he understands nothing about. Therefore, he reacts in the only way he knows, which is to try to 'make a hit'. Democracy, of course, will throw him in jail for that, toss him behind bars, and easily rid itself of the voiceless and those unable to express the injustices done to them on a daily basis, while giving immense power to fools who can easily become lawyers or police officers, for that matter. If you end up in court against a cop, his word carries more weight in the judge's eyes. It's a principle of democracy to favor the word of law enforcement, her people, of course, even if we're dealing with a complete fool and liar against a good person with clean hands. That same dime-a-dozen servant-becomes-the-master lawyer who will tear apart the poor soul who can't make ends meet and is late on his property tax payments to the municipality, will fiercely defend the con artist who exploits the elderly and Holocaust survivors and will lie brazenly on television, claiming that his client 'acted in accordance with the law,' and now you go prove otherwise. Democracy prefers to be politically correct and allow parasites who rely on other parasites to gnaw at it, to rot and contaminate it from the inside more and more with each passing day, in contrast to any animal in nature. About a billion cases a year are closed through confidential settlement agreements, and thus the filthy villain who caused harm to so many people and perhaps even death, effectively buys immunity from criminal prosecution. And this is entirely legal. Ted Bundy was almost set free were it not for a single bite mark he left on the buttocks of one of the dozens of women he brutally raped and murdered. Without that mark, there might have been room to doubt the systemic stupidity, because according to the "fruit of the poisonous tree" doctrine, if evidence against someone is obtained illegally, even if it is highly incriminating and it is absolutely clear that they are guilty, they cannot be convicted. This is because the wicked have rights, and those rights must be respected. The principle of justice in the "enlightened" democratic and Western society, which is supposed to be a fundamental overarching principle in any proper society—according to which the law should stand by those who have been wronged, leading to the punishment of liars, thieves, murderers, and rapists—has long been replaced by a principle of self-righteousness and now exists only as a hollow slogan, serving as an opiate for the masses who swallow it like fish.

The Bible is a great source for the laws of the communist society that once existed. As it is written in the book of Leviticus, "*Anyone who injures their neighbor is to be injured in the same manner: fracture for fracture, eye for eye, tooth for tooth; as he has caused a blemish in a person, so shall it be done to him.*" The commune knows how to solve its problems wonderfully, cutting down the weeds, just like every animal in nature instinctively knows how to take care of itself. If for a first offense you were to lose a hand, for a second offense a foot, and for a third you'd get a bullet in the head in front of your wife and children, within a very short period, crime in the world would drop to zero. You punished those who deserve it and who disrupt the existence of good, innocent people. But the democratic beast prefers authorities, systems, bureaucracies, committees, and other various contaminating diseases that operate together in the cacophony of a massive and sophisticated cuckoo clock, where all the gears eat and distort one another.

Say what you'll say, but at least in totalitarian regimes, there's no bullshit. Anyone who spoke against the regime, Stalin slaughtered his motherfucking mother's mother and was sent to the Gulag; the Chinese rolled tanks over protesters in Tiananmen Square; in Iran, they shot female students in the streets, and Bashar al-Assad slaughtered innocent civilians and called them rebels. 'I am the totalitarian dictator, and you can all go fuck yourselves'. And what did the enlightened democratic Western world do about it? Exactly what Enlightenment Europe did when the largest ethnic cleansing in history took place ruthlessly within its boundaries, and everyone knew: nothing. For years, they have been groveling before the Iranians, even though the Western world could free the Iranian people in a minute and a half. Who are the ayatollahs? A bunch of nobodies holding an entire nation by the balls for forty years. The American commandos could eliminate them in an hour and set the Iranian people free. In one hour. Who is Assad and the Syrian army compared to all the armies of the Western world? Who are the corrupt rulers keeping the entire African continent in horrific poverty, despite being the richest continent in the world in terms of natural resources? The same goes for North Korea and China, which hold Hong Kong, Tibet, and a billion citizens without basic human rights. With China, it may be a bit more complicated, but together, the Western world is capable. One complex month, one complex year, and the whole world would be free. But the impotence of the Western world, where everything must be politically correct, does not allow for this. And also, mainly, because every leader who ever had the balls is already deep in the grave. Yet the greatest genius of Democracy lies in the fact that it doesn't make you stop and think, because you're confident that there is law and order, and therefore—everything will be alright. It wants you to internalize somewhere, in the hidden forest deep within the back of your mind, that if you stay on the path—No ill shall befall you. Political correctness safeguards the dignity of the guilty while being lenient towards the innocence of the innocent, as it serves the interest of Democracy that one remains a fool, whose home is invaded, whose computer is blocked, who is raped, and yet can do nothing about it. And all of this is because it is the most hidden lie in history. The holy grail that is meticulously guarded by those in power, who are protected thanks to the 'bribes' they pay to the government in the form of taxes, jobs, and other such favors. Those who suffer are the ones who have nothing with which to 'pay' protection to the sovereign. There is no justice; there is law. Considerations of efficiency, considerations of policy— considerations that are foreign to justice. And this exalted in sanctity law, which was enacted by whom if not the great and wise legislator, is enforced by robots that are by law, without the right of thinking, and if you want to appeal against any of the mentioned above, you turn to the justice officials who were appointed, how else, by that same law. Incredible.

In the Talmud, it is explicitly stated that witnesses are required to identify the perpetrator by their eye witness, "the testimony of the eye is greater than a sign, for a sign can be easily mistaken, whereas there is no mistake in the eye witness." Our sages understood all too well that reality can be manipulated to appear as if. That everything is merely a game where one throws the dart and draws the circle around it. And so, a recent study found that thousands of death row inmates who confessed to crimes during interrogation, were later found to be innocent after their executions, as the age of DNA analysis began and suddenly the true culprit was identified.

But the masses nod and continue to trust that Democracy is simply a wonderful, magical, and magnificent thing. The masses pay the price because their only choice is to tear the powerful from their homes and slaughter them on the guillotine, just as was done in the French Revolution, and of course no one will do that because it goes against the law that 'protects him...' If a herd of buffalo simply stood and turned toward the predator charging at them, no buffalo would ever be preyed upon. But instead they flee, and the weakest or slowest among them pays the price for the stupidity of their crowd. The crowd also take out mortgages from the bank and rely on the bank's mortgage advisor, whose interest is, quite literally, that they lose as much money as possible, because the more they lose, the more the bank—the one paying his salary—profits. But hey, the advertisement on television looks really nice, and the crowd is crazy for advertisements. They take a famous person, pay them a ton of money, and then he or she shamelessly lies out loud that they use this or that product, causing the crowd to buy it. Amazing. And it is also perfectly legal. In Israel, state lottery and betting are legal, though casinos are not. Because unlike the extreme conservatives in Dubai who allow themselves to be smart and provide their state with a constant income while still forbidding themselves alcohol, at least outwardly, our extreme conservatives—some of whom have even served time—claim that God says gambling is absolutely disgusting and even shameful, at least outwardly. And a private investigator is legal too. Despite the Basic Law of Human Dignity and Liberty, alongside legal approval, he's allowed to invade even deep inside your underwear. And the crowd? They nod along. Our sages established that "this one benefits and this one loses—he must compensate." Yet the law allows contractors to build and wake an entire neighborhood from seven in the morning with terrifying knocks that penetrate the skull, regardless of whether someone is working a night shift or simply wants to sleep until ten. You profit from the construction; I suffer—compensate me, and then I'll decide if it's "worth it" to sleep with earplugs. But no court, no matter how Supreme, will rule against this because then they would have to compensate countless people, and the construction industry would collapse. Go seek justice in your motherfucking cunt.

That same friend of mine, the lawyer with the laptop, binders, and the loaded chick from Rishpon, once filed a petition to the Supreme Court against a government body responsible for allocating legal resources for free to those who cannot afford it. In this case, his client was divorcing someone who was quite well-off, and lo and behold, she received the requested resources. About thirty women and two and a half male pets showed up to the Supreme Court on behalf of that governmental body. It turns out this has simply become a sort of gendered junta of women looking out for women, come what may. If they had any brains, they'd realize they are actually harming women. Not only by giving them a bad name, as ones who can only succeed through deception, but also because tomorrow there won't be money for someone who really needs it—not to mention any male who truly requires help. After all, feminism is about fighting for equality, isn't it? But it quickly became clear to everyone that even in the Supreme Court, the highest court of **justice** responsible for integrity, truth, morality, ethics, and fairness in a democratic state, the place where if everyone is screwing you in the ass while whipping you, there's supposedly someone who will hear your voice. Even there, there are systemic considerations. After all, if they convict them, it's a fiasco. This is a state body; heads will roll. Na... It's a hard pass.. Unlike in communism, where every 'Tavari' reports on their friends, in the democratic arrangement, friends actually protect one another. So they had the guys from the junta promise to behave nicely and even gave them a little "tut-tut" with their fingers, but they rejected the petition. Why?? There's a par excellence corruption here, embezzlement of public funds, gender-based discrimination—whatever you want! Throw them in jail!! Do your fucking job, you bunch of pussyass fuckers!!!

In the book of Deuteronomy, there is a special commandment regarding a person who converts: "*And you shall love the sojourner, for you were sojourners in the land of Egypt.*" The Laws of Converts in the 'Shulchan Aruch,' one of the most important books in the world of Jewish law, demand even more and teach that after conversion, not only is that former Gentile considered a Jew in every aspect, but the sages say that one must be even more careful about their honor than that of a Jew by birth, because they have made greater efforts to become Jewish. Some people think that transgender individuals are merely men in dresses who wear makeup and wigs in order to deceive them and fuck them in the ass. However, contrary to the worthless judges of the Supreme Court, a transgender woman is perhaps the farthest thing from it. These are individuals who haven't just 'converted' or changed their way of life—but actually transformed their entire bodies through countless surgeries accompanied by extremely painful recovery periods, all to be authentic with who and what they truly are—the last thing anyone could say about the bunch of judges in the parodic joke known as Democracy.

In the era of the ancient judges, true sages with vast and extensive knowledge, like the Tanaim, Amoraim, and Saboraim, the parties would present their claims, and the judge, well-versed in law and wisdom, would ask questions—and make a ruling. There was no need for dull-witted individuals whose conflict resolution would undermine the very foundation of their livelihoods, routinely attacking innocent people, regardless of who gets hurt and trampled along the way, as long as the degenerate in a suit receives his fee—all, of course, under the auspices of democratic law that leaves everyone at the mercy of a judge with systemic considerations who is afraid to make decisions. In the commune, we could appoint 'tribal elders' to rule as in the past, according to standards of justice, each communine pursuing the justice they seek based on their own measures, without regard to nationality—a mere whisper lost in the roar, except for the fleeting emotional connection that pales in comparison to life itself, with all its various aspects and layers. It's incredibly moving to be Jewish on Rosh Hashanah, to light Hanukkah candles surrounded by family, to sit in the Sukkah, or to gather on Passover night when, for just one evening, we are all truly reclining together. If you're abroad, you might even celebrate like a semi-orthodox in the making. But this experience is precisely the opium for the crown that Democracy offers you—a sense of belonging to a nation woven from history, layered with the finest emotional depth. There's no doubt about that. However, it inevitably comes at the expense of, and in place of, belonging to your real group—the one with values identical to yours and a system of justice and policing that aligns with your beliefs.

But wait, go on and say, at least the media in a democratic country, unlike in dark regimes, is free, and will aid in uncovering and exposing the truth and protect us from any harm, right? Yes? No? After all, that is the journalist's role, to speak on behalf of the downtrodden and voiceless, to expose corruption and lies, hallelujah! Yet most journalists today have long since transformed into a kind of emulsion of something unclear, without giving a damn about the truth. I remember that once a senior academic scholar decided to go public with his concerns regarding the Rabin assassination events, because even without any conspiracy theory, there are plenty of question marks... But the interviewer on television simply didn't approve of it. He preferred to be 'politically neglect'. The main thing was to be considered 'okay,' to ensure he wouldn't risk his status and shout that 'The emperor is naked' if no one else is shouting. *He* wasn't about to take any risks. Therefore, he really scolded him. That 'Big Israeli Hero,' whose greatest challenge in life was getting accepted to Galei Tzahal at the age of eighteen, has the exclusive privilege of the absolute truth when the microphone is in his hand. For this is exactly what they did to Galileo Galilei, who we now know was right while the entire world was wrong. The entire world! And what do you think, that the scientists of the past didn't think they were at the forefront of technology? Did they say to themselves, 'Well, what do we know? We're in the Middle Ages'? They were convinced they were at the cutting edge of knowledge and progress, just like our scientists today. Just as we will look like Neanderthals two hundred years from now with our stupid iPhones. At the end of the nineteenth century, a prominent scientist with a worldwide reputation was asked what he anticipated would be humanity's main difficulties in the coming century. His educated response was that he was very concerned about the horse manure that filled and actually flooded the roads. A half-centimeter-sized chip once took up an entire room. If someone in those times had claimed this, they would have been forcibly committed. In that same nineteenth century, the scientific community, by a majority opinion, believed that women had smaller brains and thus men were smarter than women. The significance that the scientific community assigns to what is 'true' and what is 'correct' in our world is exactly the same as the significance of a dog arranging a blanket while it is terribly preoccupied with turning around a hundred times in its plastic bed before lying down to sleep. But for most journalists, truth and correctness have long ceased to be of interest. Their energy is concentrated solely on the pursuit of headlines. Even if the words weren't said with such intent, what matters is that they will be perceived as such. A constant striving to extract a "scoop!"—a misplaced word from the interviewee who isn't trained in journalistic tricks and manipulations. And even this is done under a veil of cowardice and excessive caution. "People will say about you that you are this and that, that you did this for this and that." No! You claim that! Say it, Herr journalist—"I think you are this and that, that you did this and that." Because the moment you say, "Some people say," it gets etched in people's minds. And usually it's the most absurd thing that you yourself have concocted in your frenzied and deluded mind. So take responsibility for it! You're a freedom fighter, right? Then say, "I say..." you worthless-coward-piece-of-shit-afraid -for-his-ass! And you also have nothing to worry about because even if you publish a report or say something that devastates a certain individual economically, mentally, or publicly, and after a few years it's proven that he actually did nothing wrong, you won't pay any price. For, if someone dares to criticize the media, it will immediately cry out about corruption and attempts to silence voices, just as it cries out day and night against nepotism, forgery, fraud, and other societal ills, while it itself is ensnared by them, whether with intent or in blissful ignorance. When we were in high school, we would travel to Tel Aviv, to an area that once thrived with garages, and today, in a stunning paradox, accumulate most of the Israeli media. They called the club 'Roxanne,' where music played that echoed nowhere else—Pantera, Sepultura, Megadeth, Iron Maiden, Paradise Lost—true heavy rock, metal at its finest. Monday nights were 'Death to Techno' nights, a threat that almost annihilated the rock scene of the '90s, dethroning the '80s pop from its coveted throne. We would dance the 'Pogo,' a circle where you'd jump in, giving and receiving not too severe kicks. Just a bit of fun—no blows leading to fights. But since we were a big crew—for as boys we needed to organize well to venture to the big city—then if someone got annoying, kicking too hard or just didn't sit well with us, he'd suddenly receive kicks from ten directions, not knowing what hit him, for we were all, in essence, watching each other's backs. Try criticizing a media person and brace for a tsunami you'd never imagined existed. And if he's really guilty and can't be silenced, they'll just turn down the heat. It's just.. unpleasant, unseemly—after all, he's their colleague, and a friend. But god forbid it happens elsewhere, then they'll unleash their loudest trumpets. The sages of the Talmud long ago proclaimed that he who declares another unfit for marriage likely carries that flaw himself, for *the one who disqualifies does so through their own blemish*. If in the past the media cried out from the shadows against oppressive regimes that silenced it, today, almost without you noticing, it itself has transformed into a tyrannical power like no other.

"*Let the youths arise and engage before us!*" declares the authoritative tone, echoing Avner Ben-Ner, commander of Saul's army in the Book of Samuel. There the opposing viewpoints clash in the studio, and the audience at home splits into factions—some for this side, others for that. And churn out headlines time and again, regardless of the blood spilled, oblivious to the truth's anguished cries and whose lives have been shattered to their very foundation. And that one's corrupt! And that one's a villain! And that one's a criminal! And he incites! And these are very serious accusations you're making now! Very serious! Yes, audience at home, did you hear that? Beware! And what you're doing here is outrageous!! Wow, yeah, let him have it, and he'll really show him in return, giving him a taste of 'the wrath of his forefathers.' Oh, what a glorious Segment! Good versus evil, evil versus good. Our eyes are blinded, drowning in the ocean of Democratic lies.

"The Blessing of Justice," the eleventh blessing in the Amidah prayer, is the central prayer in the prayer order. The Sages literature particularly highlights and emphasizes this prayer, which is taken directly from the mouth of the prophet Isaiah in the first chapter of his book. Its importance is so underscored that it is recited in a whisper, with the supplicant standing with feet close together, as if pleading—*"Restore our judges as at first, and our counselors as at the beginning!"* No more centers of power, nepotism and its cronies who will rule forever; courts operating on principles of systemic efficiency that have nothing to do with justice. A police officer, a prosecutor, and a judge who prefer to throw someone in jail and 'close the case' rather than hard work, journalists seeking headlines instead of the truth. A system that sanctifies a foul charade. Something that will work with the fewest casualties. Something that can bark, while the caravan moves on.

Not so long ago, all around the world there were fences in football stadiums. It was natural. And people would climb those fences, jump over them, and hurl insults at the players and fans of the opposing team sitting beyond the barrier separating the stands. Spitting, throwing things… Then one day, someone decided to try an experiment and remove the fences. "Have you lost your mind?" they said, "People will kill each other!" But the experiment was tried. Then another one. And today, there are almost no fences in football stadiums. When someone stands in front of you without anything in between, you act less like a lunatic and more like yourself. Just like you wouldn't start screaming at someone who accidentally bumps into you on the street, yelling, "Hope you get cancer, you bastard! Fucken son of a bitch..." But on the road most definitely. *"I*-hope-you-die-you-son-of-a-bitch- what-are-you-cutting-in-for-wait-your-turn-like-I've-been-waiting-for-an-hour-motherfuckerrrrrrrrrrrrrrrr!!!!!!!!!!!!!!!!!!!!"*. There's this crazy guy on Instagram with a farm where he raises all kinds of animals together from birth. He's got videos of lions and hyenas that are friendly, a tiger playing with a goat—things you'd never imagine. They don't see themselves as enemies because they weren't raised in a pack where everyone looks the same and knows they need to fear this kind or attack and eat that kind. They just see all sorts of creatures they've been with since day one, so no one harms anyone. *"And the wolf shall dwell with the lamb, and the leopard shall lie down with the kid,"* as it says in the Book of Isaiah, is not an unattainable utopian dream, but a possible reality. *"For behold, I create new heavens and a new earth, and the former shall not be remembered,"* Isaiah continues later, speaking the words of the Lord. *"And I saw a new heaven and a new earth, for the first heaven and the first earth had passed away,"* is written with amazing precision in the vision of John, in the verse that opens the penultimate chapter of the New Testament. If you place two dogs on either side of the dog park, they'll usually bark at each other like crazy, if you open the gate they'll play. To maintain its status, Democracy insists on erecting more and more fences between us. "Beware of what's out there!" it shrieks, instilling fear in us, "Watch out for everything beyond the fence!" For its survival, Democracy must persist in rooting in our minds the axiom that it is the best alternative. But Democracy is merely a tool—the most sophisticated one invented so far—for preserving the rule of the classes. And now, all that remains for the masses is to answer the question that their brightest minds and crowd wisdoms have yet to resolve—a dick in the ass, it's good or bad?

I once saw a video of ants carrying flower petals, creating a kind of throne for their dead queen, as in a real funeral procession. But don't be mistaken—this 'queen' isn't actually a monarch giving orders. Ants work together without any supervision. They have no 'leadership.' What we're witnessing is highly developed collective behavior for dealing with challenges without any top-down command. Those 'queens' are simply fertile females who never leave the nest because all they do is lay eggs. And do you know why this tiny, insignificant creature, from our point of view, is a billion times happier and more complete than all of us combined? Because it's part of an immense puzzle and a perfect fabric of a living, thriving, and functioning organism—functioning a billion times better, yes, a billion, did I emphasize that enough?—than our corrupt, rotten society, where extreme poverty still exists in half the world, and dark regimes suppress every attempt at revolution in the other half. At this very moment, there are millions of people who were born just like you and are trapped in a mental prison. Living under regimes of fear and terror, in poverty and sickness. Now show me one ant poorer than its neighbor, one cockroach forbidden from doing this or that. There aren't any. And so, if in the five thousand years we've existed here in some form of civilization, we haven't found better solutions, maybe it's time we learn from them. If only we paused for a moment and tried to apply this to ourselves, to allow processes to unfold without centralized control, perhaps we could solve a significant portion of humanity's problems. We don't need a king or a tyrant to force us to act, just to stay united and cohesive, as nature intended and has mastered, functioning as a single unit. And for that, we don't need Communism, Marxism, or any of Plato's and his cronies' Theories of forms —just to look downwards, towards nature. If only we were to look around us, especially beneath our feet—far beneath—we would see at any given moment a billion trillion populated colonies of organisms functioning in a brilliantly systematic manner, far beyond what you think or can imagine, that have survived and will continue to survive even a nuclear holocaust. Without poverty, without scarcity, without crime. Without depression and without suicides. A million trillion times more than you can fathom. Just because you occasionally encounter a trivial individual in the trillionth of triviality, carrying a leaf or disturbing the tranquility of your home, makes it absurd to draw the obvious conclusion that almost all of you do: that it's tiny, marginal, and redundant. It is a thousand times less marginal than you. Not a thousand, a billion. "Yes, but we made it to the moon," you'll say. So fucking what?? What has landing on the moon done for us other than killing an uncountable number of our best and brightest in the process? Is that what's going to lift your spirits right now? That once we landed on the moon and in the future, we'll land on Mars? Wow, I really give a flying fuck... What do you think, that an ant has no clue about its existence in the world? That all ants are some sort of golem or zombie, just wandering from place to place? They have communication a billion times more sophisticated than ours, and for that reason, they work together in a way that's far more marvelous and advanced than we do. Have you been aware of what ants are capable of, your mind would be blown. They prevent the spread of diseases by isolating infected individuals, collecting tree resin with antimicrobial properties, and spreading it around the nest. They even transfer a tiny amount of pathogens to healthy individuals to create a non-lethal infection that generates immunity—just like we learned thousands of years later. During floods that threaten the existence of fire ant colonies, they gather together, connect their limbs, and form a structure resembling a raft, which they use to float on the water until they reach safe ground. There are architectural structures created by ants holding onto each other, forming bridges using only their bodies to move from place to place, or giant "bongaluses" in the middle of the jungle for warmth. The legionary ants, probably the highlight of the ant family, cover distances equivalent to hundreds of meters—akin to a marathon for humans—almost every day, and they do it all while blind, communicating only through touch and chemical signals. They charge at anything that crosses their path and simply eliminate tens of thousands of creatures each day. Even a wasp nest is helpless when legionaries attack and raid the larvae for food. Just to put it into perspective, a single wasp can wipe out an entire beehive, and a legionary ant is like a fly compared to an elephant in relation to a wasp, but cooperation prevails. Crocodiles, which we refer to as a type of elongated and dangerous lizard, have existed according to science, for between seventy and two hundred million years. What are we compared to them? Nothing. Pip. A heartbeat on the counter. They have hearts, digestive and respiratory systems that we could only dream of, and they are almost entirely immune to any virus or bacteria. Water bears are microscopic creatures that can survive in the midst of a volcano, in a vacuum, at temperatures of nearly minus three hundred degrees, and in radiation a thousand times stronger than what kills any other living being. But why stop at animals? Cotton, yes, cotton wool—long before those brilliant and sophisticated humans uprooted it—had actually developed a substance on its own that it spread, which attracted and magnetized a type of insect from afar that eliminates the parasites harmful to it. With all the advanced culture we think we possess and our 'meteoric' medical and technological progress, we are a joke compared to the nature surrounding us. A breeze that, sooner or later, will pass. But we look at nature the way we look at the Indians—from above.

The craziest segment I encountered regarding the life dynamics of lions, was in a show featuring three lion prides living in the same environment. One pride was violent, let's call it "the Ganana." The second was "the Hill Pride," and the third was "the Jungle Clearing." The Ganana had herds of buffalo in their territory, and one time, they tortured a young lioness from the Hill Pride to death, not killing her immediately as they could have, but torturing her to death after she and her pride ventured into their territory in an attempt to hunt buffalo. They literally butchered her mercilessly, as if to say, "This is our territory." For them, it's a matter of life and death at every moment. The next day, the Jungle Clearing pride was plotting against a giraffe. The lionesses in this area are among the few in the world that specialize in giant hunting. There are lion prides that live near elephants, and they actually specialize in hunting elephants. It's all about strategies and tactics passed down through generations for thousands of years, with the young ones looking through their future murderous eyes with endless curiosity about that thing in which, at the end, they lick blood from one another's fur… And while the giraffe was bending down to drink, the lionesses from the Jungle Clearing approached, while those from the Hill Pride—who just the day before had experienced trauma with a lesson that left no room for doubt—watched the unfolding scene from above, from their territory on the cliff. They had learned their lesson and waited anxiously, hoping that perhaps the giraffe would run into their territory directly into a meal. What happened was that in the heat of the moment and driven by hunger and heat—which surely blurred their judgment—the Hill Pride simply began to close in on the giraffe, disregarding the fact that they were once again crossing into another's territory, because their tempting and advantageous position to flank the giraffe outweighed any other considerations. The taste of blood intoxicated them. Thus, they simply cut off the giraffe that the Jungle Clearing lionesses had already seized by the legs, and - voilà! One jumped onto its back, another one followed, and the moment it lost its balance, the poor creature sealed its fate in this life. Suddenly, twenty lionesses were on it, and the two enemy prides feasted on a giraffe together. No one needed to explain; it was clear to everyone.

It's amazing how hard it is for us to understand that they understand so much better than we do. Everything. There are clear rules for everything. But that still wasn't the most amazing thing that happened there. Suddenly, who emerged from the bushes? That's right. The baboons' screams about what was happening caught the attention of the goons from Ganana, who genuinely wanted to wipe out those from the Hill Pride and finally remove the threat to their buffalo herds. As I said, for them, every moment and every decision is life or death. Then, their senior lioness, a tough and frightening thug, silently approached the diners without fear or thought, just like a criminal coming to stab, and bit another young lioness from the Hill Pride, just like the day before. However, unlike the previous day, when the members of the Hill Pride were weaker against them and couldn't help, despite the fact that the mother of the murdered lioness stayed until the very end, watching as her daughter's chances faded, this time there was also the Jungle Clearing pride present. The very pride that had just been feasting thanks to the Hill Pride's lionesses. They simply rose and gathered around the attacked lioness, not allowing the goons from Ganana to kill her like they had her sister the day before. Although they didn't drive them away—after all, it is still the scariest group in the area—they made it clear that everyone would lose from a colossal conflict and that it would be better for them to back off. And suddenly, the three prides that hate each other with a blood feud, were eating a giraffe together.

We hold the power to exist in countless possible environments of tension, violence, fear, racism, hatred, jealousy, illness, and death. Or, if we rightly choose without anyone telling us, we can be—a kingdom of lions.

22

"But Daaa-aaaadddd!!"

"Yes, my love"

"Whaaat about the craaa-bs??"

"Right, the crabs. Well, let me tell you, my Bati. So we arrived at the hospital, and the doctor was saying about the crabs... I mean, after he heard the story, because at first, we kind of hushed it up, saying Mom just fell, because it was a bit embarrassing. I mean, why tell everyone your whole life story, right? She fell. But then he explained that it had to be very precise and that it was important. Then he laughed. And then your mother and I looked at each other, and laughed too—more out of politeness or... embarrassment. Well, not really embarrassment, more like... solidarity, you know? And then he got serious. He killed us with his seriousness. And what does this doctor tell us?"

'Tell me something, how many people do you think died from a crab attack in the last year?' At first, we thought he was joking. But he stayed completely serious—this amped-up American doctor in a tourist-upgraded clinic. 'Come on, how many?'

'Well... I don't know...?' I answered, half asking. 'Two?'

'Two?' Bati's mom looked at me with an 'Are you kidding?' expression. 'In the whole world? There must be at least a hundred...'

'Zero!' He gestured with his hand and shouted, leaning in close to us. 'Z-E-R-O! Do you hear me? Zero!'

'See-roooooo!' Bati swallowed the 'z' a bit, turning it into an 's', as she signaled the number with her hand.

'And do you know how many people died in the last decade, or in the last century, from a crab attack or crab bite? Zero to the power of zero!'

'Zee-rooo!' she said again with determined cuteness.

And then suddenly he laughed and leaned his head back, and we smiled out of embarrassment. "Now, think about how many restaurants there are in the whole world, in every fucking corner of the globe——" I swear the refined doctor said 'fucking' but I censored it because she's still small, and there's plenty of time before she's five and some kid says 'son of a bitch' or 'fucking' in preschool. "...that serve crabs in one hour! A day! A year! And we assholes..." He continued without filtering his words, "catch these innocent creatures that look really scary, and a pinch from a big one can at most take off a finger..."

"Right! My friend got his cut off!" I interrupted, but he ignored me and continued, much to my momentarily thrilled dismay.

"But besides that—which, of course, applies to any living creature one comes into contact with and attacks out of defense—they haven't done anything to us and never will. But we? We take them and throw them into boiling water.

Not less crazy than the part where the lion prides feasted together on the giraffe, was what happened the next day. After the lions—followed by the hyenas, jackals, and vultures—finished devouring the giraffe, only one bone remained—the thigh bone connected to the lower leg bone at the knee. And through the camera lens, a giraffe was captured passing by. At first, I thought the photographer had just captured a frame and was playing tricks on me, but then the young giraffe stopped, bent down, and sniffed the bone. After that, it stood for a few seconds, and only then was moving on. And then ten more giraffes followed suit! It was as if a memorial ceremony—a final tribute to their deceased friend. They're not just 'dumb animals.' They're cognitive, discerning beings, perhaps even, in contrast to us... humane. And then they walked away, beaten and downcast.

I remember someone once told me that there's a sound crabs make when you throw them into the pot, but because he loved eating crabs, he quickly explained that it's just the air escaping or something like that. 'Come on, like... it's just a crab. An animal. What does it feel? It probably just dies right away. And what does it understand about what's happening to it?'. We're ready to throw a living creature— one that feels, hurts, and worries about its family just like we do—that has emerged from the sand, where it has burrows and families, coming out to gather food for them. It scurries quickly because it's terrified of us, which is why its eyes bulge out in a frightening way, merely out of fear that something will happen to it. Then it snatches the crumbs we threw or whatever else it finds and takes them back to its wife and kids. And then we catch it and throw it alive into boiling water, and it doesn't matter to us because we close the lid really fast. And what do we care that there's a creature inside experiencing the most horrifying thing that can ever happen to any being with a beating heart?

One day I walked into Arik's apartment and noticed a tiny square jar with a single fish inside. It was a vibrant red and blue with a long, odd tail—what I think they call a fighting fish. "The girl wanted," he replied when I asked. "But so what if the girl wants? It's suffering. Can't you see it's living in a square inch?". And then he looked at me with a puzzled expression, truly not grasping what I wanted from him. "Dude... it's just a fish, what... a fish! It doesn't even have a memory..." he shrugged off any sense of responsibility. Most people are like him—unaware, thoughtless. If the fish has no memory, then how does it know to swim up when you place your finger over the aquarium? "Instinct," they'll tell you. As I said, for most it stems from ignorance or a lack of thought. The girl wanted a fish; he wanted quiet—so he bought a fish. He has a creature in his house that is locked in a square inch twenty-four hours a day and gets a tiny food pellet that, according to the seller whose sister is a whore, is enough for it, and everything's cool. Eventually it will die and be flushed down the toilet, and then they'll buy hamsters in cages, a parrot in a cage, everything in cages as long as we're free. We give them food once a day and everything's cool. We stroll about in the zoo of life, not thinking about the poor animals that are confined in cages, behind fences—living beings whose desire for life was snuffed out long ago to satisfy our appetites, and the last thing you can say about them is that they are living beings. No matter how big or 'pampered' you think those zoos or petting farms are, every day you wake up in the morning and refresh yourself with a cup of coffee, or go to sleep and cover yourself under the duvet, be it's a gloomy day or a sunny one, they are there. In the cage. "They have space and are taken care of very well," they'll tell you. Screw you! Let's see you in the aliens' zoo when they feed you in a cage. You want to see animals? Go to Africa and cruise in a caged safari jeep in the savannah! But the girl is crying, so what does he care that the parrot cries its entire life? 'Just a stupid animal, what does it understand?'. Someone looks out the window and sees a squirrel running on the tree. Although it's really a kind of mouse, you run away from mice or 'exterminate' them—which is a very nice word for catching them in a trap and then drowning them in a bucket—but it brings diseases, it's disgusting, and so forth associations that absolve us of responsibility for its bitter, not to say cruelest, fate. But compared to the 'despicable' mouse, its cousin the squirrel is actually cute. And also pretty with those ears and the tail fluttering in the wind. Running and hopping, free and happy, surely. Bullshit. Do you know how hard it is to be a squirrel? You need to constantly look for acorns to eat, find a hiding place for the acorns so you don't starve in winter, plus you have to hide the stash really well so that no other squirrel or bird steals the acorns, because that's obviously a death sentence. All this has to be done while at any moment, an eagle, a hawk, a falcon, an owl, a barn owl, or any other predator could simply sink its claws into you and carry you to your cruel death, not to mention a snake, badger, fox, or some fuckface who wants to make a keychain out of your tail. And all this without even starting to talk about reproduction and caring for the offsprings... Alongside this, they also have to build a nest. Usually, it will be a hole in a tree, but it has to be isolated enough so that they don't freeze in the winter, and believe me, I know a little about finding isolated trees. So sometimes you'll find several squirrels in the same nest even though they're not family, in order to increase warmth, they shove together, united for a common goal. Those cute little squirrels that seem to you to be happily and enjoyably running and jumping around, are alert, working, and caring twenty-four-seven while you're smoking a joint and bullshitting about your bitter fate... But we belittle everything that is not us. We treat it with disdain. Ignore it. Unlike animals in the wild that think twenty-four hours a day, we are great geniuses even without thinking. Instead of trying to learn from more successful species than us, we enslave them to our despicable cravings. We imprison them and torment them. We murder and abuse. Restaurants who serve frogs while they're still alive, their bellies wide open and their hearts still beating while the human filth, the soulless scum, sinks its teeth into them. Innocent bulls are thrown into a noisy, tumultuous arena and forced to be killed slowly and brutally by a bullfighter who's hailed a manly man—and shouldn't at all be be thrown into an active volcano—while the crowd screams en masse in a horrifying spectacle of terror called 'bullfights' that is still considered a legal and even cultural event in too many places in the world, including 'enlightened' Western countries like Spain, France, and Portugal. Sometimes they even hand out darts to the audience so that the whole family can participate in the medieval sadism dance. Horseshoe crabs, whose blue blood is capable of detecting harmful bacteria, are hung in laboratories with a syringe up their ass for several days until they are completely drained of blood. Minks and crocodiles are brutally killed to ensure the uninterrupted production of clothing and footwear made from their skins. Hundreds of thousands of living beings are condemned to entire lives in prison and torment on a daily basis, displayed for our enjoyment, as we watch them wither while still alive, pacing back and forth in the same square meter at the zoo. An entire industry takes living creatures with emotions and nervous systems, scared and in pain, and in the name of medicine, science, and cosmetics, tortures them in a way that is worse than snuff films. But why should the filthy souls of pharmaceutical companies pay millions to people for experiments when they can get monkeys cheaply? Electrodes in the brain and syringes in the eyes while still fully conscious are just the tip of the iceberg. In addition to the chilling physical tortures, laboratory animals also undergo mental tortures you wouldn't have imagined that someone thought about imagining, which is completely legal. In a covert documentation made just in the last few years at a well-known health institute in the United States, a monkey was recorded embracing and protecting its baby while the filthy scoundrel injected it with poison, all to see the baby panic, trying to shake its mother and bring her back to life with its tiny hands while crying uncontrollably. In her last efforts, she tries to rise but stumbles and falls dead. Her nipples were covered so the baby couldn't nurse, and then they replaced her with a doll, and only after the poor baby had no strength left to cry, did it hug the doll and fell asleep. This is an idea meant to create 'psychological death' to better study and delve into depressive behaviors of humans. All this and much more is not done in forsaken basements by sick psychopathic individuals who can only be seen in movies; it is done in broad daylight by 'respected' scientists in modern and prestigious facilities that are mostly funded by taxpayer money. Your money. A heinous industry operating under the auspices of democratic law, where solely due to its existence, the entire human race deserves to be extinct. "But it saves lives!" they'll tell you, "it literally saves you!" They'll explain almost as well as Joseph Goebbels did why it was simply wonderful and even a grim necessity to exterminate Jews, Gypsies, and homosexuals. Mengele looks down on the continuation of his legacy and rubs his hands in delight. There they enter through the door, stepping toward another day in the laboratory of horrors. Holding a cup of coffee in their hand, their emotions numb as those of the gas chamber operators in Auschwitz. But not long ago, they parted with a wistful glance from their children and wished them a pleasant day at school or in kindergarten, without the latter imagining that Dad or Mom, by conscious choice and free will, are the very black shadow that invokes horror and dread in other living beings.

We tyrannize every living being; we've enslaved the universe. We slaughter and sink our teeth in, locking in cages and torturing, binding, training, pitting against each other, shooting, stabbing, burning alive, squashing, crushing, and tormenting innocent and weaker beings than ourselves. We are the excrement of the universe, the instillers of fear in the galaxy. Beings from another world, descended upon a land not theirs, plundering, crushing, and gnawing at it endlessly and mercilessly. With gluttony and greed, in a diabolical hunger with wide, gleaming eyes and a smile brimming with sharp teeth, from which blood drips at the corners. Smiling and laughing, slaying while watching from the sidelines, shouting at the top of its lungs, like a monstrous terror, "Mmmmoooow wwwaaaahhhh! Mmmmoooowwwwaaaahhhh! Mmmmo ooowwwwaaaaaaaahhhhhhhhhh!" Devours the monster more and more and more! We are the devil to every other creature, with the inherent evil just like that terrifying character from the movies we thought existed only in films. Here it is, in all its glory, ingrained in each and every one of us. We are all part of the galaxy's devil's cult, serving Lucifer and praying to God.

Okay, truth is I censored this part a bit as well. I changed the story for her. I told you from the very first moment of this tale that I'd do anything for that girl. Anything. I'd alter the whole world for her. In the end, she'll understand what she needs to understand, so why shouldn't she enjoy a beautiful world filled with innocence in the meantime? So instead of recounting the exact words of the grim doctor who now shouted, "Boiling water! Do you hear me? Boiling water!" I shared that we're evicting them from their home, which is the sea, and that it's not so nice, and she agreed with me. But the ending, oh, the ending was colossal. "And all of this," he said, "so we can sit our white behinds in a fancy restaurant, eat lobster, and think we're civilized." I told you, a colossal ending.

"But... Da-aaaddd."

"Yes, sugarpie"

"But... but... then you and Uncle Arik and... and... you came back, and... and Mom stayed in India, right, da-dy?"

"Yes, my beautiful. Then we returned to Fatel."

Suddenly it transformed into an entirely different story. We understood from the looks of the locals—who are usually ultra-relaxed-Shanti-Baba—that there was also starting to be a serious supply issue, and soon, we tourists might have nothing to eat. In a fleeting moment, we morphed into being the foreign workers, 'Chinamen' and 'Cholos,' as they are derogatorily referred to. Immigrants. We tourists would find ourselves at the bottom of the food chain if it came to *that*. I realized this from the eyes of the guesthouse owner, who had always been kind. Suddenly, I sensed in his gaze that he was giving up on me. He couldn't help. A fleeting moment of truth slipped through his look despite everything he said, and at one point, he continued talking while averting his gaze, as his subconscious revealed to his conscious that my subconscious had picked up on it and communicated it to my conscious. It was as if he were telling me that the Nazis were here, and he had no way to save us. Israelis around us maintained the weight of emotions. Luckily or unluckily, none of us were the anxious type. Maybe it's because we're all from Fatel, but in any case, I was glad to discover this. We didn't panic. But the pressure cooker around us definitely began to bubble. Guesthouses started to close, flights dwindled, and we understood that we needed to take an hour-long taxi to the airport and begin our journey to Bombay and then home, like right now, regardless of what our tickets said. That's what everyone was doing. The wisdom of the crowd.

Pratiksha gazed at me with tears in her eyes, as if we were parting forever. It's time to leave.

"Aaaachoo!" Moran suddenly sneezed. And sneezing is the sign of truth. A sign that I'm lying.

"Aachoo!" Bati sneezed as well, scattering my empty words everywhere.

Empty of content? Certainly not. Of what then? Of defense. Against whom? Against what? Against herself? A plea for a pause. That's all I asked for when Moran disappeared. A plea for a pause. From my heart, from my emotions, from the world, from Arik, from Mom, from everyone. She signaled me with her finger and nail when my gaze asked again, 'What?'. We moved closer and then apart. Living like a married couple, yet far too often I felt alone. Her belly swelled. My daughter is growing within her. But I am actually here alone.

"I wanted to tell you that..." she tried to finish the sentence while we lay sweaty on the bed with only the hum of the air conditioner in the background, but I just kept on kissing.

"Hagai, the child..." she suddenly stopped moving her lips completely and opened her eyes as our mouths remained pressed together. "Take the child."

23

But before I finished telling Bati the story before bedtime and brushing teeth, knocks echoed at the door. After a few seconds, I stepped into the living room.

"Hagaichuk!" She rushed to hug me before I could move. Why does my mom invite herself to waltz freely into my home? Because that's how she is—caring for me, helping with the child. And also because in Fatel all doors are open, like in any commune that takes pride in itself. She's retired and lives next door, so she comes over every day. Even if she hasn't explicitly said she'll come tomorrow, she'll be here tomorrow. It has become her reason to rise in the morning; this is what she looks forward to all the time. For her, I could leave the child and go on a two-month trip. Suits her perfectly. And for me it's cool because it really freed me and helped. Like, the first time with a child and doing it alone… and I'm convinced it also worked wonders for Bati's cognitive abilities and made her start talking really fast. A baby is like a magnetic vacuum for information. They wake up to the world, and everything they sense through their senses, they sense for the first time. Are you sensing it? And that's what they remember now, because there's no other information in their head yet. So every day, my mom wouldn't stop chattering with her for three hours straight, and the little one would look at her in awe. Smiling, responding, she was learning. Learning every vowel, expression, and consonant. When she was a year and a half old, she was already babbling freely. I remember being really surprised that when you said something to her—then the next day she remembered right away! And you think to yourself, 'how cool that she remembered…' but she didn't 'remember'. That thing you said to her was simply running through her mind all night long until she fell asleep, and the moment she wakes up, it's still there. That tomorrow, they will buy her a new tricycle. She didn't even know if she would like the tricycle, but "tricycle! tricycle!" And it's still so fun. Making them happy. The essence of life.

"Mom!" I said as if surprised, "What, you're here?" I asked with a smile and embarrassment at the fact that I was only wearing underwear. Yes, I know she's bathed me dozens of times and changed my diapers. "Hold on, I'll put something on."

"How are you, cutie? Is she already asleep?" She kissed me firmly near the lips. She's always been like that— affectionate and emotional. An Iraqi grandma from Eastern Europe.

"Oh, no, no, we're just in the middle of the bedtime story. You're more than welcome to brush her teeth."

"Yes?" she asked with a victorious smile, as if I just announced I had won the Nobel Prize. But it was wonderful. That's what I always loved about her. "Mom, I pooped my pants in class and everyone laughed at me." "Did you?" Her smile was endless, "What a cutieeee!" And it always worked. Always. Boundless love. The secret of life. It's almost incomprehensible and completely irrational that no matter what I said, her response was always magnificent and excellent, mixed with joy and endless encouragement. I could feel hurt and think she wasn't listening to me, but all in all, it was the exact same mechanism as a child coming home from kindergarten with a hideously ugly drawing, and everyone telling him it's beautiful. And it works. Kids believe what they're told.

And while I was happily shaving in the next room, sudden screams came from the bedroom Bati and I shared.

"Not twue! You're a cheata! cheata!"

"Wow, wow, wow, what happened?" I rushed in and saw my mother holding her face, while Bati was huddled in the corner of the room, literally pressed tightly between the walls.

"Hagai, she... you..." I quickly gave her a hug and a kiss, then bent down to Bati who peeked out at me with weepy eyes and tear-soaked cheeks peeking through her fingers.

"You Cheata one! Cheata!" she screamed in a heavy storm of emotions at my mother, who looked genuinely uncomfortable but, with no other option, left me to handle the situation as she quietly walked away, lost in thought. I calmed her down with my hand, assuring her that everything was fine and that I would sort it out, whatever it was.

"Hey, hey, hey... what happened? It's not nice to talk to Grandma like that. Grandma is not a liar."

"She is!" she replied with furrowed brows, her crying bursting forth in all directions. I tried to hug her, to get closer. But she just stepped back and distanced herself from me, her gaze filled with fury and tears. "Cheata!" she pushed me with her tiny little hands. "You cheata!" she continued to scream and jump with the last of her strength, but I just stood there with open arms. "What happened, my sweetie? Tell Daddy."

"Th... Tha...!" she tried after a few long seconds, but the tears streamed down her face. "Tha..." she drew out the words that pierced my heart. I attempted to stroke her hair, but she quickly turned her head away.

"What is it, my sweetie?"

"Grand...ma said th... that... th... you took me fr... from a m... mom who lived in... in her... in her be.. lly, and also... also that... that M... Mo... ran is not my m...om, she's just a kid th.. tha..., and that my mom's na.. me is P... Patisha!"

From overwhelming emotion, a single long tear rolled down my cheek, stretching from my eye to the back of my throat. I thought she hadn't noticed; like its fatigue and all. We're always goofing around and rolling with laughter, and even then sometimes tears come out. But this tear enabled me to wrap my arms around her.

"Da-ddy?" she touched my cheek with her tiny finger when she saw my attention completely diverted.

"What, sweetie?"

"Why are you crying, Da-ddy?"

"What...? Naaa... Daddy isn't crying," I hugged her tightly so she wouldn't see.

"Then... so why do you have te-tears?" She leaned back and touched the very middle of the tear's path with her small finger.

"They're tears of joy," I replied, "tears of 'Daddy loves you.'" I surrendered and allowed the warm tear to fall and flow into my emotions.

🪲

When we were seventeen, finally in the same class after they split us into tracks, it was the day of the math exam. And she was looking her best. A completely normal Moran, who never really paid much attention to me. Definitely not like the way I regarded her, as someone so central in my life. Completely world-altering. The one who, the moment she stepped into the walls of our school, turned my life upside down.

And she, so beautiful. So effortlessly capable of making you fall in love with her. Looking back, I think somewhere in the back of my mind I knew I had no chance. That she and I were lines that would never meet. Not even parallel. We would never walk or travel any path together. They only drift further apart, slowly fading from each other's memory. Not each other's. My memories have never faded away regarding her. And suddenly, she turned to me. Right there in class, in front of everyone—all the people who grew up with us from kindergarten and elementary school in the neighborhood—and started talking to me. Moran Dagan, actually talking to me as if suddenly she knows it all, and sitting right next to me during the exam. How furious I was at her on the way home, after she fooled me, leaving me empty and ashamed. After realizing how deeply I'd been played, how she exploited my innocence. Suddenly, it all became so clear. She'd known all along. Knew that with just one word from her, I'd be completely enchanted. For years I was captivated, and all it took was a tiny match to set this overflowing fuel tank ablaze. How angry was I at her and hated. That day more than any other. And if you've suppressed it all until now, then now, after that 'algebraic manipulation', you'll surely let it loose. The sadness, the waiting, the emotional explosion… And perhaps, perhaps things weren't like that at all. Never will I know, but maybe … Never will I know if Mrs. Dagan saw that her daughter didn't look like herself and dismissed me with a glance to check if she was okay, and then suggested they go together to the clinic, where a doctor, who cannot be blamed, determined her fate. Just a normal weakness, as in ninety-nine percent of the cases, he said, and sent her back home. But Moran, Moran was always a special case. To this day, no one knows what it was. I'll never know if she really planned for… Ugh, how pathetic do I sound.

'So Young' is the opening track of that album by Suede that Moran loved so much, their revolutionary album from those days, that era of masterpiece albums like *Nevermind* by Nirvana, *Ten* by Pearl Jam, *The Black Album* by Metallica, *Siamese Dream* by the Smashing Pumpkins. On the fence by the entrance gate to the high school, there were mourning posters with the inscription 'Taken in the prime of her life.' And no one explained anything to us, neither the counselor, nor the main teacher of our grade. They just sent us all home. There was no internet, nothing, and all I had left were these thoughts in my head that I had never shared with anyone. And one picture. One picture of me and Moran from my bar mitzvah, where I insisted on inviting half of her class because I wanted her to come and didn't know how to say it. One picture of us together, as if slow-dancing because I asked her, for it was still my special party. And in the picture I'm looking at her, and she's holding a pink flower, gazing at it and smiling. Is she waiting for the song to end? Waiting for me to finally have the courage? But I didn't have the courage, Moran. I didn't have the courage... If only I could have told you it was me, the one who loves you forever and there's no need for anything else. No need to be afraid or anxious about anything. That I would take care of you, Moran. Always take care. If only I wasn't the kind that is afraid to say what he wants. That from sixth grade to ninth, was unable to tell the girl he loves— that he loves her.

I remember running home and yelling. Blaming myself for not staying at her house, standing my ground and demanding that she fulfill her promise. Maybe I would have been there the moment she collapsed; maybe I could have helped, saved her. Like a frog kissing a princess, and she transforms into the sleeping beauty who awakens! I remember that day as if it were yesterday. I couldn't see anything through my tears but I kept talking. As if wearing glasses with the wrong prescription. And I didn't get the chance. I didn't get the chance... I never even got to see what Moran's room looked like from the inside. Maybe it was a complete mess like any teenager's room, maybe it was neat and tidy, perhaps beautifully organized, or maybe ugly, painted black with graffiti. What does she have in her dresser, Moran? Should I snoop? I've always been dying to know what's hidden in there. In my imagination, I'm back here again. Alone. Leaning against the dresser while her mother is in the kitchen, easily able to lean forward, open the drawer behind me, and reveal. Reveal what lies hidden within the depths of a drawer. What is she hiding from? What does she hide? Here I shall read your secret journal, young Mrs. Dagan. Here I will know everything about you, be it the worst of all.. Yes, I know a lot of time has passed. Perhaps too much time. But pain... pain doesn't recognize time.

"*Everything is ready, and permission is granted,*" it says in Pirkei Avot of the Mishnah. Everything is prepared for you, and all that remains is to be here and now, in the present. Do not fear the future, do not dwell on the past. But the choice is yours; you are free to wander any path you choose. And if this is true, then perhaps everything has a reason. We may not know now why, how, where, or when, but one day it will happen — and it will be worth it all. Everything is written, and we are here to enjoy and experience to the fullest, to take on every roller coaster. And if something happened, it happened because it was meant to happen. I've already told you that we at Fatel believe in the cycle of souls, where every death is, in fact, the soul's own 'suicide,' and there are no mistakes in this matter; everything is meticulously planned. Each soul knows precisely what it came to experience in this incarnation and the exact second it will complete its journey, just like Sagi, who died in the army... Only once did I hear her talk for real, Sagi's mom. My aunt was at our house, and she and my mom were sitting in the living room when the phone rang, and I picked up in my room. Before the age of cell phones, if both of you picked up the receiver, you could hear and talk to each other, even in the middle of the conversation. The adults thought they weren't being heard, that we weren't paying attention, but kids have sharp ears and discernment, and we always felt it. "Come on, hang up!" I would shout angrily after a few seconds of not understanding what your parents had to quote to you, and then there would immediately be a disconnection click from the other end. But just before I was about to hang up, I realized it was Sagi's mom. She would never normally call us. She and my mom were of course Fatel and all was cool, but they weren't close friends. However, she and my aunt were. Her husband must have told her that my aunt was at our place, so she called us. That's how it used to be. And now, more than being curious about who it was, I was intrigued by what it was about. And anyway, they were both adults, so no chance they'd notice I was on the line, so I listened in. And then she started talking about little Sagi, saying he was truly a miracle for her. She was calling to invite her to his first birthday, and she didn't forget to thank my aunt for what she called the best advice she could've ever given her. She said she would have done it even at sixty, and that it was a solution she never imagined existed. While it wasn't complete, it was far better than the endless void she had been in before. Now she had something to hold on to. And that *something*, she said, may be small, but it could grow and grow, eventually filling up a lot of space. A lot of space. Which is a whole lot, she emphasized, a whole lot. And then they cried. And my mom started crying too; I could hear her from the living room. And suddenly, everyone there began crying and offering blessings to God, which confused me a bit, but I swear they were thanking the "Lorddd! Thank you, Lorrrddd, ohh... Dear Godddd!" Sagi's mom cried, " Goddd... thank you, Goddd...!" Then I gently set the receiver down, bringing it close to the two little black plastic legs protruding above the dial, so the receiver would kiss them, just touch them. Only then did I gently push it down, thus outweighing and dimming the noise of the disconnection by ninety percent. At the end of the day, even emotion outweighs wisdom and dims it. No matter how intelligent, intellectual, analytical, elite, and pinnacle of thought you are, there are situations where you can't think your way out. There are life situations where even the wisest of all cannot find their escape. Emotional states that control you. Slapping one's thigh with each dawn and dusk, especially the wisest one who is strong in the law of thought. But the true law of life is that only emotion can conquer emotion. Only love can atone loss, only excitement mends a stumble, only bliss soothes pain, and only joy—triumphs over all.

Oh God, God… Only once. Only once… I lied. And what shall I say now? That I'm sorry? I'll whisper it and press my head to her small shoulder, and she, in the boundless magnificence of her being, will hold my body and embrace me as fully as her arms can span, her feminine compassion showing the full maturity beyond her young age, until both our sorrows completely unravel and dissolve into a strength unmatched by anything in this world? God, do you hear me?! He, of course, didn't answer, but then I looked deep into Bati's eyes and suddenly experienced the answer in a deep and steady divine tone; that a child is told about the world little by little each day. This is how they learn best, adapting day by day. It becomes a natural process for them, becoming their very nature. For you wouldn't tell your little girl that everyone she knows will eventually die, and that she will too, right? She can't grasp that yet. So you tell her stories. About the tooth fairy, and Santa Claus. That this is like this, and that will be okay. All to help her sleep well at night. And little by little, she'll learn. She'll understand more, grow. 'Most of you, unfortunately, are unwilling to move forward. Seeking me in places of worship, in rituals, in prayers. Faithfully adhering to what I taught you when you were still small, when your worldview could not comprehend even a fraction of what it is capable of now. It's akin to a forty-year-old man placing a tooth under his pillow at night and expecting a gift in the morning. And at the end of the day, all I ever wanted for you - was to sleep well at night.'

They say the people closest to you accompany you through nearly every incarnation. Once they're actors in this play, and then in that, with the whole world as the backdrop. Everything is already set for you; all you need to do is go with the flow. And perhaps like Sagi and Sagi, that brother replacing the one who fell, maybe my Bati is the renewed embodiment of Moran. In a past life, she shattered my heart, and now she's here to mend it. Reappearing in my embrace in a loving, nurturing cycle, giving and healing; in which, with just one glance into her eyes - I see God. And how wonderful it is that we're here in Fatel, in our private commune. Secluded from all evil, calm and private, just ours. Only ours. Our piece of divinity. Some call it divine providence. But they look up to the heavens instead of facing straight ahead, like God told me. Only there... nowhere else do I exist. In any other place—I am not.

I tried to pry for more details, but he faded away, vanishing in the middle of the conversation. Well, he probably has a billion other things on his mind... And honestly, I got the point, so why waste precious divine time? At first, we were taught not to kill or steal from one another; later, when we understood a bit more than just what a cave and a club were, another messenger was sent our way. Amidst the thousands of false prophets surely popping up everywhere back then, just like today's reality show contestants, why is it that we remember this one for thousands of years, with over two billion believers? Over a third of the world's population, just for him? One of the most famous figures in human history, and yet he holds nothing? No message? I Once flipped through one of those books about Jesus that didn't make it into the New Testament, and that as a Jew I was of course cautioned against anything related to that false-heretic-apostate-messiah-tsk-tsk-tsk-knock-on-wood, and I remember being genuinely surprised. It was truly beautiful and interesting, and above all, wise. It was even written quite explicitly that the whole story is essentially about love. Jesus, of course, doesn't speak in the terms we use today—still God and all— but the most important commandment, in essence, is love. Love God, love others, love yourself. The rest is just nice to have. Keep being a good kid. Brush your teeth before bed, good job, sweetie. What do we say to Auntie? Tha-ank y-ou. Now wash your hands before eating, and be grateful to the universe for waking up to this beautiful world created for us. Honor your parents, enjoy holidays with the extended family, don't cheat, don't hurt others, and live joyfully. That's it. Maybe it's not the best for you to mix meat and dairy, wait a bit between them. Don't you dare skip at least one day of rest each week—steal a day and a half or even two if you can. And enjoy life! But don't become a slave to it, no gods before me. Remember to say thank you three times a day for everything you have, don't complain. Gather for meals with family or friends, don't sit home alone and eat like a dog. At thirteen, explain a bit more about life to your child, that now he's a man. Girls usually mature faster than boys, so you can tell them about the world even earlier. And always, always remember, kid—there's someone above you. Watching over you. That Dad will do anything for you. Anything.

There's only one commandment that's good to have been preserved through thousands of years. *Many do noble, but you surpass them all.* And precisely because of its unfathomable nature to the untrained eye, the masses are told that if you observe it — you'll be forgiven for everything. I stumbled upon its hidden meaning quite by accident. Like any kid at thirteen, and even though in Fatal we are light, love and fellowship, I wanted to be 'like the grown-ups who fast.' We would sit, all the friends, in the big garden, and everyone would gather. The whole village. I always looked forward to seeing her. Would I meet her? I thought as I dressed in my finest clothes, like for the Hanukkah party. What would she wear this time? Who would she talk to? Where would she be? Would she look at me or ignore me as usual? And if our eyes did meet, would I have the courage to say something to her? To approach? As the evening went on, almost all the boys from the class would walk to faraway places, on foot, not on bicycles like small children on Yom Kippur do, of course. And there, we would meet kids from other neighborhoods and places. It was there that a magical wonder of the world, remarkable in its innovation, was unveiled before us — other girls. It was breathtaking. To this day, I can't forget that girl Benny talked to. He always had the courage. She was so beautiful, new, and different. Shira. And Benny walked up like a man and spoke to her, while everyone seemed to stand around and watch. Everyone was watching. Today, when I think about it, she was just a girl like us, a little more beautiful than the others, but still just a girl. Without all those superpowers we boys always attributed to them, and the whole lot of courage that is needed to go and talk to. Later, it would just be me and Arik left. We'd walk and talk until the early hours of the morning about the world and what we wanted to be. We kept walking and talking, trying to get through the fast as best we could, so we could sleep in as late as possible the next day. Outsmarting God. I remember one Yom Kippur when we were already in the army, and Arik came back from basic training and slept through the entire fast. Slept through the whole damn thing, that son of a bitch! Left me all alone… And since then, I'm used to it. Even if I'm not doing it for some God to forgive me for something, I do it, and it feels good. But only when I'm a complete 'Frum'. One Yom Kippur I said like whatever, 'let's do the fast in the sense that I'm still a Zionist and all, but drink water and use electricity.' That's when I experienced the enlightenment! Suddenly, I understood the significance of the occasion and the real reason it was emphasized so much. Of course, like the tooth fairy, it's easiest to tell people it grants them a 'delete' on the whole year, but in a deeper sense, only when you do Yom Kippur like a true religious person do you really understand. You return home and it's dark. Only the streetlight shining through the partially open blinds lets you see something in the gloom. If you forgot to set a timer for the air conditioner, you take off your shirt, lie down on the mattress, and hope for the best. You can't turn on a light, not even glance at your phone. You have absolutely. nothing. to do! And that's the thing. This is the defining moment. For the only time in your life, once a year, it's just you and yourself. Without the background noises, without the matters of daily life. Silence. *'With darkness over an abyss'.* There's you and yourself for real. You and you. And above, this ethereal command, as if hovering over you, keenly watching your every step. And suddenly, in this silence, you hear yourself. Suddenly, there are no background sounds that your voice becomes their background. And only then are you there, with you. Because if they hadn't told us the story this way, it wouldn't have happened. None of you who don't fast on Yom Kippur will do it from now on, even if I promise you the moon. And even if you try, you'll surely cut yourself some slack at some point, and that's where it will end. And that's the thing. You need the full twenty-five hours, as we learned in our Talmud classes that *'they made a fence around the Torah,'* so even if someone slips up, at least they kept the twenty-four hours that God commanded. But only when you're committed to being fully observant for an entire day, as if your life depends on it, do the treasured depths reveal themselves. The Vipassana. The supreme meditation of once a year. The consciousness. The nirvana.

And then they quiet down. Then, I care not for their words or whispers. All those voices in my head shouting. Pathetic cowards. Cowards. I, Since, forever and ever, listen only to myself. And now as well, leave me be, you long-extinct voices from the past. Leave my tormented soul be. Oh, my soul… What sin have you committed for I lament … What have I done that you place a sharp sword at my neck? This time, this time it shall be beyond endurance—if it will not be. I ask and already answer. I know the answer. Loving the answer. Envisioning Moran kissing me, twenty years late, whispering in my ear, nearly caressing my neck. Of course I remember you, Moran. Of course I haven't forgotten. In this very garden, we were together countless times. And even if so many years have passed, no one has forgotten you. No one has forgotten you, beautiful girl. You will always remain young and in our hearts. You, Moran, are impossible to forget. And she, as if asked me now with her gaze, 'Do you promise?' And without hesitation I answered that of course I do; that I always promise you and always keep my word to you, that I've never forgotten you and never will, forgiving and absolving everything just like a good God. As in the prophecy of Ezekiel, where God sees Jerusalem wallowing in its blood, nakedness and shame, and promises to take her under His auspice in that passage during the Passover Seder that everyone avoids reading: *'And when I passed by thee, and saw thee wallowing in thy blood, I said unto thee: In thy blood, live; yea, I said unto thee: In thy blood, live…'*.

And here we are now, in the garden of Fatel, sitting and reclining forty. And suddenly her mother smiled at me and started saying something to me, and I just looked for my phone because I didn't know what to do, and all those memories suddenly rose to their feet, rising from the dust like a phoenix, rebelling against me and flooding my throat, coating it with a layer of rust that barely allows to breathe, not permitting the gullet to rise and fall. "She always liked you," she said now, as a seventy aged grandmother, no longer that protective mother of a seventeen-year-old girl from long ago. Hoarse by metal I was to the sound of the words. I couldn't help but respond. Couldn't respond. Me? My mind questioned in disbelief, are you sure she always liked me, Mrs. Dagan? Where was that all these years, this affection she had for me? Why did she never say? Never showed? Showed the exact opposite. And perhaps it was only in hindsight. Perhaps you saw from a bird's-eye view how I ran like crazy, stopping by the neighborhood's public phone, on that downhill stretch of the small road leading down from the lot that serves as a tiny parking space at the edge of the large garden where we now sit. Stopping by the phone and crying. I have coins on my keychain, but who the hell am I gonna call? My father, who will ask me why am I crying like a little kid? My mother, who will worry and hug me, making me feel truly like a small, helpless child? Who should I call, God? To God?! So I cried like a child. Just like children cry. I stood there crying, my back shaking as I held onto that part of the public phone that protects the bulky device inside. A piece of metal that was later replaced by a clear plastic cover to shield the public phone against the ravages of the weather. Never will you know how I cried. Looking sideways, not knowing who to speak to, who to address, just a stupid child standing there crying over a girl who never paid him any mind in her life. And maybe you were also just 'a stupid child'. A girl. Just a girl... And I expected you to give me all the answers as if you knew them. As if you were born with them all and just wouldn't reveal. I remember this one time in the rhythmics room at one of the Friday parties, long before I was there with Pompeos, when Moran and Benny were already a couple. After the disco dancing, the DJ would always play a slow dance. Then everyone without a partner would approach someone, and if she said yes, he knew she wanted him back. But I'll never forget that same party, where I had no one to dance with. I sat on one of the benches, leaning back, and suddenly the DJ played that song by Wham!, and George Michael sang and swore he would never dance with anyone else the way he did with *her*. I looked up, and there they were, in front of me. Embracing. Moran and Benny, during the slow dance. I remember she smiled. At that moment, it seemed to me as the height of cruelty, as if she was doing it to me on purpose. But maybe she was just an eleven-year-old girl, just a girl, slow dancing at a party.

All those years, I blamed Moran Dagan, hated her, trembled at the sound of her voice. My heart fell silent at the sight of her. But aside from being bummed out, I never said a word. I never took her hand and told her I wanted to talk. I never had the courage to approach the girl I loved more than anything.

Sometimes, what's most obvious is the hardest thing to do. Because it's obvious, it's clear to everyone that it's going to happen. And then often it weighs heavily on a person, causing them to stray off the path. You can all think what you want; I'll do what *I* want. And then you end up going for something different. A surprise. And Benny's also cute, and you had your eye on him, not even knowing if I liked you back because I never said anything, so you just went with it. An eleven-year-old girl… And perhaps all those years you hid it in embarrassment. The anger, the pain. Perhaps all those looks of yours, throughout the years, were nothing but glances of frustration and disappointment withholding unspoken questions. Why didn't you come to me? Why didn't you say anything? How did you not see that you and I were the real thing? Maybe you really did like me back, but then the announcer in the gym had already proclaimed it over the microphone, and everyone heard. And then life just rolled on and on, and it turned out that nothing ever came between us. Until it did. Until your mom said what I had always wanted to hear. That all along, you really, truly liked me.

But now I couldn't deal with it at all. What do you do with a mother of a deceased daughter who reveals a hidden truth from her past? And how can you ignore it? So I said that of course, that I had always liked her too, while inside I was screaming and crying, suppressing torrents of tears that had been stored deep in my heart for years, just waiting for the moment they could burst forth again, to explode. How impossible it is to lie to yourself. Surely it provokes a backlash, a force within the body that's hard to recover from. The internal organs simply absorb all the hurt. And what, should I just start spilling my guts and whining here at Anat's birthday in front of everyone? In front of all those who have known me since infancy? Should I suddenly just start wailing? So I imagined and made it all as true. A reality as true as can be. That I've always loved you, Moran. Always been in love. And even when you're not at all, I am still. And now, suddenly at forty, when we thought we'd all outgrown everything, here comes a voice from the past. Here is your mother in all her glory—she herself is the announcer. But this time, the message is the most volatile of it all. It's enticing. intoxicating the senses. With a delay of over twenty years, as a message from another world, distant, legendary, here you send me a greeting, gifting me a virtual kiss that transcends worlds and continents, a kiss from another realm. And oh, how sweet it is. "She always liked you." Always.

The song that concludes the first, immortal, perfect album by Suede talks about, how else, a cycle of rebirth. And Brett Anderson sings or rather whispers, that they will see each other in their next life, where they will fly away - for good.

24

When Moran returned to the room, something in her voice was strange. In the tone of her speech. Like Moran, but different. Who is this woman? I wondered to myself. I glanced to the side and Pratiksha was there, holding a newborn baby. Well, about two weeks old, to be exact.

"Yours?" I asked, still struggling. Struggling to understand. Not really getting it. Not getting it.

"Yes Mister Binder, yes? Now is good time, yes?"

Oh, shit... I remembered that... we planned that... but... Studmaster-Major, and... the opium. No, the acid... the acid?

"Mr. Binder..." Pratiksha raised her voice in a way that was so out of character. "Yes??" And then Arik walked into the room too.

"Hey man, what the..." I started to mumble my way through the situation.

"Come on, Hagai! We need to get moving, don't you get it??" He yelled at me, then immediately apologized to Pratiksha and said he'd call her in a minute.

"But Mister... I told you, I cannot... now! Please!" She stomped her foot on the floor, handing him the newborn. "Please!!"

And he, simply held the two-week-old baby. I didn't understand what was happening. "Moran?" I called towards the bathroom. "Can I come in?" I needed to wash my face. To freshen up. Maybe I should even take a shower.

"Hagai!" he yelled, stressing the word with an exaggerated emphasis. "We have to get back home. Now. With your baby. Your daughter." He shouted it in a whisper. Yes, apparently that's a thing. I didn't understand what he was talking about. "You've been on drugs for two weeks now, completely out of it. Calling people I don't know. Disappearing for days and then showing up totally high at some beach party, getting on stage during that Australian DJ's set, stopping the music, and waving to the crowd... What the fuck is wrong with you?? You realize it's barely legal here as it is... You want to get her thrown in jail because of you? Now get up, wash yourself, pack your bag, and we're heading straight to the airport. Now, got it? First flight back home, we're on it."

She shoved a pack of papers into his pocket, gave one last, lingering look at the baby, leaned in to kiss her but ultimately relented, as if pulling her head away with force to keep from kissing her, and left the room, agitated. After a few seconds, there was a knock. Moran? I opened the door. It was Pratiksha. Her beautiful face was tear-streaked. Her gaze was shattered.

"Duh, baby... please. Make up something beautiful for her... yes? Please..." She broke down in tears, "Okay?"

"Of course, sure," I replied, not understanding. Suddenly, in stark contrast to her usual easygoing and calm demeanor, Pratiksha just rushed forward, shoving me aside, and clung to the tiny baby, weeping uncontrollably. And the baby was crying too. Now they were both crying. They sobbed like a mother and daughter separated forever, their paths never to cross again. But she will have a good life, Bati, a chance for a better life than here. Indeed? I don't know why, but now tears were streaming down my eyes as well. Arik looked unusually agitated too, holding the baby in his large hands while Pratiksha lay weeping, her face pressed against the baby's, their tears flowing together and mingling, streaming warmly down his arms.

"Please..." she gives me one last look, and I nod while crying, not knowing why. It must be the drugs. And then it happened. That moment. She simply pressed against me and hugged me tight, like a mother's embrace just before her son boards the bus to join Golani, and kissed me on the lips.

"Take care, Mr. Binder..." she grasped my hand tightly, it was truly a firm hold. an unexpected gesture from someone who was supposed to act with excessive service and a smile for the guests. She pulled something from her sleeve, shoved it into my hand, and disappeared. And that was it; we never saw her again. Nor did we hear from her. "Please, Mr.," those words were now etched in my mind. "Please."

I looked at Arik in disbelief, but he didn't say a word. He just stared at me, his gaze seemingly asking, "Well, go on. What is it?" I opened my hand. A tiny pair of socks, baby size, brown in color, and their tips - red.

25

Before passing away, the village chief's daughter took her only daughter, Rita, for a close conversation. She explained that father isn't exactly father, and that she preferred her to think that way her entire life, even though she resembled the Sir like two drops of water. She explained that the accent wasn't something heavy from Moroccan or Yemeni origins. Explained it all. And when people are on their deathbeds, it's hard to be angry with them. But more than anything, she explained where she came from and where she must return. She said it was a fairly closed community, but a tiny sock would explain it all. That the other grandmothers know the story. One specific grandmother, the wife of the smuggler who risked himself. And she, Rita, already had a little girl of her own by then, Moran Dagan was her name. And what's it to her and to move away now from Kibbutz Hulda to a village near the Jezreel Valley? She said there was family there, in the Arab village. She insisted they must not know, that it was better this way, preferable even. To forget and not remember. About that sister who disappeared one night without a trace. The village girl, about whom many rumors circulated throughout the region. It was her. She was the beautiful daughter of the village chief. "My Rita, please. Please, ya binti," Moran's grandmother sobbed. "Your father," the mother said to the daughter, who had her entire world turned upside down at that moment, "your father discovered this place."

🪲

"Da-ddy…"

"Yes, sweetheart."

"I want th... I want tha... that Mommy di-dn't s.. stay in In-di-yuh, Daddy..."

"But we will always be together. right, sweetheart?" I waited a bit, and finally, she nodded. "Promise?" She nodded again.

"Bu... But... Grand-ma says that actually... th...that... we live in Giva-tayim and th... that... there's no place li... like Fa-tel!"

"Well, you know, Grandma's old, she doesn't remember."

"She does rem-em-ber!!" she yelled-laughed with a childlike giggle, covering a mouth full of teeth with her tiny hands.

"I already told you, there was a fire and everyone had to move. And we moved to Givatayim."

"N-o, w-e d-idn't!" she kept on with her curious, rolling laughter, wide-eyed, choosing to believe both stories.

"Alright, al-al-al-right... you need to go to sleep, it's already late. I'm not making you before bed no more..."

"Y-o-u w-i-ll!!!" she jumped on me.

"No!" I roared with a big laugh.

"But, but Da-ddy..."

"What, my beautiful?"

"I like your story more than... than Grandma's story. Th-that Mom kissed you on the mouth and th-then you went to In-di-yuh."

"I told you it was a fun story. A sweet story about love."

"But... but... wh-when I grow up, can we go to Fa-tel, Da-ddy? And... and... also to... Pa-tisha? Grandma says we can't!"

"And what do you say? Do you want us to go?"

"Yessssss!" She looked at me with a playful, bright smile.

"Alright, but first you need to put on your socks so you don't get cold, right? And only those who wear the special socks can enter Fatel, remember?" She nodded in the cutest way ever.

"Alrighty then. So one sock... the other sock..."

Every evening, just before she goes to sleep, I wrap her tiny feet in socks. Sometimes she makes a fuss in the middle, but the one time I told her that if she didn't want to then she didn't have to, she woke up screaming that she didn't have any socks on. She was missing that something, the one thing that symbolizes her entire world and how she got here. I could tell her. Wait for her to be six or eight or whatever the educational counselor, the therapeutic guide, or the experiential therapist would say. But no. "The righteous know the soul of their beast," it says in the Book of Proverbs, and I knew my daughter's soul from the moment our eyes met. I knew that for her, I would create the most artistic work I could, even if it was made of precious wood that the world had never seen. They say children know, that they feel. And she knows. We both know she knows. And over time, she will learn to separate and understand, just like one realizes on their own that there's no such thing as a tooth fairy. But she also knows that I did it all for her. And also... also for Moran.

Here we are again in India, our late honeymoon. And she embraced my love. As if to make up for all those years. Everything I endured because of her, all the suffering. In the name of that unrequited love that tears your young heart apart. a true crime against humanity. What was I, after all? A cute oversensitive kid, slim, with muscular legs and a sweet reddish haircut that loved you, Moran. Loved unconditionally. Without preconditions. Without checking if you'd be this way or that, without inquiring about you, hearing about you, hearing you, without knowing what your voice sounded like. But I knew it sounded wonderful. And when I heard it for the first time — it was simply mesmerizing. Much more wonderful than I had thought. Much more intoxicating than I could have imagined. Young and a bit chirpy, but with a pinkish and delicate tone. Unique. My unique one. You are the one I want. And I know in the same breath that I will never have. But I want. I want and want and want and want and want. Now that I've felt it all, I want.

And in the evening we went to that market located on that street that transforms into a kind of lively night bazaar on that side road along the route leading from Palolem to Patnem that I had found during one of my wanderings from and to "The island of demons," and that I promised I'd take her. We sat down to eat in a place where someone was performing with a guitar. Probably just some fool, I thought to myself. But at that very moment, he began to sing 'Kinky Love' by The Pale Saints. For me, it had always been one of those romantic love songs that have accompanied me since I was fourteen when Pompeos brought back this rock collection from his cousin, songs that no one knew, that weren't played on MTV. Over the years, whenever the name of this song came up, I realized that no one really recognized it. But the truth is, that made it even more special for me. A crazy love song that felt almost exclusively mine. And suddenly, there he was with me. And immediately after that, he began to play David Bowie's 'Soul Love', and then Nirvana's 'Pennyroyal Tea'. Later in the evening, he also sang 'Halo' by Depeche Mode, and 'Soma,' one of my all-time favorite Smashing Pumpkins songs, and even 'Busy Bee' by Ugly Kid Joe, which we used to listen to like all the time in high school! It really felt like someone was signaling to me. And She turned and kissed me back. Embraced me, and kissed me again. We kissed a lot, for long stretches of time. I'd been waiting for this my whole life. I couldn't let go of those lips, fearing this might be the last time. I wanted to bite and taste that fruit that had been forbidden to me for so many years. More and more and more I am sipping on her luscious lips. And she kissed just like I did. Wanted just like I did. Her spark shines through a rock. Soon it will be seen glowing in all splendor. It may not yet reveal itself to her, yet she knows it's there. I felt it. There's a song by Sting called "If You Love Somebody Set Them Free." And now, for the first time in my life, I fully understand what he means. Here's Moran Dagan returning and penetrating my thoughts, my bones. "How can one live any other way?" she asks. And I, still haven't found the answer.

"Fatel is a nice place, Da-ddy?"

"Of course, my beauty. It's a place where everyone is always happy to help each other, always. At any time."

"What... everyone, everyone, Da-ddy?"

"Everyone, everyone. So much so that it's always bright, even at night."

"At... at night?"

"Yes, my beauty. There's a very big moon, in a really big shape, that shines a very, very beautiful light."

"And... and is there also... also... a king and queen and... and... a palace, Daddy?"

"Of course. And the king of Fatel loved the queen of Fatel very much. Even before she loved him. Long before."

"What, long, long, long before, Daddy?"

"Yes, my sweet one. Years before. And then one day the queen, um... fell... and... and... her head hurt, and then she went to sleep and didn't wake up."

"And then... then she didn't wake up, Da-ddy?" she asked, turning her head from side to side.

"And then the king swore that he would always love her. Because true love is forever and ever. And that he would never love another queen."

"Never, ever, ever, Daddy?"

"Never."

"But, but, Da-ddy..."

"What, my beautiful one?"

"So... but... but... and how will he have children, Da-ddy?"

"Well, he promised to travel far, far away. To a magical kingdom. And from there, he would bring back a special girl who would be only his. And he would love only her."

"What, more than... than... the queen?"

"More than the queen. More than anything in the world."

"But... but, Da-ddy...?"

"What, my sweet one?"

"But...but... he said he wouldn't love, Daddy."

"That's right, my beauty. But that was before he met his princess. And from the moment he looked into her eyes, he knew he loved her more than anything in the world."

"Any-thing in the world??" she smiled sweetly.

"Anything in the world," I said, seeing exactly what God meant.

"What, and... and... the queen just kept sleeping and sleeping and sleeping, Da-ddy?"

"Yes, my sweet one."

"But... until when she... will sleep, Da-ddy?"

"Until... until today, even."

"Really?"

"Of course. And one day she will wake up, because she promised me. She promised that..."

"But, Daddy..."

"What, my love?"

"So... th... that the queen will wake up and then... then you will hold hands, Da-ddy?"

"Yes, my sweet one. Then we will hold hands."

Epilogue

There she stands in the doorway of her room, looking at me.

"Moran... you surprised me," I say, hiding my alarm. I almost got caught red-handed. I nearly ruined any chance of going back from here. To snoop around like this in someone's drawer? My Morani's private drawer??

"Get up, come on. Why are you sitting on the floor like that?" She smiled and laughed, and suddenly her mother joined from behind her shoulder. I stood up, leaning and lightly bumping my back against the shelf and the drawer. The hidden drawer of secrets, so deeply coveted and yearned for.

"No reason... I stood before her, gazing at her from a mere inch away, dying to kiss her.

"Come to eat," her mother said, turning away.

I continued to gaze into her eyes. Those eyes that I was afraid to say a word to my entire life. I was afraid.

"What?" she looked at me with a questioning gaze and a playful grin. "Why are you suffering so much?"

Moran, it's not... You don't understand... I... I'm excited, Moran... My left eye turned red, bracing itself. What? No, no... don't cry now, don't cry... don't you dare cry!

"Not suffering, relax... all good," I smiled at her, a knowing wink dancing in my eyes.

"Okay, then I'm relaxed," she replied, nodding her head sideways.

"Great."

"Great."

"Then give me a kiss."

"Mmmmmm…" She suddenly pressed her lips to mine, as if it was she who had been longing for this moment so much.

"Mmmmmm…" I kissed her back with fervor.

"'Come on, let's go,' she gently pulled away, smiling. 'Until my mom finally cooked?'"

"You're right," I turned to head toward the kitchen when she stopped me, grabbing and holding on tight. "What?" I asked, dying to say "Morani" or "my Moran" or "my sweet one" at the end of the sentence but still not daring.

"Nothing," she replied with a smile that gave her away.

"Nothing?" I asked, my heart racing, and asking for more.

"I wanted to know where you feel from."

"Where I what?" I asked, still wrapped in her embrace, until she let go.

"Where you feel from," she repeated, reinforcing her words.

"Okay, and what does that mean?" I thought to myself and said out loud too.

"That most people feel from their head. It's good for them—they're afraid to lose what they have, so they end up feeling their emotions through their mind, not their heart. They're scared she'll leave when she realizes he's just some conman who somehow managed to win her over when she was in a moment of weakness."

"A moment of what? A moment of weakness?" I laughed. "No, like.... I... I'm... you know." "Ugh, shut up already! My Moran Dagan's excited and confused presence. I mean, I meant my *self* in the presence—not my *Moran*... even though... Well luckily, she again cut my entangled thoughts.

"Anyway, you're not. You're real. And that's what I love about you. You—you feel from the body."

"O-kay..." I started stammering again.

"Ugh, just shut up and hug me."

She grabbed me, and I grabbed as tightly as I could. The tightest I've ever held anyone. Well, maybe except for my mom after returning home from my first two weeks in the army. She was always the hugging and kissing type. But I was a kid, a distant, messed-up kid who didn't hug back too much. But after two weeks of suddenly being yelled at from the moment you wake up until you go to sleep—if you could even call it sleep, considering the ridiculous reasons we had to get up to guard the barracks, the classroom, that ladder, that tank, and our damn, fucking asses—after all that, I found myself hugging her, and I swear it was the happiest moment of her life. Well, maybe until she got the news about her first granddaughter that's on the way.

Here I was, coming back from another two weeks of recruit training—now with the respectable experience of at least a month and a half under my belt, since I'd already done the unit's badge march. It was Friday afternoon, and as I walked toward home in Fatel after getting off the last bus that comes anywhere near the village, she suddenly drove by. Her small red car was the height of style then—a kind of compact, cool Mitsubishi, reserved for the finest of our pleasure-loving, trendiest girls of the '90s. I looked at the window, and suddenly, in a single flash, it all came back to me. "Come on," she stopped and opened the door. "All the way home." And I got in. The year was 1994 and the radio was playing track four from Suede's newly released second album. With all the emotional explosions—how this boot camp was hell, and I still had no idea what my role was there, in every sense of the word, suddenly, I had no way to even contain Moran Dagan. Where did you pop up from now? Isn't it bad enough for me as it is, that I need you on my aching, burdened head during the forty-eight hours I get to be home? Really, thanks a lot for the ride. Do you think I haven't found myself fighting that annoying little demon again who woke me up again saying 'Hey, maybe this will happen now'? There you are again with that look that says nothing. Silent, unresponsive. Impossible to decipher. Pathetic me. Every time, no matter how much I managed to convince myself otherwise, whenever I saw you, I still wanted. Again, I wanted. Always, I wanted. Like an unrelenting tremor that grips the heart and arouses at the mere sight of your gaze. Is that what you mean, Moran? Is that what you mean when you say to feel from the body?

"Yes," she replied, "This way. Hold me this way".

Printed in Dunstable, United Kingdom